THE
SHAMAN

BY CHRISTOPHER STASHEFF
Published by Ballantine Books

A WIZARD IN RHYME
Her Majesty's Wizard
The Oathbound Wizard
The Witch Doctor
The Secular Wizard

STARSHIP TROUPERS
A Company of Stars
We Open on Venus
A Slight Detour

THE STAR STONE
The Shaman

THE STAR STONE

BOOK ONE

THE
SHAMAN

Christopher
Stasheff

A DEL REY® BOOK
Ballantine Books • New York

A Del Rey® Book
Published by Ballantine Books

Copyright © 1995 by Christopher Stasheff

All rights reserved under International and Pan-American Copyright Conventions. Published in the United States by Ballantine
Books, a division of Random House, Inc., New York, and simulta-
neously in Canada by Random House of Canada Limited, Toronto.

Library of Congress Cataloging-in-Publication Data
Stasheff, Christopher.
The shaman / Christopher Stasheff.
p.   cm.—(The Star stone ; bk. 1)
ISBN 0-345-39242-6
I. Title.   II. Series: Stasheff, Christopher. Star stone ; bk. 1.
PS3569.T3363S48   1995
813'.54—dc20   95-17985
CIP

TEXT DESIGN BY DEBBY JAY

Manufactured in the United States of America
First Edition: September 1995
10   9   8   7   6   5   4   3   2   1

THE
SHAMAN

PROLOGUE

"Ohaern was only a man, then," said old Lucoyo. "But that was *then*."

Lucoyo was a lean old man with long, pointed ears, still spry, still quick in limbs as well as wits. His eyes still glowed as he told the tale to the five small children, their ears only slightly pointed. Beyond them, near the roaring fire, an old woman and a young one chatted, looking up occasionally with fond smiles. Long hair hid their ears, but there was something of the old man's quickness, of the mischievous glint in his eye, reflected in the younger woman. She was shorter than the older.

"You said last time that he was a big man, Grandfather," said the oldest child.

"So he was, so he was! The biggest man in his village, both in height and in muscle. He was warrior as well as hunter—but he was not an Ulin."

Here and there in the long house other members of the family looked up, then began to move toward the old man and the children, their eyes alight with interest. They had all heard the tale before, of course, but when the winter wind was howling about the eaves, old tales and a fireside held a kind of comfort that went beyond heat and companionship.

"The Ulin were gods," said the eldest girl. She must have known where to push, for the old man reddened and cried, "Not a bit of it—though everyone thought so at the time, even Ohaern! Even I! Dariad told him otherwise—told him the Ulin were only bigger and stronger than we, and were all born with magic. But Ohaern said to me, 'I cannot see much difference, Lucoyo. Supermen or gods, what matter? They can still kill you as soon as look at you.' The sage told him otherwise, though, and then Ohaern believed."

"How he meet shage, G'amfa'?" the smallest child lisped. Even he knew how to deliver a cue.

"Ah!" The old man let his face sag into a properly tragic expression. "In a time of sadness, a time of trouble, that is how Ohaern met him!"

The children settled back, eyes shining.

"They have him going now," the younger woman whispered to the older.

"Yes, but it never took much, dear, did it? Let us listen awhile, and see how the tale swells this time." But the old woman's eyes danced as she settled back to listen to her husband tell the tale of their meeting yet again.

CHAPTER 1

The blood roared in Ohaern's ears, and the room seemed to
darken. His grip tightened around Ryl's little hand as if it were the
only thing real in this world-suddenly-turned-horrible, by her very
own words. He tried not to hear them, but they echoed in his ears.

"Do not wait—" Ryl broke off with a gasp of pain as another
contraction seized her. When it slackened, she went on as if she
had never broken off—but Ohaern winced at the agony in her eyes.

"If I am dying, do not . . . wait . . . for my spirit to leave me . . .
Cut my body . . . slit with the knife . . . and cut the child free . . ."
She broke off with a cry as another contraction seized her. Ohaern
held tightly to her, trying not to squeeze the pale hand too hard,
her agony reflected in his own misery. When it passed, she
moaned, "If I must die, at least let her . . . live."

It seemed that the baby had been battering to be born for hours
now, assailing the gates that would not open for her. Ohaern felt a
stab of anger and scolded himself—surely the child did not know
what it was doing to its mother! It only wanted life, as all people
did. Ohaern swallowed against the rock in his throat and caught
both her hands in his. "No, dear one. While we live, the gods must

5

still be guiding. Time enough to take the child after your breath has stilled—for surely it shall not! Surely the child is safest in your body! We must believe that the gods could not be so cruel as to take you so soon, so young." But he knew they had taken others, even younger. He showed no sign of that misgiving, only said, "Remember, if we take the child now, you might not live—and neither might she! But if you can keep the breath within your body until she is born and her own breath begun, both of you might see the springtime come."

Ryl started to speak again, but he pressed a finger over her lips. "For now, be still. Work when your body must, and rest while you can—for the child's sake. For mine."

Her body tensed and she cried out, clinging so tightly to his hand that he was amazed to find so much strength in such frail fingers. When her body relaxed again, she lay panting, wild-eyed, gazing up at him with death in her eyes. He stared, shaken, but was saved by the hand on his shoulder. He looked up, almost as wild as Ryl, but the gray-haired matron gazed down at him with compassion and beckoned, then turned away. Ohaern stared, then looked back at the little hand that lay limply in his now, at the closed eyes in the perspiring face. "Rest, beloved. Mardone summons me away—but I shall come back to you as soon as I may."

"Go then," she whispered, but did not even open her eyes. She seemed so exhausted, so spent, that Ohaern had to shake off a paralyzing fear before he could rise and go after Mardone to the doorway, following the shaman through the hides that kept out the wind.

Outside, the snow lay windswept and clean; the sky was clear, as if the stars were suspended in ice. Ohaern did not even notice the cold, though, for he saw the doom in Mardone's eyes. "She must live!" he cried, then remembered himself, swallowed his fear and whispered, "She must!"

"If she does, it shall be the work of the gods," Mardone told him grimly. "Be sure that I shall do all I can to seek their aid, Ohaern— but I fear the worst."

Ohaern almost seized the older woman, but again caught himself in time. "It must not be!"

"Then pray," Mardone said simply. "That is the best you can do for her now. Pray to Lomallin—and leave her to us. There is little you can do inside, Ohaern, and she will sense your fear."

Ohaern gave a choking cry and sank to his knees.

"Pray," Mardone advised again. Then she was gone, back within the lodge.

Ohaern knelt in the snow, rigid, his mind as frozen and empty as the sky. Then one of the stars within that void began to burn more brightly. He looked up through the naked branches, let his gaze drift to the void between the cold, cold sparks, and spoke inside his mind: *Lomallin! God of people, lover of humankind! Be with us now, I pray you! Do all you can, that Ryl may live! O Lomallin, send wisdom to Mardone, send skill to her hands, send Ryl a birth!*

There was more, much more, unuttered but issuing from his agony and fear. How long Ohaern knelt there in the snow, he did not know—but finally, he looked up . . .

. . . and saw the figure coming out of the woods a hundred cubits away, cowled robe light against the darkness of the firs, staff rising and falling in a clenched hand.

Hope sprang in Ohaern's heart, a hope that he was almost afraid to feel, but he let it rise and himself with it, stumbling, stepping, running to the robed figure, crying, "Welcome, stranger!"

The cowled head rose, and merry eyes twinkled within its shadow. "Good night to you, hunter!"

Ohaern skidded to a halt, suddenly awkward and at a loss for words. "It . . . it is late to be abroad."

"Very late," the stranger agreed. He had a short ruff of beard that hid his jaw, and a long straight nose. His eyes were large, and his eyebrows as bushy as his beard.

Still fighting for words, Ohaern asked, "From where do you come?"

"From Lomallin," the stranger answered. "Five nights ago, in a dream, Lomallin knew, and I knew, that a woman would be in peril of her life, from hard birthing, here."

Ohaern cried out, as if he had been run through, and sank at the stranger's feet.

"Get up, get up, hunter!" The sage reached down and lifted him, as if his huge bulk was of no more weight than a bird's. "You are her husband, then?"

"I am—and if you can save her, stranger, I shall be your bondsman for life!"

"Not *my* bondsman, but Lomallin's," the stranger corrected sternly, "though he does not want slaves, only loyal followers. But do not count the lives until they have been saved, hunter. What is your name?"

"Ohaern!" The warrior stared.

"I am Manalo. Who is the woman who labors so long and hard?"

"Ryl, my wife, my darling, the star in my night!"

"Take me where she lies, then," the stranger urged.

"Done!" Ohaern turned and went into the birthing lodge.

Ryl cried out as they entered—raw and ripping, a cry that tore at Ohaern's heart. Her back was arched, every muscle tense, so tense that Ohaern feared they might pull loose from the bone.

Manalo stopped, watching—not staring, just watching, and Ohaern snatched a frantic glance at him, wondering how the man could be so calm as he watched another's agony. But then, it was not *his* pain, or his wife! Ohaern had to stifle an impulse of angry resentment—but before he could begin to speak, the scream ended and Ryl's poor, tired body collapsed in exhaustion. Ohaern started forward, but Mardone saw and held up a palm to stop him. Ohaern froze, darting an agonized glance at his wife—and the sage stepped forward, throwing back his hood and holding up a palm in answer to Mardone's. "I am Manalo."

"I am Mardone," the shaman said in answer; then, "What do you here? Know you not this is a woman's place and time?"

"I, too, am a shaman," Manalo answered.

"One sent by Lomallin!" The cry ripped loose from Ohaern, and Ryl looked up, startled, and in sudden hope.

"I heard Lomallin's call some days ago," Manalo acknowledged, "and came because he had left the knowledge in me that a woman of the Biri people would be in pain."

"What can you do that we cannot?" Mardone demanded.

"Perhaps nothing," Manalo admitted, "but then, perhaps a great deal. May I touch the woman?"

Mardone glanced at Ryl, who gave a frantic nod. Mardone looked up at the woman's husband.

"Surely!" Ohaern said.

Manalo nodded, handed Ohaern his staff, and went to kneel by Ryl.

Ohaern was amazed at the feeling of calm that seemed to flow into him from the sage's staff. Suddenly, he could bear to watch Ryl's pain as she screamed again, watch it with less fear, for he knew somehow that she would live.

Manalo laid his hands on her distended abdomen, gazing off into space as his fingers seemed to walk over the taut flesh by themselves. His voice was distant as he said, "The child is tangled in the cord; it pulls her back when she seeks to descend."

Mardone's eyes widened. "How could you know that?"

"I see with Lomallin's eyes," the sage answered, his voice gaining life even as he spoke. He came from the trance and turned to Mardone. "The child is so wound about that the whole length of the cord is taken up, and it pulls against the womb as the woman's body squeezes."

"The poor lamb!" Mardone cried. "But how can you save them?"

"With this." The sage took from his cloak a long slender rod with a small blade on the end. "We must cut the cord before the child is born—but I must reach up inside to do it, and it must be I, for I must look as I did even now."

Mardone stared at him, her pride in her own reputation warring with her concern for Ryl. Finally, she nodded, and Ohaern breathed a sigh of relief.

"Have I the father's permission?" the sage asked.

"You have!"

"It is well." Manalo nodded. "But you must go outside the lodge, Ohaern. You may not witness."

Ohaern hesitated.

"Do not be anxious for compulsion," Manalo told him. "If she dies, you may tear me limb from limb then—and there is only the one door."

"I would not!"

"Then go."

Ohaern bowed his head and went.

Even as he passed through the door, Ryl screamed again. Ohaern forced his feet to keep on walking, his eyes to keep looking forward.

Then he was out in the clean, dark chill again, filling his chest with the night air. He shivered, but not from the cold, then looked up at the stars and breathed a prayer of thanks to Lomallin.

Ryl's scream rent the night again, then again and a third time— but after that the shrieks merged into groans that came again and again, punctuated by Mardone's voice calling encouragement. The hide door rustled, and Manalo stood beside him. "The babe is engaged as it should be," he said. "It will not be much longer, perhaps an hour."

Ohaern did not ask what the sage meant by "engaged," he only said fervently, "I thank you with all my heart, Manalo!"

"And you are very welcome," the older man said, with a smile. "Thank Lomallin, too—it is good for the heart. But pray also that the babe will be born with no further obstacles, Ohaern—she is not safe yet."

"I shall," Ohaern assured him fervently.

"That is good. I must see to your wife again—though if all goes as it should, there is nothing that Mardone cannot see to as well as I, and perhaps better. Be steadfast." Then the sage was gone again, back into the birthing lodge.

Ohaern breathed a silent prayer of thanks for his presence, then threw his whole being into another prayer, and another, while the moans sounded again and again behind him, then finally grew into screams once more—one final scream that made Ohaern whirl about, poised and ready to plunge back into the lodge. Before he could, though, Manalo emerged, smiling, and beckoned. Ohaern bolted in after him like an arrow from the bow.

There, in the light from the fire, Ryl lay, face pale and damp, eyes closed—but her breast rose with breathing, and Ohaern felt something loosen a little within him. Then he saw Mardone, holding a small and squalling bundle, murmuring to it, then smiling up at him.

Ohaern wasn't aware that he had moved—he only knew that he was standing next to Mardone, that she was moving aside a fold of fur and he was staring down into a little, wizened, red face with eyes squeezed shut and a mouth opened in protest. It seemed to him that he stared at the miracle forever, then finally looked at Mardone, wide-eyed and incredulous.

"A son, not the daughter you expected," she said, "but whole and hale—and Ryl is worn out, poor thing. She has lost much blood, but not enough to be in danger. She must rest, rest long, but she will be very well within the week."

"I cannot thank you enough!"

"Of course you can—by being good to her and helping her in anything she asks. Kiss her now, for I must give the babe back into her arms for a few minutes—what it seeks, I can no longer give."

Ohaern turned away and sank down on his knees, then reached out with a trembling, gentle touch. Ryl opened her eyes, gave him a very weary, very exultant smile, and his kiss lingered long on her lips. But he had no sooner lifted his head then Mardone was nudging him aside and laying the baby on Ryl's breast. Ohaern stared, fascinated, as the child began to nurse, and a wave of tenderness engulfed him, then bore him up on a surge of desire.

No. Time enough for that when she was well—in weeks, in a month. For now, he turned to the sage, who stood watching and smiling in the firelight. Ohaern bowed. "How can I thank you, Manalo? Ask anything of me, and I shall give it!"

"Some food, and a bed," Manalo told him, "for I am wearied."

"The best of beds, and the best of food! Come!" Ohaern led the sage out into the night, where the sky was burgeoning with the light that spread before the sunrise, making the branches stark and skeletal against the washed sky. Across the clearing they went, past the great central lodge and into the one that was Ohaern's. He swept the hides aside with a forearm and bowed Manalo in. "Enter my house!"

The sage gave him a weary smile of thanks and went in. Ohaern hurried after him, kneeling by the fire pit to add kindling and blow the coals aflame, then leaping up to open the smoke hole. The flames leaped up, revealing a neat, clean home that fairly breathed of Ryl—the dried flowers, the fragrant herbs, the neatly mended curtains around the wall-bed.

Manalo eyed it and shook his head. "I cannot take your bed, Ohaern. Make me a pallet on the floor, if you please."

"Surely, Manalo! A pallet, just as you say—but I shall rest there, not you! No, do not protest—you have saved my wife! After so long a journey, and such a night of watching, you must have a proper feather bed and blanket!"

Manalo opened his mouth to protest, but Ohaern said quickly, "I shall not sleep in any case. I am too excited, and too much relieved."

"Very well, if you will have it so." Manalo gave in with a smile. "I shall rest, then."

"But first, you must dine!" Ohaern snatched flat bread and cheese, and began to cut thick slices with his belt knife. "It will be poor fare, only bread and cheese and beer. It would be much, much better if Ryl were here—but since she is not, and since I think you would rather have plain food quickly than—"

"Bread and cheese will be a blessing." Manalo hung his cloak on a peg, then sat down on the bedside and kicked off his boots with a sigh.

"Plain fare, but quick!" Ohaern presented the meal on a wooden platter, with every bit as much deference as if he served a god himself, or a southern king. Manalo took the platter, and Ohaern pressed a tankard of ale into his hand. "Dine and sleep, O Sage! Then wake and dine, and rest again! You must stay with me several days at least, that I may show you my gratitude!"

"I am nothing loath to stay awhile, to not go upon the road again," Manalo admitted, "for my life is given to wandering from village to village. I would be glad to stay with you some days."

"Wandering?" Ohaern asked, puzzled. "So worthy a man as you? Why would you not stay and become a chieftain?"

"Because I am devoted to Lomallin's cause," Manalo explained, "that of serving humankind, of uplifting them and bringing light to their souls."

"You are a teacher!" Ohaern cried.

"I am. And I go where Lomallin sends me—to this village, then that, staying until the Ulin tells me to go to another."

"As he has told you to come to us! Praise Lomallin!" Ohaern knew the term "Ulin," of course—it was the kind-name of the beings humankind worshiped as gods. It was seldom that anyone used it, though, and he wondered why Manalo had.

"Praise Lomallin indeed, for the woman lives." Manalo handed back platter and mug with a sigh. "Now I shall rest—then tomorrow, I shall teach."

Well, it was not the next day, for Manalo slept through half of it, then hovered over Ryl until he was sure she was well and would be so without him. After that it was time to dine again, and time to sleep, so it was the day after before he began to teach.

But once he had begun, there was no stopping him. He taught the arrow makers how to twist the feathers to make the arrows fly more truly; he taught the women new plants to gather and showed them some seeds that they could bury in the earth, promising that when they came to this village site again the next year, the seeds would have grown into plants, assuring them food. He showed Ohaern a strange sort of glittering rock, then showed him how to build a fire that made part of it melt into grooves dug in the earth. When that part had cooled, it was a metal stronger than copper, and Manalo showed Ohaern how to heat it again, then take a hammer-stone and beat it into any sort of shape he wanted—an arrowhead, a spearhead, or even a knife, and, wonder of wonders, a great long knife called a sword. For, "You shall need such things," the teacher assured him, "if the creatures of Ulahane should come against you."

Ohaern shuddered—even he, the mighty hunter and warrior— for he, too, had heard of the twisted, misbegotten shapes that the evil god, the human-hater, had made to plague the younger races. He bent to the work with a will, learning how to make weapons far better than any he had ever seen, for he had a wife to protect, and now a child.

Ryl continued to thrive, and the child grew even in those few days, while Manalo taught the women new medicine and new ways of healing. But the truly esoteric lore he saved for Mardone and Chaluk, the shamans.

He taught the hunters new signs to seek out when they tracked game, new ways to trap the wolves and wildcats that stole the quarry, and a new way to ask the bear for its meat. He taught the children new games and a set of signs they could draw in the earth with sticks, to talk to one another when the other was not there. He taught everyone everything; there seemed to be nothing he did not know.

Then, one day, he said to Ohaern, "Lomallin summons me away. This will be my last night among you."

Ohaern cried out in protest, but the sage was stubborn—go he must, but this last night he would teach something new to all the village. So they all gathered around the great fire in the big lodge, and Manalo sat in the chieftain's chair and told them a tale they already knew—but told it in a way that made them feel they had never heard it before, and surely he told them parts of it they had never heard. They sat spellbound half that night, the youngest child and the oldest grandmother and everyone in between, hanging upon his words as Manalo told, all over again, and all anew, the tale of the Ulin.

CHAPTER 2

"Before He created humankind," said Manalo, "the Creator made the elder kind, the Ulin, from the four elements of Earth, Air, Fire, and Water—not in equal parts, but in those most suited to magical beings, who would be best equipped to enjoy the world that the Creator had set before them. He gave each Ulin-man a mind of his own, each Ulin-woman a mind of *her* own, and did not compel them to thank or worship their Creator in any way—and being so well-suited to pleasure, they set themselves to worship that instead."

"Therein was a mistake," said one of the men.

But Manalo shook his head. "The Creator does not make mistakes, though it may seem so to humankind—and of course, to the Ulin, it seemed that *humankind* was the mistake."

"Would they not then challenge the Creator?" another asked.

"No more than you—for you, too, are each born with minds of your own, and it would do you well to remember that. Oh, to us they seem to be giants, each born with the power to work magic, each a hundred times stronger than any of us, with far greater minds and senses—but intelligence by itself does not confer wisdom, and greater perception does not bring insight."

"But the Ulin are immortal," a woman objected.

Manalo nodded. "Left to themselves, they will not die—nor can any mere mortal slay them. But they can slay one another, yes, which is why there are so few of them left—for none of them saw any reason why he should not take all the pleasure he could, even at another's expense."

An old woman shook her head, muttering, "Surely they had pleasures enough at their beck and call, without slaying one another!"

"They did indeed. They drew their sustenance from the elements themselves, so they did not need to work; though they enjoyed eating the fruits of the earth, they did so only for pleasure, not from need. They only hunted for the joy of it and gathered what they wished to dine upon—but they enjoyed fighting, too."

"And their greatest fighter was Marcoblin!" a boy cried with excitement.

Manalo nodded. "Marcoblin was the best with sword and spear, and stronger than any but Agrapax the wondersmith—and Agrapax had no interest in fighting, of course."

"But Marcoblin could compel him!" the boy insisted.

Manalo shook his head. "None could compel Agrapax, for it was he who made the weapons, and no warrior dared risk his displeasure. Those who did, saw their swords break in their hands in the midst of battle, and died. But Marcoblin could slay others, and many were the Ulin who thought twice about defying him if he told them to do something."

"Only thought twice?" the boy frowned. "Did he not rule them all?"

"You do not 'rule' an Ulin," Manalo said slowly, "no matter how great a fighter you are, for all Ulin work magic, and few indeed were equally skilled with both weapons and spells. Marcoblin certainly was not, and himself had need to beware of those mightier with magic."

"Then he was not truly their king?" a man asked.

"Not truly, but he was as much of a king as the Ulin ever had. Still and all, he could not truly command any who did not willingly follow him, especially since there were many Ulin who did not wish to fight at all, and withstood him by magic alone, or by banding together against him."

"But he formed his own band," the man insisted.

"He formed his own band," the sage acknowledged, "and foremost among them was Ulahane—not quite so skilled with weapons as Marcoblin, but that was no wonder, for there had been many who had not been quite so skilled as he. The difference was that Ulahane still lived."

A ripple of uneasy laughter passed through the throng. "But Ulahane was still mighty," the man insisted.

"Still mighty, but by virtue of his anger and the intensity of his vindictiveness," Manalo said.

"And Marcoblin's band fought another band?"

"They did," Manalo confirmed, "and many died on both sides—but none won, for where Marcoblin's band assaulted with weapons, Harnon's band excelled with magic. In the end, both bands stepped back, leaving many dead, but none a clear winner. There were no more fights between bands after that."

"Lomallin was Harnon's lieutenant, was he not?"

"No, but he was one of the magic-workers who repelled Marcoblin's band."

"Was that when the enmity between Ulahane and Lomallin began?" asked a woman.

"No, it had been there for some time already, but that is not saying much, for there had been enmity between Ulahane and nearly every other Ulin almost since the beginning."

"Then after that, the only Ulin who fought one another were those who enjoyed it?" another boy asked.

"That is true, but there were many who enjoyed fighting. Indeed, it seemed that the greatest pleasure of most Ulin men was combat."

"And coupling," an old woman said dryly, "but not marriage."

Manalo shrugged. "No Ulin woman needed to marry, for she had no need of a huntsman to bring her food, nor of a protector, for the Ulin women were as mighty as the men."

"But not so bloodthirsty," the old woman reminded him.

"Not bloodthirsty, no," Manalo admitted, "though they enjoyed a good fight now and then. Indeed, the few who are still alive are the ones who enjoyed fighting most, or least."

"Is that not true of their men, too?" an older man asked.

Manalo nodded. "Lomallin can fight well, but takes no joy in it.

Ulahane delights in battle and hates to lose—and revels in his victims' pain."

The people shuddered, some glancing over their shoulders as if to make sure the sinister god was not there. "Did not the Ulin women need protection from such as he?" another grandmother asked.

Manalo shrugged. "Some yes, some no. Certainly any Ulin woman could defend herself long enough to summon help, and if none else, there were enough other women to side with her to overpower even such a one as Ulahane."

The crowd murmured with foreboding and wonder at the might of the Ulin women.

"So no Ulin woman ever coupled with any man she did not desire," Manalo summarized, "though that is not so much to say, for there were few the Ulin women did not desire."

The crowd murmured again, the women with disapproval, the men with appreciation. "If they coupled so often," a younger woman challenged, "why are there so few Ulin left?"

"Magic," said Manalo. "The Ulin women could control whether or not they conceived."

The women murmured with amazement and envy—this was something they had not heard before. Mardone frowned. "I have never heard that said of the Ulin before."

"There is much that is not known of them," Manalo agreed, "but that Lomallin knows, and may reveal to those who truly seek to bond their hearts to his purposes."

"And you are such a one?"

"I am, which is why I go where Lomallin directs."

"But if it was magic," a young man demanded, "could not the men control whether or not there would be children born of a union, too?"

"They could, so there were few children born indeed—only when both parents wished it, and few Ulin had much instinct for parenting. In those who did, it was easily satisfied—especially since they quickly learned that children bound them to their houses or, at least, to the children themselves. They found they could no longer go gadding about whenever they wished, or engage in amorous play whenever the urge came, or spend endless hours with their grown companions, whiling away an afternoon with wine and talk. In a word, they had to think of someone else before they thought of themselves, and few Ulin found that agreeable."

"They were very selfish, then!" a mother said indignantly, for her children were glancing at her and at their father uneasily.

"Very selfish, so marriage was rare, though liaisons were frequent."

"But short-lived!" the grandmother snapped.

"A few weeks for the most part, though many lasted only a night, and some lasted years—so there were a few little Ulin born to replace those who died."

"Was there so much fighting and killing as that?" one boy asked, eyes huge.

"Oh, there was enough of it, you may be sure," Manalo said bitterly. "They killed each other in rage or cold revenge; they killed each other to see who was the stronger, or who the better fighter. They killed each other in games that grew too rough—but it was not all killing of one another. There were some who died hunting the giant beasts of those dawn days of the world—and some grew weary of life, so bored and so overcome with a sense of purposelessness that they slew themselves."

"Why, they were no better than we!" another grandmother cried indignantly. "At least, if what you say is true—but I have never heard this before, Teacher!"

"Then be taught by me, for so says Lomallin, and he was there from the first, to see it."

"Then how dare they call themselves gods?" she demanded.

"They did not—it was humankind who called them that." Manalo pointed a finger in accusation. "Be not deceived—the Ulin are not gods! Only the Creator is God! The Ulin are an older kind, a bigger kind, a mightier kind, aye—the Ulin can work wonders, and bring disasters. But they are only beings, like yourselves but greater—immensely greater, but still creations, not the Creator! They are not gods!"

Most of the people stared, amazed—they had certainly never heard *this* before! Some even frowned, looking at the teacher askance—but they did not voice their doubts.

For himself, Ohaern saw no distinction. What was the difference between greater men and lesser gods, after all?

As if he had read Ohaern's thoughts, Manalo said simply, "Gods do not die. They cannot be killed. Ulin can."

"But it is Ulin who kill them," one woman objected, "not mere men."

"More than men, but less than gods?" Ohaern asked.

Manalo nodded. "Even so. The Ulin were many at first, but as the centuries rolled, there were fewer and fewer—and even those who delight in life, when they are young, may find it growing to be tedious and wearying and a heavy burden after a thousand years."

"Could people *want* to die?" a little girl gasped.

"After a thousand years, with no children to cheer them?" Manalo smiled down at her fondly. "Yes."

The little girl looked somewhat reassured.

"But it was the war that killed the most of them, was it not?" asked Ohaern.

"More than anything else, though one out of every three Ulin was dead before it began. New creatures began to appear upon the earth—elves and dwarves and dwergs and humans, who looked very much like the Ulin, though much lesser in every way. The Ulin realized that the Creator had brought forth a smaller, shorter-lived, but more prolific race, like the Ulin in appearance, though born without magical powers. They could learn magic, but it did not come naturally to them."

Mardone nodded slowly on one side of the room, and Chaluk on the other.

"But why did the Creator bother making the elves, when the world housed beings so much better?" a young man demanded. "And why, having made the elves, did he make dwarves and dwergs and *us?*"

"So asked the Ulin," Manalo answered, but waved a forefinger slowly. "Do not think that *bigger* and *longer-lived* and *more powerful* means 'better.' The Ulin were far more proud than they should have been, to neglect their Creator so, and very selfish indeed not to want children. In fact, you could say truly that very few of the Ulin could love anything more than themselves. Is this 'better'?"

"No!" a dozen women chorused, and most of the men nodded agreement—but the young man who had asked the question looked unsure, and so did many of the other youths and maidens.

Manalo explained, "The Ulin were the elder race, and they had magic that could waive barriers, and make even two separate species produce offspring—without any love at all."

The people muttered with apprehension and disapproval, and one man asked, "That is how Ulahane bred up his monsters, is it not? Goblins and trolls and lamias and sphinxes—"

"And many others too numerous to mention." There was disgust in Manalo's face and tone. "Aye, the poor things, who never wished to be born—and their poor parents, who were forced into couplings they did not desire! But Ulahane delights in pain and grief, and persists in making more of them, even though the monsters cannot produce offspring of their own. Never go into the woods alone, young women—and young men, too! You never know when Ulahane's minions will be lurking about to seize new living toys for his cruel delights."

There was an outbreak of angry talk, and people shivered with apprehension. One young man cried out, "Is that all we were made for? To amuse the gods?"

"The Ulin," Manalo corrected, "and though some thought that, most also thought the new breeds were made to challenge them or replace them when they had all slain one another. They thought the humans could not control their urge to have children—"

"*Can* we?" an older woman asked in an acid tone, and a few laughed, but quickly silenced themselves.

"I spoke not of the urge to couple," Manalo said, "but of the urge to have children. Indeed, the Ulin saw quickly that humankind could not control when they would or would not conceive—"

"They were right in that," the woman said with a sardonic tone.

"They are, but the human need for children goes beyond mating and conceiving." Manalo's glance lingered on the small ones nearest him. "The Ulin had no idea that human beings might be capable of loving something else more than themselves, you see—the notion was foreign to them, alien."

"Inconceivable," the woman said dryly, and everyone gave an astonished laugh, though it was sharp and short-lived.

As it died, Manalo nodded. "It was indeed, for even the few Ulin who had wanted children, and birthed them and reared them, had quenched that desire long since. To have children by human mothers, though, was another matter, since the women either could not or did not object, and could very easily be deserted."

"It did not take a god to discover that!"

"Are you sure?" Manalo fixed her with a glittering gaze. "Did the men of your kind invent the notion of leaving a woman with child to fend for herself? Or did they learn it by the example of the ones they called gods?"

The woman frowned. "I begin to think you are right—that the Ulin are no gods, but only more able to be vicious than human men!"

"Or Ulin women?" Manalo smiled sadly. "I fear they, too, used humans as toys—though never very many, for they found that such babies tied them down just as badly as Ulin infants."

"Why, then, did any bother with human males at all?" a different woman asked, puzzled.

"Because Ulin men no longer wished to have to see to the rearing of children," Manalo explained. "Oh, they were ready enough to sire them, so long as they did not have to care for them, or for their mothers. Often enough, though, they found human men who were honored to take such a woman to wife, for there was no small standing in having a half-Ulin son or daughter, and it was of advantage to his own children."

No one said anything to that, but men and women glanced at one another uneasily. Finally, a grandmother said, "Were not the goddesses jealous?"

"Most jealous indeed, and they sought revenge on the Ulin men."

"Surely there was danger in that!" the grandmother gasped.

"Danger indeed, so more often they took their revenge on the women who had lain with the Ulin men, or took human mates themselves in spite. Most frequently, though, they sought to revenge themselves on the children of such unions."

"Thus were made the Ulharls," a grandfather said, his voice low.

"Thus the Ulharls came," Manalo confirmed, "and that is why so many of them fled to the protection of their fathers, even though it meant serving them in every slightest wish. And they are doughty servants indeed, for they are half again as tall as any human man or woman, half again as strong, and many are born with powers of magic. All can learn magic easily, and most of them wish to."

Everyone shivered at the thought of the vindictive superhumans. "Why are the Ulharls so cruel?" one woman asked.

"Because they hate you for being free, when they are not," Manalo answered. "Those who were taken by their Ulin fathers—which some Ulin did only to anger their fellows or former lovers—and grew up among the Ulin, despised and mocked and ever the object of the women's spite—these grew up bitter indeed, and are ever seeking weaker targets for their anger and hatred."

"But there are good Ulharls!" a youth cried.

"Oh, some Ulharls grew happily enough," Manalo said, "for they are honored if they grew up among humans—or are happy and spoiled if they have Ulin mothers and grow up with them. But they are few, very few."

"The Ulharls can have children by human wives, can they not?" one young woman challenged.

"They can have children, yes," Ohaern answered, "though I have never yet heard of an Ulharl who bothered to wed—or dared to, without his father's consent."

"Would not such a one be human?"

"Not the child of an Ulharl—such a one would be too huge to be mistaken for a man or woman. But a grandchild or great-grandchild might be mistaken for a human, yes. A very big human, a very strong one—but a human nonetheless."

Ohaern felt a chill as several glances sought him out.

"Do you all know who your great-grandparents were?" Manalo challenged. "A son of a son of a son of a son has little resemblance to his ancestor, after all. Any among you could be of the Ulharl."

A rash of coughing and clearing of throats ran through the great lodge, and everyone turned away from Ohaern. In fact, everybody tried not to look at any of his neighbors—and hoped they weren't looking at him. Ohaern smiled, amused, and grateful to the sage.

"It is their safeguard, ironically," Manalo told them, "the Ulin's guarantee that their race will never truly perish, so long as human beings walk the earth. You who are their victims, and the butt of their hatred, shall ensure that something of them survives."

"You do not mean that the gods are dying!" Chaluk cried, shocked.

"Oh, yes," said Manalo softly. "They have died from slaying each other in rage, they have died by their own hands when life became too dull—but the greatest number of them died in their war. There are only a handful left now, perhaps fifty—of whom many disdain the world of men, and some even disdain the other Ulin."

"And Lomallin and Ulahane are the most powerful among them?" someone asked.

Manalo shrugged. "Perhaps only the most powerful of those who concern themselves with the destinies of mortal folk. If Lomallin has greater power than most, it is only by dint of his compassion for humankind, and his concern for their welfare, which focuses all his energies—and if Ulahane has greater power than most, it is sheerly by virtue of his will." He shook his head slowly and sadly. "Oh, make no mistake—the Ulin are a dying race, while mortals are still growing, still becoming more and more numerous."

"And they hate us for that?" a young man asked, and the girl next to him shuddered.

"They do," said Manalo. "Many of those Ulin who are left regard the younger human race with spite and jealousy. All of them are concerned only with their own satisfactions—and for many of them their greatest satisfaction is venting their revenge on humankind."

"For no greater crime than that we exist?" a young woman asked, her voice quavering.

"For no more than that," Manalo agreed.

"But what of Lomallin?" asked another. "Surely *he* is not concerned only with his own pleasures!"

"His only fulfillment, rather," said Manalo, "and yes, he is. It is fortunate for humankind that his notion of reward, his reason for staying alive, is seeing us thrive."

"Would he kill Ulahane, then?" another young man asked, eyes wide.

Manalo shrugged. "Not willingly—but if he must kill or be killed, I do not think he would hesitate."

"So other Ulin are yet more important to him than us," a mother said bitterly.

"Of course," Manalo said. "What else would you expect?"

"Does he not think of us as his children, though?"

"No," said Manalo, "for he did not make you—well, not very many of you, and those few were Ulharls. No, he thinks of you as ones who need his protection, but not as being of his kind."

"His pets," the woman said, even more bitterly.

"Something more than that," Manalo answered. "Remember, though, that Ulin are not gods, and Lomallin is certainly not the Creator. If he favors humankind, it is because he wishes to, not because he must."

"But how can you say they are *not* gods," Ohaern asked, "when their powers are so far-reaching, and they have so much to do with our destiny?"

"You, too, Ohaern?" Manalo looked up sadly, then thumped his staff against the floor and pulled himself upright. He rubbed his back. "I should not sit so long with my legs folded at my age. Come, my friends, let us go to bed. I must be up before the sun tomorrow, and on the road as it rises."

A chorus of protest answered him, but he stood firm against it, and it turned into a tide of regretful good wishes for his journey. Finally, Ohaern ushered the rest of the clan out and left Manalo to his bed by the fire in the great lodge.

CHAPTER 3

The tribesman caught Lucoyo by either arm and slammed him back against the rock. "Bind him fast," the chief ordered, and his captors turned to their work with a will, wrenching tight the rope of twisted hide—around one wrist, around the back of the slab of rock, and around the other wrist.

"So much for your pranks, halfling," Holkar grunted. "Laugh, why don't you?"

"Yes, laugh," snapped Gorin the chief. "Laugh while you can. If my daughter dies, you will scream soon enough—and long enough." The back of his hand cracked across Lucoyo's face.

"It was only a jest," Lucoyo said, then had to pause to spit blood. The bruises on his face were burning, and he knew they were already swelling. "Only an idle prank. The spider wasn't supposed to bite. I didn't know it *could* bite."

"You knew it well enough!" Kragni's fist caught him on the cheek, sending the bruises aflame and adding his mark to the others'. "*Everyone* knows that the white crone has a bite—and that it can kill!"

It was true enough—but the huge, hairy spider was also the

most frightening of its kind, which was why Lucoyo had chosen it to hide among the rushes Palainir would use for weaving. If truth be told—which Lucoyo was determined it would not be—he *had* hoped the crone would bite. Palainir deserved it, for not only had she spurned his invitation to go walking out to watch the sunset, which he had expected—she had also given a shriek of laughter and called her friends to come see the stub of a halfling who had the temerity to approach a real woman. Burning with shame and seething with anger, Lucoyo had gone away and thought long about the manner of his revenge. He had made sure to be near, currying a pony, when Palainir had taken out her basket of rushes to begin weaving a hat; he had barely kept himself from laughing out loud as she jumped back with a shriek. But even he had been appalled when the shrieks went on and on as she flapped her hand, trying to throw the spider from her. Her mother had seized the whole basket and knocked it against her hand, which was fine, but she had also turned and pointed a trembling finger at Lucoyo while she tried to soothe her daughter's sobs, which was not. None doubted he had done it, though none had seen him—and Palainir now lay laughing and crying by turns in fevered delirium.

Actually, Lucoyo couldn't blame the spider. After having been tumbled among the rushes, it had no doubt been frightened and angry; he would have bitten, too. In fact, he wished he had. But he *could* fault the crone for bad taste, considering how long it had held onto Palainir's hand. On second thought, perhaps he would have, too—the girl was very pretty. On third thought, no—he would not have wanted to keep that taste in his mouth. If beauty was in the heart and soul, Palainir was sadly lacking.

Lucoyo turned his head to spit more blood. "You wrong me, Gorin. I, too, hope she recovers."

"I am sure you do—now that you are caught and bound. For the fright you gave her, you have been punished with blows and kicks, and you deserve it richly."

Well, Lucoyo could have argued that—but it didn't seem like the time or place.

"But for her illness, you shall be punished with the ordeal of fire!" The chief's eyes blazed. "And for her death, you shall be punished with your own!"

That, Lucoyo just couldn't abide. "Go to Ulahane," he croaked.

The back of the hand rocked his head again. Through the ringing in his ears he heard Gorin say, "No. That is where *you* are bound."

Holkar and Kragni laughed richly, though Lucoyo could see little humor in the remark, and surely no wit. Gorin spat in his face—surely a subtle piece of satire, that—and sneered. "Ponder the ways of your wickedness, half-elf! When my daughter's agony is over, yours begins!"

He turned away, and so did Holkar—but Kragni lingered long enough to slam in another blow that made Lucoyo convulse against his ropes in agony, and said, "Point-eared jackass!" with malice and satisfaction before he, too, turned away into the night, leaving Lucoyo to hang alone in the dark.

The old, old insult, Lucoyo thought as he struggled for breath and waited out the waves of pain that radiated from his groin. How he hated the tired old phrase—they could not even invent a new one! He had been hearing the same worn-out curses ever since he was old enough to understand words—or, at least, for as long as he could remember. "Half-elf!" "Point-ear!" "Jackass!" "Monster!" "Halfling!" and half a dozen others, always greeted with roars of laughter by the rest of his crowd of tormentors, as if they were bright, new, fresh—and funny.

Lucoyo knew just how humorless they were, those insults—and those tribesmen—so he had bent his mind to thinking up really amusing insults to answer theirs. Unfortunately, that had brought beatings—but he had fought back, and watched and studied the big boys as they fought, and bit by bit began to win now and then. To win, when he was always smaller and lighter than the others! But they had an answer for that—they came at him in threes and fours, and never gave him an honest chance at a fair fight. So he had learned to fight back with pranks that made others laugh until they realized who had done them—he learned to set the burr in the saddlecloth, to drop the sharpened peg in the boot, to substitute the sandstone arrowhead for the flinten one and the green shaft for the seasoned bow. He had learned to answer their clumsy japes with true wit.

"A rabbit's ears, and a rabbit's heart!" Borek had sneered.

"But a man's brain between them," adolescent Lucoyo had answered, "whereas you have a man's ears and a rabbit's brain!"

Borek turned on him, looming over him. "We shall see a rabbit skinned for that!"

"Skin?" Lucoyo stared at the hairy chest in front of him. "Have you really a skin under all that fur?"

"Lucoyo, you go too far!"

"No, it is *you* who go to fur . . . No, no, I am sorry, Borek!" Lucoyo held up both hands in a parody of pleading. "Have it as you will, suit your pelt—I mean, your *self*!"

"I shall see *your* pelt stretched to dry!" And Borek waded in with a roundhouse punch.

Lucoyo leaped back adroitly, then ducked under the next punch and came up fist first and hard. The blow cracked under Borek's jaw, jarring his teeth; he staggered back, and Lucoyo followed close—face, belly, face—punching hard.

Borek's friends roared anger and leaped in.

Lucoyo jumped aside just before they landed—so they landed on Borek, who howled with anger, and Lucoyo leaped away, running. Borek and his friends shouted in rage and came pelting after.

Lucoyo ran like a river in flood, with quick glances back over his shoulder. Borek lumbered along, farther behind every minute, with most of his friends a dozen yards ahead, almost keeping pace with the sprinting half-elf—but Nagir was catching up, coming faster and faster, closer and closer . . .

Lucoyo slowed down, just a little bit, just as much as might come from tiring . . .

Nagir shouted and kicked into a wild dash.

At the last second, Lucoyo pivoted and slammed a fist into Nagir's belly. The bigger boy doubled over, eyes bulging, and Lucoyo hooked the fist into his jaw. Nagir straightened up, and Lucoyo hit him with three more punches before he fell. Then he had to turn and run, for the other boys were catching up.

"Run, rabbit, run!" Borek bellowed in fury as he plowed to a halt, shaking his fist. "Run, rabbit-heart! You cannot outrun the council!"

That didn't worry Lucoyo. He came home at dusk, confident the men of the tribe would realize that when it was five against one, the one was rarely at fault.

He was wrong.

As the men beat him with sticks for having beaten one of their sons, the fatherless half-elf learned not to trust in authority, not to rely on the law.

But quick fists and fleet feet were only one way. Lucoyo learned also to wield truth as a weapon. He learned to answer scorn with the loud announcement of things his tormentors thought secret, learned to ferret out each person's covert shame and charge them with it aloud, in answer to their sneers. It earned him beatings, yes, but the insults did slacken a bit. More importantly, he felt the fierce elation of revenge.

Thus had Lucoyo learned to be the jester—but the jester whose tongue was barbed and poisoned, whose jests were edged and honed. They hated him for it, of course, but by their own law, they could do nothing as a clan, take no action against him.

In private, of course, they could beat him, and did—if they came in threes and fours. In fact, he decided they had kept him so long because they needed something to punch.

Oh, he hated them! Why had *he* stayed with them so long?

Because his mother still lived, that was why—his mother, seduced by that wicked elf, who must surely have mocked her when he was done. Oh, she had told Lucoyo that he had bade her come to dwell with him, but she had been loath to leave her own kind—wisely, Lucoyo was certain, for what could she have been but a servant in an elfin hill?

But perhaps, the traitorous hope whispered, as it always did, *perhaps they would have honored her—honored you, if you had grown up with them! Perhaps he would have married her . . .*

Ridiculous! Lucoyo was actually grateful for the stab of pain that came with his angry shake of the head; it helped him deny the thought. His mother would have been a concubine when she was young, a wet nurse as she aged, and would now be a scullery maid to an elf-wife! No, she had done unwisely to have gone to that blasted elf's bed, but had then done as wisely as she could to come back to her nomad clan's camp and endure the shame of their censure.

Her clan . . .

It had never been his, not really. He had always been the outsider, the odd one, the detested stranger whom they could not quite exile with a clear conscience . . .

Until now.

He had made his fatal mistake, he had played one prank too many, taken one revenge too vicious. He had to admit, facing his inner heart, that he had hoped the spider would bite, hoped the chief's daughter would die as she deserved, for the mockery she had heaped on him, that they all had heaped on him. True, she had been only one among many, and it was not right that she suffer for all of them . . .

Then make them all suffer, something wicked whispered inside him—Ulahane's voice, perhaps; but Lucoyo was ready to listen to it now, ready and more. *Revenge,* it whispered, *on them, on all the other mortals who would have treated you just as badly, on the elves who would have treated you worse! Revenge, on every human of every race and breed! Revenge on anything that lives!*

It was a worthwhile thought, and Lucoyo promised he would give it serious consideration—if he lived.

But who was he promising?

Surely only himself!

Lucoyo was short, slight, and sharp-faced. Even without the ears, anyone would have known him on sight as not wholly human—and, of course, everyone in this tribe of nomads knew what he was and what his mother had done. No man would touch her after that—he had heard them talk about how none would take an elf's leavings! True, his mother had told him that she was too plain to have attracted a husband, that the elf-man had been her one chance of gaining the baby she had so ached to hold, but he did not believe her.

He *must* not believe her—or Lucoyo would have to blame her, too, for this bitter, constant torment called "life."

So when the clan folded their tents and followed the great herd of aurochs, it was Lucoyo's mother who bore the heaviest burdens, Lucoyo's mother whom Gorin's wife commanded to watch over her own children as well as Lucoyo.

"Is your pouch filled with stones, Kragni?" little Holkar asked— little, but four years older than toddling Lucoyo, and already bossing others about.

"Filled!" little Kragni answered. "Where is the rabbit?"

"There!" Little Palainir pointed at Lucoyo, laughing.

Her two brothers laughed, too. The little half-elf stared at them, not understanding, then started to laugh, too. Whatever the source of the jest, it must be funny, since they were all laughing.

"No, sister," said Holkar, from the lofty superiority of eight years. "Rabbits have big legs and cotton tails. Lucoyo has only very spindly shanks."

Palainir pouted. "How then *do* you find rabbits?"

"By their noise," Kragni told her. "They thump the ground with their feet."

"*He* can find them!" Holkar pointed at Lucoyo. "With those big ears of his. Go find us a rabbit, Lucoyo!"

And little Lucoyo, not understanding the insult, not realizing the slight, had actually gone out and tried to listen for a rabbit— then endured Holkar's scorn for not being able to find one. He had felt that he was a failure, deeply and truly, when he could find no game.

He remembered that now, convulsed in pain, and the old humiliation burned in him again. Once having found their choice insult, they used it over and over again, until, compared to it, a dry bone would have been fresh. They had mocked him, calling him "Rabbit!" and "Hare!" The worst humiliation of all had come when he found that someone had sewn a rabbit tail onto his leggings.

That had been the pattern of their growing: Lucoyo alternately befriended and insulted by Gorin's children. For all that, he had thought them friends, until he grew big enough for them to side with the other children against him. For all that, he had loved Palainir in his heart of hearts, from the straw-haired child she had been then to the shapely, golden-haired young woman she was now. But he had always had sense enough to keep his peace, to endure her mocking and teasing in silence. Now, though, when he had brought down an aurochs by himself, with nothing but his own arrows, not even a horse beneath him—now, when he had brought home the beast's head, though the other young men had taken the meat as their own right for hauling it on their ponies—now, he had dared not even to tell her of his love, but only to ask her to walk alone with him in the sunset. And it was good he had dared no more, for she had mocked him, and spurned him, had called her friends to laugh at the temerity of this little half-elf who would dare woo a real woman!

Lucoyo managed to straighten up against the pain in his groin, drawing a deep and shaky breath as he searched his heart for some trace of that love he had felt all his life—but it was gone now, transformed into the flame of anger that was burning down into hatred. No, there was no love left there now, and he was a fool to have ever let there be. She had deserved the spider's bite, and even now, facing death, he felt a grim, exultant satisfaction in it.

Surely he could not really die! Surely there must be a way free of these bonds! He was half an elf—surely he had half an elf's magic?

But he had thought that before, had wished it many times, had yearned, had learned a rhymed curse and uttered it—but nothing had happened. Perhaps, if he'd had an elf to teach him how to work elfin magic . . .

Perhaps. Oh, there might have been much that was different if his father had stayed with him! But he had not, and Lucoyo had always had to face life alone . . .

Even as he now faced death alone.

Looking up, he was amazed to realize that the sky had lightened with dawn. Could another day really come? Could he live so long?

"Down, elf-get!" Hard hands tore at the knots, snapped the thongs from his wrists, scraping them raw; hard boots kicked him away from the rock, kicked him down to the ground. Lucoyo started to shout a curse, but one of those hard hands pressed down on the back of his head, grinding his face into the dirt, filling his mouth with loam. "She lives, elf's bastard!" Gorin's voice hissed in his ear. "She lives, so you will only suffer as she has suffered—and perhaps die, as she might have died. Turn him over!"

The hard hands lifted him up, flipped him, and slammed him down again; Holkar and Kragni pinned his arms to the dirt while two more held his feet and a dozen others stood about watching, eyes burning with gloating satisfaction.

Gorin tore Lucoyo's shirt open and slapped a cup of bark down, open side against the skin. "*Three* white crones, woman-striker!" he said between his teeth, and began to drum on the bark. Lucoyo felt one of the spiders bite and stifled a curse. But Gorin saw his pain and his fear, and grinned. "Now let us see whether or not the bite kills *you!*"

Lucoyo twitched again, pressing his lips tight.

"Did another bite?" Gorin jibed. "Or did you only pretend? No, I think I will play my drum a while longer, dagger-nose—long and long, until your skin is freckled with their venom."

And he did.

At last he took the cup away and snarled, "On his feet!" Holkar and Kragni yanked him upright and threw him forward. Lucoyo stumbled on feet gone numb from squeezed ankles, then fell. A boot dug into his side, harsh laughter echoed around him, and the hard hands yanked him upright again, then sent him stumbling once more. "Out into the world, traitor!" Gorin bellowed. "If the company of your . . . of this clan does not suit you, go find one that does! If any will take in a bastard halfling. If you cannot respect your betters, go leave us!"

"*What* betters?" Lucoyo grated, even though he knew he was too lame to dodge the blow that came and rocked his head. Through the buzzing, he heard the massed bellow, and the chief's shout, "Go! And do not linger within ten miles of us, for from this day forth, any who finds you may kill you out of hand, without breaking our law! Go find life if you can—or death, as my daughter might have!"

Lucoyo limped away, not deigning to humiliate himself by asking if he could have food or water; he knew the answer, knew how savagely they would delight in denying him. He limped away,

jaws clamped tight against the savage insult he ached to return—
for in spite of it all, he wished to live. He limped away, hearing the
woman's keening behind him, back where she could not even
see him, knowing it was his mother, barred even from saying
good-bye.

His heart filled with scarlet fury, and in that heart Lucoyo
swore revenge. *Ulahane,* he prayed silently, *I am yours henceforth. Only give me vengeance, and I will serve you in every way I
may! Vengeance against these small minds and hard hearts,
vengeance against all who mock the weaker—vengeance against
all their kind! Human-hater, save my life—so that I may slay humans, aye, and slay them in torment!*

But Ulahane did not answer. Why bother? Lucoyo realized that,
with sick irony, the god's answer would be in his own life or
death.

Palainir had been bitten by one spider, but Lucoyo had been bitten by three. For days he lay in torment, the fever burning him,
the chills shaking him apart. For a week he lay in the little cave by
the water under the oak's roots, sipping from the muddy drops
that trickled near him when he could, shivering and cursing when
he could not, and dreaming, always dreaming—of the huge and
mighty Ulahane, surging forth to battle the human-lovers, roaring
with rage, dwarfing even his own bastard sons by human victims;
dreamed of the reeking sacrifices that were the sinister god's delight; dreamed of the agonies and tortures in which he reveled . . .

Dreamed of revenge.

Revenge against all that was human, revenge against all that
was elfin—revenge against all that lived but was not Ulin.

Then, finally, the fever passed, and Lucoyo woke to discover,
with amazement, that he still lived. So the scarlet god had saved
him after all! He still had to crawl out in the mud to grub for roots
to sustain him, he still had to lie hidden for weeks while slowly,
slowly, he gained his strength again. He still had to crawl down to
the river to drink as dogs drink, crawl back up to hide in the
bracken—but finally he was once again strong enough to throw

stones and bring down rabbits and squirrels to eat. They were the only food that came near, other than tubers, but that was enough, and it felt good to kill. He dared not kindle a fire that might attract men to kill *him*, but that, too, was as well—he found that he enjoyed the taste of blood. Enjoyed the taste, and reveled in the thought of human blood to come.

Lucoyo ate and rested and regained his strength, planning his revenge.

Ulahane, he prayed, *send me someone upon whom to vent my anger! Send me a victim for vengeance! Someone of my own erstwhile tribe, by preference—but I will take whomever you send me! Only let it be human!*

He liked to think that the scarlet god heard.

CHAPTER 4

Ryl gave a racking cough, then thrust herself up to catch Ohaern's hand. "Husband . . . please . . ."

"Hush, dear one. Lie still." Gently, Ohaern pushed her back down on the pallet. "You are ill, my love. Conserve your strength."

"But, Ohaern . . ." Her hand tightened on his, and he fought against the sudden tears in his eyes. "Husband, hear me. I . . . if I . . . die . . . our son . . . who shall . . ."

"Hush, hush!" Ohaern spoke through the tightness in his chest. "I know I am a great worthless hulk when it comes to small babies, but there are women enough in this village to see that the child is well cared for. Rest, and recover; your friends shall ward your babe for you."

"But if I should die!"

"You shall *not* die," Ohaern commanded. "The fever will break!" But his stomach was hollow within him, for he knew it might not.

Ryl started to speak again, but he pressed a finger over her lips. "For now, be still. Lie and sleep during the hours of darkness—for the child's sake. For mine."

Her body tensed to struggle against his hand again—but she saw the pleading in his eyes and sank back. He took a deep breath and murmured, "Rest, and gather your strength to fight the illness. That is the greatest thing you can do for all of us now."

She swallowed, eyes closed, then nodded. "As you wish it."

"Dear lady." His hand closed around hers and he bent to kiss her again, then straightened—and saw Mardone watching him, eyes stern.

Ohaern nodded, patted Ryl's hand again, then rose and stepped aside, so that Mardone might kneel by the sick woman, bathing her forehead and face with a cold, wet compress.

A touch on his arm startled him. Ohaern looked up and saw Chaluk, the clan's other shaman. Chaluk beckoned, and Ohaern followed, with one last, anxious look back at Ryl.

By the doorway, Chaluk whispered, "That was well-spoken—but you must not stay here any longer. She will feel more fear from your fear, and that will keep her from the sleep she needs. Go outside, Ohaern."

"No—"

But Chaluk held up a hand, and Ohaern closed his mouth, biting back a refusal.

"Be sure, I shall summon you if she nears death—but step outside, Ohaern. You can do no more here. Leave her to sleep, and to those of us who know the spirits that bring illness."

"What spirit plagues her now?" Ohaern hissed.

"One sent from Ulahane, of course." Chaluk frowned. "What else?"

What else, indeed? Just as Lomallin did all he could to bring humans happiness, love, and life, so Ulahane did all he could to bring them misery, loneliness, and death. But why Ryl? Why this one poor woman, twice in three months?

There was no answer to that, nothing the shamans could tell him that he did not already know—because told him they had, and several times each. Ryl had been weakened, that was all—and where there was a weakness, Ulahane would seek to break through and destroy. He was a god and could do what he pleased; all that stopped him were Lomallin and the gods who were Lomallin's allies.

Ohaern looked back at the still form of his wife, so small, so frail, her eyes so unnaturally huge as they fluttered open and gave him another stare filled with the agony of helplessness. Fear wrung his heart again, then a surge of tenderness followed. He turned back to Chaluk, closing his eyes and nodding in submission. "As you will, Chaluk. But tell me." His fingers bit into the shaman's shoulder. "*Will* she live? Can she?"

Chaluk gazed steadily into his eyes, then slowly turned away to look at the young woman. "That is a matter for greater shamans than me," he said, as if the words were dragged out of him, "but they are not here." Then he spun on his heel, pushing through the hides that covered the doorway, out into the night air. Ohaern swept the skins aside with a forearm and followed.

Out in the chill of the early spring night, Chaluk turned back to Ohaern. "Can you not bring Fortor? All the Biri clans are under his care. But his dwelling is four leagues away."

Ohaern thought furiously. "It would take all the night, and most of tomorrow . . ."

"And you might return to find her spirit sped." Chaluk nodded, lips tight. "And the chief shaman of the nation is farther still." He turned his head slowly from side to side, holding Ohaern with his gaze. "No, Ohaern—we are not the greatest of shamans, Mardone and I, but we are all that the clan has. Ryl's illness has surpassed my knowledge, and Mardone's, and our skill. She is in the gods' hands now."

"What then can I do?" Ohaern cried in agony.

"Pray," Chaluk told him. "Stay here, outside the lodge, and pray. If Lomallin hears you and can bring all his forces to combat Ulahane, and if Mardone and I can give Ryl strength enough, the fever may slacken and she may live. Stay, Ohaern, and pray with all your spirit to Lomallin."

Ohaern held the shaman's gaze for a long minute, then bowed his head. Chaluk turned away, stooping through and brushing aside the hides, leaving Ohearn to the cold, crisp air of a night of very early spring, and to the company of his own soul.

Ohaern took a deep breath, filling his lungs with the chill freshness, and felt a stab of guilt at the relief it gave him—but there was peace out here, peace in gazing at the hills, and the bare oaks and elms climbing their sides to the pines above. He turned slowly, surveying all the land about in a circle, then finally felt his lips quiver with the urge to smile. Chaluk was right—he must let his soul rest, that he might have strength to give Ryl, if the unseen Guide came near her in the night. He filled his spirit with the peace of the deeps of the night, the sweep of the hills, the well-beaten trail leading up over them . . .

And remembered how, in the depths of winter, he had seen Manalo come forth from the trees. Ah, if only he would come down that trail now! If only he were within the forest, if only he would step out from the pines once more . . .

Ohaern waited, hoping against hope, his whole soul surging upward in a silent, unvoiced prayer to Lomallin, that the sage might come, might yet save Ryl . . .

He waited, he waited, the tension drawing his soul out thinner and thinner . . .

But the pines stayed obstinately dark, and the sage came not.

Ohaern relaxed in defeat; his heart twisted within him. Of course he could not summon Manalo, nor compel Lomallin.

But he could petition. And he did, all that cold, dark night. His soul yearned upward as Ryl lay bathed in sweat; he prayed to Lomallin while the land was coming alive around him and Ryl was dying; prayed for a miracle, prayed for Manalo . . .

But the sage came not, and at last the sky lightened with the coming of dawn . . .

And the coming of Chaluk, from out of the lodge, to lay a heavy hand on Ohaern's shoulder and say, "We have done all we could, Ohaern, but it is not enough. Come then, to say good-bye."

Ohaern still knelt, rigid as iron. Then, slowly, he rose and went back into the hut.

Chaluk followed.

They came forth again as the sun broke above the horizon, to welcome Ryl's soul to the sky. They came forth in silence, Chaluk in fear and alarm, Ohaern with a face filled with thunder and a heart filled with rage.

"Ohaern," the shaman pleaded, "we could do no more."

Ohaern chopped his hand sideways in an impatient gesture. "It is not you who deserves my anger, Chaluk. Indeed, you and Mardone made Ryl's passing as easy as you might. No, it is not you who merits revenge."

"Who, then?" And Chaluk was instantly sorry he had asked, for Ohaern grated, "Lomallin!" and strode away to his forge.

There he picked up the hammer and struck blow after blow on the anvil, until the hammer broke and the metal bore the imprint of his anger. Still, unslaked, he turned to glare into the fire, silently berating Lomallin, hurling insult after insult at his god—and slowly, as his anger began to abate, the notion of a fitting revenge began, the idea that he could strike back at Lomallin only through Ulahane, and that surely it would serve the human-lover right if Ohaern were to turn to the worship of his rival . . .

He howled, throwing his head back and sinking to the floor. What nonsense, to give obedience and worship to the god who had taken Ryl's life! But to whom could he turn? What god could he worship? Ulahane was his enemy, and now he swore a deep and dark revenge upon the human-hater, swore that he would fight Ulahane in every way that he could, frustrate his schemes wherever he saw them. He knew which god to fight, well enough . . .

But with whose power? What god would lend him strength for such a revenge? If Lomallin had failed him, to whom else could he turn?

Finally, worn out with his rage, he tumbled to the floor of his smithy and wept his way into sleep.

The excited clamor brought Ohaern back to wakefulness. He looked about him, astonished, and saw the long golden streak of sunset striking through the doorway to stripe the smithy floor. He looked about him, astonished that he still could live when his grief was so great, that the world still could exist when Ryl was gone from it.

The remembrance of her death made his chest feel suddenly hollow again, as if his heart were gone with Ryl. In a desperate search for distraction, he stumbled to his feet and fled outside.

The clansmen were gathered around a pony laden with a double pack, accompanied by four men who carried staves and wore long knives at their belts. Everyone was speaking at once, demanding news, wanting to know what goods the men had to trade, or bringing out their own amber beads or caches of the tin that they had dug from the cliffs a day's travel away. Ohaern watched with dull disinterest, and was amazed that he could feel only leaden sadness when, always before this, the coming of the amber traders had been an occasion for excitement and delight. But what joy could there be in a world without Ryl?

One traveler was standing in front of the pony's head and he held up his hands, laughing. "Peace, my friends, peace! We cannot answer all your demands at once! We will stay a day or two, if you will have us, and will have time enough to hear your news and give ours, to take your tin and amber and give you the pottery and cloth and jewelry of the south! Have any of you found any gold?"

"None was in our round this time," answered Rubo the chief. "Why you southerners are so fascinated by that yellow metal, I cannot see! Oh, it is pretty enough when you polish it, and works well to make trinkets for the ladies, but what good is it otherwise?"

"As much good as the amber we seek," a second trader answered. "The people of the cities will give us yards and yards of cloth for a piece of amber, because it makes such pretty ornaments."

"The tin, though, they need for making bronze." The lead trader held up his own blade. "We have saved some of these for you, even though we have come so far north!"

"You need not have bothered," Rubo said proudly. "We have found iron ore, and we have a smith!"

The trader wrinkled his nose at that. "Iron! It will break under a blow from a bronze sword forged by a really good smith! No, you may keep your iron, and I will keep my bronze."

"Well, some of us might want it," said another man.

The head trader shrugged. "I will trade gladly—that is what I brought it for. But tell me, who taught you to forge iron in this one year since I came last?"

"The wise man, Manalo," Rubo answered. "He came in the winter, stayed a month, and taught us much."

"Manalo?" another trader said, frowning. "Is that not the name of the wanderer who angered the captain of the soldiers of Kuru at their trading fort of Byleo?"

Ohaern stiffened, suddenly paying close attention.

The lead trader nodded. "Yes, it is. He had the foolishness to preach the virtues of Lomallin to the Kuruite soldiers. The captain threw him in their jail and swore that the sage would forswear Lomallin and worship Ulahane, or be sacrificed to him."

"Manalo imprisoned?" Ohaern leaped forward, catching the man by the shoulders. "Are you sure?"

"As sure as I am that you squeeze too tightly." The lead trader frowned, trying to twist free, but Ohaern held him in a vice grip.

"Where is this Byleo?"

"Atop a hill where your Segway River flows into the Mashra, and a town has grown up about its walls already. Surely you have heard of Byleo!"

"I have." Ohaern scowled. "And what I have heard is not good."

The people muttered in agreement. Ominous stories were told of the soldiers at Byleo—how strangers disappeared there, but shrieks were heard coming from the fort at midnight; how no pretty girl dared be seen by one of the Kuruite soldiers; how they had taken hostages to compel several tribes of hunters to bring in every ounce of food they could find. Of course, they paid those hunters well and promised them that Ulahane would make them rich—but they were no less compelled for all that.

Hostages—Manalo! That was why they had imprisoned him instead of killing him out of hand! But why would they then threaten to kill him for their sinister god's pleasure?

"When do they mean to sacrifice him?" Ohaern demanded.

"Take your hands from me and I will tell you."

Shame-faced, Ohaern withdrew his hold—but there was still frantic urgency in his voice and in his face. "No wonder he did not come!"

"Not come?" the leader asked. "Did Manalo promise to visit you again?"

"No, but . . . Never mind! My wife is dead because he came not, and that I will revenge upon these soldiers!"

The trader looked up at Rubo in alarm. "Is the man mad? You cannot fight the soldiers of Kuru!"

"Oh, I can fight them well enough," Ohaern said grimly. "I may die from that fighting, but that matters little. Tell me, when do they mean to sacrifice the sage?"

"They had not named a day when we were there," the trader said, "and I doubt that they will do it at all, for several of the tribes who serve them love Manalo for the good he has done them. He is of far more worth to them in prison than upon the altar of Ulahane."

"If he is alive, he shall be free," Ohaern said grimly, "or I shall be dead!" And he turned on his heel and stalked away.

Alarmed, Chaluk started after him, but Rubo caught his arm and shook his head. "Let him be, Chaluk. Solitude is the medicine he must have now."

He was right, though not for medicine—Ohaern needed to be alone to pray to Lomallin. He took station beneath an oak, looked up into its budding branches and thought, with intense concentration, *Lomallin, forgive me! I have wronged you in laying Ryl's death upon your shoulders, I see that now! It was the servants of Ulahane who held Manalo from us! O Lomallin, give me strength, give me wisdom, give me insight! Aid me, and I shall free your sage!*

For surely, it had come time for him to show his thanks to Manalo—the sage had refused all other rewards, but Ohaern did not think he would refuse thanks for his child, thanks for saving Ryl from death in childbed. He could only repent his anger, his rashness, in doubting Lomallin when she died—but he could also haul Manalo out of that sink of depravity called Byleo!

When Ohaern came back to the village, dusk was falling, and the travelers, done with the day's trading, had settled down to telling the news of the wondrous cities of the south. But all fell silent when Ohaern came out from the trees—fell silent and stared at him in apprehension, feeling his grim purpose.

He came into the center of them, stood by the fire and looked all about him, his face stone. Finally, he said, "I will go up against Byleo. I shall bring back Manalo, or die there."

They stared at him, riveted by his words. The traders inched away, watching him warily, thinking him mad.

"Who will come with me?" Ohaern demanded. "Who truly feels the need to thank Manalo for his teaching?"

"Ohaern," Rubo said darkly, "this is—"

"I." Geht stepped forward. "Manalo withdrew the demon that could have burst my child's belly!"

"I!" Farren stepped forward. "If he had not spoken to her father, I would not be wed to Oril!"

"I!" Toan stepped forward. "He saved my wife from the raging fever that not even Mardone's herbs could abate!"

One by one they stepped forward, and with each, Ohaern stood a little straighter, smiled a little more firmly, and Rubo's misgiving seemed to lessen a little. Finally, nineteen men stood before the clan, and Ohaern's eyes glowed, his chest expanded with pride. Rubo nodded grudgingly, and there was a gleam of pride in his eye, too. "It is well," he judged. "Manalo has given much to this clan. I would be sad indeed if any of you did not come back—but it is our due to him." He raised his head, a faraway look coming into his eye, and Ohaern said quickly, "No. You are the chief. What would the clan do without you? Leave it to us, Rubo. We shall come back with Manalo, or not come back at all."

"I cannot ask you to go if I am not willing myself!"

"You are willing," said Geht. "We are all witnesses to that. But you must not go, Rubo."

So the chief did not. Ohaern set forth from their forest village with nineteen men behind him and burning purpose in his heart.

There was burning purpose in Lucoyo's heart, too, as he trudged quickly down the roadway. He had recovered from the fever almost completely—enough to have made himself a bow and some arrows, to have chipped a flint head and lashed it to a pole for a spear. There was fire in his eye and fury in his heart. How he knew where to go, he could not say—but know he did. It must be Ulahane at work within him, he thought, just as it was Ulahane who had brought him back to life after the spider bites.

He came to a crossroad—to a place where five roads met. He stared at it in surprise for a moment, then grinned. Such a meeting was rare indeed, and fairly spoke of Ulin magic working within human beings—and since the five roads could be the vanes of a pentagram, Ulahane's symbol, the Ulin in question must have been the blood-god! Here, then, was the goal to which Ulahane had been leading him—but where were the people to slay?

Coming, something within him seemed to say. Lucoyo raised his head, smiling. Of course! Ulahane had even brought him here ahead, so that he might find the best place for ambush!

He looked around him. The roads met not far from the forest, and there were tall trees overhanging the crossroads. One was a pine, and looking up, Lucoyo could see a large branch clearly, thick where it joined the trunk, thirty feet up. From such a perch, he thought, a man might shoot down upon any who came by either of these roads—and falling from such a height, the arrows would strike even harder.

He grinned and went to the tree. Leaping, he caught the lowest branch and pulled himself up—groaning and gasping; he certainly had not recovered his former strength! In fact, he had to rest a few minutes, sitting astride the branch and holding to the trunk to steady himself. When he felt restored, he stood carefully, then stepped up and sideways to the next branch. From this point it was easy.

Finally, he settled down upon his chosen branch, leaning against the trunk. He slipped his bow around from his back to string it, then took an arrow from his quiver and set it against the string. Then he relaxed. Of course, Ulahane might have brought him here a day or more before his quarry came—but somehow Lucoyo didn't think so. He settled down to wait.

The sun was halfway down the sky when he heard the chanting. Looking up, he saw a group of men approaching from the northeast—not a very large group, he counted twenty as they came closer, and mere hunters, not even so advanced as his own . . . *as the people who reared me!* he corrected himself angrily. But these hunters were human, and he had no doubt that if it had been they who had reared him, they would have treated him just as badly as his nomad clan. He raised his bow and pulled back the string, taking aim at the leader, a big fellow with massive shoulders and arms and a chest like a basin, if the archer was to judge by the bulk of his furs. He couldn't miss, Lucoyo thought.

Just as he was about to loose, though, a shout broke his concentration—a shout from the south. Lucoyo flinched, and barely managed to hold the arrow on the string. Relaxing the bow, he turned to see . . .

A troop of soldiers who came striding toward the crossroads, wearing the scarlet kilts and bronze pectorals of Kuru, their heads protected by coiled-rope caps—protected, and warmed; other than that, they had blankets draped around their shoulders, but even from a bowshot's distance, Lucoyo could see how thin those blankets were. Those soldiers must be cold indeed! He was surprised that the southerners had not learned to deal with this northern chill any better than that. Of course, he could see their point— those pectoral tabards would turn an arrow easily enough.

Fortunately, their sides were unprotected under the flimsy cloth. Lucoyo raised his bow.

The lead soldier, the one with his arms left bare so all could see his armbands of rank, shouted angrily at the hunters and motioned his men to speed up. They broke into a quick-step, leveling their spears.

Lucoyo looked back and forth from one band to the other, delighted and confused. Which should he attack?

CHAPTER 5

Ohaern grinned—how considerate of the Kuruite soldiers to come to meet him, still two days' march from Byleo! "Charge!" he called to his men. "If they do not give way, cut them in half!" He drew his sword, swinging it high then down, to point at the soldiers as he leaped into a run.

The soldiers arrived first and clustered at the crossroad, a rough oval of thirty men, spears forward. "Halt!" the leader snapped. "Give way to the soldiers of Kuru!"

"The roads are free to all!" Ohaern shouted. "Give way before *us*, outlander, for these forests are ours!"

"Brave talk, from a bush-crawling barbarian!" the soldier sneered. "We are thirty to your twenty! Surrender or die, and those who survive shall be permitted to live as our slaves!"

"No Biri warrior shall be a slave!" Ohaern roared, and in the tree above, Lucoyo suddenly knew which humans to begin slaying.

The two forces crashed together, the Biriae with wild war cries, the Kuruites with ritualized shouts of anger. The Biriae beat the spears aside with axe and sword and cut at their owners. The Kuruites, though, proved more adept than they looked, blocking swords with the copper bands on their spear shafts, then striking down with the sharpened edges of the points. Here and there a spearhead found its mark, plunging deep or leaving a red trail behind—but there and here an axe chopped through a spear shaft and a sword plunged past into flesh. In minutes the two forces had become a churning melee of single combats.

Above them Lucoyo swung his arrowhead back and forth, sighting along the shaft, waiting for a clear shot at a Kuruite soldier . . .

There! A Biri fell with a red gash along his upper arm, his sword falling from nerveless fingers. The Kuruite lifted his spear high.

Lucoyo drew and loosed. Even as he watched his arrow strike home and the soldier fall, he was pulling the next shaft from his quiver and nocking it to the string. There again! Another Kuruite soldier turned away from a fallen, bleeding Biri, looking for another foe . . .

An arrow shaft appeared in his chest as if by magic. He shouted with pain and died. With savage elation Lucoyo nocked another arrow. Revenge had begun! None could exile him for it now—and his head was already any man's for the taking. He could kill and kill and kill, and none could do any worse than they already had. He sighted along the shaft, aimed just to the right of another Kuruite pectoral, drew, and loosed. The feathers blossomed in the soldier's side like a deadly flower. The soldier stared down at it, amazed, only just beginning to feel the pain when his eyes rolled up and he crumpled. Lucoyo nocked his next arrow, reveling in the slaughter, sighting on another soldier of Kuru, drawing, loosing, watching avidly as the blood welled out around his arrow, feeling like a true servant of Ulahane, then finding the next foe, and the next, and the next . . .

Suddenly, there were no more. Suddenly, the men of Kuru were all fallen, except for the half dozen who fled across the meadow as if all the wolves of all the northern forests were at their heels. They almost were, for a half-dozen Biriae charged after them, but stopped at the big leader's call. "Enough! We needed the road clear, nothing more! We are Biriae! We do not kill for pleasure!"

That, Lucoyo thought, *is the difference between you and me, Biri.*

But the Kuruite leader looked up with dying eyes and saw his nemesis in the trees above him. He tried to shout, but it was only a croak—a croak that carried. "May you die in agony, barbarian! I lay Ulahane's curse upon you! May Ulahane shred your flesh and grind your bones!" Then his body went loose and his eyes went dull.

Lucoyo stared, feeling his stomach sink, feeling a raw and empty gulf of dread within him. He had chosen the wrong side! He, who thought he served Ulahane, had fought against him! And he knew, with a hollow certainty, that whatever god he worshiped in the future had better be strong enough to protect him from Ulahane.

But perhaps he could even the score, win the scarlet god's forgiveness! Frantically, he snatched another arrow from his quiver . . .

But the Biriae were looking up, too, pointing, finding the slender archer among the leaves and calling to one another. Silently, Lucoyo cursed his luck—so much for the thought of continuing the slaughter with the Biriae!

"Come down, friend," the big leader called. "We must thank you mightily for aiding us against our enemies."

Lucoyo hesitated. He had never heard anyone thank him before—except his mother.

"You are our ally, and a brave man, to dare the wrath of Ulahane," one of the other men said. "Come down, halfling."

Rage spurred. Lucoyo's eyes narrowed as he bent the bow.

"He mislikes the term," the big leader said in astonishment.

"I pray you, pardon me, friend!" the other Biri said quickly. "I meant no offense."

"To us, the half-elfin are honored," the leader explained, "for we worship Lomallin, and they are his allies."

Lucoyo stared. Could it be true? Had he chosen the wrong god after all? But Lomallin was so gentle! How could he stand against Ulahane?

The big leader smiled, holding out a hand. "Take the risk," he urged. "We will not even ask you to unstring your bow, or set the arrow back in your quiver. Here, we will give you room." He waved his men back a good thirty feet from the trunk, then looked up at Lucoyo again. "If we seek to betray you, you can be back up that tree before we can reach you—but we are friends, and you will be safer with twenty allies than you would be alone, even if some of us are wounded. I am Ohaern." He held out his hand again.

Lucoyo wavered, looking down at the open, honest faces smiling encouragement, and felt the longing within him surge up. He quashed it sternly—but told himself that he knew a good bargain when he saw one. He relaxed the bow and said, "I am Lucoyo."

The hunters cheered.

"Come down, then, Lucoyo," Ohaern urged, "and let us take what little loot we can from these Kuruite dogs, then march on a little way and break bread together."

Lucoyo forced a smile—at least, he told himself it was forced—and began to drop down, branch by branch, but still holding the bow, and saying, "I like the sound of loot well enough. As to the bread, I can only gain by the bargain, for I have none."

"Well, ours is hard journey biscuit, but it *is* bread." Ohaern held up an open palm as the half-elf landed on the ground. "Peace and alliance between us!"

Lucoyo pressed his palm against Ohaern's, never taking his gaze from the war chief's eyes. "Peace," he said slowly, "and alliance."

"It is well!" Ohaern grinned, then gestured to his men. "These are my clan-mates—Glabur, Sotro, Vlanad . . ."

Each nodded as he was introduced. In spite of himself, Lucoyo found himself smiling as he returned the nods—and concentrated intently on each hunter's name and face, memorizing; if these men were to be his allies, he would need to know upon whose name to call—and if they turned and betrayed him, he would need to know upon whose face to visit revenge.

"Welcome among us." Ohaern clapped him on the shoulder. "Now let us see if these dogs of the Byleo kennel carried anything worth reiving."

They turned to the looting, what little there was. Lucoyo limped along, keeping a sharp eye out for arrows or anything else worth stealing—but there were only journey rations and the excellent Kuruite bronze knives, almost long enough to be short swords. Ohaern gave Lucoyo two of them because, he said, "There is easily one for each of us, and several more besides. You slew more of these men than any of us, friend, so you shall have an extra knife."

"But I suffered less risk," Lucoyo protested, and was amazed to hear himself say anything to lessen his own position.

"That is true," Ohaern said judiciously, "but if you *had* been discovered, where could you have run to? One cast of a Kuruite spear would have finished you."

A chill seized Lucoyo's bowels as he realized the big hunter was right.

Then, wonder of wonders, the hunters turned to burying the enemy dead! "Why do you do them such honor?" Lucoyo demanded.

"Because it is an offense to Lomallin to leave a dead man unburied," Glabur explained, "and in hopes that a weight of earth and stone will keep their ghosts from roaming."

Lucoyo watched the digging in disbelief. "What if one of them were still alive?"

"Oh, have no fear of that," Glabur said grimly. "We shall make very sure they are not."

When they were done, Ohaern shouldered his pack again and called, "We march!"

They did, but he slowed his pace to match Lucoyo's limping— the half-elf was mortified that even the hunters who were wounded could still move faster than he. "Why did you not ask me to help with the digging?" he demanded.

"Because I could see that you are not yet recovered from your last wounds," Ohaern replied.

Lucoyo looked up, astonished—not by Ohaern's having noticed the limp and the easy tiring, but by his consideration.

"No doubt that is why you fired from hiding," Ohaern said generously.

Lucoyo's eyes narrowed. "That," he admitted, "and a wish to kill as many enemies with as little danger as possible."

Ohaern laughed, clapping him on the back—but he remembered to pull his punch at the last minute, and the slap landed lightly. "I cannot argue with that, since it saved our lives. Indeed, not one of my men is dead, thanks to you."

The other men grinned their appreciation, and Lucoyo felt a surge of unreasoning anger. Did not the naive fools realize he had come within a hair's breadth of shooting *them*? "You would not have been so thankful if my shafts had gone astray," he said acidly.

Ohaern laughed out loud, and so did his fellows. Lucoyo decided, right there and then, that he was going to make them lose their tempers, each one of them, individually and collectively, before they reached their destination. *Then*, if they still wanted him along, he might begin to trust them. "Where are you bound?"

"To Byleo," Ohaern said offhandedly. "We have a quarrel to settle with the soldiers of Kuru."

Lucoyo stared. And they called *him* twisted! "Have you taken your brain to the shaman lately? It does not seem to be working well."

"Really?" Ohaern looked down at him, a grin hovering at the corners of his mouth. "Why do you say that?"

Behind him, Lucoyo heard Glabur whisper to another Biri, "I have not seen Ohaern smile this fortnight. The half-elf is a tonic for him."

Lucoyo felt anger rise again and determined that if he was a tonic, they would not like his taste—at least, his taste in pranks. "What makes me say that? Oh, merely the fact that you are going a long distance, with a great deal of effort, to seek a death that you might just as easily have found at home!"

"You think the Kuruite soldiers are unbeatable, then?" Ohaern asked politely.

"When there are five hundred of them to your twenty," Lucoyo said, "yes."

"Come, friend Lucoyo!" Glabur stepped up beside him. "Have you never stolen anything from an enemy?"

Lucoyo turned on him, face burning. "And what if I have? If it is an enemy, there is only honor in it, not shame!" He did not tell them that the enemies had been within his own clan.

"Exactly," Glabur agreed. "And if the thing you steal is something they stole from you, the honor is greater."

Lucoyo looked up at him in silence for a moment, then gave a short nod and said, "Even so. What do you go to steal?"

"A sage," Ohaern told him, "a teacher who had given us great aid, saved our lives, and taught us much—even the forging of iron."

Lucoyo looked up shrewdly. "Was his name Manalo?"

"Why, yes." Ohaern looked startled. "Do you know him, then?"

"Somewhat. He taught our clan, too." But not enough, Lucoyo added silently. Manalo had been the only man who ever spoke kindly to him, without trying to intimidate him the next minute or enlist his aid so that he would take the blame for a rule-breaking. Lucoyo had felt himself drawn to the man very strongly, though he tried to fight the feeling by playing prank upon prank, and jibing, and striving to find a question Manalo could not answer. The sage had borne it all with a good grace and seemed to persevere in liking him in spite of it all. Yes, he had tried to teach Lucoyo's clan his own easy tolerance and kindliness—but the teacher is not to blame if the students reject his teaching. "What has he to do with Byleo?"

"They have locked him up in their prison," Ohaern said, "for he will not worship Ulahane. My wife died because he could not come to save her." The sadness, the darkness, suddenly settled about him again, like a mantle.

The contrast was so great that it shocked Lucoyo, and he felt a quite uncharacteristic urge to banish that gloom from the big man's face. "Oh, well, then." He turned away nonchalantly. "Of course, if you only go to steal, then I am your man!"

"Are you really?" Almost against his will, Ohaern smiled again, ever so lightly. "Are you the master thief, then?"

"Quite the master," Lucoyo said airily, "and if it is only a matter of sneaking past their guardsmen and breaking into their prison, I am quite willing to take *that* much risk."

"Well, there may be need to do more than sneak, when it comes to their guardsmen," Glabur said, and Ohaern agreed. "We cannot risk one raising the alarm. It may be necessary to take one out here and there—perhaps even to kill."

Lucoyo looked up at him with a fox's grin. "Oh," he said, "I think I can accept that." After all, he really didn't care who he killed—anyone would do, as long as he was human—or elfin. He would be just as glad to make Byleo the butt of his revenge as his own tribesmen.

No, his own tribesmen would be better—much better. But any other human being would be acceptable after that—except, possibly, for these hunters. He would delay judgment on them.

Of course, he would try them first. When they pitched camp an hour or so later, Lucoyo volunteered to gather kindling, while others set out to hunt. There were few trees on this side of the river, and they all clustered by the water—the flow marked the end of Ohaern's forest country and the beginning of Lucoyo's grasslands—but Lucoyo found sticks enough to start a fire, and some thick enough to keep it going.

He also found a stand of curious fanlike plants with cones that he knew well.

He brought them all back to the campsite and started laying the fire to roast the pig the hunters brought back. Then he stacked the larger sticks to the side, hiding the cones in them.

"Well done, Lucoyo!" Dalvan knelt beside him, opening the greenwood box that hung at his belt and emptying the living coal out into the pile of kindling. Lucoyo watched with interest and saw the box was lined with clay, hardened and blackened from the heat. His folk always carried along a smoldering pot, but when they journeyed from place to place, they went as a clan, not by ones and twos. He realized he could learn much from these hunters . . .

And they from him.

When the pig was roasted and the carcass taken from the spit, Lucoyo said, "I will stoke the fire."

The Biriae looked up, agreeably surprised. "Well, thank you, Lucoyo!"

"None can say the ha—the stranger does not do his share of the work."

"Stranger? No more! Let us call him . . . the archer!"

Lucoyo almost felt guilty as he set a few sticks on the fire— with the cones among them. But he steeled himself with the thought that these Biriae's goodwill must be tested—never mind that he wasn't really acting as a friend should.

He went back to his place, gnawing on a bone and listening to the talk. Glabur was in the middle of a tale about a huge boar and a sharp spear when—

The fire exploded.

Loud reports rang out, and sticks and flaming coals flew everywhere. Dalvan shouted with pain and brushed a burning stick from him as he jumped up. The others were already on their feet, yards away from the fire and still moving, calling to one another, "What was it?"

"A spirit!"

"The wrath of Ulahane!"

"A fire demon!"

Ohaern was as surprised as any of them, but as he leaped back, his hand was on his dagger, his left up to guard, and the expression on his face neither angry nor frightened, but only very alert. While the others looked at the fire, he looked at the trees around, then at them, and noticed that Lucoyo was silent, though moving just as fast as any of the band. He caught the halfling's eye, and Lucoyo's face went blank with innocence.

Ohaern laughed.

The other Biriae looked up at Ohaern in surprise, then followed his gaze to Lucoyo, then looked at one another with sheepish grins as they all began to laugh, too. "It was a famous joke," Glabur told Lucoyo, "or will be. What was it? Resinous wood? But here there are no pines."

"No," Lucoyo admitted. "Cones."

"Cones?" Glabur stared in surprise. "What kind of cone makes a noise like that?"

"We call it 'the podium,' " Lucoyo told them. "It is a low branching plant with a few cones at the top. Crickets sit on them to play their tunes, looking like chieftains standing up high to address their people."

" 'Lucoyo's podium' it shall be to us from this day forth," Ohaern averred.

"You will have to show it to us before we will truly know it," Glabur said. "We have never seen it before."

Lucoyo frowned. "Why, how is that?"

"It must be a thing of the grasslands," Ohaern said. "And you really *must* show it to us, Lucoyo—we might find a use for such a thing as that."

"Use?" Lucoyo asked, disbelieving. "What use could it have other than to play a prank?"

"Well, it was a humorous prank indeed," said Glabur, shaking his head. "I have not jumped so high since an aurochs tried to gore my shins!" He chuckled, shaking his head.

"It was indeed." Dalvan chuckled, too. "But can we go back to our meal now, archer? With no more alarms?"

"I promise." Lucoyo held up a hand. "For this meal, anyway."

"Oho!" Glabur cried. "Watch out, my lads! We have a prankster among us!"

They laughed and averred that they would be careful as they sat down to eat.

Lucoyo could scarcely believe his ears. They were actually laughing! And no one seemed to be angry with him—at least, after the initial shock. He took his place in the circle slowly and tentatively, unable to believe that people could be capable of such simple goodness.

There had to be a reason for it. They had to have a motive.

Lucoyo determined that he would find that motive. He would test these people very thoroughly before he would begin to trust them.

But they will turn away from you, that nasty voice whispered inside him. *They may be friends, real friends, and you will make enemies of them by your tricks.*

Lucoyo realized that, and had to admit that perhaps the ill-will among his clan-mates had not been entirely due to their villainy. Nonetheless, he had to test these new friends. It was stupid, he knew, but the urge to revenge his hurts on anything human was too strong for him still; he would confine it to attacks that could be construed as jokes—heavy-handed, perhaps, but jokes nonetheless.

Lucoyo tried them, well and truly. He put dried burrs in Glabur's leggings; he put riverbank clay in Ohaern's boots. He put a cricket in Dalvan's coal box, and when Dalvan opened it and cried out in alarm, Lucoyo laughed with delight and produced the coal, live and hot in a makeshift box of his own. He was careful never to do any real damage—and was always amazed that, after the initial shout of anger, the hunter would look up in surprise as his clan-mates began to laugh, then would grin sheepishly and begin to laugh himself.

Of course, Lucoyo hadn't stopped to think that *they* might play pranks on *him*. He didn't even think of it when he shoved his foot into his boot and felt something cold and supple move against his foot. He yelped and yanked the boot off, dumping the little snake out, then beat the sole furiously to knock out anything else that might be there—and suddenly realized that the whole band was laughing. He looked up, astonished and enraged, leaping to his feet with words of denunciation on his lips—then remembered the sheepish grins and grudging laughter of his victims. Indignation shot through him, pushing out the rage—he would be hanged if one of these crude hunters would show more tolerance than he himself! He forced the grin, then managed to hack a laugh—and found that the second came easier than the first, and the third even more easily, and by the fourth he was really laughing.

Ohaern clapped him on the back and cried, "There's a man for you! He can swallow it as well as he serves it!"

Lucoyo laughed even louder, realizing that now it was *he* who had been tested—and had passed the test. But he resolved to reserve a very special tidbit of humor for the big barbarian.

Of course, he jibed at them constantly, calling Glabur "ox-high" due to his epic leap, and Dalvan "coal-carrier." They responded in kind, calling him "arrowhead" and "limpet," to which he replied that all should be as limpid as he, and answered their chorus of groans by saying that he could walk as quickly with a bad leg as Racol could with a good one, which of course led to a race, and when he lost, Lucoyo could always protest that he would win the rematch when his leg recovered. Ohaern pointed out that perhaps he should not have picked out the fastest runner among the Biriae, but Lucoyo answered that there was no honor in challenging any but the best. "True," Ohaern answered, suddenly somber. "It is therefore that we go against Byleo."

Lucoyo was shocked to find himself alarmed at the leader's gloom and determined once more to banish it. "No," he said. "It is therefore that Byleo sent troops against the Biriae."

Ohaern stared, astonished, then joined in the chorus of laughter and slapped Lucoyo on the back again. He forgot to be gentle this time, but he caught the half-elf before he hit the ground.

So, what with one thing and another, Lucoyo was feeling quite a part of the band, and very much the honorary Biri, by the time they came to the river.

CHAPTER 6

Lucoyo looked out over the River Segway and could barely see the opposite shore. "How do we cross?"

"We do not." Ohaern nodded at Glabur and Dalvan, who had taken huge leather bundles out of their packs—indeed, the packs could have held very little else. They unfolded the leather, while other men prowled the small stand of trees on the banks, cutting down saplings and pruning limbs off larger trees. As Lucoyo watched in astonishment, they bent the saplings, lashed them together, bound others around the top, then stretched the leather over them.

"Skin baskets!" the half-elf cried. "*Huge* skin baskets! But what is their purpose?"

"They are boats," Ohaern said, grinning. "We shall ride them on the water."

Lucoyo stared up at him, appalled, then whipped about to stare at the water, swiveled to gape at the boats, then the river again. Finally, he backed away, shaking his head. "No, never! They will turn over! The water-spirits shall drag us under! We shall all drown!"

Several of the Biriae laughed aloud, and Lucoyo swung about, staring, then turned to Ohaern, glowering. "It is a prank! It is all a ruse, to see me tremble!"

"It is not a ruse," Ohaern told him, grinning, "but your panic is amusing—the more so since each of us felt it the first time we rode in a coracle. No, you shall not drown, Lucoyo—and if you keep your seat, making no sudden movements, neither shall we capsize. We shall ride all the way to Byleo in these boats, or nearly—and you shall find the trip less tiring and far quicker than it would have been otherwise."

He spoke truly. Lucoyo managed to keep up a brave front— though he was jelly inside—as he took his place in the center of one of the boats. Four other men climbed in beside him and pushed off from the shore with their staves—slotted spear shafts into which they had bound broad wooden blades. With these paddles they guided the rocking boat out into the middle of the river.

Lucoyo was terrified. He had seen bodies of water this size before, had even bathed in them, near the shore, but had never been in a boat of any kind, not even a raft. He sat rigid, eyes huge, expecting any minute that the boat would roll over, that he would feel the bloated hands of drowned men in his hair, that he would be dragged down to the bottom, to become like them . . .

But the boats did not capsize, and after a while Lucoyo became used to the rocking, and realized that the coracle would roll only so far in one direction, then just so far in another—provided his companions plied their paddles well. But they did, and he began to loosen a little, becoming accustomed to the rocking, no longer feeling it was dangerous. By sunset he had almost relaxed, and when they stepped ashore to camp for the night, he was surprised to find that solid ground felt unnatural.

That was the only night they camped, though. The next day, a man in one of the left-hand boats gave a shout, pointing, and they all looked to see a dozen canoes putting out from the western bank, moving toward them. Ohaern called out a greeting, but it was answered with a flight of arrows. The arrows all fell short, woefully short, but Ohaern called, "Into the middle of the river, and paddle hard!"

The current moved faster in the center of the river, and the pad-

dlers dug in with a will, united by Ohaern's war chant. Lucoyo un-
limbered his bow, strung it, and asked, "How can I look over the
side?"

"Carefully," Glabur answered, and Ohaern nodded, never slack-
ening the chant.

Dalvan said, "As you move higher, archer, I shall move closer to
Ohaern, and we shall yet be steady. Ready? Up, now—carefully,
carefully . . ."

Lucoyo inched his way up the side of the boat, his heart in his
throat, but it did not capsize—and when he arrived there, he was
surprised to see the canoes far away behind them and growing farther, the men in them shaking their fists at the Biriae. Dimly, he
could hear their curses. "Why did I bother?"

"In case they proved to be better boatmen than they seemed,"
Ohaern told him, "and this sluggishness only a ruse to draw us in."

"It is no pretense," Jannogh said from his place in the rear.
"They are so clumsy it is ridiculous—but surely they would not
pretend so when they see us escaping!"

Ohaern frowned. "What manner of men are these, who have canoes but know not how to use them?"

They rowed in silence while each man pondered the notion.
Then Lucoyo offered, "Thieves?"

"There speaks the voice of experience," Glabur grunted, "but I
think you have found it, archer."

"He has," Ohaern agreed. "These are plainsmen who have conquered a river village, and its canoes with it, but have no idea how
to use them—or have just begun to learn, at least."

"I hope they will not have learned better when we return,"
Glabur said.

"They *are* five to our one," Dalvan admitted.

"But what kind of archers are they, whose shafts fall so far
short?" Ohaern wondered.

But Lucoyo had an answer for that. "They are plainsmen who
follow the great herds. My clan has met some of them, and kept
our weapons in our hands as we traded insults, then finally began
to trade goods instead. Their bows are made of aurochs' horns,
with only an arm's length of wood to connect them. They will

send an arrow with great force, but for some reason it will not travel far."

"More likely, then, that they do not know how to make arrows," Dalvan opined.

"Do they know how to wield swords?" Glabur wondered.

"It grieves me to say it, but I trust we shall not have to find out." Ohaern sighed. "We cannot spare the time; each day we tarry is a day Manalo comes closer to being sacrificed to Ulahane. Perhaps we can fight them *after* we have saved him."

But the plainsmen had other ideas—or their first cousins did. The next day, the river narrowed, and the canoes started out from the shore as soon as the Biriae came in sight. By the time they neared the village, there were a dozen canoes already in mid-river, with more following from both banks. Lucoyo readied his bow, and one man in each coracle readied his spear.

"Keep them from us, Lucoyo," Ohaern bade him, and the half-elf did his best. He filled the air with arrows, arrows that would have found their mark if the attackers had not dodged so well—they seemed as supple as eels. They were close enough to see clearly now—stocky, swarthy, bearded men with black or brown hair coiled under leather caps. They wore copper armbands and leather jerkins, and were shouting obscenities at the Biriae.

"I have come this way before," Glabur said, "and I have never seen such as these!"

"Whoever they are, they are cousins to those who chased us upstream," Lucoyo said. "Duck!" He took his own advice, and a short arrow arced into the coracle. Ohaern shouted in anger as it struck his boot.

"Are you hurt, Ohaern?" Glabur cried.

"A fly's bite, nothing more—but my boot will need mending."

"It will." Lucoyo plucked the shaft out of Ohaern's boot heel and sent it flying back to its source. "I have only two more arrows, my friends!"

"There are more in my pack," Glabur answered. "Put them to good use, Lucoyo."

The archer did.

Shouts rang out from the other boats as the Biriae caught the strangers' arrows on their paddles, then handed them down to the spearmen, who threw them back at their attackers. Those were only fly bites, of course, so the stocky men pulled closer and closer, no matter how clumsy they were in their canoes.

"Give me a boat like that, and I could fly like the wind!" Dalvan cried.

"Why, then, I shall!" Ohaern replied as a canoe lurched up alongside. The stocky men sprang to their feet, and the canoe lurched beneath them. They shouted in alarm, flailing for balance, and Ohaern slashed with his sword. Bright blood answered him, the wounded man howled and fell—and the canoe capsized. Over they went, and the Biriae cheered.

The other coracles had met with similar fortune. All but three of the canoes had capsized, and the attackers floundered in the water, eyes white, too proud to call out in fear but very obviously sinking. The water was churned to froth by men who could not swim. The few canoes still afloat were doing the best they could to pick up their drenched friends—with comical results as first one canoe, then another, flipped over when men tried to climb in.

Through his laughter Ohaern called out, "Bid them hold to the sides! A canoe will hold you as well upside down as right side up!"

One man must have understood him, for he bawled something in a language the Biriae could not understand, and the men in the water seized hold of the overturned canoes like leeches grabbing onto warm flesh.

"Grapple two of those empty canoes!" Ohaern called to the coracle coming after him. "Spoils of war!"

So they left the barbarians behind, and the river bore them south. It broadened again within the mile and stayed broad enough so that they could easily hold off any more attackers until they had passed them. With the two canoes and the lighter load in the coracles, they seemed to be traveling faster than word of their coming could, for none of the other tribes were lurking in midriver waiting for them. Indeed, most of them did not even try to paddle out—they only shot arrows, which almost invariably fell short.

"Why do they bother?" Lucoyo asked, looking over the edge of the coracle. He had tried a canoe once, and had quickly opted for the coracle again. "Why shoot when they know they will lose their arrows?"

Ohaern shrugged. "Perhaps they wish to make it clear we are not welcome."

"Well, they have succeeded in that. Will we find them doing so all the way to Byleo?"

They did not; a day's march from Byleo, the riverbanks became reasonably peaceful—but also amazingly cultivated. The grasslands and the forest ended as if cut off by an axe, or turned into open fields of bare ground, with men and women alike out digging.

"What are they seeking?" Lucoyo wondered.

His boat-mates exchanged glances; apparently the nomad knew nothing of farming, in spite of Manalo's visit. "They are opening the earth to receive seed, Lucoyo," Ohaern explained. "Manalo showed us the way of it. They put grains of oat and barley in the ground and cover them over. Then, late in the summer, they will have oats and barley to reap by the basketful."

Lucoyo stared. "And they *live* on that?"

"If they have to. It is better than starving. But I suspect they still hunt when they are done with the planting, and after the harvest."

"Hunt *where*? They have cut down the forest—and the great herds do not come so close to the river!"

"That is true. They must hunt small game, and perhaps deer. Those crops must attract a great number of such."

"They certainly must! There is so much of them! When do these people find time to do anything else?"

"It does make you wonder," Ohaern admitted. "At least they are peaceful."

But the fields did not leave much room to make a landing. They ate hard biscuit and dried meat, and drank from the river. The next morning they came to Byleo.

"Lucoyo, awake!" Something nudged the half-elf.

Lucoyo looked for something to throw, found nothing, and grudgingly levered himself up. "Why?"

"We must go ashore and hide the boats! Quickly, before the sun rises!"

Lucoyo frowned up at the big hunter. There was urgency in Ohaern's voice, but also eagerness. The half-elf decided it was not time to argue. He pulled himself up to look over the edge of the boat and saw, on the horizon, the shapes of lodges—for surely those odd, squared shapes could be nothing else—dark against the false dawn.

But so many! They spread out on the eastern shore as far as he could see—long and low, but very many. A hill thrust up out of their center, a low hill with a black crown of many points. "What is that atop the slope?" Lucoyo asked, feeling a chill of dread.

"It is a wall made of trees set upright side by side, and sharpened on top," Glabur told him. "I was here once before, to trade furs for bronze blades. They would not give me bronze, but they offered me a great deal of elegant pottery and pretty beads."

Lucoyo gave a snort of laughter. "You did not come again, did you?"

"No, I did not!" Glabur said grimly. "Pots are useful, but not worth the trip, and we can make beads enough at home. But it is more than that—these Kuruites are so suspicious, they give off such an air of malice, that you shudder just being near them—and whenever they look at you, you cannot help but feel that they are gauging how good a sacrifice you would make, to their scarlet god Ulahane."

Lucoyo felt another chill, but he forced a sour smile. "They will not do much business, will they?"

"I hope not," Glabur answered, but he did not seem sure.

They clambered ashore, stowed the coracle skins, and sank the frameworks under a bank, where few would think to look for them. Then the hunters set to hiding the canoes, muttering about it being nearly impossible without forest cover. But Lucoyo was amazed—before his very eyes the canoes disappeared. Soon there was nothing left but a long, low mound on the bank, of dried grass and last year's fallen leaves.

Glabur turned to Ohaern. "What now, chief?"

It was the first time anyone had said it, but Lucoyo realized it was true—Ohaern was the chief, at least of this little band. The term raised his hackles, but he reminded himself that this was Ohaern, not Gorin, and let the antagonism subside.

"Did you go inside the stockade?" Ohaern asked Glabur.

"Yes, for that is where they do their trading."

Ohaern smiled. "It was well for you that you were willing to trade, or you might have walked out of there without your furs after all."

"And lucky to walk out with his life," Dalvan said darkly.

Ohaern nodded. "They must have had sacrifices enough that month. It is large, then?"

"Large enough to hold two villages the size of ours! Indeed, it does hold one—if you can call four long houses of Kuruite soldiers a village. There is a fifth house, too, for their women."

Ohaern frowned. "Odd that the wives would not live with their husbands."

"I did not say they were wives."

"But how else—" Ohaern broke off, shaking his head. "Never mind. The ways of these southern city-people are such that I will never understand them. Is there only the one gate?"

"No, there is a smaller one, wide enough for only one man at a time, at the back, behind the temple."

Lucoyo stared. "They have a temple in there?"

"Did I not say it could hold two villages? Yes, they have a temple, to worship Ulahane. The prison is next to it—in fact, they share a wall."

"All the easier to make sacrifices of criminals," Ohaern said grimly. "Are the gates shut at night?"

"They are, and held closed by a tree trunk squared enough to be a great bar. There is a small gate on the southern side, but it, too, is closed and barred."

"What can be closed can be opened," Dalvan growled.

"Without question," Ohaern agreed, "but I would rather open a small gate than a big one. There should only be one guard there, for one thing, or perhaps two. Well, then, my friends—which of you wish to go into the fortress and trade?"

There was a moment's pause; then all eighteen called, "I!" After a minute, so did Lucoyo. It was just his bad luck that Ohaern chose him for companion.

They went into the city when the sun was low, entering by twos and threes. Lucoyo was amazed at the extent of it and the overwhelming number of people—amazed and repelled that so many people could live together with so little room for each. It showed; there were quarrels on every hand, and he saw two fights break out as they walked along.

Byleo had grown up between the riverbank and the fortress on its hilltop. The houses varied between the lodges of the hunters, new and strange to Lucoyo, and the tents of the nomads, which were more familiar to him, though not quite like those among which he had grown up. At least the street between them was a good twelve cubits' wide, though it was only dust; there was no grass and few enough trees, but there were weeds a-plenty, if the dried remains of last year's crop were anything to judge by.

After fifteen minutes' walk through a warren of such streets, they came into a broader one, at least ten yards in width. The houses here were built of mud brick, something that Lucoyo and Ohaern stared at. "Surely it will wash away in one good rain!" Lucoyo protested.

"Surely," Ohaern agreed. "What are these pictures painted on the walls?"

Lucoyo frowned. "That one is a fish—and surely that is a joint of meat. I see a sheaf of grain, but what is that foaming bowl next to it?"

"I cannot say," Ohaern said, "but I do recognize a bunch of grapes, there. What can such drawings be for? Surely not mere decoration!"

"They show what goods we have to trade, outlander," a fat man called, lounging in the doorway under the sign of the foaming bowl. "Mine shows a bowl of beer. If you have goods to trade, you may taste of it."

"Beer? What is that?"

The merchant grinned. "A drink made of grain, though it must be made by a special recipe, and takes a week and more to prepare. I will let you drink all you want for only one small piece of amber, if you wish it."

"Perhaps tomorrow," Ohaern said, interested, "but for now, we must go to the stockade and learn how we are to go about our trading."

"Ah, well!" the merchant said with regret. "You had best hurry, then, for they close the gate when the sun sets."

"Thank you, stranger." Ohaern hastened his steps, asking Lucoyo softly, "Surely the amber traders would give us more than a few bowls of drink for a piece of gem?"

"It would seem to be a bad bargain," Lucoyo agreed. "Why do you suppose this street is so wide, Ohaern?"

"Look!" Ohaern pointed at the stockade, straight in front of them, though still much higher. "It goes directly to the gates! It is wide so that a troop of soldiers may march down it side by side!"

Lucoyo lifted his head slowly. "Yes, that would make sense. Well, let us go to it side by side, then."

They came to the great stockade gates just as the sunset reddened the sky. "You have come too late," the sentry told them. "There is no more trading today."

"Can we not come in and stay the night?" Ohaern peered in through the gate. "I see that other traders do, and we would prefer to be here when the trading begins in the morning."

"Well, you can if you wish," the Kuruite soldier said, "but you shall have to barter for your dinner."

Ohaern nodded. "I have amber."

The soldier's eyes gleamed with a covetous light. "Give it to me and I shall see you fed!"

Ohaern reached into his pack and pulled out a lump of amber the size of his thumb. "Is this all?" the soldier asked contemptuously.

"No, but I must save some to trade in the morning, must I not?"

"There is that," the soldier said reluctantly. "You will need breakfast, too. Very well, enter."

Ohaern and Lucoyo went in, and found Glabur and his two men already waiting. Not far away, Dalvan and Jannogh lounged and gossiped. They were careful not to acknowledge one another, pretending to be strangers. The soldier was true to the bargain and brought them dinner—if bowls of cold porridge can be called dinner. Ohaern pointed this out to the man, but he only said that he would bring it to them hot, for breakfast. Then he walked away, chuckling to himself.

Lucoyo tasted the mess and made a face. "I hope that soldier is still on duty when—"

Ohaern cleared his throat rather loudly.

"—the moon rises," Lucoyo finished hastily. "It will be good to know we have a protector."

"What?" said another barbarian sourly. "Do you think that man would care whether you lived or died?"

"So long as I had amber or fur to trade him? Yes."

"A point," the stranger admitted. "Have you?"

Lucoyo saw the covetous gleam in the man's eye and grinned. "Whether I do or not, friend, he will learn in the morning. But what trade goods have you?"

"It is too late to talk." Ohaern gave Lucoyo a warning glance. "We should be abed."

"What, when the moon is not yet risen?" Lucoyo gave him a wink. "Surely it would be quite unnatural for traders far from home to forgo the pleasures of talk and news any sooner than that!"

Ohaern lifted his head, understanding coming into his eyes, and Lucoyo turned back to strike up some gossip—and just incidentally learn a little more about Byleo and its Kuruite soldiers. He discovered, for example, that they changed the sentries an hour after sunset and again in the middle of the night; that the sentries tended to gossip and nap at their posts; and that there were always two stationed by the prison door, and one by the southern gate. The gleam of approval in Ohaern's eye told him that he was doing well.

For his part, Ohaern looked around at his men, noting that they had done as he said—spread themselves out at the edge of the crowd, nearer to the long houses where the soldiers dwelled. There were nine of them, two for each of the soldiers' houses, to strike down any who might respond to an alarm, and one to knock down any who might come stumbling out of the women's house at the wrong moment. Ohaern nodded, feeling the tension mount. He knew that five more of his men were hidden in the maze of houses below, all within sight of the main road, all ready to come out and attack any who sought to follow him when he emerged with Manalo—if Manalo were still alive and well, pray Lomallin! There were two more of his men at the edge of the crowd near the prison, and two more opposite them; they would account for the guards. One last Biri was chatting with a stranger not far from the small, one-man gate; he would be the one man, when he had struck down its guard.

That left Lucoyo and himself to drop any sentries who might be on duty inside the prison. Ohaern had a little mistrust of the half-elf still, but not much, and knew that Glabur would be watching from his post by the barred door, anyway.

They were ready. He prayed for moonrise—and for clouds.

CHAPTER 7

The moon rose, a thin sickle, and though there were no clouds, it was still dark enough to hide their movements.

"Now!" Ohaern said. "We shall take the guards at the prison door!"

"What?" Lucoyo looked up, startled. "Do you mean to charge them?"

"Aye." Ohaern frowned down at him. "What else?"

"What else? They will raise the hue and cry before you are halfway to them, that is what else!"

"It is dark."

"Not dark enough to hide a hulk the size of yours! Only think— if you saw a man of your bulk charging at you with Glabur and Dalvan behind him, what would *you* do?"

"You do not mention yourself," Glabur said with a tone of menace.

"Me?" Lucoyo spread his hands. "Slight, short me? Who would take notice of *me*? Who would feel threatened? Nay, you fellows creep around to the sides, so that you may pounce *after* they have not noticed me!" And he was up and away, walking swiftly toward the prison.

Glabur started to shout after him, but Ohaern caught his arm. "No, let us trust him. He has done nothing to earn anything else."

"But if he should turn traitor now, with hundreds of Kuruite soldiers about us—"

"If he should not, he will have us into that prison without noise. See! He changes his gait!"

Glabur looked where Ohaern was pointing and saw the half-elf stumbling, almost staggering, toward the prison. "What stratagem has he in mind?"

"Only a prank, like as not. Do you and Dalvan circle to the left; I will take the right."

Keeping low, Glabur and Dalvan went to the shadow of the wall and followed it until they were out of the guards' line of sight. Then they dashed across a small patch of open ground into the shadow of the prison wall and crept along it to the corner.

Ohaern, however, had no obliging wall to shield him—but a happy thought struck him, and he stood up and strode openly and boldly toward the temple. The prison guards looked up, stiffening, and so did a sentry on the wall—but they relaxed as he went to the temple portal. No one thought twice about a worshiper going to Ulahane's temple in the middle of the night.

But once in its shadow, Ohaern flattened himself against the wall and crept to the corner that overlooked the prison door. He arrived just in time to see Lucoyo stagger up toward the door.

Two spears were leveled at his midriff. "Stand!" a guard snapped. "Where do you think you go?"

"Latrine." Lucoyo followed the statement with a loud hiccup, then explained, "Burshting."

"The latrines are over against the western wall, fellow!"

"Can' make it," Lucoyo slurred. "Flood. Here."

"If you dare to think of it, I'll see you inside that door for good and all! Then you can manage in there, where they *have* no latrines—or where every scrap of dirt is a latrine!"

Lucoyo stared at them, owl-eyed, then shook his head slowly. "Dirty," he said. "Sick."

"What matters illness, to those who go to Ulahane? They will not live long enough! Nay, and the few who *are* kept alive, awaiting judgment, deserve death anyhow—so what matters illness, indeed?"

" 'Deed," Lucoyo echoed. "You go in there?"

"Only to serve the prisoners their slop! How dare you say that a soldier of Kuru should dwell amidst such filth!"

"Oh ... I dunno ..." Lucoyo joined his hands, twiddling his thumbs. He seemed to have heavy going of it—they kept tripping over one another. But he rolled his eyes up, pursing his lips as he contemplated the moon, and the two guards stared at him, beginning to grin, wondering what this foolish drunk would say next.

"The barbarian hasn't tasted beer before," one of them grunted to the other.

"The first time always takes them like this," his partner agreed.

"Ah!" Lucoyo stabbed a forefinger upward. "Found it!"

The guard stared. "Found what?"

"Why Kuruite soldier might go in prizhon!"

"Oh, have you really," the one soldier purred, and the other demanded, "Why?"

" 'Cauzh he might *fall on 'em*!"

"Fall on them?" The soldier grinned, and his mate laughed. "You talk nonsense, fellow! Why should we fall—"

The big shadows that loomed behind them raised war clubs and struck down with dull cracks. The two guards stiffened; then their eyes rolled up and they slumped to the ground.

"That is why," Lucoyo hissed.

"Well done, archer!" Ohaern's eyes glowed with excitement. "Now! You three hold the door!"

"Can you two wear these soldiers' helmets and pectorals?" Lucoyo asked Glabur. "I am too slight—no one would believe it."

Glabur nodded. "A good thought."

"And I shall bring out Manalo!" Ohaern turned to the door.

"Alone?" Lucoyo stared at him.

"Yes, alone. The guards are out here—why should there be need for more than one? But if anyone comes near, friend Lucoyo, do you carry on more of these antics you used on these guards."

Lucoyo nodded. "No one will think anything of a fool entertaining a couple of bullies. But how shall you get in? There is no latchstring, nor any other means of unlocking it that I can see!"

"Like this." Ohaern laid hold of the handle of the prison door, set himself, and heaved. Every muscle in his body stood out; for a few seconds his form was a gigantic bow, straining against wood. Then something snapped, and Ohaern nearly stumbled as the door shot open. But he caught himself, chest heaving, and turned back to his three friends, who were staring, wide-eyed. "Close it after me, but be ready to open when I knock like this!" He struck the door in a brief, complex rhythm.

Glabur jolted out of his daze and nodded. "We shall, Ohaern!"

"Good. I should not be long." Ohaern glanced down at the two prone and now naked soldiers. "Oh, and—hide the refuse." Then the door closed behind him.

Lucoyo jolted himself out of a daze. "Has he always been that strong?"

"Only since he grew up," Glabur told him.

Lucoyo shook his head in amazement, then said, "Well, we had better do as he said. You two stay on duty, in case anyone looks this way. I'll haul." He laid hold of a guard's feet and began dragging.

Glabur glanced at Dalvan and said, "The halfling is trustworthy."

"So it would seem," Dalvan replied. "I pray Ohaern has no difficulty!"

Ohaern was having a little trouble finding his way in the dark, but the body he tripped over cursed him in his own language, and he bent down to say, "My apologies, Biri. How came you here?"

"I got drunk," the Biri snapped, "and they robbed me of all my trade goods. Then they claimed I could not wander the town with no substance, so they threw me in here. They tell me I go to Ulahane tomorrow night. And you, man of my nation?"

"I have come to free you." Ohaern groped in the dark, and as the Biri was still whispering, "What? Free me? How can you? There is a chain, a copper chain, that holds me to the wall!" Ohaern found the links, took a firm hold, and heaved with a grunt. The links parted with a sharp report, and Ohaern panted, "Now you are free!"

There was silence a moment, then the Biri hissed, "Are you a god?"

"Only a man, but a very strong one." Ohaern was beginning to wonder at his own strength. "Do me a favor in return. There is a wise man here, a sage named Manalo. Has he gone to Ulahane yet?"

"No, praise Lomallin!" the Biri said. "Come, I will bring you to him!" He pressed cold links into Ohaern's palm and chuckled. "Hold my chain!"

He set off with the air of a man who knows every inch of a familiar room. Ohaern stumbled along in his wake. His eyes had adjusted to the gloom now—there were only two small windows set way up high, but they did let in a little of the moon's wan light. Tripping and stumbling over objects that cursed, Ohaern followed his guide to the far wall, which was taken up by stout wooden doors with tiny windows in them—slots, really, such as might be used for pushing through a little food. They were held closed by copper hinges and metal hasps that must have been taken out and replaced every time the door was opened—a good sign that they were opened rarely indeed.

"What are these stalls for?" Ohaern whispered.

"For criminals they deem especially dangerous," the Biri answered, "ones who might kill us others, when we might better be offered to Ulahane instead."

"Manalo is no murderer!"

"No, but he served the Kuruites poorly in another way—by never ceasing to preach the virtues of Lomallin as he nursed us in our illness or sought to heal our hearts."

"Dangerous indeed!" Ohaern said with a grin, then raised his voice a little, more by urgency than loudness. "Teacher! Sage! Manalo! Do you hear me?"

There was a second's silence, then the clank of chains and finally Manalo's voice itself! "I hear you indeed, Ohaern."

Ohaern's heart leaped with gladness, and he suddenly realized how deeply afraid he had been that Manalo might have been dead. "Teacher, I have come to take you out of this place!"

Manalo's laugh was as gentle as always. "Well done, Ohaern, and I will follow you gladly—if you can open this door and sunder my chains."

"The door? Is there a door?" Ohaern waved the Biri away, set one hand on the little window and the other on the handle, braced a foot against the wall and heaved. For a moment nothing happened; then a groaning sounded, and the nails in the hinges began to move. Faster and faster they came out, then sprang loose. The door jolted wide, ripping the copper hasp. Ohaern staggered backward, then tossed the door aside and called, "Teacher! Come out!"

"I cannot," Manalo answered simply. "There is a spell on this cell that I cannot overcome with any magic of my own—and I am bound down."

Ohaern mouthed an obscenity and went in. The darkness was total here, but his hands found Manalo's body—or at least, the cold links that wound around his chest. Ohaern took hold of the chain, but Manalo said, "There are five of them, one around my shoulders, one around my elbows and stomach, a third around my wrists and hips, and a fourth around my thighs. The fifth binds my ankles and is fastened to the wall."

"They really *do* fear you!" Ohaern exclaimed. "Well, that last shall be no problem." He bent down, groped over Manalo's knees and shins, then found the chain. He set himself against it and pulled. The cell was silent for a moment, then the links popped. Ohaern staggered upright, saying, "It will take too long to break each of them—and they are so tight about your body that I cannot get a proper grip. They shall have to wait until we are far from the town."

"But how shall you take me there?" Manalo asked. "Your strength is amazing, Ohaern, but surely not—" He broke off as the darkness tilted around him and Ohaern slung him over one hip. Then, holding Manalo fast with one arm, Ohaern said, "Quickly, that is how! Come, Teacher, before we are discovered!" He strode out of the cell.

The Biri gaped. "No human man is that strong!"

"There was an accident at my birth," Ohaern said impatiently. "Guide me out, friend!"

Other men were coming awake and beginning to cry out.

"Silence, all of you!" Ohaern hissed. "If I escape, you may follow me! Come, but be quiet, or the soldiers will charge upon you!"

The prisoners fell silent and crawled to their feet, following him like a host of dim shadows. The Biri guided Ohaern through the near-darkness, back to the door. There, the big hunter turned to the prisoners and whispered, "Go soft-foot, and bring down the sentries at the gate! If you can be gone from the stockade before they can raise the alarm, you may live! Give them warning sooner, and you are dead men!"

"We will be as silent as a fox stalking a wood hen," someone promised.

"Be so," Ohaern said. "Do not attack the guards on this prison's door—they are my own men."

"Your own men?" another prisoner asked, astonished. "What happened to the Kuruite guards!"

"They still live—I think. Now, go quietly!" Ohaern turned away, but heard a last whisper at his back: "None can defeat a Kuruite soldier!"

"None *could*," someone else answered darkly.

They stole out of the prison, and Ohaern caught the Biri by the elbow, steering him aside. "Wait with me." They joined Glabur and Lucoyo, and watched as the prisoners stole out into the night, several laughing maniacally but in whispers, many limping, but all burning with lust for freedom, and revenge.

"We all feared to attack the soldiers, for they could not be beaten," the Biri whispered, amazed.

"They do not fear them now," Ohaern returned. He shifted Manalo's weight to the other hip, saying, "Forgive the indignity, Teacher."

"Perfectly all right," Manalo answered in a strained voice.

"Come!" Ohaern turned away toward the back gate. Glabur, Dalvan, and Lucoyo fell in behind him. In amazement, the Biri came, too.

They had just reached the postern when the yelling broke out at the main gate.

"I feared they would not contain their elation," Ohaern said. "Come quickly!" He tore open the little gate, stooped, and led the way through.

They stayed in the shadow of the wall, moving around toward the front of the fort—toward it, but not to it. Fifty feet away the sentries were all riveted to the mob of filthy prisoners storming the portals. The soldiers were shouting back at them in return, hurling rocks and, when a prisoner managed to climb up too high, hurling spears.

"Will they never wrench the gate open?" Lucoyo asked, staring in horror.

"It *is* open," Manalo replied, his voice strained by Ohaern's arm. "Those who wish freedom more than revenge have already fled. The ones who are left are those who cannot forbear the chance to strike at their tormentors."

"If we seek to aid, we are lost," Ohaern said. "Come!" He turned away from the wall, running down across the slope to the shelter of the nearest house. He skidded into its shadow and leaned against the wall, chest heaving, as Glabur, Dalvan, and Lucoyo came pounding up beside him. They leaned, too, except the half-elf, who sat on his heels, panting. "Where to now . . . O Chieftain?"

"The river!" Ohaern heaved Manalo upright. "Apologies, sage, but it was necessary. Now I think we can afford you some slightly greater comfort."

"I have not complained," Manalo assured him, smiling. "I am free; what more matters?"

"Not free yet! Not free till we have put this accursed midden behind us!" Ohaern hoisted Manalo up to sit on one shoulder. "Lead, half-elf! Find us the broad way!"

Lucoyo bristled, but realized quickly that, from Ohaern, the term was no insult—rather, it referred to the elves' legendary powers of sight and memory. In his case it was true—that much, at least, he had inherited from his scoundrel of a father. "Follow!" he whispered, and set off between the houses. He was going only by dead reckoning, a memory of where the broad path was. He took what seemed to be the most direct route to it, but the houses were set in such a jumble that his path was very crooked.

Then, suddenly, a huge dog leaped out at them, barking furiously.

Lucoyo shrank back, as much from surprise as fear. Just as he was collecting himself, Glabur stepped between them, his sword swinging down in an arc to strike the animal broadside on the head. The beast broke off in mid-bark and fell.

Lucoyo felt frantic anxiety—dogs had been among the few good creatures in his boyhood! And this one even looked like the dogs of the plainsmen—almost half wolf. But the animal's chest moved with breathing, and he relaxed. He would not want to be party to the murder of an innocent beast who had only been doing as he had been trained to do.

A person, now—that would have been another matter.

Ohaern beckoned, and Lucoyo stepped around the dog, following the big hunter with the man sitting on his shoulder. How odd Ohaern looked—and how unfathomably strong! Surely he was himself more than mortal!

But not in his emotions—nor, Lucoyo thought privately, in his wit.

They came to the broad path, and Ohaern stopped in the shadow of a house, nodding to Glabur, who made a hollow ball of his hands, blew between his thumbs, and made an owl's cry that was so real it startled Lucoyo. Then Glabur looked up, waiting, expecting something. Lucoyo began to fidget; what was he waiting for? After a minute, he heard a nighthawk cry, and realized that one of the other hunters had answered.

They went out onto the path, though surely there must be some grander name for a stretch of packed earth thirty feet wide. Glabur made another owl's cry, and this time it was answered immediately by another owl off to their left, then a minute later on the right by some other night bird, one Lucoyo did not know. So they went on down the path, with Dalvan and Glabur taking turns making birdcalls, until the other two Biriae had answered.

"Where are . . . the nine who . . . watched the soldiers' . . . houses?" Lucoyo asked, panting as he ran.

"Following," Ohaern answered. "More slowly. Between . . . the houses."

Suddenly, a half-dozen soldiers rounded a corner ahead of them.

Glabur halted, but Lucoyo pushed him back into a run. "Keep going! They may think we are on a lawful errand!"

Glabur stared in susprise, then grinned, even as he lumbered back into movement.

But the soldiers did not come to that conclusion—they saw running men, heard shouting and the clash of arms from the citadel behind them, and came to the sensible conclusion. They shouted and charged.

"Do we fight, chief?" Dalvan asked, grinning as he hefted his axe.

"We fight!" Ohaern drew his sword.

There was no room for a bow. Lucoyo, heart in his throat, drew one of his new long knives.

Then the soldiers were on them, shouting and jabbing their spears. Glabur chopped through a shaft, but another spear scored his left arm. Dalvan drew his dagger with his left hand, using it to deflect a spear, then seizing it with his right and wrestling it out of the soldier's grasp. Blows rang on Manalo's chains but glanced off; Ohaern thrust and cut fiercely, knocking spears away, chopping through shafts—but three streaks of crimson adorned his chest and arms. Lucoyo ducked as a spear thrust over his head, then he came up right next to the soldier, jabbing with his dagger. The soldier twisted aside and cursed as the knife scored his ribs, then dropped the spear and wrapped his hands around Lucoyo's throat, squeezing. Lucoyo felt panic rise as the pain choked off air, but brought the knife around to stab at the soldier's side. Then another soldier shouted, and a spear shaft cracked down on Lucoyo's hand. Agony shot through his fingers, and the knife clattered to the ground. The soldier's face, the whole street, seemed to darken, and sparks of light shot through it as his lungs clamored for air, his face growing hot with pent-up blood—

Something struck the soldier's forehead; redness welled up, and the soldier slumped, his hands loosening. He fell, revealing one of the Biriae who had been guarding the soldiers' houses. The rest of the nine seemed to rise up behind the Kuruites, axes and swords chopping down. The soldiers fell, senseless, some pumping blood.

"Glabur! Dalvan! Lucoyo!" Ohaern looked about frantically, reassuring himself that his men were still alive. He found Lucoyo last and sprang to him. "Are you well, halfling?" Amazingly, he sounded afraid.

Lucoyo nodded, too busy letting the breath rattle in down his throat—then tried to answer, but all that came was rasping.

"He lives," Manalo said from his perch on Ohaern's shoulder. "He will be well."

"Praise Lomallin for that!" Ohaern looked about. "You grow too heavy, Teacher, and I fear for you if there is another such brawl." He set Manalo down. "Here—let us take these chains from you now!" He grasped the top links, his hands on either side of the rivets, and pulled. Again, for a second, he seemed to be frozen, muscles standing out in huge curves; then with a sudden *spang!* the rivets popped out and went flying away. Breathing hard, Ohaern broke the second chain, then the third, then the fourth. At last there were only the shackles on Manalo's wrists left. "I hesitate to part that one, for fear of hurting your hands," Ohaern said. "Come, kneel and set the chain on the ground. Glabur, your axe!"

CHAPTER 8

Manalo knelt, holding his hands far out in front of him, the chain stretched taut between them, without the slightest sign of fear. Ohaern stood facing him, swinging the axe above his head. He took careful aim, holding the axe in one hand, then brought it sweeping down. It cracked into the copper and sliced it cleanly through. Manalo breathed a shaky breath and held up his hands. "I shall wear bracelets till we have come to your camp, Ohaern. Now quickly, let us go!"

"To the river!" Ohaern set off trotting, and the Biriae followed him, all twenty of them alive and functioning. It seemed a miracle to Lucoyo—but perhaps these Biriae were better fighters than he had thought. Not that he had thought badly of them—but the soldiers of Kuru had a reputation that was ferocious indeed. That, at least, seemed to have been inflated like a blown bladder—either the Biriae were excellent fighters, or the Kuruites were nowhere nearly as good as rumor had them.

Or, a voice whispered inside him, *you had the protection of a god.*

But so had the Kuruites, had they not? They worshiped Ulahane, after all. Was Lomallin stronger than the God of Blood?

He decided to worry about it later—right now, he needed to devote his mind to staying alive. After Glabur and Dalvan he went, and was surprised to see that Manalo was not only keeping up—he was even keeping pace beside Ohaern to say, "I can run faster."

The chief only grunted, but picked up the pace; down the road they ran, the gleam of the river coming closer, closer . . .

With a roar, a monster erupted from the water, some sort of huge lizard, fifty feet long, with a crested head and as many fins as legs, with a twenty-foot tail that ended in huge flukes and jaws five feet long by three feet wide.

"A dipsosos!" Manalo skidded to a halt, throwing his arms out to stop the tribesmen. "One of Ulahane's unnatural creatures! Beware—it spits poison!"

Ohaern glanced back at the hilltop and saw a troop of soldiers erupting from the gate. "We cannot go back! Surround it, men! Some must die, that others may live!"

The Biriae paled, but they spread out around the monster, swords and axes in hand. Manalo held his ground, hands out in a fan, chanting in a language they did not know. Lucoyo strung his bow, nocked an arrow, and stood directly in front of the dipsosos, waiting for a clear shot, hoping for it to open its mouth.

So, of course, it was at him that the monster rushed. Its mouth gaped wide—and Lucoyo loosed his shaft, then leaped aside just before a gout of dark liquid struck the ground where his feet had been. The earth smoked, then boiled, and Lucoyo turned pale, so riveted that he did not see the huge tail swinging around. It struck him behind the knees, and he fell with a shout. He landed rolling, rolling up to his feet, but his knees wouldn't hold; they gave way, and down he fell again—just as the huge tail swished back, sizzling through the air above his head.

Then Ohaern's hand caught his arm, Ohaern hauled him bodily to his feet, Ohaern held him up with one hand while he brandished the axe against a monster that turned away from a torn and sectioned body, blood dripping from its jaws, to lunge at the chieftain . . .

. . . and froze in mid-movement.

Ohaern and Lucoyo stared; so did all the Biriae. Then, as one, they looked up at Manalo, whose fingers writhed as he brought his hands up from his hips to his shoulders in a slow, graceful arc—and as they watched, the dipsosos began to fall apart, right before their eyes.

First it began to shake, faster and faster. Then scales fell off, then bits of flesh—but there was no blood, for the whole body seemed to have solidified, like mud under the heat of the sun. Like mud indeed, for its shreds crumbled to flakes even as they fell to the ground—and in minutes there was nothing left of the monster but a pile of dust.

Ohaern drew a long, shuddering breath. "Teacher," he said, "you know magic other than healing!"

"There is seldom need for it," Manalo answered. "Go, Ohaern! You must run, for the soldiers rush down upon you!"

Ohaern looked up, startled—he had completely forgotten the Kuruites, but sure enough, here they came, halfway down the hill and howling like wolves. "Come!" the chief snapped. "Along the riverbank, till we find a place for crossing!"

They turned to go, but Glabur lingered by the torn and bloody remains. "Alnaheg . . ."

"We cannot take his remains home for burial—there is no time! We shall have to gather the tribes and come back to raze this pest-hole in his honor! Come, or you shall join him!"

Ohaern started up the riverbank, and Glabur reluctantly turned away to join him. Lucoyo felt an odd sadness tug at his heart, odd because he had scarcely known the man—but he consoled himself with the thought that if they only lost one, they would have come out of this very well.

Still, he wondered that he should feel any grief at all.

He followed the chieftain down the path by the water, feeling the strength ebbing from his limbs, feeling his injuries flame up, but not daring to slow—especially since, ahead of him, Manalo kept pace with Ohaern without effort and, Lucoyo thought, Manalo was twice his own age at least!

"Here!" Manalo seized Ohaern's arm, skidding to a halt. "The water grows shallow, no deeper than your chest at its worst!"

"We can swim more quickly!" Glabur made as if to dive, but Ohaern checked him with an outstretched hand. "Teacher—the dipsosos! Had it any cousins? And would they not wish revenge?"

"They might," Manalo agreed, "but I shall distract them with a spell, and they shall not notice you."

Ohaern frowned. "How shall you do that while you are swimming?"

"I shall wade," Manalo said simply. "I have told you it will not come above your chest."

"My chest, and your shoulders! Besides which, with those manacles still on your wrists, you cannot gesture long without wearying!"

"Long enough," Manalo assured him.

"I trust your honesty, Teacher, but not your limbs." With a sudden heave, Ohaern hoisted Manalo up on his back and waded into the water.

"Ohaern! This is not necessary! I can walk, I can—"

"You can keep the monsters away! Enchant, Teacher, and I shall wade for both of us!" Ohaern stepped down, and the water rose to his knees.

Manalo knew when to give over. He began to make passes in the air, chanting in a strange, singsong rhythm.

Behind them, the Kuruite soldiers raised a shout as they came into view. As one, the Biriae threw themselves into the river. They were halfway across by the time the Kuruites came close enough to cast their spears. Shafts cut the water to left and right, but the Biriae swam with an eye back toward the bank, and twisted aside ere the points landed. Each soldier bore three spears; each threw them all. Here and there trails of blood stained the water, but only one Biri sank, then rolled up again with a spear through him. Dalvan seized his arm and towed, oblivious to what the blood might bring—after all, there was flow enough from his own chest. Manalo saw, and his chant grew louder, more commanding. A Kuruite soldier howled a curse, and a last spear shot toward the sage, now only above the water from his belly up as Ohaern labored beneath him. Manalo snapped out a word, and the spear suddenly veered aside, sailing over Lucoyo's head to splash into the water beyond the Biriae. Something roared in pain, making the whole river shake, and a mighty form surged out of the waves, then threw itself toward the Kuruite soldiers. They howled in alarm and ran.

"Well-aimed . . . Teacher!" Ohaern gasped.

"A fortunate coincidence," Manalo assured him. "I should bear my own weight, Ohaern, ere you founder!"

"Only five yards . . . more!" the chief gasped.

Lucoyo was overwhelmingly glad to hear it. His legs were leaden, his whole body ached, and each arm seemed to weigh as much as the dipsosos; he could scarcely lever it out of the water and throw it ahead to propel him another foot. Then, suddenly, he saw Ohaern's form rise up before him, wading higher and higher, till the water was only at his waist. With a glad cry, Lucoyo swung his feet down—and felt the mud slide out from beneath them. He toppled face first into the water.

He floundered in desperation, trying to thrust his head into air again, but his weary arms seemed no longer to answer his commands. Panic was just beginning to seize him when a huge hand closed upon the back of his jerkin and hauled him upright. "I have . . . lost two men . . . already tonight," Ohaern panted. "I . . . do not wish . . . to lose you . . . too."

Ohaern scarcely had enough breath left to protest as Manalo hopped down off his shoulder and waded the rest of the way ashore. Ohaern followed, hauling Lucoyo and himself up onto the bank, where he dropped the smaller man and stood panting, chest heaving. Lucoyo simply flopped down onto the grass and lay gasping like a beached fish. All along the bank the other Biriae hauled themselves out and threw themselves down on the grass, limp with relief, drawing huge lungfuls of air.

"Do not rest too long," Manalo cautioned. "They have barges— huge flatboats that can carry both horses and men. They shall cross, and they shall pursue you with small carts pulled by their horses!"

Ohaern frowned, still panting. "What is a . . . cart?"

"It is a sort of half pot on wheels, big enough to hold a man."

"Like a . . . travois . . . I think he . . . means." Lucoyo levered himself up on his elbows.

"What is a 'travois'?"

Lucoyo started to explain, then said, "Never mind. It will be just as quick for him to tell us what a 'wheel' is."

"Think of a log," Manalo said. "Now think of cutting off a slice of it, as you would cut a slice off a roast."

Ohaern still frowned. "Why would anyone want to do *that*?"

"Because the log rolls," Manalo answered, "and if you put a heavy load on top of two logs, you can move it easily as the logs roll."

"Interesting," Ohaern allowed, "but it will roll off the log."

Manalo nodded. "So they take two log slices, fasten them to each end of a pole in such a way that they can turn freely, then fasten the pole to the bottom of a huge basket—and the basket will not roll off the pole, but will roll along with it."

"What an ingenious idea!" Ohaern's eye lit with delight.

"Is it not? And the Kuruites have such things—they call them 'carts,' and when they are drawn by horses, they can go much faster than a man can run."

"And they will catch us with them, as soon as they can bring them to this side of the river!" Ohaern turned to his Biriae. "Up, men of mine! We must flee while we can, and find a place to hide that the Kuruites cannot discover!"

Groaning, the men came to their feet, complaining but mobile. Two of them lashed a cloak to two spears and slung their companion's body between them, then set off after Ohaern.

Lucoyo marched next to Glabur. "Why did you not use your spears on the soldiers?"

"Swords and axes are for men," Glabur answered. "Spears are for animals."

"As I said—why did you not use them on the Kuruites?"

Glabur stared at him, then guffawed and gave him a slap on the back that sent him stumbling. "Well asked, Lucoyo, well asked! I shall have to remember that as a riddle, as a famous riddle! Oh, well asked!"

Lucoyo reflected wryly that it was nice to be appreciated, but these Biriae took it to an extreme. One would think they had never heard jests before, that he himself had invented humor.

Well, perhaps he had—for them.

•　•　•

Since they had crossed back to the western shore, it wasn't long before they found themselves back in forest country. By morning they were among stout old oaks, and there was still no sign of the Kuruites. The Biriae were weary, but nonetheless stood a bit straighter, walked a bit more firmly, looked with a brighter eye, for being back in their natural environment. Lucoyo, on the other hand, was edgy and apprehensive. He felt as if the trees were closing in on him, as if the very air were thick in his nose and throat.

Ohaern stopped by a tangle of bushes and brambles among some oak trees. "Here," he said, and his men set to, some cutting at the underbrush, some gathering more to heap upon it. Lucoyo watched them, wondering if they were mad, wondering what they hoped to accomplish.

"Now! Your bracelets!"

Lucoyo turned to see Ohaern setting Manalo's wrist atop a big rock, though not so big that the two did not have to kneel. Then Ohaern took a small, dull gray tool from his pouch and a war club from his belt. He set the beveled edge of the tool against the top of Manalo's cuff. "Your pardon in advance, Teacher, if I cut your flesh."

"You are pardoned, Ohaern—but I do not think you will need it; I trust your skill as a smith. It is a matter of pride for the teacher when the student surpasses him. Still, I would ask you to cut at the side of the wrist, so that if you do slip, you will not sever one of the great veins."

"Done," Ohaern grunted, and reset the tool, then raised the war club only as high as his shoulder, lowered it to rest briefly against the end of the chisel, then swung it up to his shoulder again, hard and fast, and struck down harder, all with only a snap of the wrist.

The copper parted with a sizzling sound, and Manalo sighed with relief as Ohaern peeled the metal off the sage's flesh. "Do not look for blood, Ohaern—there is none, not even a scratch, or I would have felt it."

"Not always." The smith still sounded anxious.

Manalo held up his wrist, displaying smooth, unmarked skin.

89

"You struck well and truly, Ohaern." He set his other hand down on the rock. "Do so again."

Glabur came up just as the second manacle came off. "It is done and ready, Ohaern."

Ohaern looked up at the thicket and nodded. Lucoyo couldn't discover what he was so pleased about—the thicket looked just as it had, except that there was more greenery atop it, woven into its sides, and heaped along the bottom of its roots.

"The plainsman sees nothing," Glabur said with a grin. "Let us hope that the city men see nothing, too. Come, archer—look upon our handiwork."

Frowning, Lucoyo followed the hunter. Kneeling down, Glabur pulled aside a bush—and Lucoyo saw a leafy tunnel with open space beyond it. "Enter," Glabur invited.

"Quickly, too," Ohaern said from behind him. "Others of us wait to go in."

Lucoyo scrambled through, doubled over—then was amazed to find that he could stand up after only two steps! Oh, he still had to hunch over a bit, but there was a good five feet of height beneath the roof of leaves and vines twined around branches.

"Thickets are often hollow inside." Ohaern stepped up beside him, stooped beneath the roof. "Or hollow enough—it takes only a little clearing to make a shelter of them. Mind you, it will not keep out the rain—but it will shelter us from Kuruite eyes." He turned and said, "Dalvan! Take first watch with me!"

"Well, what matters two hours more without sleep?" the hunter sighed. "Even better, once I do nod off, I shall sleep till dusk, by Lomallin's grace and aid. You poor folk who take second watch will only have two hours' sleep."

"Far better than none at all." Glabur pulled out some jerky and began to share it around. Each of the other men sat down and began to take food from their packs. Lucoyo looked around—they were all there, somewhat crowded, but all there. The thicket had been larger than it had looked.

"Be not overly concerned." Manalo had taken a stick and begun to sketch arcane symbols in the dirt. "I shall lay a spell that will distract them—unless Ulahane sends one of his poor bastard sons to lead the Kuruites."

"Well, we shall post guards, anyway." Ohaern looked thoroughly reassured, though. "Who will take second watch?"

He looked around, but not a single Biri waved. The chief frowned, disappointed in his men. He was about to speak when Lucoyo said, "Second watch."

Ohaern looked surprised. "Are you sure, outlander? I have watched you during this flight—you have tired quickly . . ."

"I shall be refreshed quickly, then," Lucoyo snapped, "if we can be done with this infernal yammering and get to sleep!"

Ohaern nodded, still taken aback. "Very well. Dalvan, let us go!"

Dalvan sighed and followed Ohaern out of the tunnel. One of the band pulled the bush-door back into place, and Lucoyo lay down with a grateful sigh. There was a bit of low-voiced conversation going on, but he was able to drift off anyway.

It was another sort of low-voiced muttering that woke him. There was very little light—the hunters had not seen fit to start a fire, for fear it would alert the enemy to their presence—but in the dense gloom there was a soft glow emanating from Manalo's symbols. The teacher even now moved his hands over them in strange, mystic passes, chanting very softly. As Lucoyo watched, the chanting died, the hands stilled, and the glow faded away. Then, in the stillness, Manalo's voice murmured, "Fear not the eldritch, Lucoyo. The spell will shield this thicket from the notice of the soldiers of Kuru, that is all."

Lucoyo felt the hairs on the back of his neck prickle. "How did you know I watched, O Sage?"

Manalo shrugged off the question. "To those with wisdom, many things become clear, including sight with an eye that is only in the mind. Sleep peacefully, Lucoyo."

Anxiety prodded the half-elf. "But the Kuruites worship Ulahane. Will he not cancel your spell?"

"I invoke the power of Lomallin," Manalo answered, "and where Ulin are opposed, human vices and virtues turn the tide. By the Biriae virtue and cleverness at hiding and watching, they will be less likely to be seen; by the Kuruites' arrogance and contempt for the forest and plains, they are less likely to see. In fact, they will perceive only what they expect—and they expect a campfire with a ring of men about it. Either that, or plodding fugitives dragged down with weariness. Here they expect nothing but a thicket, so they will see nothing but a thicket—if they ever come this far into the wood. Sleep without care."

"If you say it." Lucoyo laid his head down again, but he was still frowning.

"Waken, half-elf."

Lucoyo sat bolt upright, eyes blazing—but Ohaern knelt over him, saying, "And I hope your elfin half has elf-sight, to pierce this gloom about us. Are you alert enough to watch?"

"I am now," Lucoyo grumbled, floundering up off the pine-bough bed.

He found his place in a tree, from which he could see the thicket if he turned and looked back over his shoulder, and all the approaches to it from the east. He settled himself, carefully choosing a branch that was not terribly comfortable, and started fighting off the urge to sleep. He hadn't quite dozed off—and the proof of it was that he was still in the tree, not lying crumpled at its foot—when Dalvan came to relieve him two hours later. Lucoyo made his way back into the thicket and sank down onto his bed with a grateful sigh. Even the constant, steady murmur from Manalo and Ohaern did not keep him awake any longer than it took to wonder how the two of them would manage with no sleep—but perhaps Manalo knew a spell that would let them keep marching a day or two without . . .

It seemed he had not quite fallen asleep before Dalvan was shaking his foot and saying, "Rise, Lucoyo. The gloom lightens, and we must be abroad."

"A broad what?" Lucoyo snarled, but he rose anyway. Sure enough, Manalo and Ohaern were still talking. "Be sure you remember these spells," Manalo was saying.

"I shall, Teacher," Ohaern promised, "as I have remembered everything you have taught me."

"Do so, for you will need them."

Lucoyo hoped one of them would banish the need for sleep—and that Ohaern would sing it over the whole band. The chieftain looked as if he could use some of that himself.

The dawn light was beginning to filter through the leaves as the

Biriae emerged from their tunnel. They split into bands of three, to meet at the northern edge of the forest, as Ohaern had told them. Lucoyo went with Ohaern and Manalo—and two other Biriae accompanied their party to guard the sage.

Through the forest they went, sometimes on a deer trail, sometimes without one. Lucoyo was amazed at how silently these hunters moved; even he could scarcely hear them, and he was right next to them! There was little conversation, and what there was, was low-voiced.

In late afternoon they emerged from the wood into a meadow— and heard an ear-piercing, warbling sort of howl. The Biriae all stiffened, and those of the remaining eighteen who had not already come out of the wood surged crashing into the grass. "What cry was that, Ohaern?"

The chief shook his head, staring in amazement. "I know not."

The cry came again, chilling each of them with fear where he stood—these brave hunters, not even daunted by a charging aurochs!

"It is the cry of the Klaja," Manalo said grimly, "creatures of Ulahane's making."

Then people burst into sight, running.

"Biriae!" Glabur cried. "Loghorix! Marntile! Atroyo!"

"They are wounded!" Dalvan cried. "And the women run with them!"

On came the Biriae, panting, terrified, limping and slogging with weariness. Then their pursuers burst into view behind them, and Lucoyo didn't know whether it was their cry or the sight of them that sent fear shooting through him anew. They were men, big, brawny men—except that they were covered with fur, they ran on jackals' legs, and their faces were human faces, but with jackal's noses, jaws, and ears—and teeth, as he saw when their mouths opened and long tongues lolled out.

They howled again, flourishing spears overhead, and charged at the sagging, exhausted Biriae.

CHAPTER 9

"Forward!" Ohaern bellowed, swinging his sword to point. "Make a wall for our kin!" He bounded forward. The Biriae answered with a mighty shout and charged after him.

The fugitives looked up in shock, the men automatically bringing up weapons—then staring, their faces going haggard with relief. In an instant they were behind Ohaern's men, but were turning, weapons at the ready to help in the fight.

Ohaern stopped, holding up a hand. The Biriae ploughed to a halt, weapons ready, forming an inverted V, point toward the enemy. Ohaern, of course, was that point—with Manalo right behind him. "What are they, Teacher?" the chieftain asked.

"They are Klaja, Ohaern—bred by Ulahane from the seed of a jackal and a human. They are vicious, but if they see the tide is against them, they will show themselves to be cowards."

"Beware, Ohaern!" gasped one of the fugitives. "They are vicious indeed! They have destroyed our village and slain fifty of our kinsmen!"

"Fifty out of two hundred!" Ohaern shouted, outraged. "Revenge, my men! Justice!"

The Biriae answered with a shout. Then the Klaja struck.

The fight was short and ruthless. The Klaja attacked with spear and fang and claw, and the Biriae were in no mood to show mercy. Lucoyo ducked a spear thrust and jabbed upward with his long knife. The Klaja convulsed, folding over the agony in its stomach—and bit Lucoyo on the shoulder. He shouted in rage and pain, jerking the knife out, then jabbing up under the jaw, and the beast-man's bite opened as the Klaja fell away. Lucoyo kicked the body aside, stooped to catch up its spear, and felt another graze his back. He straightened with a shout, his knife ripping sideways, and another Klaja folded over his blade. But this time Lucoyo knew enough to sidestep those jaws, to yank out his knife and dance free, brandishing the spear to guard with his left hand. The pain was dim and seemed not to matter; he wielded the sword as efficiently as ever. But another pain scored his side, and he whirled to see a Klaja lowering a hind leg with dripping claws, spear poised to plunge.

It was off balance. Lucoyo threw himself forward, striking with his shoulder. The Klaja went down with a howl, and a Biri axe chopped its head off. Lucoyo didn't see that—he was whirling to catch the next attack on his spear, parrying a thrust. For a moment he faced fangs. But this Klaja used two hands to Lucoyo's wounded one. It beat down his guard and thrust—just as a savage face with a manic grin rose up behind, and its sword plunged home into the Klaja's spleen. The beast howled and fell, and the Biri woman stood panting, glaring at the new corpse in wild vindication.

Lucoyo stared. No woman of the nomads would have done such a thing. That face was seared into his brain—blond hair bound into braids, fine-featured face with huge blue eyes and a neck like a swan's, cheeks aflame with exhilaration, tip-tilted nose smudged with a streak of dirt that might well have been war paint.

Then a snouted face charged up behind the blond plaits; a spear stabbed down.

Lucoyo shouted and leaped past the girl, coming in low, pivoting as he thrust with his knife, ripping the Klaja's belly open, then dropping to his knees, bowing low. The Klaja stumbled over him, gagging, and Lucoyo just barely saw the sword chop down, saw the

Klaja's head drop sharply, saw the sword chop again, and the head roll away. The woman grinned with savage glee, her eyes alight with a glow of revenge. Lucoyo felt an answering surge of joy in the act. Revenge indeed, revenge on all those who had wronged him all these years, revenge—though it be only these warped abominations who must bear his wrath. He leaped to set his back to the woman's, looking about him for more foes . . .

They were running, three score and more—running from twenty men and fifty exhausted fugitives!

"They truly are cowards," Ohaern panted, staring after them.

"Jackals ever were," Manalo answered, himself a bit disheveled, "though they are savage enough when they are sure their prey cannot fight back overly hard."

"Then how could they have destroyed a village of Biriae!"

"Because they came a thousand strong," the woman panted, "and you and our other best fighters were gone."

Ohaern stood rigid a second, then began to make a strange keening sound in the back of his throat.

"Be of good heart." A wiry man with a weathered face limped up to clap Ohaern on the shoulder. "You could not know—and you could not let the Teacher languish in prison, or be fed to Ulahane."

"For that, I thank you," Manalo said.

Lucoyo's head came up as a realization struck him. "Ulahane sent them *because* he knew your men were gone to assault Byleo!"

"Then would not Ulahane have warned the soldiers?" Glabur asked.

"Be sure, he did," Manalo answered grimly, "but where Ulin are opposed, human courage and shrewdness turn the fight. Well did Ohaern plan his assault, well did he . . ."

But Lucoyo missed the rest of it, because the adrenaline of battle suddenly ebbed, fire exploded in his bitten shoulder, and the surge of pain banished consciousness.

He woke, in a bleary sort of way, or perhaps he dreamed, for he saw the blond woman's face floating over him, hair now unbound, arms and shoulders bare of those bulky furs, upper body bound in soft skins, and that bare arm reached toward him, that gentle hand pressed a cold compress to his forehead. Lucoyo was aware of gibbering a stream of nonsense at her, but he managed to contain it long enough to say "Thank you," before sleep claimed him again.

When next he wakened, it was Manalo's hand that rested on his forehead, then moved to his wrist, and his face hovered beside the girl's. "It is the poison in the jackal's bite," the sage was saying.

"But that made the others ill for only a few hours, and he has been thus for two days!"

"He was weakened sorely not long before he joined Ohaern's band and had not fully recovered. He has been pushing himself ever since, determined not to hold them back."

Hold them back! Lucoyo frowned; this man understood very little! He had hidden his weakness out of sheer vanity, that was all! He had been determined not to let these Biriae see that he could not keep up!

He must have spoken aloud, for both faces looked surprised, then amused, but there was respect in the girl's eye, and a gleam. "That is the sort of thinking we Biriae can understand," she said.

"Laudable, in its way," Manalo allowed, "but borrowed strength must be paid back, soon or late. Rest, archer." He touched two fingertips lightly to Lucoyo's eyes, and sleep reclaimed him.

When he woke next, he was astounded to find he was fairly clear-headed. He was in a type of enclosure, with a very little light filtering through some sort of woven wall. He forced himself up on one elbow, saw there was no one around him, and pushed himself out of bed. He staggered up to his knees—and fell.

The wall of branches burst apart, and the girl came running in. She hauled Lucoyo up, sitting on her heels and dragging his upper body onto her thighs, then levering him over to the pallet from which he had risen, saying angrily, "Cannot a girl leave you alone at all, but you must try to be up to wear yourself to death? Lie still, half-elf—your eldritch blood may give you more strength than a mortal, but even that is spent."

Half-elf again! The surge of anger lent Lucoyo energy before he remembered that here the term was not an insult. He used it to ask, "What does it matter to you? I am a stranger, not even one of your own kind!"

"Kind enough," she answered. "You saved my life in the battle, and I yours, I think. That is bond enough for me to care quite strongly. Let us be strangers no more. I am called Elluaera."

"I am Lucoyo." Lucoyo had to work to show the smile he felt. "You do well to care for me, for if I were to die, I would not be there to guard your back when other monsters come."

She smiled, the wicked gleam in her eye again. "Or for me to strike a blow to save. Rest, half-elf—regain your strength, for if you seek to know me better, you shall need it."

She turned away, for which Lucoyo was inordinately glad—he was sure he was staring like a fish. Had she hinted at what he thought she had hinted? Not at bedding, no, nor even caressing, but at keeping in her company enough to interest her in the idea! A woman, attracted to *him*?

But now that he thought about it, she was shorter than most of her kind, perhaps not much taller than himself . . .

He had time to compose his face before she turned back, holding a bowl of soup. "Eat, outlander."

"Outlander, forsooth!" he snapped. "We are all outlanders, so near to By—" He broke into coughing, for she had thrust the spoon into his mouth between words and held it hovering in front of his face, smiling with glee.

"Eat first, outlander—all right, *fellow* outlander! Regain your strength with something besides crossness. *Then* we shall talk."

The invitation thrilled Lucoyo, even through his weakness. He subsided and drank the broth she fed him, hoping the bowl would not empty soon. As he drank, though, he marveled at the resilience of these Biriae—or perhaps it was only at the resilience of this one woman. To fight and lose to a horde of half-canine bandits, then flee and fight again, and only hours later be able to smile, and hint at wishing courtship! Most amazing indeed!

Some of that resilience was Elluaera's, but if Lucoyo had been awake the hour after the battle, he would have been almost as much amazed at her tribesmen's ability to rebound as at her own. When the wounded Biriae had been tended, the wounded Klaja dispatched, and the three dead Biriae buried, Ohaern turned to the oldest of the fugitives and said, "Now, Cordran! How did it transpire that you and three score of my countrymen came fleeing so far from home?"

The light of triumph faded from the weathered old face, and Cordran said, "Home is no more. Sit, Ohaern—sit, all of you! For it is not a pretty tale that I must tell!"

It had begun like any day in the life of the hunters—women out seeking nuts and berries, a few men coming in from the hunt with a dead boar slung on a pole, small children playing in the dust and larger ones howling through the wood as the trackers found the tracked and threw themselves into a mock battle.

Then they were drowned out by another sort of howling altogether. A horde of furry bodies burst from the trees, brandishing spears, canine teeth dripping in long, pointed muzzles. The children's cries from the forest broke into shrieks, and the attackers tore apart the first few women and elders. But the extra time spent in wanton cruelty cost some of them their lives; the hunters turned from the carcass of the boar with their own spears stabbing, and some Klaja howled as flint blades transfixed their chests. Others only gurgled as the spearheads found their throats.

Then their pack-mates surrounded the hunters and stabbed from all sides, drawing back bloody spears as more and more Klaja poured out of the wood.

But the villagers set up a uluation of their own, high and vibrant, as they drew the new iron swords Ohaern had forged for them, cut through the Klaja spear shafts and sliced through fur as Cordran bellowed, "To me! Women and children inside! Form the circle!"

The circle was the shape sacred to Lomallin, and now it proved its strength. Warriors herded women and children into the center and took up posts about them, parrying and slashing, each easily a match for his half-furred opponent, each slaying and slaying as iron sword bested bronze spearheads and wooden shafts. But for each Klaja that died or fell wounded, two more sprang up in its place.

Suddenly, Biriae warriors burst from the forest, bolting quickly back from the hunt, and fell on the rear of the Klaja clustered around the villagers. They did not roar their battle cry until their swords had bitten deep; then they cried indeed, loud and hard. The Klaja screamed with fright, bounding away—and old Cordran shouted, "To the trees!"

The Biriae circle began to back away toward the trunks. Emboldened by the sight of retreat, the Klaja surged back with renewed vigor, howling for blood—then falling back and choking on it, choking on their own.

"Surround them! Engulf them! Do not let them escape!" thundered a huge voice, and a human shape lumbered from the wood—human, but ten feet tall and three feet wide, its face handsome, but with a brutish gleam to its eyes. It wore a torc—a collar of metal about its throat—and the draped cloth, bare legs, and sandals of the south. There was a sigil in his torc, an emblem of inlaid stone—a stylized jackal's head—and the sigil also gleamed in the band about his curly hair, hair as red as blood. "Slay them!" he bellowed. "Blood for Ulahane!"

He drove the Klaja nearest him with blows of a huge whip, and they howled in fright and turned upon the humans in their rage. The circle backed closer and closer to the trees, gathering stray villagers as it went—chanting praises to Lomallin as the warriors' arms grew heavy.

Suddenly, the Klaja found that only a few of them could come at the circle at any time—and those few died, and those who came after them died, again and again. What they did not see was the groups of Biriae, five at a time, who were sprinting from the circle to the shelter of the huge evergreens and climbing into their branches, nor the women who wore swords across their backs and perched on lower branches, watching, waiting . . .

Then Cordran barked, and suddenly the circle burst apart, the warriors leaping back into thickets and dodging behind trunks. Amazed, the Klaja stood for minutes staring, for now there were no more Biriae to be seen.

Then the giant roared in anger and waded in among the trees, showering the Klaja with blows. He could not bring his whip into play among the trunks, so he struck with a huge fist, and the Klaja dodged out of his way, but the slower ones slammed back against bark and slid to the ground, crushed. The others turned, noses to the ground, and began to sniff.

In a while they had all joined together on one common trail, and were off to follow it. The giant caught a dozen of them, slapped them back toward the village and barked commands in a language the Biriae could not understand. The Klaja ran from him, ran to obey him, back to the village—and within minutes the houses burst into flame. Then there were a few more human shrieks, but only a few, before the only sounds were of fire and wind.

The pursuing Klaja passed out of sight toward the south. Then the trees rained Biriae, who landed lightly and fled, off to the east.

But the clan had been split apart, and Ohaern's infant son was not in this band.

Now, two days later, Ohaern had mastered anger and grief enough to ask, "Who laid the false trail?"

"Borin," Cordran answered. "What befell him and the men who went with him, we cannot tell—but be sure the trail faded after a league or so, and the Klaja floundered in frustrated rage."

"So Borin and his men are likely well, but just as much wanderers upon the earth as you are," Ohaern summarized.

"More," said Cordran, "for they were only a handful, and we are a hundred. But the village is lost to us, and a quarter of the clan with it."

"This must call up a strong revenge," Ohaern said darkly.

Manalo raised a cautioning hand. "He who thinks of revenge, Ohaern, blinds himself to tomorrow. Let yesterday be as if it had never been; think only of how you and your clan-mates may survive to see another sunset, then another and another."

"Is there to be no justice?" Ohaern demanded.

"There will be," Manalo assured him, "though it may be long in coming. In any case, if you wait to see it, you will waste your life."

Cordran spoke from anger then. "Is Lomallin so much weaker than Ulahane that he cannot give justice?"

"The Creator's power is stronger in Lomallin than in Ulahane,"

Manalo answered, "and by itself will act as a wall, witholding Ulahane's malice from humankind. But human wickedness and perversity can breach that wall and give Ulahane a way in, to harass people and make them suffer. Then humankind can magnify Ulahane's power, so that his strength is balanced against Lomallin's— and human beings must determine the balance according to where they throw their weight."

"Fair words," Cordran scoffed, "but where was the human wickedness that breached the wall of virtue that guarded our village?"

"Far away from you," Manalo told him, "far to the south and the east, where nomad tribes with too many children became greedy for their neighbors' lands and the crops of the farmers, and offered maidens in sacrifice to Ulahane. From those poor girls, and the jackals who follow corrupted meats, he wove these depraved beings and sent them against you."

"Then the fault was not ours! Why therefore are we punished?"

"You are not punished, you are assaulted. Cleave to Lomallin and bring as many other human folk with you as you can, and Lomallin will gain strength to prevail against Ulahane."

"But how can he," Ohaern demanded, "if the Ulin are equal to one another in strength?"

"By dying," Manalo said, "and ask me no more than that, for I do not understand it. An Ulin bard, inspired by the Creator, spoke that prophecy in a trance, and all the Ulin have shuddered to hear it—for how can one gain strength by dying?"

"Surely you must have gained *some* notion," Glabur protested.

Manalo shrugged. "Only a guess—and I have told it to you. If enough mortal beings put their trust in Lomallin, no matter how badly he fares against Ulahane, the strength of their faith will magnify his spirit even after death—and having died once, he can die no more, and will be invulnerable to Ulahane's assaults."

"So," Ohaern said, frowning, "Ulahane dares not slay Lomallin, for fear he will become greater in death."

"You are quick to perceive," Manalo told him, eyes glowing with pride, "and yes, that is so—though if he thinks he has turned all but a handful of human folk against Lomallin, I think Ulahane will risk the fight."

"But how if it is *not* human belief that will strengthen Lomallin?"

"Then," Manalo said softly, "Ulahane will have a very nasty surprise."

"Surely Lomallin dares not slay Ulahane," Cordran objected, "for if one Ulin will gain strength by dying, will not another?"

"Oh, no," Manalo said, very quietly. "Lomallin would quite willingly die if it would rid the world of Ulahane."

"But how if it did not? How if Ulahane gained strength after *his* death?"

"The prophecy spoke not of that," Manalo told him.

Ohaern frowned. "Strange that Lomallin should gain strength after death, when Ulahane will not."

"Perhaps," Manalo said, "or perhaps it is only that Lomallin seeks union with the Creator, while Ulahane seeks to overthrow Him."

The Biriae were silent, appalled at the audacity and arrogance the statement implied. Then, finally, a woman gasped, "Surely he dare not!"

"Ulahane dares anything," Manalo told them, "and right and wrong have nothing to do with it, nor even wisdom and folly. Therein lies his eventual doom."

"Eventual," Ohaern said, with a sardonic smile. "It shall not come soon enough to save us."

"Who was the giant, O Sage?" another woman asked, and shuddered at the memory of that handsome, brutal face.

"He was an Ulharl," Manalo answered, "half human, half Ulin. Which one, I cannot say—but by the sigil in his torc, it is clear he was one of Ulahane's."

"One of his own bastard sons, then?"

"In all likelihood," Manalo said, "though since the Ulin do not marry, the term 'bastard' has little meaning among them. What is more to the point is that Ulahane's by-blows are almost without exception the children of rape. It is for that, and for his harshness to them, that they hate their father—but since the other Ulin despise them and will injure them if they can, Ulahane's progeny are dependent on him for their safety."

"So they hate him, but must serve him," Cordran said.

"All except Kadura, the first of them," Manalo answered, "for he was the child of seduction, not rape, and his mother was honored among humankind, those who followed Ulahane. So was her son—until she died and Ulahane took back his own."

"He cannot love his father!"

"No, for Ulahane has dealt as cruelly with him as with any. Still, he is the strongest of the Ulharl, and will gladly discipline any who grow rebellious."

"Would not their father's death free them?" Ohaern demanded.

"In some measure," Manalo said slowly, "though all know they would instantly war upon one another, to see who would win command—and it is not certain that Kadura would rise from the chaos, for his siblings are like to league against him before they fall to warring upon one another."

"What a sweet family," a woman said bitterly.

"Are they not? And Ulahane would have us believe that this is the natural order of things—for the son's hand to be turned against the father, the father's against the mother, and all the children's against one another."

"It is to our advantage, then, to see Ulahane dead," Ohaern said judiciously.

All held still in shocked silence. Some of the Biriae glanced nervously over their shoulders, as though to see if Ulahane had been listening—but Manalo nodded, unperturbed. "It is so," he said, "and therefore is it apt for you to give your allegiance to Lomallin, and to persuade all you meet to do so, for only an Ulin can slay another Ulin."

"But from what you say, it is Ulahane's worshipers who grow in number, not Lomallin's," Lrylla said.

"It is even so," Manalo agreed, "for your village is unique in that three quarters escaped. Only imagine the lot of those who lose!"

The villagers, wide-eyed, exchanged looks of mingled dread and fascination.

CHAPTER 10

❀

Manalo gave them time to recover, though, time to tend their wounds and begin to heal in spirit as well as body, before he told them the fate of those tribes who had not died fighting. The next day, Ohearn put the question to him after the evening meal, and Manalo replied, "The Ulharl bade their subject peoples turn to the worship of Ulahane and serve the Klaja—who served Ulahane—for all their days, by laboring to grow crops in the fields, by building his temples, and doing any other work they were given."

The Biriae rumbled, and a woman demanded, "This was a boon?"

"To the Ulharl's way of thinking," Manalo said, "yes. Those who served the scarlet god long and well, with full devotion, might one day win the right to wear his torc of honor, such as the Ulharl wore."

An ugly mutter sprang up among the Biriae, and one of them growled, "What honor is this, to wear a dog's collar?"

"The Ulharl counted it so, as it was the sign of their rank—so it would likewise be a sign of rank and authority among the humans who worshiped the Scarlet One."

"How if they did *not* wish to serve Ulahane?" Cordran demanded.

"Then they would serve him with their deaths, on his altar."

"Sacrificed?" a woman cried in horror, eyes wide.

"Even so," Manalo said, "and it is from just such a fate that Ohearn and his band saved me—though perhaps the price was too great, for surely Ulahane knew when they departed, knew the time was best for striking down your village when the strongest of its warriors were gone."

Again, an ugly murmur, and here and there a woman muttered to another that the men should have fulfilled their greatest responsibility and stayed at home to protect kin and kind—but none could bring themselves to say it aloud, realizing that Manalo then would have gone to Ulahane's altar, and not as an acolyte.

But the sage had excellent ears, or else knew their thoughts. "I regret the loss of your village, my friends, and of your kinsmen. If I had known, I would have bade Ohaern and his men stay at home, for surely my life is not worth your fifty dead, nor the loss of your homes."

The Biriae were silent for a moment; then Cordran said, "You gave us much, Teacher, and it was a debt that we needed to repay. There was no question of Ohaern staying at home."

The tribesmen rumbled agreement, and the women, too. Manalo smiled, warmed by their support—but it was a sad smile, too, for he knew their loss.

"If it is the price of freedom," a woman cried, "we will pay it! Would that I had died, rather than my sister!"

"What of those other tribes given the choice?" a man asked. "Did any convert?"

"Most," Manalo said, lips thin.

There was a babble of consternation. Cordran summed it up. "Free hunters and warriors, accepting slavery to the scarlet god?"

"The sacrificing was not merely death, look you," Manalo told them, "but death by torture!"

"Even so," a woman cried, "they were free hunters!"

"Some," Manalo agreed, "though some were free nomads, and there were tribes of several nations who were taken. But most chose the side of the one whom they thought must be the stronger god, for they valued winning above all else—and some chose slavery rather than death in agony. Do not censure these last, I beg you, my friends, for you have not stood where they stood. If you had heard the screams from the temple of Ulahane, as I have, you would not be at all quick to blame."

The Biriae shuddered and exchanged looks of dismay.

Lucoyo came limping out of the thicket that had been his temporary sickroom, leaning on the arm of Elluaera, his self-appointed nurse. He pretended disdain, but occasionally stared at her for a moment, as if he could not believe she really existed. Whenever she caught one of those stares, she gave him a roguish glance, then turned her gaze away with a toss of her head.

But the words of the people by the campfire electrified Lucoyo, making him turn all his attention to Manalo.

"What of the Kuruites?" a woman demanded. "Were *they* conquered, and did they turn away from their ancestral gods to the Scarlet One?"

"They turned their backs on their parents' gods, yes, and embraced the worship of Ulahane," Manalo told her, "but they were not captured. No, they were seduced by Ulahane's promises borne by the Ulharl—promises of wealth and power, of dominion over all the 'barbarians'—"

"The word is infuriating," Cordran said, "and I have heard traders, and now an Ulharl, use it as an insult. I know that we are barbarians, but—"

"Not really, no," said Manalo. "You are savages—that means, 'wild,' which is to say that you are hunters who are not ruled by the king of a foreign nation. Barbarians are folks who drive the great herds—"

"Like me!" Lucoyo cried.

"Yes, like Lucoyo and the tribe that reared him." Manalo turned to the half-elf with a nod. "The Kuruites, on the other hand, deem themselves to be 'civilized'—but that word, taken strictly, means only the ways and customs of people who live in cities."

Cordran spat. "That for the cities! If that is the meaning of the words, Teacher, I will be a savage, and proud of it!"

"Even so," Manalo said, amused, "but when folk speak of civilization, they generally mean that such customs are more cultured, and their behavior less brutal, than that of folk who do *not* live in cities."

"Not to judge by the Kuruites," a woman sneered.

"Quite so," Manalo said, "quite so. In fact, I have met many savages and barbarians who are more civilized than the people of Kuru."

"So, then," Lucoyo said, "Ulahane may be a god of cities, but he is not a god of civilized ways."

But Manalo shook his head. "He is not a god of cities alone, for the Klaja are wild, and so are the Vanyar, the nation of tribes who are swarming over these western lands to beat them into subjugation for Ulahane—you met them on the river, and I promise you that, though they be foolish in boats, they are very clever indeed with horses."

Lucoyo snorted. "Their arrows fall short."

"But on land they will be much closer to you," Manalo reminded him. "They, like the Kuruites, have been won over by Ulahane's promises—but they seek land and slaves, where the Kuruites seek empire."

"And the Klaja?" asked Ohaern.

"They seek to stay alive."

"So we face the Kuruites, the Klaja, and the Vanyar," Lucoyo summarized. "Which of these is worst?"

"All," Manalo said grimly, "though if I had to choose one who is even more my enemy than the others, I would choose the Kuruites, for they have been seduced so thoroughly, and won over so completely, that their city of Kuru is virtually Ulahane's capital."

Ohaern tensed. "Is that his seat?"

"There he dwells," Manalo confirmed, "for in Kuru is his largest and most luxurious temple—and there it is that a human man or woman is sacrificed to him every single day, not once a year or once a month, as is the case in his other temples."

"Never a Kuruite, of course," Lucoyo said with irony—and to his amazement, the people laughed.

"There are some few Kuruites," Manalo said somberly, "who

have been bred to the sacrifice, and who have dedicated themselves to Ulahane so completely that they go willingly to the torture and the death—but these are given drugs that make the pain far less than it is for foreigners such as us."

Lucoyo frowned. "Do even they who are bred to be sacrifices spend their lives, then, in murdering and torturing their fellows?"

"No, in prayer and service in the temple."

"Then when they die, how can they be of Ulahane?" Lucoyo asked. "Their lips may worship the scarlet god, but their lives worship Lomallin!"

The Biriae cried out with glee at his words, slapping their knees. Lucoyo almost bolted with shock, but caught himself and sat straighter, with affected calm.

Manalo nodded, and waited till the people had quieted before he said, "You speak truly, archer. Those good souls are deceived and blameless, so upon their deaths they flee to Lomallin, who protects them from Ulahane. Then from Lomallin, they fly to the Creator."

"But their fellow city-men, who do Ulahane's real work, are far less devout," Lucoyo said grimly.

Manalo grinned. "By your own mark, Lucoyo, they are quite devout in the way they live their lives—in murder and rapine, and secret laughing at the ones who spend their lives preparing themselves to be sacrificed."

"Why, what a sweet devotion is this!" Lucoyo cried, and was very glad he had mistaken his way out of Ulahane's worship. "Those who pursue it most devoutly go outside its reach, and they who are most hypocritical fall most squarely within it!"

The people crowed with delight, and Manalo returned, "What says that for its god?"

"It says that he prospers by knowing his worshipers' greed, and by persuading them that their self-interest is his! It says that any worshiper of Ulahane's who thinks himself smart and worldly is a fool, for by believing in Ulahane, he is a thorough gull!"

The Biriae hooted and stamped and applauded, and Lucoyo was completely amazed. He thought he had spoken in anger, not in wit.

Then he realized that the two could be completely compatible.

"There is truth in that claim," Manalo admitted.

"So!" Lucoyo cried. "By seeking their self-interest of empire, and thinking they let Ulahane do their work for them by granting them victory, they truly spread *his* empire, bringing more and more lands and tribes under his sway and into his service, willingly or not!"

"Far too willingly," Manalo said darkly.

"When will they discover how he has used them?"

"They will discover it when it is too late," the sage told him, "when all the free lands have been conquered and Ulahane has no shortage of ruthless, depraved servants of all lands and tribes. Then will he grind down the Kuruites to the bondage and subjugation in which he delights—and too late, they will know their folly."

"Well!" Lucoyo's eyes flashed as he forced himself to his feet—and nearly fell, but Elluaera was there to steady him. "Well! Let us do what we least delight in, and try to save the Kuruites from the discovery of their own folly—by seeing to it that this tribe, at least, remains free!"

The people leaped to their feet, shouting and bellowing their approval.

Manalo waited until the shouting had passed its peak, then spread his hands to quiet them and said, "It is well. Let us seek sleep, then, for you cannot do Lomallin's work if you stagger with exhaustion. To bed, and on the morrow we must move, for we have tarried in this place a day and a night, and if we stay longer than another night, we shall surely see Ulahane's jackals upon our heels. Good night, good friends."

They answered with calls of good night and wishes for fortunate dreams as they moved back toward their brush huts. A stout young man clapped Lucoyo on the shoulder and said, "You are witty, friend."

"I thank you," the half-elf said warily. "Who are you?"

"This is my brother Lafgar," said Elluaera.

He turned to her in astonishment, then back to Lafgar, all wariness now. "I owe your sister great thanks, Lafgar. She has nursed me through a most pitiable state."

"I have always had cause to be proud of her, and hope that she is proud of me," Lafgar returned. "I love her dearly and would take it amiss if anything untoward happened to her."

"Lafgar!" Elluaera said indignantly, but Lucoyo only threw back his head and laughed. He slapped the bigger man on the shoulder and said, "Friend Lafgar, I would I were well enough to be a threat of any kind!"

Lafgar stared at him a moment, then grinned sheepishly.

"Have no fear," Lucoyo assured him. "Her honor is as sacred to me as my own."

"That is what I feared," Lafgar said.

Lucoyo's eyes flashed with anger; then he realized the joke, and smiled. "So, a man after my own taste in words!"

"So is she," Lafgar warned. "Beware."

"I will rejoice in it—for at the moment I can rejoice in little else. Have I your permission for her to escort me to my pallet?"

"Do you need it?" Elluaera demanded indignantly.

"Need it or not, he has it," Lafgar told her, and struck Lucoyo a mock blow on the upper arm. "Our family is honored by your friendship, half-elf—but I pray you, learn of our customs ere you flirt with my sister. Good night." And he was gone into the gloom.

Lucoyo frowned after him, then turned to the maiden, who burned with embarrassment. "What customs did he mean?"

"Why," she said, "our silly males hold that a man must prove his worth ere he can ask a woman to be his wife."

Lucoyo stopped, staring into her eyes. "I see no silliness in that."

She stared back at him, startled, then turned away, blushing. "As if you had any interest in me other than in my nursing!"

"Yes, as if I had," Lucoyo murmured. "Imagine that."

"I cannot."

"You should," he told her, and she looked up, staring in surprise. "But if I were a well man, and a whole man, and one who might think of more than flirting," said Lucoyo, "how would I prove my worthiness to be a husband?"

"By gaining wealth," she said slowly, "furs and amber to trade, and perhaps even some of the southerners' golden coins. In our tribe, if a hunter has built a house and brought back meat for the clan and gathered furs and amber for two years together, he is deemed worthy to take a wife, for he has shown that he can feed her and her children, and house them."

"Is that all?" Lucoyo asked in surprise. "Must he not also go forth to battle, and come back alive?"

"Well yes, but there may be no battles in his time," Elluaera said. "Besides, you have already proved your worth in that fashion, by the accounts of Ohaern and his band—and no one will doubt their word in *that*."

Lucoyo stared, amazed and grateful to his fellow raiders. It felt odd. "But I fell down in the battle!"

"After it," she reminded him, "and you were already worn down when the band met you."

Lucoyo stiffened in indignation. "I walked as tall and ran as far as any of them!"

"You did," she agreed, "and they spoke of it with great respect when they told your tale around the campfire. But they knew you were not in the fullness of your strength even then."

And they had never let him know they guessed! "So—I have proved my worth as a warrior . . ."

"And need only prove that you could husband." Her eyes twinkled. "But that would be if you had the wish to marry."

"Why, yes." Lucoyo caught her hand and looked into her eyes. "And if I did, and if I had proved worthy by hunting and building, would you wish to marry me?"

Her eyes widened, seemed to swell as she swayed forward, and her lips tasted sweet on his, sweeter than any honey or syrup he had ever sipped, sweeter yet as the kiss deepened, and he closed his eyes, the better to savor the taste, the touch, the feel . . .

Then her lips moved away, but her eyes were still huge, still very close, and shining into his. "I might," she said, "but no woman may answer such a question till the man may ask it."

"But I have not," Lucoyo breathed, "only asked, 'what if.' "

"Then what if you proved your worth as a hunter first?" she asked. "What if you dwelt with my people for two years, to show them you would willingly dwell among us all your life?"

"Why, so I would," Lucoyo said fervently. "But for me, a far greater question is: Would *they* have *me*?"

"Oh, yes," Elluaera said softly. "From the words I have heard around the fire, they would very willingly have you among them all your days."

Some little while later, Lucoyo returned to the brush hut that had been his sickroom—and found Ohaern reclining on the other pallet. He sat up, smiling, and said, "So you have found your nurse a pleasant companion, outlander."

"Very pleasant indeed." Lucoyo sat slowly on his pine-bough bed. "But how is it you are come, Ohaern? I need no nurse any longer, and if I did, I would not choose you!"

"It is because you no longer need one, that I am come," Ohaern said with some irony. "We must speak of the future, Lucoyo."

Lucoyo braced himself. "Speak, then."

"Will you return to your own tribe?"

"Never!" Lucoyo spat. "They have cast me out bodily—but they cast me out in their hearts, the day I was born!" He sat trembling, amazed at his own venom.

"The more fools they, then, and the greater our gain," Ohaern said. "Would you be a Biri, Lucoyo?"

"Aye, willingly," Lucoyo said slowly, "but can a fox become a wolf? My ears will always be long and pointed, and my feet shall always be that of a nomad!"

"So long as they return to a Biri village, there is no bar in that," Ohaern said, musing, "and so long as the rest of your body cleaves to no woman but one. The fox can be adopted by the wolves, Lucoyo."

"I have never seen that, nor heard of it!"

"Nor have I," Ohaern admitted, "though I have heard that wolves have raised human children and treated them as their own. Will you be an honorary wolf, Lucoyo, and mingle your blood with that of our clan?"

Lucoyo stared, his whole body stiffening, trembling, unable to believe his good fortune.

"Come, the choice is not so great as that," Ohaern said, his voice low. "You have already mingled your blood with ours on the battlefield. Do you not wish it?"

"With all my heart!"

"Then it shall be done." The big smith stood up, grinning, and reached down to clasp Lucoyo's arm and hand. "When we have returned to our own land and reclaimed our village, we shall take you into our tribe with ceremony—but we have already taken you in, with our hearts. Sleep well, Lucoyo."

He left, but the half-elf did not sleep for an hour and more. He only sat, dazed by his good fortune and trying to persuade himself that it was both real and true.

At last he lay down, but lay awhile longer staring into the darkness, seeing visions of harmony and companionship and love and marriage, trying desperately to quell the fear within him, the fear of hoping, of feeling delight, the fear that if he did, all would be taken from him. So when, at last, he did sleep, worn out by warring jubilation and anxiety, he was not surprised when he was wakened by the angry shouts of alarm and the clash of iron on bronze.

He clasped his knife belt about him, caught up his bow and quiver, and charged out into a night lit by burning brush huts, hearing the cries all about him.

"The Klaja! The Klaja!"

"They have come back, with more!"

"More Klaja, and their master!"

Lucoyo was scrambling upright when a running body struck him and sent him spinning. The body fell with him, howling, and sharp teeth snapped shut an inch from his face. In panic, Lucoyo yanked out his knife and struck. Crimson streaked across the human cheek and the jackal's snout, and the monster howled again, but this time in fear, then scrambled away. Hot with blood lust, Lucoyo pursued—and saw his quarry duck between two more of his kind, who advanced, snarling, with spears raised.

Lucoyo fell back a few steps, then bent to string his bow and came up with an arrow nocked. The Klaja hesitated, giving him stable targets, and he loosed one arrow, then whipped another across the bow even as the first struck a Klaja chest. The beast fell howling, and its mate scrambled away.

Burning with fury and the elation of victory, Lucoyo spun, looking for new quarry . . .

And a huge hand slapped him aside as if he were a branch of leaves. Thunder filled his head as he fell, the thunder of a huge basso voice bellowing in a foreign language, as much bark as words. Dazed and terrified, he saw the giant, half again the height of a man, wading through the fight toward a knoll where Ohaern stood with Manalo behind him. The giant struck Biriae and Klaja alike, sweeping them aside with huge backhanded sweeps of his arms, slamming them against trees to slide broken to the ground.

One of those blows struck Elluaera.

She stood bravely, a spear in her hands, jabbing at the giant. Then she was flying through the air, head snapping back, striking the bole of a huge oak and sliding to the ground in a heap of bright hair and tumbled limbs.

Lucoyo screamed.

He screamed, bent his bow and loosed. The arrow flew straight and true, and stuck jutting out of the giant's shoulder, right next to the cross straps of his black leathers. He did not even seem to notice, just kept ploughing through the fight.

Lucoyo went mad. He screamed obscenities, running around the giant, stabbing and slashing at any who came in his way, not caring if they were human or half beast, for he was almost a beast himself now. Twelve feet in front of the giant and five to the side, he knelt and loosed an arrow. He aimed for the eye; it struck the cheek, and this time the giant felt it. He roared in anger—a broad, blond-haired, high-cheeked face that might have been rudely handsome another time, but was now ugly with rage and gloating anticipation. He advanced even as Lucoyo was drawing again, and struck the half-elf a backhanded blow that sent him caroming off an elm. Dazed and aching, Lucoyo scrambled to his feet—and saw the circle of men about Ohearn and Manalo, only yards to his left. Ohaern stood shouting, a sword in each hand, cutting down any Klaja who came near him. Most huddled back, spears ready, wary of coming within the big smith's reach. One by one the Biriae rallied to their chief, those who still lived. As they came, Manalo gave each an iron sword, which he produced from beneath his cloak in seemingly endless profusion; even in mid-fight, Lucoyo had the crazy notion that the sage could not possibly have carried so many.

But he needed a sword himself, and his arrows could reach those Klaja who were careful to stay beyond Ohaern's grasp. Lucoyo ran toward them—or tried to run, but his legs kept giving way beneath him, and a Klaja, mistaking that weakness for vulnerability, struck down at him with a cry of glee, the firelight gleaming off its teeth. Lucoyo struck upward with his knife, ripping skin and muscle; the jackal fell back howling in pain, clutching blood. Lucoyo paid him no attention, but stumbled toward Ohaern, dodging legs and striking with his blade. Twice spears struck him, but he twisted aside at the last instant, and they only left red streaks; twice, blows caught him and sent him spinning, but they threw him in the right direction, toward the knoll, and the protection of the Biriae.

But the Ulharl reached them first.

Chapter 11

The Ulharl reached them first, or came close enough. He roared and swung up a hand, a hand that suddenly cupped fire in its basket of a palm, a hand that shot forward, hurling that fire, hurling it straight toward Manalo.

The sage whipped one more sword from beneath his cloak—a sword of bronze, with strange patterns etched in the metal. He shouted some words the Biriae could not understand, slashing the sword between himself and the Ulharl. Fire traced that arc, flames burst from it—flames that engulfed the Ulharl's fireball. A loud, sharp report sounded; then the flames roared, swirling up higher than the Ulharl's head and billowing toward him. The giant fell back with a cry of alarm, then growled as the flames died. He lurched toward the sage.

But Manalo was chanting again, gesturing as if lifting handfuls of grain, and snakes came writhing out of the ground to twine up about the Ulharl's legs, dozens of snakes, scores of snakes, thicker and thicker as they followed one another, twining about the giant's limbs and swarming over him. He thrashed at them, bellowing in anger, and managed to trample a few underfoot, but the others held fast, tightening their coils.

In rage, the giant shouted a spell of his own, and the snakes melted like spring snow in a shadowed pocket, touched suddenly by sunlight.

But Manalo was still chanting, hands paddling like a mole's, and the ground beneath the Ulharl rumbled, then sank. Roaring in surprise and anger, the giant dropped into a pit that had not been there a moment before, as the ground gave way beneath his feet.

"Their champion is down!" Ohaern bellowed. "Cut these jackals apart!"

The Biriae roared agreement and blocked spears on their shields while they slashed the owners with their swords. One Biri began to chant their old war song, and others joined him. In seconds the whole throng was belting out the words of doom, while their swords reaped death all about them. Biriae fell with spears in their chests—but far more Klaja rolled on the ground, yelping with fear and pain as they clutched at crimson wounds, or lay silent and lifeless. Even though they outnumbered the Biriae three to one, the Klaja began to give way, their circle widening.

As they did, Manalo held his palms out toward the hole as if he were warming them at a fire, and chanted words of power.

But the Ulharl was chanting in his pit even as he was gouging handholds, then kicking them into footholds and climbing up toward the rim. He surged up the last four feet, head and shoulders shooting into sight, right arm swinging down, fingers widespread, as he shouted his own enchantment—and a thousand dripping teeth shot through the air to englobe the sage. But even as they flew, Manalo shouted his imperative, and a thousand needle-sharp daggers flew to stab at the Ulharl from all sides.

They scarcely seemed to concern him. He roared anger at the annoyance, swatting the blades out of the air with palms that must have been as hard as oak, while his roar turned into a chant that brought the thousand knives tinkling down.

Manalo banished the dripping teeth with a snapped phrase and a gesture of irritation. They did not fall, but simply ceased to be; the air around him was suddenly clear. Instantly, he began to chant again, molding something invisible in his hands, forming a large ball that gradually became visible, then began to glow, brighter and brighter.

The Ulharl bellowed as he threw himself out of the pit.

The globe in Manalo's hand burst into flame as he hurled it into the Ulharl's face.

Snarling, the Ulharl swung a huge hand to bat the fireball out of the air—but as he did, it burst into five separate brands, each hurtling toward him. He swatted at them, hands a blur, lips pulled back in a snarl of pleasure as he sent one, then two, caroming back toward the Biriae, then three, four . . .

And the dark sphere in their midst, which had rocketed on unnoticed, struck his chest and exploded.

The Ulharl only began to scream; the sound was cut off as he fell, a huge dark sunburst across his chest—but only across, not within. The Klaja froze, staring, struck dumb by the fall of their leader—or, perhaps, their herder, for as the fact of his falling sank in, they threw back their heads and howled—though it was a howl that seemed to have as much of elation as of fear.

Then the Biriae shouted with triumph, and the howl definitely became one of panic. The Klaja dropped their spears and ran. Biriae pounded after them, shouting their battle cry.

"Stop!" Ohaern cried. "Do not pursue! They may lead you into division and fall upon you piecemeal!"

The eager Biriae hesitated.

"We cannot be sundered now!" the chieftain called. "There are too few of us left!"

"Too few, indeed," Manalo answered him, speaking loudly, "and those few must needs seek out the others, whether they be slain or fled. Quickly, there is little time! My fireball has only marked this Ulharl and sent him to sleep; he shall waken all too soon, and we must be gathered and gone!"

That pulled the Biriae back, and they fanned out in search, looking for signs of tribesmen who might have fled.

But Lucoyo was looking frantically among the bodies, heaving Klaja forms up and away until he could look into the face of the Biri beneath. Then, whether it was dead or merely stunned or wounded, the nomad moved on, searching again and again, growing more and more frantic as he did.

"He does as he should," Manalo said to the startled clansmen. "Seek for your scattered fellows, for many fled the Klaja and many have fallen to their onslaught. Bring them together, those who have hidden—but quickly, for there is little time!"

"The Klaja will not come back while their champion lies dead," Ohaern objected.

"I have told you he is not dead, but only unconscious, and Ulahane still shields him enough to keep my spells from slaying him! We must be gone ere he awakes! Speed you!"

They sped, the Biriae fanning out in every direction, heaving the dead Klaja aside and slaying those who were badly wounded. Dead Biriae they left where they lay, in sorrow, for there was no time to bury them. At last Manalo summoned them back, and they came, with five women, two old men, three girls, and a boy. "These are all we found, O Sage," Dalvan said.

"But Elluaera! Was there no trace of Elluaera?" Lucoyo cried.

"None," Dalvan said, his face heavy with pity.

But, "I saw her fall," one of the old men said. "A Klaja spear transfixed her, and I threw myself against the knees of the beast; he fell, and I cut his throat, but another came on us in an instant. I saw her crawl into a brake, and the Klaja thrust into it with his spear. Her scream was short."

The half-elf threw back his head, keening grief, and sank to his knees, burying his face in his hands.

"But I did not *see* her die!" the old man amended.

"Do not give him false hope," Ohaern said heavily. "It is far more cruel than the harsh truth."

"But we have not found her body," Dalvan objected.

"She may have crawled deeper into the underbrush as she died," the chief answered, "or even into the stream, and the current may have whirled her away." But he did not say what was uppermost in his mind, what all of them were thinking—that the Klaja might have borne her body away for feasting. Certainly there were many bodies missing.

The fallen giant gave a single rasping groan. Electrified, everyone whipped about, staring at him—but he still lay on his back, though with no more movement than the silent rise and fall of his chest.

The sound brought Lucoyo staring up from his grief. "Can you not slay him?" he demanded of the sage.

"Yes, given enough time," said Manalo, "but he would waken before that. They are incredibly tough and hard to kill, these Ulharl—they are half immortal, after all, and though their father can be slain, it would take another Ulin to do it."

"Hard to kill, eh?" Lucoyo glared at the supine giant, eyes narrowing.

"Very," the sage answered.

With a cry like a bird of prey striking, Lucoyo threw himself onto the giant's chest, stabbing down full-armed—but a hand's breadth from the Ulharl's hide, the blade turned aside as if it had met curving steel. Lucoyo screamed in frustration and struck again, again . . .

"Peace, archer, peace!" Ohaern seized the half-elf and wrestled him away. "Ulahane's spell protects his get; you can do no good!"

"I can do a great deal of good for my aching heart!" Lucoyo cried, struggling. "Release me, Biri! Let me at least wear out my anger on his unholy body!"

"There is not enough time for that, there will never be enough time for that! I know the depth of your passion, outlander, I have seen it in the way you smite your enemies! The Ulharl would waken to find you on his chest, and I would lose a valiant fighter!"

"Lose me! Let me be lost!" Lucoyo cried, throwing himself back and forth against the smith's arm. "If Elluaera is lost, let me be lost, too!" And he thrashed about from side to side, a howl tearing at his throat—until suddenly he went limp and slid from Ohaern's grasp to the ground, where he knelt, sobbing.

"Pick him up, and take him with us," Manalo commanded, "for we cannot stay here, and we must not lose so greathearted a man."

Glabur and Dalvan moved in to gather up their fallen comrade, almost tenderly, and Dalvan carried Lucoyo off over his shoulder.

Manalo turned to the assembled Biriae. "We have searched and we have found only a few. Pray to Lomallin to aid those others who have escaped these Klaja, and pray that most of your tribesmen have done so—but pray for your dead when there is time, for we must flee now, and quickly, ere this Ulharl awakes and rallies his poor twisted pack. Come, away!" He turned and strode off, robes billowing, staff rising and falling with his steps. Ohaern turned back to beckon only once, then set off after the sage. More slowly, the others followed—but followed faster and faster the farther they went.

They vanished among the trees, leaving the fallen giant alone with the dead.

Then the Ulharl grunted and groaned, and his huge body shivered. One arm jerked up, then fell back—and the giant lay still again, lit dimly by the ruddy glow of the still-burning campfire.

As they walked, Ohaern stepped up beside Manalo and asked, his voice low, "Is Ulahane, then, so much stronger than Lomallin that you, who draw on Lomallin's power, cannot slay one who draws on the power of the scarlet god?"

"Ulahane and Lomallin are equal in power, Ohaern," the sage answered, just as softly.

"Then why could not you, who serve the green god, escape from Ulahane's prison?"

Manalo sighed wearily. "Because the two are equal in power, as I have said; it is the lesser beings, the humans and Klaja and others whom they can each sway to their sides, that will decide the conflict."

"As Ulahane prevented you from coming to the aid of my wife, by imprisoning you?" Ohaern scowled blackly. "Or do I accord myself too much importance?"

"Every human being is important to Lomallin," Manalo answered sharply. "But yes, you are more important than most, Ohaern. You are the pivot on which a battle shall swing, perhaps more than one—so if Ulahane can seduce or cripple you, he will."

Ohaern looked up, staring, appalled. "Then may Lomallin protect me! Am I truly singled out for the spite of the Scarlet One?"

"You are," Manalo answered, "but you are also elected for Lomallin's special protection. He is wise in that, for even as Ulahane thwarted him in his desire to save your wife, so you thwarted Ulahane by freeing me."

"Is there no way for Lomallin to become stronger than Ulahane?" Ohaern protested.

"Only by dying, as I have told you before. He can only become stronger than Ulahane if the Scarlet One kills him."

"Only Ulahane?" Ohaern frowned. "He does not become stronger if another Ulin kills him?"

"I suppose he might—but who among the few Ulin who remain would do such a deed? Be sure that if Lomallin dies, it will be Ulahane who slays him. And since Ulahane, too, has heard that prophecy, he takes great care not to murder Lomallin. To wound him, to maim him if he can, perhaps—certainly to defeat him in every other way, to hinder and frustrate and oppose him—but he will not slay the Green One, for fear of that redoubled strength."

"But how can Lomallin become stronger by dying?"

"Only the Creator knows that, until it shall come to pass," Manalo returned. "For now, it is a prophecy that both Ulin accept, though they do not comprehend the way of it."

Ohaern glowered at the ground ahead of them, gnawing over a point that troubled him. "If the Creator knows how Lomallin shall gain strength, could it be that he truly prefers Lomallin's way to Ulahane's, and lends him strength enough to win in the end?"

"I devoutly hope so," Manalo replied.

"But we cannot *know*, can we?" Ohaern lifted his head with a grimace of distaste. "Gods are so stingy with knowledge of why they do as they do. Does even Lomallin know whether the Creator has given him greater strength than Ulahane?"

"No," Manalo said, with full certainty. "None of us can *know*, Ohaern—we can only strive to our utmost to accomplish what we believe is right. And that, perhaps, is the reason the Creator does not reveal the knowledge."

"I feel that I am a toy being played with," Ohaern grumbled.

"Do not we all?" Manalo smiled. "Nevertheless, we can strive until we know our circumstances, and work to use them to best advantage. That is still a great deal, Ohaern, and if our circumstances make us toys, then certainly our manipulation of them must make us a great deal more."

Ohaern looked up at him, frowning. "You speak as if our lives were a game of jackstraws."

Manalo laughed and clapped him on the shoulder. "Perhaps

they are, Ohaern—perhaps they are like to jackstraws. But remember—only 'like.' " His hand still on the smith's shoulder, he steered him onward down the woodland path.

They had been on the road perhaps half an hour when they heard shrill yips ahead. Lucoyo's head snapped up; then, with a growl, he drew his long knife. About him, bereaved husbands and fathers likewise drew swords and raised spears, the whole group emitting an angry rumble.

"Nay, down!" Manalo said urgently. He waved them back, saying, "In among the trees, quickly! Their master summons them back, and if they do not come, he shall know where we are!"

"Let him know," said a grizzled veteran. "Let him come. We shall carve his dogs for his dinner."

"We must not," Manalo countered, "for though we may prevail, we shall pay heavily for the victory. You are diminished by half already; if the victory costs you the other half, it is no triumph at all, no matter how few Klaja survive. This Ulharl may lose, but his master shall win. Into the brakes with you now, so that you may fight tomorrow, and again the day after, and whittle down the enemy shaving by shaving, till there are none of them left, but many of you! Hide!"

The bereaved stood a moment, glowering and wavering; then Ohaern stepped forward to herd them off the track and into the underbrush. Unwillingly, they went.

Other Biriae were already climbing the trees. When they had, they held spears poised, and Lucoyo strung his bow.

"Strike only to defend yourselves," Manalo counseled. "If they do not strike you, let them pass."

"How can they miss us," Glabur demanded, "with their jackals' sense of smell?"

"It is clouded by the aroma of blood in their nostrils, by their eagerness for it. They do not expect you here and are therefore less likely to see you." Manalo stepped into the undergrowth, too.

The forest path stood empty, but a voice from among the leaves said sourly, "The lust for blood may cloud their senses, but it is your spell that clouds their minds."

"Even so," said the sage's voice. "Be silent now, and let them pass." He began to chant softly.

"Revenge tomorrow shall be as sweet as revenge today," Ohaern assured his tribesmen. "Bide in patience."

"All well and good for *you* to say," snarled a young widower. "You have had your revenge!"

"Not enough, I assure you," Ohaern said. "Not even a beginning."

His voice was so grim, so thick with banked anger, that his tribesmen fell silent in sheer surprise. In his thicket, Lucoyo's grin drew his lips back from his teeth; he knew in his own heart the depth of hatred from which the chieftain spoke.

The wood stood silent a while, except for the occasional scrape of leather against bark. The chorus of yipping grew louder.

Then they came, pushing the leaves aside, treading stealthily even though their conversation was loud—anthropoid torsos and limbs with jackals' feet and fur, yapping to one another and snarling back and forth. There was a tension to them that might have been either apprehension or leashed eagerness. On they went down the trail, oblivious to the Biriae hidden all about them. They passed between ranks of men, every one of whom crouched with naked blade, yearning for a single Klaja to turn aside and stab at him—but none did. Under tree limbs freighted with Biriae they padded, but never once looked up. Lucoyo tracked the biggest one with a barbed arrowhead, but the beast never even glanced into the undergrowth, only snarled at the other Klaja about him.

Then they were gone, vanished into the forest's gloom.

The path stayed silent for a few minutes; then a voice demanded, "How long, O Sage?"

"Wait yet a while," Manalo told him. "When we are sure there are no stragglers yet to come, we shall resume our journey."

"I could have carved out that big one's liver," an older Biri growled.

"I would have been happy enough to see my arrow through his heart," Lucoyo answered.

"Yet you withheld your hands." Manalo's voice was warm with

praise. "Well done, O Biriae. Your forbearance today shall win a greater vengeance tomorrow."

There was some grumbling at that, but nothing with any real heart to it.

After a while, leaves rustled, and the sage stepped out onto the path. "There are no more to come, and the band is far enough past not to hear. Away!"

One by one they emerged; fifty strong, they followed the sage and the smith along the path in the direction opposite to that of the Klaja.

Twice more they hid and waited while groups of jackal-men went past them toward the Ulharl. Then, as twilight darkened the forest, Manalo held up a hand. "Hist!"

The Biriae halted, some glowering resentfully at the man who had deprived them of revenge, some glancing apprehensively at the foliage around them.

"They come hot-foot," Manalo told them, his whole body taut, "with their master whipping them on. Now must you hide in earnest, Biriae—but be ready to strike your hardest if they discover you!"

"We could have diminished their strength with safety!" Dalvan howled.

"No," said Manalo, "for then they would not need to search for us—they would *know*. There is one party seeking us in this direction, yes, but they are one among many quartering the forest, for they have no certain knowledge even of the direction we have taken."

"Then we may strike at them?" a younger man asked eagerly.

"Not unless they strike us," said Ohaern, "for that would bring the whole host down upon us, and the Ulharl with them. We must hide again, my friends, and trust in the sage's magic to conceal us."

"But what of the Ulharl's magic?"

"As ever, it is Lomallin's power against Ulahane's," Manalo told him, "locked against one another in balance, with the spirit and effort of mortals deciding the issue. Hide, and have your weapons ready!"

Once again they hid in a thicket; once again Ohaern posted sentries, changing by watches. Once again the sage wove his spell of concealment, and the night passed in fear mingled with longing for battle. Many were the eyes that closed, but few were the warriors who slept.

Four times during the night they heard the yipping and growling of Klaja coming nearer and nearer, and men grasped weapons in fierce hope of discovery, determined to sell their lives dearly, for the only reason they had now for living was to slay as many Klaja as they could. But soon enough the noises receded again, the barks and growls and occasional gutturals that the jackal-men used for speech, as the Klaja passed by. Disappointed, the Biriae relaxed again—a little.

Finally the forest lightened with a foretaste of dawn, and Manalo banished the concealment spell with a mutter and a gesture. Ohaern rose up. "Come, men of mine! We have survived the night and can press onward to some true vengeance."

"Press onward!" a grizzled warrior cried in disgust. "Six times now you have cheated us of the chance to sell our lives in that pursuit!"

"To what purpose?" Ohaern replied. "We would only have taken a small number of the Klaja, and there is no point in that. They are not the enemy."

A chorus of protest answered him. "Not the enemy? They have slain our people, they have destroyed our village! If they are not the enemy, who is?"

"The one who drives them," Manalo answered, "and the one who drives the driver. Ohaern speaks truth. The Klaja are tools, and unwilling ones at that; I doubt that any of them has even the ghost of a notion of choice, between obedience and death at the Ulharl's hands. Ulahane warped the union of jackal and human to bear fruit; Ulahane made them; Ulahane drives the Ulharl who drive the Klaja. It is with Ulahane that your quarrel lies, not with his poor victims."

The glade fell silent, each Biri glancing at his neighbor, then away, feeling the touch of terror in his vitals. "Who can fight a god?" Glabur whispered. "Who could dare to go up against Ulahane?"

"A fool mad for revenge," Ohaern answered, "and such a fool am I. Who will go with me to strike against the Scarlet One?"

The clearing held in silence, the Biriae staring at the big smith as if he had taken leave of his senses.

"Remember," said Manalo, "that the powers of Lomallin and Ulahane are equal, and locked in balance. It is mortal folk who may decide the issue, whether they be Klaja or human or Ulharl—and the Ulharl may be very hard to kill, but they do die."

"Then if we wish to strike against Ulahane," Glabur said, "ought we not to strike against his mortal minions?"

"So we must," Ohaern agreed. "Where is he strongest in human followers?"

The Biriae muttered and shifted, for they all knew the answer. Finally, Dalvan spoke it aloud. "In Kuru," he said, "for that is the Scarlet One's citadel."

"You have spoken well and truly," Ohaern answered grimly, "and therefore shall I go up against Kuru. Who will go with me?"

CHAPTER 12

There was no silence, not a moment's hesitation; fifty voices cried, "I!" with a savagery that surprised even Ohaern. But it braced him and set him a broad smile. "Well, then, we go, we who are left of the Clan of the Hawk!"

"There may be others who fled, and hid so well we could not find them," said one of the grizzled veterans. "Oh, I pray to Lomallin, let it be so!"

"Let it be so," Ohaern agreed, "but if it is, they are so well hid that even we could not find them."

"Pray the Klaja will not find them either!" the veteran cried.

"I shall," Ohaern told him, "so that the clan may not die. But to better their chances, let us give Ulahane a greater concern. Southward! We march to the river, and ride it to Kuru!"

The men answered with a ferocious shout and followed the smith—a smith no longer, but a war chief now.

Lucoyo strode with searing anger and hatred rekindled: the anger he had felt for the clan that had reared him, redoubled and double-heated now, but directed at Ulahane. How temeritous of a man to assail a god! How impossible a task, how hopeless! But how else was he to find any meaning in life, or any reason for living?

As for Ohaern, he forced his steps, hiding the deep and bitter depression that dragged at his heels and bade him lie down and wait for death, for Ryl was no more, and the child she had birthed, Ohaern's son, was lost with the rest of the clan, probably lost in death, never to be seen in the world again. He had never even named the babe! Yes, Ohaern had indeed a strong grievance against Ulahane—and no other reason to live.

Unlike Lucoyo, though, it never occurred to him to think of attacking a god as arrogance. He only knew that Ulahane was the true source of his misery, and must suffer for it as Ryl had suffered—and, more importantly, that the Scarlet One must be eliminated, or humanity would never be happy again. Indeed, if Ulahane lived, humanity would die.

The question was whether humanity could be saved. From what Manalo had been telling him, more and more people were devoting themselves and their lives to Ulahane, out of greed or due to false promises, and they very well might overwhelm the good folk, who were dedicated to Lomallin. Ohaern set his face toward the south, determined to find out for himself just how much evil there was in the world, and how much good to set against it. Unlike other men who have undertaken that quest, he had a very practical reason.

Of one thing he was certain: the evil of the city of Kuru must not be allowed to persist.

When they stopped to rest at midday, Ohaern asked, "Where are we bound for on our first stage, Teacher? To the river, surely—but where shall that river take us?"

"To Cashalo," Manalo answered. "It is a city two hundred leagues from Kuru, but which is loyal to Lomallin and has thus far held steady against Ulahane and his minions. There are many cities in the south, and only a few have fallen to the worship of the Scarlet One. When you come to any city, be circumspect until you have discovered to which Ulin it is devoted. Some, such as Cashalo, will shelter you for no better reason than that you are strangers who might wish to trade, or to work among them."

"But none will shelter us for being Ulahane's enemies?" Lucoyo asked.

Manalo smiled sadly. "Alas, no—they may not worship Ulahane, but they fear him. And be wary of thinking of yourselves as Ulahane's enemies, archer."

"Yes, I know," Lucoyo said sourly. "Are the flies who seek to drink my blood my enemies? Are mice? Surely I am theirs—but are they dangerous enough to be mine?"

"Say, rather, the serpent who sinks his fangs into your flesh," Ohaern returned, "who bites your heel even as you seek to crush him with your foot!"

The Biriae rumbled agreement, but Manalo shook his head. "Do not embrace the viper in your hearts, O Biriae. Remember that your totem is the hawk, who strikes boldly and suddenly, and does not slink upon you in secret. Be mindful that the hawk pounces on prey—he does not seek revenge."

"But how can we do anything else?" Ohaern erupted. "We, who have lost all we love because of Ulahane's malice!"

"You can wipe out a menace," Manalo replied, "as you would slay a rabid wolf. But do not feed your hate, or dote on vengeance, for then is Ulahane in your heart, and you are half swayed to the Scarlet One even by your own hatred for him. If you must slay his slaves and his servants, do so to ensure that they will not slay more innocents, not to slake your thirst for vengeance."

"But if a man has hurt me," Lucoyo said, "I must hurt him in return, so that he will know not to hurt me again!"

"Ulahane will ensure that there are always more who seek to hurt you, no matter how many hurts you give in return," said Manalo. "He hates you for no better reason than that you are human—even you, Lucoyo, for he hates all the younger races almost as much as he hates humankind. No, revenge against Ulahane and his pawns will not lessen his will to hurt and slay you and your kind—but it will lead you into his power."

Ohaern scowled. "You do not mean that lust for revenge on Ulahane will make us his worshipers!"

"No," said Manalo, "but it will give him a handle by which to grasp you, and once having a hold on you, he will draw you in, to slay you."

"So." Lucoyo leaned forward, brow wrinkled with the effort of understanding. "We should fight Ulahane's creatures because they are a threat, not because we wish to punish them, or are angry at them."

"Even so," said the sage.

"We are not to strike in anger, or in hatred, or because they have hurt us."

Manalo nodded. "Evil motives against evil enemies ensure evil results. If you wish to defeat Ulahane, you must not use his weapons, or they will turn in your hands, turn against you and cut you apart."

"Well, I can accept that," the half-elf sighed, leaning back. "It rankles, mind you—it will go hard, but I shall manage it. At the last, I care not why I kill Ulahane's creatures—so long as they die."

"That will have to suffice." Manalo hid a smile of amusement. He rose and addressed himself to the clan. "Come; we must be on the road again. If you go up against Kuru, you must begin by visiting the most northerly of the southern cities—Cashalo—for there you will find ships and captains that can take you to the eastern lands far more quickly than you can walk."

"Cashalo?" Dalvan frowned. "I have heard of that city. But how shall we find our way?"

"You have but to journey down the Mashra River; it will take you into the heart of the city itself."

"Up and away, then!" Ohaern came to his feet. "If the road to Kuru begins at Cashalo, then to Cashalo we go!"

"It is time to divide into small bands, though," Manalo told him, "for so large a force as ours will be noticed by Ulahane's sentries, and he will send his creatures against us. Divide yourselves into bands of three and four, and journey to Cashalo separately."

"But will we not then be easy meat for any Klaja or wicked men?" cried Lucoyo, dismayed.

"The Klaja will not trouble themselves for so few," said Manalo, "for their Ulharl drives them toward one particular goal that his master has set him, and only that one. As to bandits and enemy tribes, have you never dealt with them before?"

"Aye," Glabur said slowly. "We hide when we can, and fight when we must."

"So you must do again. Believe me, there is little to fear—

none will take you for a threat when there are so few, but there are enough to give pause to any who might wish to prey upon the weak. Go to Cashalo as secretly as you can, but do not skulk so obviously as to arouse suspicion. Meet there, and rally to Ohaern. Choose your traveling companions and go by different roads."

Lucoyo lingered, reluctant to push himself onto any of the groups, but wishing ardently that some would invite him. It seemed none would—Glabur and Dalvan united with two other Biriae, and all around him others joined in threes and fours, by bonds of kinship or long-standing friendships. But before everyone had clustered, Ohaern beckoned the half-elf to him. Lucoyo's heart leaped—did he truly have a friend? He went.

"You shall travel with us, archer," Ohaern told him. "I need your nimble wits and nimbler hands, and with my bulk to back you, we should be unbeatable."

Lucoyo grinned, sensing genuine liking beneath the excuse. "Why, thank you, smith! I will be glad indeed of the protection of your hammer! But with whom do we travel?"

"With me," said Manalo. "Or will that make you uneasy, Lucoyo?"

The half-elf looked up at him slowly, and admitted frankly, "A little—but I shall master it. Where do we wander, O Sage?"

They wandered to the west, away from the path and between the great trees—but they left last, watching the other dozen bands go off one by one, each waiting, chatting and resting, until the one before it was a goodly distance ahead. Three went by the path; three to the east through the forest and toward the river; four to the south and southeast, to circle around and find the stream; and three to the north, to swing down to the flood in their own turn. Only Manalo, Ohaern, and Lucoyo went west, to take the longest circle and come last to the river, so that they might catch up and aid any who might come to grief.

"The Klaja will have a merry time trying to track *this* band, if they seek to," Lucoyo said with a grin. "Why do we wait?"

"For magic." Ohaern pointed at Manalo, who leaned upon his staff, looking back at the campsite and singing softly as he watched. Lucoyo frowned, watching, too, wondering what the sage was up to now. He waited and waited, growing more and more impatient, and was about to demand they leave when he saw a small animal come hesitantly from the far edge of the clearing. It was a stoat, and another joined it from another quarter, then another and another. They came forward, meeting in the center of the clearing. The sage nodded, murmuring, encouraging. The little creatures looked up at him, then at one another, then began to spread their scent all over the clearing and back into the trees.

Manalo turned away to join the two Biriae, chuckling. "Let the Klaja try to track our bands by scent *now*!"

"I could almost feel sorry for them." Lucoyo wrinkled his nose, trying to fan away the rancid, musky smell.

"I could indeed," Ohaern agreed, "if I did not remember what they would do to one of our bands if they found them. Where did you learn *that* trick, Teacher?"

"That is a story in itself, and too long to tell now," Manalo said. "But the spell is short, and worth learning. Repeat the words after me, and I will tell you their meaning."

He began to recite syllables that seemed like nonsense to Lucoyo, and that would not stick in his mind, even when the sage explained their meaning in an ancient tongue—but Ohaern scowled in furious concentration and nodded again and again, repeating the syllables perfectly time after time, until Manalo was satisfied that he had memorized them. Lucoyo stared at the smith with surprise, and not a little awe. What manner of man was this? He was supposed to be merely a hunk of muscle, with a brain that worked only for hunting, fighting, and forging weapons! Was it possible that a man could be more than he seemed—more, perhaps, than even he himself knew?

In mid-afternoon they came out of the forest and into a rough land of rocky outcrops, low bushes, and tough grass. Lucoyo looked about him and shivered. "What place is this, Teacher?"

"The Hard Country," Manalo replied, "and though none live here, it is a sacred place to many tribes."

"Sacred?" Lucoyo looked up, startled. "How could so bleak a place be sacred to any?"

"It has a rough beauty all its own," Manalo answered, "though that is easier to see at sunrise and sunset than it is now. Wait until we come to higher ground and look about you."

Lucoyo followed. He was willing to wait, but he doubted he would see anything to glory in.

They wound their way up a rocky trail, and Ohaern found himself wondering who had worn this pathway in the rock and hard-packed earth, if none lived here. Surely there could not be so many wild tribesmen wandering this land as to leave trails!

They came out onto the top, and Manalo stopped them with an upraised hand, suddenly tense. Ohaern and Lucoyo looked up—and saw them, rank upon rank of bleached rough human forms, like those a mother makes from a dough of meal and water to amuse little children. Their heads were devoid of hair, they were so lumpy that they seemed to have no joints, and their hands were rough mitten shapes with no fingers. Their feet were long lumps, and for faces they had only two pockmarks for eyes, another where a nose should be, and a slash for a mouth. But those mitten hands held clubs and primitive spears, sticks shaved to a point and hardened in fire, lethal for all their rudeness.

"What are they, Teacher?" Ohaern asked.

"The homunculi Agrapax made for Ulahane," Manalo answered, his aspect somber, "and whom Lomallin fought to free."

The gashes of mouths yawned open to issue a warbling wail, and the homunculi charged.

"Archer, your bow!" Ohaern cried as he drew his sword. As Lucoyo strung his bow, Ohaern leaped in front of Manalo and slashed in a frenzy—but every wound that opened in the dough bodies failed to bleed, or even to show muscle and veins. Instead it showed inside only what was outside—bland flesh—and the wounds closed, healing even as Ohaern cut again. The pointed sticks, though, scored his chest and arms, and the clubs struck bruising blows on his arms and legs. The homunculi were not strong enough for any one blow they dealt to break a bone, but they struck the same places again and again . . .

Lucoyo dropped to one knee, nocking an arrow, and loosed. It lanced into a dough-man who was swinging a club, and threw the swing off just enough so that it missed Ohaern—but the homunculus did not drop his weapon, nor cry out in anything but anger. Lucoyo followed the first shaft with another that skewered the homunculus through the center of the chest, if a chest it was—but the dough-man did not even notice. He only swung his club again, and this time it struck Ohaern's head. He staggered and fell.

With a keening cry, Lucoyo dropped his bow and sprang to stand over Ohaern's body, drawing his long knife and bracing himself for the onslaught of the homunculi—but Manalo stood forth between the host of pale bodies and the fallen chieftain, holding his hands up and crying out in an ancient tongue. The clumsy advance slowed and halted. The leader of the homunculi replied in the same incomprehensible syllables, and from the intonation, it seemed to be a question. Manalo answered, and the leader—or perhaps the one to his left, or the one to his right, or two or three away; they looked identical to Ohaern and Lucoyo—responded with a statement. Manalo answered at some length, and Lucoyo began to grow impatient. Ohaern must have seen the signs of it, for he said, "Patience, archer. His words are our best shield now." He made to sit up—and a dozen homunculi raised their weapons at his first movement, but held them still as he continued to rise, very, very slowly.

Manalo turned to speak down to them. "The homunculi understand now why you thought they attacked you. For their part, they could not understand why *you* seemed to be attacking *them*."

"Our apologies, then," Ohaern said. "It is not good for those who could be friends to fight one another."

Manalo spoke to the homunculi, and there was general muttering, in thin and tinny voices, with nods of agreement.

"Do nods mean the same to them that they do to us?" Lucoyo asked.

"Yes," Manalo told him, "and that is what they mean—'yes,' or in this case, agreement and acceptance."

Ohaern began to stand. Again the homunculi braced their weapons, but did not strike. Slowly, he regained his feet. "Archer, give me an arrow."

"I thought we did not intend to fight them." But Lucoyo passed him an arrow anyway—then bit back a cry of alarm as Ohaern gave the shaft to one of the homunculi. They made noises of approval, and the leader presented his spear to Ohaern, making a long, metallic-sounding speech.

"He thanks you for your gift," Manalo said, "and gives you one in return. He realizes that by giving him the means of wounding, you have shown trust in him, so he now shows trust in you."

"Tell him that I thank him," Ohaern said, "and trust him indeed, for I think we must be friends who fight the same foe." He passed the spear to Lucoyo. "I give his weapon to the friend who gave me the shaft to give him, in token that we both give and accept the trust of the homunculi."

Manalo translated. The homunculi set up a positive buzz of approval this time.

But Lucoyo gave the spear a jaundiced glance. He wasn't all that certain that he wished to be an ally of such creatures, no matter how doughty. However, he reminded himself that he did not wish them for his enemies, at least not in such numbers, so he took the shaft, forced a smile, and made a slight bow.

Then the leader beckoned. Manalo said, "He asks that you hold to both shafts, as he does."

Lucoyo was only too glad to give back the spear.

Ohaern held it out, and the homunculus clasped it a foot above Ohaern's hand. He held forth the arrow; Ohaern grasped it, but the homunculus held fast. With both of them holding both shafts, the homunculus began to drone.

"He says that you are comrades in arms now," Manalo said, "and that if his people call upon yours, you will come to their aid."

Lucoyo stared in alarm, but Ohaern said, "We shall set forth on the instant."

Manalo translated, and the homunculus nodded, eyes glinting, and rattled on again. "For his part," said the sage, "he promises that he and his people shall do likewise, that they shall come on the instant at which you call them, and that if you have need of them, you have but to call out this phrase . . ."

The homunculus proceeded to make a series of sounds that, to Lucoyo, sounded like nothing so much as the chipping of flints and the clatter of metal.

"Repeat it," Manalo advised, "so that he knows that you know."

Ohaern tried, but apparently had it wrong, for the homunculus shook his head and repeated the phrase, much more slowly. Ohaern tried again, and Lucoyo could have sworn he had duplicated it, but the homunculus corrected him and repeated the phrase in pieces, waiting for Ohaern to repeat each section, then recited it all again, and Ohaern recited it, too. After two more repetitions, the homunculus nodded, satisfied, and let go of the arrow.

"He is satisfied that you can call him at need," Manalo said. "Surrender the spear to him again and go your way."

Ohaern let go, saying, "Shall I not give him a gift?"

"It is not necessary, and might be misunderstood. He has your goodwill; he knows, and has felt it. That is all that is necessary."

Then, with much bowing and mutually unintelligible protestations, they took leave of the dough-men. When they had disappeared around a rocky outcrop, Lucoyo let out a long breath and suddenly felt wobbly in the knees. He clutched at the nearest boulder for support.

"Buck up, my friend." Ohaern's arm was about Lucoyo's shoulders, though he did not look terribly well-braced himself. "I am sure we shall see more strange sights than that before we are done."

They saw the next when darkness fell that night.

They camped in the lee of a rocky outcrop, but as Lucoyo knelt to lay the fire, Manalo said, "Not so close to the stone, archer."

"Why not?" Lucoyo looked up in surprise. "When the sun goes, the fire will warm the cliff and give us heat from back as well as front!"

"That is true," said Manalo, "but this cliff face is no ordinary stone."

"No, I see that—it is black, and glitters so that I could swear I see my face in it!"

Manalo nodded. "'It will also burn."

Both men stared at him as if he were insane. Then Ohaern asked, "Burning rock?"

"There are many marvels in this world," Manalo told him, "and this is one among them. Be sure, this rock will burn. If you doubt me, gather up the pebbles that have fallen at the base of the cliff and use them to feed your fire. But first, I pray you, kindle it farther away."

They did as he asked, and sure enough, the black rocks began to send up flames themselves. Oh, they sat in the wood fire for a goodly while indeed before they began to burn—but burn they did, and Ohaern knelt marveling, staring into the flames.

Lucoyo, however, clapped his hands in glee, cried out in delight, then turned to skewer the bird he had shot during the afternoon and set it upon a spit over the flames.

When they were done with their meal, Ohaern knelt to bank the fire for the night—but it roared, and shot up as tall as a man.

"Back!" Manalo cried, but Ohaern had already leaped away, and Lucoyo was farther still. The sage retreated slowly, though, still facing the blaze.

The flame shot up higher and higher, twice the height of a man and higher still, till it towered as tall as a tree.

"What has happened, Teacher?" Ohaern cried.

"Ulahane has sent more evil magic against us!" Manalo called in answer.

Then Lucoyo realized that there were eyes near the top of that flame hill, eyes that glowed more brightly than the fire itself, white-hot amidst orange, glaring down at him. He stared back, rooted to the spot, suddenly unable to move, for he could not find the will. The flames drew in, shaping themselves into a tall slender shape that tapered to a point at the bottom, was rounded at the top—and, dimly, Lucoyo could perceive some sort of a snout below the eyes, a snout that opened to let a ruby tongue of flame lick out to taste the air.

"What it is, Teacher?" Even Ohaern's voice shook.

"It is a salamander," Manalo replied, "a creature formed of the element of fire. Indeed, you might say that it is the spirit of fire itself. O Spirit! Wherefore do you visit us?"

"Why, at the behest of Ulahane," the creature replied, in the voice of a furnace blast.

"How is it that you serve the Scarlet One?" Manalo's voice did not shake.

"I do not serve!" the furnace-voice roared, and the eyes shot jets of flame. "I do as I please, and Ulahane has told me that there is fuel for my flame here. He has asked me to consume the overwhelming mortals I shall find around this fire! Who are you, small and kindling-fat, to question a salamander?"

"I am Manalo, a teacher among the human folk!"

The salamander's eyes brightened to actinic sparks, and the elemental boomed, "Perhaps, but I can see that you are more; it hovers about you like a mantle twice your size! Will you burn?"

"My body will burn as readily as any, I doubt not," Manalo answered, "but I hope you will not consume me, nor my friends."

"Wherefore should I not?"

"Why, because it is not your pleasure."

Lucoyo couldn't believe it; the elemental hung in midair, humming and roaring for long minutes. Then, at last, it said, "Consuming fuel is always my pleasure."

"True," Manalo agreed, "but there is so much water in these weak human bodies that it would cost you as much to ignite them as you would gain by their burning."

"Nay, more," the salamander admitted.

"Then wherefore should you do it? Out of friendship to Ulahane?"

"He is no friend of mine!"

"No, nor of any, and that is his boast. But if it is not your pleasure to do what he wishes done, then you should not."

"That is true." The salamander bent, swaying down over the sage. Manalo braced himself and stood firm. "Let me look more closely upon you," the monster said, "for I seldom see living creatures that make so much sense."

"I thank you," Manalo said simply.

"There is no need; I but speak my mind. Yet my thoughts are such that, if I have come to this camp, I would not waste the effort. What can you give me to make this journey other than useless?"

"Black rock," Manalo answered.

Chapter 13

"Fetch more, quickly!" Manalo told Ohaern and Lucoyo as he stooped to catch up pebbles from the pile they had gathered to feed the fire. "Chop it from the cliff face with your sword, if you must—it will only dull the blade, and we can sharpen it later!" Without waiting for an answer, he threw a double handful of the black pebbles into the flames that were the salamander.

The flames roared higher for a moment, then sank lower. "Good," the elemental judged. "Very good indeed! More, mortal, more!"

"More you shall have!" Manalo began to toss the pebbles one by one, aiming as high as he could, near the salamander's mouth.

But Lucoyo and Ohaern had already turned away, hurrying back to the cliff face. Lucoyo drew his knife, but Ohaern caught his arm. "No, we need speed! Let us try this first!" So saying, he picked up a boulder as large as his own head, hefted it high, and hurled it against the cliff face. The crack of its impact was drowned by the salamander's cries for more, but as the stone rebounded, a shower of fragments fell loose and a huge slab of the black rock fell to the ground.

"Take it!" Ohaern grunted as he hefted the boulder again. Lucoyo darted in, caught up the huge shard, and hefted it back to Manalo. In a lull between the salamander's calls, he heard the boulder crack into the cliff face again.

"Hurl it in anywhere!" Manalo said, and Lucoyo heaved. The giant flake of black stone arced high, then fell into the salamander's belly. A grin of fire spread under its snout, and it smacked unseen lips with a sound like the falling of a burning branch. Lucoyo shuddered and hurried back to Ohaern.

The smith was just lifting the boulder again, but as he saw Lucoyo coming, he lowered it to the crook of his arm and stood panting. "Aye, take another for him, Lucoyo! Belike I shall join you soon enough—my arms feel leaden already. I cannot keep this up much longer!"

"I hope you will not have to." The half-elf dashed in, then grunted as he heaved a huge lump into his arms. He was amazed to see how the pile of black boulders had grown. He turned away and lugged the second lump back to the salamander, hearing Ohaern's boulder crash into the cliff behind him.

Manalo nodded, and Lucoyo heaved the great rough stone into the salamander's belly. Again came the crackling of appreciation, and the elemental grunted, "More!" This time Manalo turned away to accompany him. "Not a great deal more, I suspect."

Lucoyo looked up with hope. "How do you know?"

"Because it only said 'more' once this time."

Ohaern stood bent over, hands on his thighs, heaving great lungfuls of air. His hammer-stone lay on the ground by his feet. Manalo surveyed the black heap and nodded. "That will be enough, I think."

"What . . . wizardry is this," Ohaern wheezed, "that can make . . . stone burn . . . or satisfy . . . a salamander?"

"The burning stones are no magic of mine, but that which the world itself fostered as it grew. As to the salamander, fire will always feed on what it finds next, but it can be assuaged by banking."

"And we are . . . banking it?" Ohaern gave him a keen glance.

"That we are. Come, Lucoyo! Bear up!"

"I bear," the half-elf grunted, staggering under a huge piece of rock.

"That . . . is mine." Ohaern plucked it from Lucoyo's grasp. "Do you take . . . another."

The half-elf squalled protest. "You are wearied, Ohearn!"

"I recover," the smith said grimly, "and we have need of haste. Do not make me lift, Lucoyo. Take another."

Grumbling, Lucoyo turned back—but he had to admire Ohaern's tact. The big man had managed to make him feel guilty at the thought of taking the bigger lump. Still, to show Ohearn, he took another almost as large and lugged it to the salamander.

Back and forth they went, hauling huge lumps to throw into the elemental. When the pile was gone and only rubble remained, Manalo said, "Will that content you for a time, O Fiery One?"

"A time," the monster allowed. "In truth, the taste and the bulk inclines me to warm feelings toward you."

"What other kind could he have?" Lucoyo muttered, but Ohaern shushed him.

"I would repay this kindness," the salamander told them, "when you have need of my flame. If you do, call me thus." And it made a sound like a series of explosions, such as come from green, resinous wood thrown into a blaze. Lucoyo stared, incredulous that the monster could think such sounds could be made by a human throat—then even more amazed as Manalo imitated them exactly.

The sage turned to Ohaern. "Do you say them, too, Ohaern. Like this." He repeated the pops and booms, one by one, until the chieftain could imitate them perfectly, both singly and in series.

"It is well," the salamander told them. "You are friends now, and need never fear me again! Farewell!" Then the blaze of his form seemed to double, roaring upward toward the heavens. The mortals leaped back, raising their forearms to shield their faces— but the blaze shrank as swiftly as it had swelled, then dwindled away to a mere campfire again.

Ohaern breathed out a shaky breath. "You have a most amazing gift for making friends, Teacher!"

"It is convenient," Manalo admitted, "though there are many with whom I have failed."

"How is it done—making a friend of an enemy?"

"By first being sure he *is* an enemy." Manalo turned to him with a smile. "Those Agrapaxians we met held no ill will—they simply happened to be in your path, and the two of you startled one another. In similar fashion, this salamander had no personal reason to wish us ill, so I asked him why he did. Always ask, Ohaern. If they will talk, they may become friends, or at least not enemies."

"I have known many who would talk all day and still slit my throat if they could," Lucoyo said darkly.

"So have I." Manalo's face turned grim. "And if a man seeks to kill you, of course, you must disable him before you can ask him questions."

"You may kill him in the disabling," the half-elf reminded.

"You may, and you must take no chance that he will slay you," the sage agreed. "However, if he does not attack at once, but takes time to threaten, you can usually find an opportunity for a question. Come, let us seek something calming, then sleep." He turned away to the fire, drawing a small bag out of his robes. "Set a pot of water over the fire again, Ohaern."

They drank an infusion of herbs in hot water as they sat and discussed the day's events. Whether it was the talk, the heat of the fire, the brew, or all three, Ohaern and Lucoyo soon found themselves growing sleepy. They rolled up in blankets, feet toward the fire, and slept, while Manalo watched, meditating.

In the morning, when they had breakfasted and buried the fire, Manalo took up his staff and turned to them. "I am now confident that you can survive any danger that comes your way. Remember only to be careful and quick, ready for any mishap that may befall."

"Or any enemy that may spring out at us," Lucoyo said.

But Ohaern frowned. "You speak as if you would leave us, Teacher!"

"And so I must," the sage said. "You Biriae cannot go up against Kuru alone and hope to win. There are many other tribes who would join you if they knew of your venture: those with grievances against Ulahane or Kuru, those who fear one or the other only from what they have heard, and those who are ready for any quest so long as it promises glory."

"And those who are ready for any quest that promises loot," Lucoyo said with a wicked smile.

"Such as they are usually dedicated to Ulahane already, though they may not know it yet. At any rate, no tribe that might aid us can rise and march if they do not know of the campaign."

"So you must go to bear word to them?" Ohaern asked.

"Word, and a bit more," Manalo admitted. "Some will not come unless they see it is I who ask it; some will not come unless they are given good reason. Nay, it is I myself who must go, and accompanying me would delay your progress intolerably. Go south without me, Ohaern. You have much to do on the way."

The smith frowned. "What manner of doings?"

"You shall find them as you go." Manalo turned to the half-elf. "Do not be so desolate, Lucoyo. You can manage well enough without me."

Lucoyo smoothed his face on the instant. He had not known that his feelings showed so.

"He feels no worse than I." But Ohaern looked somber, not bereft. "Still, we managed without you when we went to Byleo to bring you out of prison, and we shall manage again if we must."

"Stoutly spoken!" Manalo clapped him on the shoulder. "Be sure you shall see me again, at Kuru if not before. When the time has come for the attack, I shall be there—but by the same token, I shall ask you not to assail Ulahane's city without me."

"Oh, we promise," Lucoyo said fervently. "Be sure, Teacher— we would not wish to begin the festivities without you!"

Manalo laughed and set a hand on the half-elf's head. For a brief instant Lucoyo felt a strange tingling, as if something flowed from the sage into him—but Manalo took his hand away and it was gone.

The sage turned to Ohaern. "You must give me your promise, too, Ohaern."

"Oh, I promise." The big smith grinned. "I am not so much a fool as to attack a city without you, Teacher, or with only one tribe behind me. Nay, we shall wait for you, and for those you bring."

"Well said! Then I shall go to find them. May your journey be smooth and your road straight!" So saying, the sage turned away, striding off toward a huge wind-sculpted bluff. Beneath it he turned back to wave once, then set off around the huge outcrop and was gone from sight.

Lucoyo felt a surge of panic and started after him, but Ohaern put out an arm to stop him. "Let him go, Lucoyo. We are not children, after all, nor he our parent. Come, let us find the southern road." He took up his pack and turned away.

Lucoyo felt as if the smith's words had plunged his head into an ice-cold pool. Smoldering within, he shouldered his pack. Of course Ohaern was right—of course they needed none but themselves—and the smith could not have known how the mention of a parent would galvanize him.

He had fared without a father thus far, and he would go on faring without one surpassingly well! In fact, now that he thought of it, he was reluctant to have so much as a single road companion, even one so likable as Ohaern.

Reluctant, but not foolish enough to bid him farewell. Lucoyo, too, fared south, pacing quickly to catch up with his friend.

"It is ridiculous!" Lucoyo protested. "The sun has set; soon there will be only darkness and stars! We should have pitched camp before the orb even started to sink! Why do we still wander?"

"Are your legs so tired as that?" Ohaern returned.

Well, yes, they were, actually—but Lucoyo wasn't about to say so. "Ulahane's minions are more active at night—all know that! Why do you insist that we keep marching?"

"I do not know." Ohaern shook his head with dogged persistence. "I only know that we must. Call it a feeling, call it certain knowledge from some god or spirit, but it is there—a certainty that we may not yet rest. Stay if you wish, Lucoyo. I will come back for you when it is right."

Camp alone, on this barren plain? The man must have thought Lucoyo was out of his mind! Who knew what might come upon him, or how defenseless he would be with none to watch and none to guard his back? "Oh, you know I will not leave you!" the half-elf grumbled. "Who would ward your right arm if I did?"

Ohaern answered with a smile. "Why, then, I thank you, my right arm. Be content—I do not think it shall be much farther."

Lucoyo eyed the huge jumble of rock that reared out of the plain before them on their right. "I hope not." It unsettled him, how masses of granite could rise so suddenly out of this tableland—especially since the trail they followed almost always ran around those huge masses and right near them. Lucoyo could only think what an excellent place it would be for an ambush, just the sort he would have chosen. Of course, there was no sign of any living creature here, if you did not count the birds and small rodents—

Sudden shouting broke out ahead, with the clash of arms.

Lucoyo stared. Somebody else had noticed it was a good place for an ambush!

"Yes, not much longer to march, at all," Ohaern said grimly. "Come, archer, and keep your bow to hand! Let us see who fights whom!"

They sprinted ahead, and Lucoyo went dancing up the rock slope as nimbly as a lemur—and with just as good a night vision; at least he had some gift from his nameless father. He dropped down to his belly and stuck his head over the edge of the rocky shelf.

"What do you see?" Ohaern's voice was tense behind him.

"A band of men, beset by goblins!" Lucoyo hissed. "See for yourself, but move softly! Those big-eared monstrosities can hear a gnat's landing!" He squirmed backward, then up to stand, as Ohaern crawled past him.

Below, he saw torches ringing a half-dozen men with packs on their backs and swords in their hands. They slashed desperately at the bloodred monsters, half their height but four times their number, who sprang in on their huge frog legs, landing on great splay feet to stab with spears held in short, musclebound arms and knob-knuckled hands. Their huge dish ears were turned toward the knot of men, though, not listening for sounds of rescue.

"Can you shoot the goblins without slaying the men?" Ohaern demanded.

"Aye, if I shoot at those farthest from the humans."

"Then do so—and take care not to hit me!" Ohaern vaulted

over the edge. Lucoyo almost cried out, but caught himself in time and leaned to see his friend land, then go skating down the talus slope, drawing his broadsword as he went. Lucoyo cursed under his breath and strung his bow.

Ohaern hurtled toward the fight, a silent juggernaut come to doom the goblins. He slammed into their rear ranks, laying about him with sword and buckler. Goblins screamed as they fell. Then, the surprise gone, Ohaern roared with a berserker's anger. Goblins gave way around him in sheer fright, and he turned to mow them down.

Above him, Lucoyo cursed again and bent his bow. If it had not been for Ohaern, he certainly would have gone his way and avoided this fight—or sat and watched, enjoying the spectacle. Personally, his sympathies lay with the goblins—but if his friend fought for the humans, what could he do? Even if Ohaern had not exactly given him a chance to express a preference . . .

The humans, seeing a champion charging in to their rescue, let out a glad shout and began to lay about them with renewed vigor. One sheared off a spearhead; the goblin dropped the shaft and leaped at the man, teeth yawning wide in its noseless face. The traveler slashed, but the goblin somehow twisted aside and sank his fangs into the man's forearm. The traveler cried out, dropping his sword, and a second goblin sprang for his other arm.

Cursing anew, Lucoyo aimed and loosed.

An arrow sprouted in the goblin's back. It screamed and fell short of the beleaguered traveler. One of the human's fellows chopped through the first goblin's neck; the body fell, and the head opened its jaws in one last scream as it fell to the ground to be trampled underfoot.

At the edge of the ring goblins were dying, arrows in their necks and transfixing their bodies. One goblin turned back to call up more of his fellows, saw the windrow of bodies and let out a screech. A dozen of his fellows turned, saw, and howled, scanning the rock face for their enemy. Lucoyo flattened himself against the stone, imitating its stillness, but they saw him anyway, and with a howl of vengeance the dozen goblins surged toward the bluff, leaping and hopping far faster than a man could run.

But a man ran anyway—Ohaern, leaving the travelers to their own devices. He could afford to—only half a dozen goblins remained to fight four still-standing men, and three of the monstrosities held broken spears.

Lucoyo saw he was discovered and knew there was no hope but fight. He stepped up to the shelf's edge and began to shoot, a stream of arrows flowing down toward the goblins. They saw the flight and dodged aside, hiding behind rocks, then leaping from one boulder to another, coming inexorably closer and closer—but much more slowly.

Ohaern caught up with them, chopping one head from its shoulders. The monster had scarcely any neck, but the cleft between shoulder and head was enough to guide the sword. As the body fell, Ohaern cut backhanded at another—but the creature saw him and screeched just before the blade struck. The other goblins whirled about to look, and Ohaern roared as he strode forward. The goblins yelped in fright and leaped around to put the boulders between him and them—and Lucoyo's arrows struck between their shoulders.

A goblin bent backward, keening as he died. The others looked up, realized their only hope was attack, and went leaping up the slope toward the archer, howling for revenge. Lucoyo picked off another and another and . . .

Groped at an empty quiver.

Cursing, he threw down his bow and drew his long knife. He crouched at the edge of the shelf, knife in his left hand, right finding a stone and throwing.

It struck the lead goblin in the face. The creature went down, and his two companions leaped on past him still howling—but Lucoyo threw another stone, and one goblin dodged.

Ohaern caught him.

The last sprang on, unaware that he was alone. He leaped high, and needle-sharp fangs closed on Lucoyo's left arm. The archer shouted with pain and stabbed; the goblin face fell away, but Lucoyo's arm dripped blood.

Then Ohaern was there, catching him up. "How badly are you hurt, Lucoyo? Ah, a curse upon my slowness!"

"It is only flesh," the half-elf groaned, watching the even flow of blood. "I do not think he caught a vein, and certainly not the bone. But anything so ugly must have poison in its bite!"

"Come, down to the travelers!" Ohaern said. "I see packs on their backs; perhaps they have medicines."

Lucoyo picked up his bow and clambered off the shelf, then stared at Ohaern. "You are not unscathed yourself!"

"What, these?" Ohaern glanced down at the runnels of blood on his chest, forearms, and thighs. "Mere scratches. They do not even pain me—yet. Come, Lucoyo. If there is medicine for your hurt, there is medicine for mine."

They skidded down the slope arm in arm—but Lucoyo stopped next to the first of the dead goblins that had an arrow in him. "I must have back my bolts!"

"Then the travelers who are not injured can gather them for you!" Still, Ohaern bent to wrench the arrow out of the goblin, then wiped off its ichor in the sand. They labored down the hill, and Ohaern drew and cleaned every arrow they passed. When they reached the plain, he was able to draw a few from the ground.

"Every archer misses now and then," Lucoyo said testily.

"Yes, especially when his targets see the arrow coming and leap aside—or hop away from a sword stroke at the wrong moment. I think we will camp here for the night, Lucoyo. We can look for other shafts in the morning."

So they came to the travelers, who had already gathered the goblins' torches into a campfire and were tending one another's wounds. They looked up as Ohaern and Lucoyo neared. One of them leaped to his feet. "Welcome and thanks, brave rescuers! How did you know we had need of you?"

"A lucky chance," Ohaern said, but Lucoyo told them, "A god talked to him in his heart. It must have been his heart, for surely, anyone with a brain would have thought better of fighting these imps! Have you medicine for a goblin's bite, traveler?"

"Aye, in plenty, and you are welcome to it! Come, join our healing circle."

Ohaern looked about as they came up to the fire. One traveler lay prone, his face blue, gasping, and Ohaern knew him for a dead man. One of his legs was bound with cloth, but there was a great deal of blood dripping from it, and Ohaern knew the great vein had been cut. Two of his fellows gathered by him, murmuring, though one had an arm in a sling and blood and bandages in a dozen places.

"Only two real casualties, praise Lomallin!" the leader said. He waved the two guests to seats by the fire. "My other two comrades are out finishing off the wounded goblins and gathering your arrows. Two to slay, two to guard, one maimed, and one . . ." He glanced at his dying companion, and his face darkened. "It is bad indeed—but it would have been worse without you, much worse." He turned back to them and yanked up Lucoyo's sleeve. The archer nearly cried out, but managed to stifle it to a gargle. The traveler held up a small clear cylinder with liquid inside and pulled its stopper. "Bite hard; this will hurt."

Hurt? It was worse than the goblin's bite, as bad as fire! Lucoyo nearly strangled on the shout of pain that his grinding teeth throttled. It *was* fire, liquid fire that sank into his arm and shot up to his shoulder, down toward his heart—but its heat faded as it coursed, and in a minute it was only an ache.

The traveler turned to putting drops of the fluid onto a white puffball, then dabbing it onto Ohaern's wounds. The chieftain bit down against the pain, but when it eased, he asked, "How is it you came with an antidote for a goblin's bite?"

"We are men who travel for a living," the stranger answered, still dabbing. "We trade the stuffs in our packs for whatever goods people have. We bring baubles from the cities of the south and trade them for furs and tin, amber and gold. When we have traded our goods for three donkeys and enough amber, gold, and furs to load them fully, we shall wend our way back to the south, where the city folk shall trade us more baubles—and other things we want, many more—for the goods we bring from the north."

"You are traders, then?"

"Yes, and as such, we carry medicines for every danger we can think of—even the bites of goblins."

"Wise." Ohaern nodded. "You should prosper, with such forethought."

"Those of us who come home alive and sound may say so," the

trader answered darkly. "And you, strangers—who are you, and why have you come?"

"We are men of the north, bound for the cities of the south," Ohaern told him, but did not say why.

The trader apparently felt no need to ask; it only made sense to him that anyone who did not live in a city would wish to. "If you go south, then beware of the Vanyar."

"The Vanyar?" Ohaern traded glances with Lucoyo. "We have heard something of them, but only a little. Tell us more—for example, why have they come to our lands?"

CHAPTER 14

Lucoyo leaned forward, frowning. "We have seen them from a distance, but know only that they are robbers on a large scale—and very poor rivermen. But what are they?"

"Who, rather," the trader corrected him. He held out a hand, palm forward. "And as to 'who,' I am Brevoro."

"I am Ohaern." The smith pressed his palm against Brevoro's.

"Lucoyo." The half-elf pressed hands in his turn. "He is a Biri, and I am an adopted Biri."

"Ah, yes, the nation to the north and west!" Brevoro nodded, lowering his hand. "I have traded with men of your nation, though not, it would seem, with your clan. I tell you, your people are much more hospitable than the Vanyar."

"I have not heard of them before this." Ohaern frowned. "Are they a southern people?"

"They are a *new* people—at least, in this part of the world. They tell me they have come from the Vanyar homeland, which is to the south and far to the east, in the plains that view a mountain range a thousand leagues and more from here."

"A thousand leagues!" Lucoyo sat bolt upright. "They have come a long distance in a little time!"

"Not so little as that, for these tribesmen told me they have never seen their homeland—only one among them had, and he was very, very old. He was determined to return, but no others were, at least not from anything more than curiosity. They wanted new lands in the west, with new peoples for slaves, so that each of them might live like a king."

Ohaern snorted. "They have little humility, have they?"

"They are supremely confident, and claim that they will prevail against every enemy, for the source of their strength is Ulahane himself."

Ohaern and Lucoyo sat very still. Then the half-elf said, "Poor hosts they must have been, indeed! Did they seek to murder you in your sleep, or only to rob you?"

Brevoro gave him a thin smile. "Neither one, though they might have done both if their smith had not had the foresight to realize he would want our trade not just this year, but next year, too. As it was, we kept a vigilant guard day and night. None threatened us, though many gave us cold stares, and covetous glances to our goods. In truth, we did not know how strongly their chief held them leashed, the more so since every man among them is proud and overbearing—so we felt that our lives were in danger every minute, and did not truly breathe easily until we had been two days on the road again, with no offer to injure us." He gave a hard smile. "I should not say 'no offer,' for after we had left their camp and were about to rest at midday, we saw a dust cloud. One of our party climbed a tree and saw a raiding party following us."

"Did their chief know?" Ohaern demanded.

Brevoro shrugged. "Perhaps—or perhaps he might have punished them if they had slain us. It would not have helped us then."

"You did not rest, I gather," Lucoyo said.

"Oh, we did—but deeply buried in thickets and high in trees, with slings ready. The Vanyar rode right past us, for they are steppe riders and know little of woodcraft, whereas we had been careful to cover our tracks. No, we stayed where we were for an hour and more, then moved through the wood away from the path. When we came out into open land, we saw them against the sky, returning. We hid again, for we did not wish to go back to their camp—in pieces."

"There was some talk of strange monsters who were half bald yellow men and half pony—surely not big enough for a horse— who struck like lightning, with complete and utter cruelty, striking down every living being before them. I did not place much credence in that, though, since there was also talk of there being too many Vanyar for the herds, even the huge herds of aurochs that they followed. No, they are hungry for land, these chariot-riding barbarians with their double-edged axes; there were far too many of them for their ancestral lands, so they began raiding and conquering, and have overrun the steppe lands north of the Land Between the Rivers."

"I have heard of that land." Ohaern frowned. "They say the plain between those rivers is rich beyond belief, so much so that people live in the same place year after year and do not hunt, but only push seeds into the ground."

"It is true, and those villages have grown mightily, so that the plain is thronged with cities, from Merusu at its northern edge to Kuru at its most southern."

"Surely the Vanyar dare not challenge the might of those cities!"

"Surely they do, though they have sent one wing of their horde to make sure these northern lands will send no armies against their rear when they turn south."

"Only one wing?" Lucoyo stared, aghast. "There are *more* of them?"

"Three times as many, at least—and their elders speak of cousins who rode south and east, instead of here into the west. No, it is three-quarters of their host who will ride south. They learned of the wealth and luxury of the cities from their newly conquered slaves, and decided to capture and loot them. Their first target is to be Cashalo, a rich city on the eastern shore of a strait between two inland seas, a strait that opens out to become a tiny sea in its own right."

"A city west of Merusu?" Ohaern asked.

"There are several along the eastern shore of the Middle Sea. They are the homes of seafaring trader folk." Brevoro grinned. "I would resent their competition if I did not know that they only trade with seacoast towns, whereas my people trade with river vil-

lages and those inland, wherever there are roads, or even paths."
He took a small flask and three beakers from his pack. "This is the
wine of Cashalo. Will you drink to my hope that they will with-
stand the Vanyar?"

"Aye, right gladly!" Lucoyo said.

"Pay him no mind," said Ohaern. "He will drink to anything."
He took up a beaker. "Is their situation hopeless, then?"

Brevoro shrugged as he poured. "I have not heard of the Vanyar attacking a city yet—but I had not heard of the Vanyar at all, until this
last month." He shook his head sadly. "We traders feel saddened
by the doom coming on Cashalo, for the people there are good—
hospitable to traders, and fair, though hard in their bargaining."

Ohaern stared. "City dwellers who are *good*? Are they not all
like those of Kuru?"

"No, not really. It is a matter of which god a city worships—in
their hearts, even more than with their mouths. Kuru worships
Ulahane, heart and lips and soul. But Cashalo holds the Scarlet
One in disdain."

Ohaern sat still, numbed by amazement. He had met the soldiers
of Byleo, and Manalo had cautioned them to wariness with regard
to the people of Cashalo. But the notion that there might be city
dwellers who were really good disturbed him in some deep way that
he could not fathom. He felt a sudden, almost angry desire to see
these people of Cashalo for himself, that he might judge whether
they were truly good, or merely not as evil as those of Kuru.

"It is a shame to see good folk despoiled and debauched,"
Brevoro sighed, "and worse to think of them maimed and slain—
but what can a man do?"

"Exactly." Ohaern bent a stern gaze on Lucoyo. "What *can* a
man do?"

"At the least," Lucoyo said slowly, "a man might bring them
word of their peril, so that they might have time to prepare for the
onslaught." He turned to Brevoro. "Are the pleasures of the cities
everything they say?"

"Well, the streets are not paved with gold," Brevoro said, nor
even paved at all, for the most part—but the most important
streets are paved with stone."

"What is a 'street'?"

"Like a road, only it runs between houses. And the people of Cashalo are clean—each sweeps the street in front of his house every day, and they bury their wastes. In some cities they let the wastes mound up, to harbor flies and their maggots, and fill the air with stench."

"But the women," Lucoyo pressed, with a glint in his eye. "Are they as willing as rumor says?"

Ohaern stared at his companion, shocked. Could he truly have been wallowing in grief over the death of his beloved Elluaera only days before?

Then he realized that Lucoyo was one of those men who bury their grief in soft flesh and smother it with caresses. If he were sorely injured in a fight, he would not even wait for his wound to be fully healed before he would be off to battle again. In fact, Ohaern realized, that was what Lucoyo *had* done.

"Rumor speaks falsely," Brevoro said slowly, "or at least builds a fruit of illusion around a kernel of truth."

"Fruits are delicious, and I am fond of kernels, if there are enough of them. What is this one?"

"Cashalo holds Lomallin and his ally, the goddess Rahani, in highest reverence," Brevoro explained, "but the people there worship many gods, Handradin among them. She is a goddess devoted only to erotic pleasures, and on her feast day the women of her cult will give themelves to any man who asks, for thus, they believe, they will gain merit in her eyes."

"Then I cheer for Handradin! When is her feast day?"

"In a month's time." Brevoro frowned, looking from the one to the other. "Are you bound for Cashalo, then?"

"We are *now*," said Ohaern.

The next morning they bade farewell to the traders and set off for the south—or, at least, for the Mashra, the river that ran south, past Byleo and down to the sea whose waves lapped the docks of Cashalo. It was less than a day's march, so they were able to cut the saplings for Ohaern's coracle before nightfall. In the morning, they stretched the skins over the bent poles, set it in the river by a shelf that jutted out into hip-deep water, and began to paddle. Lucoyo was nervous; the swaying and dipping of the fragile craft still bothered him; but he had a bit more confidence than he'd had on his last ride and was able to master his fear well enough to take a hand with a paddle himself. He was sure they could have gone twice as far in the time it took Ohaern to teach him how to propel the craft, so he vowed silently to make up that distance, and more, by having two paddles drive the craft instead of one. Of course, Ohaern had to caution him not to paddle so hard.

Down the river they went in the dawn, with the mist rising off the waters and the newly wakened sun setting the ripples and wavelets to dancing gold. Lucoyo took a deep breath of chill air, amazed at the beauty around him, at the broad expanse of water and the distant green mounding of the forest, amazed even more that his soul seemed to swell and rise in response. He gave his head an angry shake; next he would be as much a believer in the goodness of Lomallin as was Manalo himself!

Toward evening they saw trails of smoke striping the sky ahead. "What moves here?" Lucoyo asked.

"People," Ohaern said, somewhat unnecessarily. "When we came this way before, they rowed after us in canoes."

"Have we come so far so quickly?" Lucoyo shipped his paddle and strung his bow. "Let us hope they are no better with boats than they were before."

But they were—still not terribly good, but then, neither was Lucoyo. Ohaern, however, was quite skilled, and drove the coracle on alone while Lucoyo, bow ready, watched the men approach. "They come faster this time."

Ohaern spared a glance. "No wonder. They do not do their own paddling."

Lucoyo's face hardened. The men doing the paddling were being driven with whips; he could hear the smack of leather against flesh. The paddlers were gaunt, their faces emptied of hope but filled with fear, and there were only two of them, two for a huge canoe that carried also four warriors. "I think," he said, "that we have found the Vanyar."

"Well, they shall not find *us*," Ohaern said between his teeth, and drove the coracle on with his huge smith's muscles. A cry went up from the Vanyar as the Biri passed the point of intersection, with the canoes still distant from the spot. A flurry of arrows rose into the air, but fell far short of the coracle. Lucoyo tensed, raising his bow to answer, but Ohaern panted, "Not . . . yet. Do not shoot . . . unless they become . . . a threat."

Against his liking, Lucoyo lowered the bow. The Vanyar would be easy shots—but Ohaern was right; they needed to keep his bow secret until it was needed. Besides, if they shot one of the barbarians, the others would follow them forever, if they had to, to exact revenge.

Onward Ohaern drove, with the canoes falling farther and farther behind. Finally, the Vanyar must have realized their mistake, because they pulled two boats together and traded two more paddlers for two warriors. Then there was only one to attack, for the other had to watch his captives—but the rearmost paddler must have been exceptionally strong, because the canoe actually began to gain on the coracle.

Of course, by that time Ohaern was resting, chest heaving.

"Ought we not to paddle again?" Lucoyo asked uneasily. "That one canoe is moving much faster now."

"Let them think I have tired," Ohaern said. "They will not be far wrong."

Lucoyo glanced at him uneasily. "Even with a few minutes' rest you cannot keep up such a pace for long."

Ohaern nodded. "Whereas they can, with four paddles. But I have a stratagem in mind. Do you see that island ahead?"

"Not really; I have been watching astern." But Lucoyo turned and looked ahead. There was a sizable island coming up on the starboard side, big enough to be covered with tall trees, crowding each other so badly that many leaned far out over the water.

"We will pass from sight around those leaves," Ohaern said, "and they will speed all the more, to catch us before the river bends."

Looking ahead, Lucoyo saw the water curve and the eastern shore round beside it. "That is not what I would call the most reassuring news."

"Ah, but we shall disappear from sight *before* we come to the curve," Ohaern explained, "for once past those leaves, they shall not see us."

Lucoyo smiled, a smile that grew wolfish. "Paddle, then!"

Ohaern brought them from around the far end of the island and in toward the shore. Lucoyo grasped the leaves, then the branches of a tree that leaned almost parallel to the water's surface. He grappled hand over hand until they had a screen of leaves between themselves and the expanse of water stretching to the eastern shore.

In a few minutes the canoe came into sight. The Vanyar in front held a short, recurved bow with an arrow already nocked; the one behind shouted abuse as he drove on the paddlers with a whip made of short, knotted thongs. The paddlers were bending every effort, but they looked to be on the verge of exhaustion—except for the one in the stern. There was something odd about him; he was short and lumpy, and . . .

"Now," Ohaern whispered, and waited just long enough for Lucoyo to release two arrows before he drove his paddle into the water.

The rearmost Vanyar screamed in anger as an arrow sprouted in his chest; then he toppled over the gunwale and into the river. His mate whirled to see, which saved him from an arrow through his heart; instead it lodged in his shoulder, making him drop his bow, and Lucoyo cursed almost as loudly as the Vanyar.

But the paddlers had stopped, frozen in astonishment, and Ohaern drove his coracle up beside, to grapple the canoe to him. The Vanyar caught up a big double-bladed axe with his left hand and chopped at Ohaern, shrilling a battle cry—but the smith chopped, too, with his sword, clear through the shaft of the axe, and the head flew into the coracle. The Vanyar dropped the shaft with a curse and caught Ohaern by the throat—but the big smith seized his wrist and twisted. The Vanyar gave a high, whinnying cry and loosed his hold—but his right fist came around to buffet Ohaern on the ear. The smith rocked, and Lucoyo realized that if the Vanyar had not been wounded, that blow might have knocked the smith cold. He bobbed back and forth in a frenzy, holding his bow bent, looking for a clear shot, but losing all chance of one as Ohaern and the Vanyar grappled one another.

But the rearmost paddler swung his blade high, and the edge of the paddle cracked into the Vanyar's skull. He folded, and Lucoyo turned to thank the man—then froze, staring at the squat figure, the shorn remains of a huge beard, the bald head, the muscle-knotted arms, twice as long as they should be . . . "Ohaern!" he cried. "The fools! They have captured a dwerg!"

"Fools indeed," the dwerg answered in a voice like the grating of boulders on gravel. "All dwergs shall be their enemies now, no matter where they travel."

Now Ohaern stared, too, he and Lucoyo together—for though the words had been heavily accented and hard to understand, the dwerg had spoken in the language of the Biriae.

CHAPTER 15

The dwerg explained it by the campfire that night. "We are creatures of stone," he said, "and speak the language of rock and
earth—so we speak also the languages of all those who live in harmony with the earth, and the plants and creatures it nourishes."

"But do not the Vanyar live as part of the earth?" Ohaern
asked.

"They did, before invaders chased them out of *their* homeland,"
the dwerg replied. "Then, though, in their bitterness and hatred,
they turned against the earth and its creatures and sought to im-
pose their will upon the land. They are apart from the earth now,
not a part of it. They are separate by their own choice and have
lost the harmony of the seasons."

"If they have, then so has the jackal." Lucoyo jerked his head
toward the imprisoned Vanyar. "That one is tattooed with the
jackal's head."

But the dwerg shook his head. "The living jackal is a part of all
that lives, and has his place in cleansing the earth of offal. These
Sons of the Jackal seek to be lions, and thereby lie by their lives.
No, the jackal's head is the sign of Ulahane."

Ohaern nodded, his mouth a tight line. "The last of his servants we met wore jackals' heads on their shoulders."

"Another tattoo?" the dwerg asked.

"No," said Lucoyo. "Living heads."

The dwerg stared. His beard grew so high and his eyebrows so bushy that it was hard to see his eyes—but they were clear enough now.

The campfire was secreted in a cave from which ran a stream that flowed into the river. The dwerg had led them to it unerringly, for he knew all the secrets of stone. The stream itself was hidden from the river by a screen of brush and leaning trees, and Ohaern would never have guessed it was there if the dwerg had not led them.

The Vanyar lay beyond the firelight, trussed up tight and gagged. He glared at Ohaern and Lucoyo and would not leave off straining against his bonds. Two of the rivermen lay nearby in the sleep of exhaustion, but a third still sat up with them, fingering the Vanyar axe Ohaern had given him—they had hauled in the body of the dead Vanyar long enough to loot it of weapons, and taken the living one's, so the rivermen now carried each a bow or an axe. This wakeful one had cut a new shaft, fitted it to the axehead Ohaern had clipped, and now sat fondling it, his eyes burning into Ohaern's as if pleading to be allowed to use the weapon on the living Vanyar. The big smith had already prevented the gaunt rivermen from taking final revenge, though he had seen no reason to prevent their taking turns with the whip. However, it now hung on *his* belt.

"No," he now said.

The riverman laid the weapon aside with an exclamation of disgust. "I do not seek to slay him now—only to make you see that you must go back and chop these Vanyar down!"

Lucoyo could well understand the burning desire for revenge that drove the man to stay awake and plead, though all his limbs must be heavy with exhaustion. The rivermen had been completely naked until Ohaern and Lucoyo had found furs for them to wrap about their loins, and Lucoyo had seen for himself that Brevoro had not exaggerated when he told what the Vanyar had done to the few warriors they kept alive. He had also seen that they could not stand; the Vanyar had hamstrung each one of them. Oh, they had made very sure that their male captives would not be able to fight their new owners! Lucoyo could only think that the poor rivermen must have waited on their captors by walking on their knees, or even crawling. His hatred for the Vanyar began to equal his hatred for the clan that had reared him.

Of course, you did not need to stand up to paddle a canoe—and that was probably the greatest reason why the Vanyar had kept a few of the rivermen alive. They could not paddle as quickly as they had before the conquest, however, for they were all gaunt, from short rations, and stretched to their limits by the exertions of the day.

"They made us watch what they did to our wives and children," the man protested.

Ohaern shuddered at the thought, but said doggedly, "It is more important to eliminate the source of their power first. When we have done that, we will go back and see to the Vanyar themselves."

"What source is that?" the dwerg asked in his grating voice. He was scarcely four feet tall, perhaps not even that, and his hands hung down to his ankles—but his shoulders and arms were hugely muscled, and his short, bandy legs were like the trunks of small trees. The muscles of his chest and back strained against the leather straps that held the kilt that was his only clothing. It was stained and spotted with the holes of cinders, for the dwergs had been smiths for longer than men had known iron. Their works of bronze were said to be miracles of loveliness, their weapons miracles of death, and there was nothing they could not make. But human folk almost never saw them, for they labored in their hidden homes inside mountains and rarely came out into the light of day.

"How is it you were captured?" Ohaern asked in return.

"We cannot find all the materials we need inside our hills," the dwerg answered. "Now and again we must venture out, to mine the rare earths that lie on the surface, or to trade for things such as saltpeter and the sulfur that gathers near steaming springs. It was my misfortune that a group of Vanyar chanced near my band. The other three they slew with their arrows, but I lived, and they kept me for their amusement. Then an elder of a tribe they had conquered, hoping to win leniency for his people, told them I was a smith of wonders, and they set me to forging for them. But when they discovered that I knew the craft of boats, they set me to paddling, for I am strong."

"Let me do to the Vanyar what they did to me!" the riverman pleaded.

The bound Vanyar squalled in rage and thrashed at his bonds.

"If you will not allow that, and you will not slay them all, then let me at least slay this one!" the riverman pleaded, raising his axe.

But Ohaern shook his head. "We need the knowledge in his head, but we will not find it by breaking open his skull." His gaze strayed to the Vanyar. "Though perhaps I *should* let this riverman have his way with you, if you will not tell me what I wish to know."

The Vanyar went still and his eyes turned to ice. He stared back at Ohaern with contempt and a mute challenge.

"He is stubborn-hard," the chief said in disgust, turning back to the riverman. "If he would not answer when you and your friends had your exercise with him before, he will not talk no matter how much pain we give him."

"It is their pride." The riverman turned and spat on the Vanyar, whose eyes blazed at him with cold fury that told how *he* would treat the riverman if their positions were reversed. "He will die in pain rather than speak. They fancy they will go to a palace that Ulahane keeps for heroes, if they find valiant deaths."

"It is a lie," Ohaern replied. "Ulahane has no use for the dead, save those few souls that he keeps as slaves to his magic."

The Vanyar gargled something in a contemptuous tone.

"Oh, believe me, I know!" Ohaern rose and went to the man, and Lucoyo would never have guessed, from his tone and face, that he was lying. He stared; this was an Ohaern he did not know. "I have learned something of the scarlet lord." Ohaern yanked the gag from the man's mouth. "Let me show you what I have learned of his worship!" He bent low, and all Lucoyo saw was that he squeezed the man's leg—but the Vanyar let out a piercing shriek, and kept shrieking.

"Tell me what your people want with the cities, and I will stop the pain," Ohaern said.

The Vanyar clamped his mouth shut against the scream. It still gurgled in his throat, but he would not let it out.

"That will not move you? Then perhaps this . . ." Ohaern seized him near his neck, and the man brayed with pain—but the bray formed into a single word, repeated again and again: "No! No! No!"

Ohaern left off and glared down at the man. Then he came back to the fire. "It is as I said—he will not speak. We could waste three days in the attempt, and I have not so much time."

"I have," the riverman said, his eyes smoldering. "The rest of my life is waste! Let me have *some* purpose in it!"

"We shall find you purpose enough," Ohaern promised. "You and your friends shall come south with us, for we shall be all the stronger for a second boat, with three armed men."

"Where did you learn that torture?" Lucoyo whispered.

"The techniques of healing can be used for pain." Ohaern turned to him. "As to the will for it, I had only to remember my village and my people after the Klaja found them, then imagine what the Vanyar did to this village of fishers. But for now let us seek a swifter and more certain way of unsealing this man's lips." He took his pack and began to rummage within it. He took out a small pottery jar and a bark kettle, filled the kettle with water, and set it over the fire. As it heated, he chanted softly in an unintelligible language, adding pinches of powder from the jar.

The riverman stared, then sidled over to Lucoyo. "What does he do?"

Lucoyo wasn't at all sure himself, but he thought it best to put a good face on it. He shrugged and said, "He knows some magic; he is a smith."

"So am I," said the dwerg, "but I have never learned magic of this kind."

"Our teacher taught him some healing, too." But Lucoyo doubted that this magic would make the Vanyar any more whole.

Ohaern put the jar away and began to chant more loudly, watching the kettle boil. Lucoyo suspected that his friend did not know the meanings of the words he said, for he recognized their sounds. "He recites a spell our teacher taught him."

The dwerg nodded, reassured. "He does; I comprehend the words—though I have never learned this chant."

Ohaern went to yank a hair from the Vanyar's head—the man grunted with surprise—then brought it back to the fire, cast it into the kettle, and followed it with another pinch of powder as he shouted a last phrase. Finally, he took the kettle from the fire and brought it to the Vanyar. For a moment he stood, looking down with narrowed eyes at the invader, whose eyes showed white all around the iris now.

Then Ohaern dropped to one knee beside him, hauled his head up by the hair and held the kettle under his nose. The Vanyar tried to turn his head away, ignoring the pain in his hair, but Ohaern held him too closely. The captive tried to wrench his head away, but the kettle followed, staying under his nose, and Ohaern laughed. "Why do you seek to avoid it? The scent is pleasant enough!" Then he sang softly in the foreign tongue as he watched the steam waft up into the Vanyar's nostrils, filling the invader's head until the fumes thinned and disappeared as the brew cooled. Then Ohaern handed the kettle to Lucoyo and jabbed the Vanyar in the belly, just below the breastbone. The invader's eyes bulged and his mouth gaped—and Ohaern snatched the bucket, yanked the captive's head back, and poured the brew in over his tongue. The Vanyar instantly clamped his jaw shut, though his eyes still bulged with pain, but reflex made him swallow. He set his jaw, even though he still struggled for breath, but Ohaern only poured the rest of the brew onto the earth, nodding with satisfaction. He whistled between his teeth until the Vanyar inhaled again with a long, loud gasp, then demanded, "Why did your people take the village of the rivermen?"

"Because the traders—" The Vanyar clamped his mouth shut, wild-eyed, shocked at himself—but the words still struggled for escape inside his mouth.

"It is none of your doing, but that of the brew," Ohaern informed him. "Its fumes have settled in your brain, and will ensure that you speak only truth. Tell me, then—why did you take the fishing village?"

Still the words struggled, but the Vanyar held his jaw tight against them. Ohaern threw him down in disgust and did not bother replacing the gag. "Now he will not answer at all!"

"So much the better; the sound of his voice would sicken us," Lucoyo replied.

"But we must have what he knows!" In a rage, Ohaern turned, dropping to one knee again as his huge fist rose high for a buffet that would surely break the Vanyar's knee . . .

Or would have, if Lucoyo had not caught that fist and held it back. "No, no, softly, blacksmith, softly! He is not iron, nor is there an anvil beneath him, that you should seek to beat him into a shape more to your liking. After all, what does he know? He is only an ignorant cart rider, and surely holds nothing of any importance in his ugly head!"

The Vanyar's eyes flared with anger at the insult.

Ohaern glared up at Lucoyo, but withheld his blow.

"Do you know why he has not spoken?" Lucoyo said. "He is ashamed of the sound of his voice, afraid that we will learn that he knows no answers at all!" He gestured at the bound man. "His people are so bestial that they scarcely have gods! Why, he could not even tell you the totem of his clan!"

"The viper!" the Vanyar snapped. "I am of the Viper Clan! And beware, soft woodsmen, or my fangs shall pierce your flesh!"

Lucoyo laughed in savage mockery. "Fangs, is it? Your fangs are drawn, viper, though I could believe there is poison in you. What else could there be, to make you slay so many good and innocent folk?"

"Trade!" the Vanyar cried. "Trade, the word you stupid westerners use for your custom that lets us steal your beads and pots for bits of worthless yellow stone! The traders' boats come up and down the river three and four times in a moon, and already the Vanyar grow rich from their exchange! These stupid fish catchers only gave them the river's harvest, taking cloth and iron spearheads in return—and what did they use those spearheads for? Catching more fish!"

Ohaern stared, but had the sense to keep his mouth shut and leave the questions to Lucoyo.

"Stupid, is it?" the half-elf sneered. "Not so stupid as a cart rider who takes a clay pot for a piece of amber that is worth a thousand pots in Cashalo or Kuru! But godless men would not know that."

"The Vanyar are not godless!" the invader shouted. "And well you know it! We worship the great god Ulahane! The great god who will make yours cower in the dust!"

"Cower, forsooth! How can you say that, when you know not who our gods are?"

The Vanyar grinned. "I have heard you speak of Lomallin. Stupid, am I?"

"Most stupid indeed, to think that speaking of a god means you worship him! Stupid even more to worship Ulahane, who will gobble you up into his foul maw when you die, and swallow you down to the fire pit of his belly! Why would you worship such a god, if you were not stupid?"

"Because Ulahane has promised us wealth beyond our wildest dreams, fool! And surely he keeps his promise, for we have already gained wealth, great wealth—*your* wealth, that of all you effete westerners!"

"So you are nothing but bandits?" Lucoyo sneered. "The only way you can gain wealth is by stealing it? Why, you are no better than river pirates—petty land-robbers, all of you!"

"*Great* land-robbers!" The Vanyar's face swelled red with anger. "We steal land by the mile! Land enough for all the Vanyar, and all our descendants! This Ulahane has promised us, if we will worship him and, in sign of that, give blood—much blood, oceans of it—piling high the soft corpses of slain villagers, and giving him the best of the people we conquer, in living sacrifice!"

"Living?" Lucoyo braced himself not to shudder or show his horror. "You mean you kill them by slow torture!"

"Even so! Even thus would Ulahane be worshiped!"

There was some sudden lurch of motion behind Lucoyo, but he stayed Ohaern with a hand. "With tortured villagers, yes—but not the tender city folk, for ignorant cow-catchers like the Vanyar would not dare to assault the great cities!"

"How little you know!" the Vanyar sneered. "Aye, we dare! Even now our cousins mass to attack Cashalo!"

"Ridiculous," Lucoyo scoffed. "What use have you cart drivers for great buildings?"

"None." The Vanyar grinned like a jackal indeed. "But we have great use for their wealth—oh, yes. And when that is taken, we shall tear down their obscene masses of hardened clay, we shall camp on the high ground to watch the spring floods wash it away, and we shall stay till the waters dry up, that we may see there is nothing left of these boastful city dwellers!"

"You will conquer it only to destroy it! How wasteful! How like an ignorant cow-catcher!"

The Vanyar's face darkened with anger again. "We shall lay them waste indeed! The Vanyar have no use for cities! We shall cleanse the earth of them, we shall tumble them and grind them down—for these stupid city dwellers may think their warrens are only places for trading and for pleasure, but the Vanyar know the truth! They are strongholds, every one of those cities, guarding all traffic on a river or even two or three! They would pen the Vanyar in, imprison us in a ring of clay, prevent our coursing up the waters with our captured fish-eaters—" He paused to spit at the river-man. "But they shall not hold us back! The Vanyar will take them and destroy them, root and branch, stone and clay, every one!"

"These are no villages you speak of," Lucoyo said, as if he spoke to a five-year old, "but great masses of houses and temples! It is not so easy to take a city as a village!"

"It is *every* bit as easy, for your foolish villagers have not learned to build walls—nor have your cities, we hear! None but Kuru! And they have great, broad, hard pathways, our spies tell us! Oh, yes, we have spies—did you think we would charge a city, knowing nothing about it? We shall speed our chariots down Cashalo's great broad streets, striking down every living being; we shall send our warriors running in among their warren of huts, slaying all the men before they know what has struck them! Oh, be sure, the Vanyar shall chew up your cities and leave not even enough to spit out!"

"Except yourselves." Finally, Lucoyo let the loathing show in his voice and face as he turned to Ohaern. "Have you heard enough? Or is there more you would know?"

"Nothing," Ohaern said with full contempt. "He has said it all."

The Vanyar stared, then howled with rage, thrashing against his bonds. "You have tricked me! You have made me say what your magician wanted to know! A curse upon you! A curse!"

"A curse indeed—you are a curse upon the land." Lucoyo turned away to the fire. "What shall we do with him now?"

Ohaern turned with him. "I care not. What use is he to us or to the world? Let him shrivel and die! Let the jackals he esteems take him and chew his entrails!"

The riverman took the hint. His eyes gleamed as he took up the mended Vanyar axe and crawled back to its owner. Ohaern and Lucoyo hunched their shoulders, trying to ignore the shouts of anger, then the sudden terror-filled screams that were so abruptly cut off.

"Revenge, or justice?" Ohaern muttered.

"I care not," Lucoyo said with sudden ferocity. "So long as the latter was served, what matter the former?"

"What matter indeed?" Ohaern muttered, then looked up at Lucoyo keenly. "I would have tortured him harshly if you had not stopped me. You knew that, did you not?"

"I had some inkling," Lucoyo admitted.

"It was well done, for he would not have spoken no matter how much pain I gave him; it was well done, for your trickery drew from him all the knowledge that torture would not have."

Lucoyo nodded. "I have some experience of the game."

"A game well played," Ohaern said, "but why did you stop me? Mind you, it was the right thing to do, but I would not have expected it from you."

The trickster shrugged. "As you said, torture would have been useless with that stubborn Vanyar anyway, and would have served only to vent your rage. Besides, as you heard from him, torture is imitation of Ulahane, doing to one another what the Scarlet One will do to all humankind if he gains the chance. If you begin to use Ulahane's methods, you will put yourself into Ulahane's power— and I have very personal reasons for wishing to avoid that."

They departed in the false dawn, leaving the remains of the Vanyar for the jackals, even as they had said. Ohaern told the dwerg to return to his mountains, that he was free—but the wondersmith, loyal to those who had freed him, followed on the shore and would not be turned away. Finally, concerned for his safety, Ohaern bade the fishermen take him into the canoe. They went more speedily after that, and Ohaern had to check them, or they would have left his coracle far behind.

Thus they traveled south on the broad river. There were a few more challenges from the shore, but none of any consequence— and, two weeks later, as the sun was sliding down the sky toward evening, they saw a smudge upon the horizon, like a very low-lying cloud.

Ohaern shipped his paddle and beckoned the canoe closer. As the rivermen grappled his gunwale, he asked, "What is that stain upon the sky?"

"The smoke of many, many cooking fires," they answered—and that was their first sight of Cashalo.

CHAPTER 16

T hey camped for the night, then rose before the sun and came
into Cashalo with the dawn. The first thing that struck Ohaern
was that there was no wall around the city. He had thought the
Vanyar mad when he talked of the possibility of building a wall
around a city, though after seeing the palisade around Byleo,
Ohaern had understood his captive's meaning—but it seemed in-
credible that people might surround a whole city with a wall! At
least, if cities were as large as rumor said.

It seemed that they were, to judge by Cashalo.

Lucoyo wasn't thinking—he simply stared in amazement. The
mist rising from the river obscured the city, making it seem a
faery realm, half real and half dream—and Lucoyo could well believe it a dream, for he had never seen so many huts; and even
though there seemed to be a great deal of room between the stone
and timber structures, he felt hemmed in already. Some of the
buildings were huge, ten times the size of one of his people's
dwellings, tapering step by step as they ascended toward heaven.
Had the people of Cashalo built homes for their gods?

As he came closer, the city spread as far as he could see to east and west. The mist burned off as the sun's rays struck through, and as the travelers came closer, he could see more clearly. There was some turbulence as they passed the mouth of a smaller river, and Lucoyo had to clutch at the sides of the coracle, but he still could scarcely take his eyes off the huge buildings that crowded either bank of the smaller river. The people of Cashalo had actually built some sort of hut that crossed the smaller river from shore to shore, like logs fallen to bridge a stream—if a log could be a hundred feet long or more, square at the sides, with dozens of people going back and forth across it, carrying heavy loads! Some of them worked in pairs, carrying their loads atop poles between them. He could only see their silhouettes against the bright morning sky, but remembered it well, for it was his first sight of city people—not counting the soldiers of Byleo, of course, which he didn't.

"I see a place to tie our craft," called one of the rivermen. Ohaern looked where the man pointed and saw a wooden wall rising out of the water, anchored by stout upright logs, to which were tied boats—but what boats! Some were small as their own, but others were large as houses, made of plain wood or painted bright colors, some with no paddles, some with a dozen, and some even with huge square sheets of cloth hung above them on a great, thick pole! Such expanses must have been very expensive, for he knew how long it took a Biri woman to weave even a small blanket from the sheared hair of the wild goats.

Then the city seemed to tower on either side of him, or rather, to loom hugely, for they were coming in between great huts, four and five times the size of the largest tent he had ever seen. But they were not made of stretched hides, no—they were made from stones cunningly fitted together, as high as a man's chest, with stacks of split logs rising twice higher yet!

"Catch a rope," Ohaern called.

Lucoyo looked down, startled, and saw that the smith had paddled them in against the wooden wall—not a wall only, he saw now, but the side of a great flat floor, just below his chin! There were ropes hanging from the tree trunks, and he caught one.

"Hold us fast," Ohaern told him. He shipped his paddle, then took the rope from Lucoyo. "I will hold us tight against the wall. Up with you, now, and out!"

Lucoyo did not need to be invited twice. He seized the edge of the wooden floor with relief and, being careful not to jump and swamp the coracle, hauled himself up waist-high, then rolled over and up to his knees. The view of the river was quite different, even so little higher as this! He found himself looking down at the rivermen in the canoe as one of them caught a rope and pulled their boat in against the wood.

"Steady the coracle," Ohaern called, and Lucoyo dropped down onto his stomach to hold the skin boat tight against the wood. Ohaern levered himself up and out in the same fashion Lucoyo had, then reached down to pull the coracle out of the water. He began to loose the leather bindings from the saplings.

"Let me do that," Lucoyo said. "You help our friends up!"

"A good thought." Ohaern passed him the coracle, then leaned down to catch the rivermen, one by one, and haul them up to sit on the edge of the wooden floor.

"It is a larger dock than I have ever seen," one said, looking about him.

" 'Dock'? What is that?"

"What we are sitting on." Riri thumped the wood. "It saves us having to wade out pushing the canoe each time we climb in, so we have built short, low, wooden docks at our fishing village—but only two of them, never so many, and never so high or wide as this!"

"So we have come to Cashalo," one of his friends said, looking about him with wondering eyes. "So many years I have dreamed of it, and at last I have come!"

"Much good may it do you, Orl," Riri said bitterly. "What pleasures can a cripple have in Cashalo? What manner of life?"

"Aye," Hifa said on Orl's other side. He looked about him somberly. "We have escaped from the Vanyar—but how shall we live?"

"How should we live anywhere?" Riri retorted. "Who has use for a lame man?"

"Who has use for a skilled fisherman?" Ohaern countered. He climbed to his feet and strode down the dock to a large boat, whose crew were just now boarding. The deck was piled with nets. "Ho, men of Cashalo! Do you fish?"

The oldest man looked up in surprise. His face was seamed leather, and his only garment a swath of blue cloth draped over one shoulder and belted to form a kilt. He grinned and answered in strongly accented Biri. "Aye, stranger, we are fishermen! Most of the folk of Cashalo still fish for their dinners, though we labor hauling and carrying for the traders, too—and the richest among us do nothing but trade."

"Working for the traders? I had not thought of that." Ohaern straightened, stroking his chin. "Where do they wander to trade?"

"Everywhere," the fisherman said, "or the young men do— north and south, east and west, wherever the rivers bear them. But when they have gathered enough wealth, they stay at home and the river brings the trade to them."

"How can the river bring trade?" Lucoyo came over, curious.

"Because it bears traders." The fisherman pointed a little farther down the dock, where men in sheepskin vests were tying up a long, low boat. "They are from the north, and will doff those woolly pelts for honest cloth quickly enough, I warrant. They have already left off their hats."

"Small wonder," Ohearn grunted. "It is hot!"

"And those!" The fisherman pointed across the dock, and Ohaern turned to see small, dark men with straight black hair and light cloth loincloths tying up a high-stemmed boat that seemed to be made of nothing but bundles of reeds. "Those are from the south and west! All come to Cashalo, if only to pass through to the Dark Sea—but if they do, they stop here to trade for jars of beer and hard bread, and a night's pleasure, too. Most trade their goods here, though for the pots and weapons and metalwork of Cashalo— or of the east, or the cedars of the west and the ivory of the south, for that matter. Then they go home, and trade the freight of Cashalo for four times as much as they set out with—and while they do, the traders of Cashalo are trading their cotton cloth for the amber and furs of the north. See! There are northmen now, of your own nation, or I miss my guess!"

Ohaern looked, and sure enough, there were Biriae, tying up a fleet of coracles. He made a note to ask them their clan and tribe and discuss the depredations of the Vanyar and Klaja with them—but there were friends to dispose of first. He turned back to the fisherman. "Have you work for fishermen who cannot walk, but can paddle well?"

"Paddle?" The man looked up, startled. "Aye, for a man need not stand for that. In truth, in our boat he need not stand to haul in the nets! They would be useful indeed, for I have only my two sons today—my three neighbors are working for Gori the trader. Where are these men?"

"Yonder." Ohaern turned to beckon. Startled, Riri looked up, then pushed himself to his knees and, face flaming with shame, came walking on his knees.

The fisherman frowned. "What has befallen him?"

"The Vanyar," Ohaern said. "His village was one of peaceful fishermen. The Vanyar overwhelmed them, slaughtered many, and kept a few to paddle—but they maimed and starved their captives, as you see."

For a moment pity lined the old fisherman's face, but Riri saw, and his own face turned to flint. The old fisherman made his own face board-smooth and said, as Riri came up, "Can you row?"

"What is 'row'?" the riverman spat.

"It is like paddling," said the elder, "only you sit with your back to the bow and set the paddle between two sticks we call an 'oarlock.' The shaft is longer, though, and the blade shorter, so we do not call it a 'paddle,' but an 'oar.' "

"It is an odd way to send a boat," Riri said.

"It lends greater power to your strokes, for you can use your back as well as your arms. Would you learn?"

"For dinner and a bed?" Riri shrugged unwillingly. "I will."

"Have you fished with a net?"

"Have I? Aye, and made them, too!"

"Then I may have much work for you, indeed," the elder said thoughtfully. "When I do not, others will. Nay, friend, lash your craft here, and none will disturb it, for it is the mooring of the family of Stibo. Come with us for a day's fishing, and your canoe will be here when you come home."

"I thank you," Riri said slowly, sounding as if he were uncertain as to whether or not he should be grateful.

"And I shall thank you," Stibo returned, "if you fish as well as your friend talks. I have need of your mates, too. Bid them bring the canoe, and we shall row out."

"Ho! Ori! Hifa!" The alacrity with which Riri turned to beckon to his friends belied his coldness. "The canoe! Hurry!"

His friends stared, startled, then lowered themselves back into the canoe, slipped the mooring, and paddled around toward the fishing boat.

"There is nothing crippled about them in the water," Stibo said, watching the canoe—so he could affect not to see Riri look up with surprise that turned to satisfaction, even pride, as he nodded and turned back to his friends.

"Into the boat!" Stibo said. "We must row out a little before they can paddle in! What is your name, stranger?"

"Riri," the riverman said.

"Then into my boat, Riri, for we've a day's work to do!"

"That I will!" Riri reached up to catch the gunwale, then hauled himself over. "Show him his bench and his oar!" Stibo called, and one of his sons nodded, pointing the way for Riri.

"I thank you, Stibo," Ohaern said softly.

"You are welcome, stranger," Stibo said. "I am glad to do it, for I serve the goddess Rahani, and thus would she have me do. Nay, we shall be back here at sunset, if you wish to speak to your friends—but they shall have beds in my house tonight, and work on the morrow, so you need not fear for them."

"I am Ohaern," the big smith said. "I can forge both bronze and iron. Call on me if I can aid you."

"I shall." Stibo nodded. "Good luck in Cashalo, my stranger friend—and if you have gold on you, keep your hand away from it, but know where it is at all times." Then he vaulted into his boat, and it drew away from the dock. The canoe tied up; then Ori and Hifa reached up for Riri and his new shipmates to draw them over the gunwales.

"The people of Cashalo are good," Lucoyo said, "if they are all like him."

"Even if most are," said Ohaern. "But come now, Lucoyo. Let us speak to our countrymen." He turned away to the Biriae, and Lucoyo followed, secretly thrilling that Ohaern no longer seemed to remember that he had ever been anything but a Biri.

Ohaern's tribesmen were already talking to a trader, who stood beside them with a small slab of clay in his hand, pressing tally marks into it with a pointed stick as they laid marten pelts before him, adding them to a stack set on a clean square of pale cloth. "One hundred and seven!" the trader said. "We agreed on one gold bead for each five pelts, so that is twenty-one beads."

"Twenty-two." The Biri held up two more fingers. "Or I shall take back two of the pelts."

The trader shrugged. "What are two out of one hundred seven? Still, I would rather have them than lose them—so I will give you a silver bead for them."

The Biri nodded. "Silver? Yes, I will take that." He was a grizzled, scarred old warrior who looked to be as hard as an axe blade—and the three young men with him were all hale and muscular. Ohaern could understand the trader's reluctance to cheat them.

"Then, praise Ulahane, it is agreed!"

Ohaern's head snapped back; he felt as if he had been dealt a blow across the face at the mention of the scarlet god's name. He stared, watching as the trader slipped the beads onto a string. He did not look at all evil. How could he be Ulahane's?

The elder Biri took the string and bit one bead.

The trader smiled. "Do you not trust me?"

"I like the flavor." The Biri looked down at his own toothmark in the gold and grinned. "Praise Ulahane indeed, if he gives good bargains to us both!"

Ohaern felt as if the slap had been repeated, nay, doubled.

"Indeed he does, for he is the god of prosperity!" said the trader. "Come to his temple tonight and you shall find great pleasure in his worship!"

"Pleasure in a temple?" The Biri frowned.

"Pleasure indeed, for in every ritual, we consecrate women to Ulahane's service, and he fills them with uncontrollable lust. When the worship is done, they mingle with the male worshipers, and there is a merry time indeed! Nay, come and learn our manner of worshiping the trader's god."

"Let us do so, Father, I beg you!" one of the young men said.

"Aye, let us do so indeed," said another, "for the journey has been long, and it will be years before I have enough battle scars to claim a wife!"

"I am scarcely loath, myself," the older man agreed, "though I might have been so before your mother died."

One of the sons seemed disconcerted at that, but he made no protest as the father said, "Aye, let us go to worship Ulahane!"

Ohaern turned away, shaken.

"Will you not speak to your countrymen?" Lucoyo demanded. "If anything, I should think they need your words now more than ever!"

"They would not listen," Ohaern replied, but kept his face turned straight ahead. "Perhaps not all of these Cashalo men are good."

"Or perhaps they are," Lucoyo said, "but are becoming less so." He gave himself a shake. "I can certainly understand the appeal of their god!"

"You have been too long without a woman," Ohaern grunted, and was appalled at the surge of desire he felt within him, at the memory of Ryl. Remorse and grief followed on the instant.

"Will Ulahane really give us the better bargain?"

Ohaern's head snapped around. The accent was thick, but he could understand the words—though those speaking were not Biriae, but Myrics, the short, broad-faced men from the far north, with whom the Biriae sometimes fought and often traded. In fact, there were two Biriae climbing into the barge with the Myrics, which was why they were speaking the mixed trading language the two nations had developed.

One of the Biriae shrugged. "We are his worshipers now. We shall learn quite quickly whether he will favor us in our dealings or not."

"Even if he does not," said the other Myric, grinning, "his ritual was well worth the conversion!"

"It was indeed," the other Biri agreed. "We shall have to see to building him a temple and beginning his worship at home."

Ohaern could only watch, stone-stiff, stone-cold—watch, and listen.

"He has certainly brought us good bargaining," said a Myric. "The priest was right, telling us to press for as many beads as we could, and to give none to the beggars."

A Biri nodded. "One of the acolytes told me some word about Lavoc the cloth trader, that he would not wish his wife to know."

"What—that he had been playing with the women in the Street of Lantern Houses?"

"Yes, and trading his wife's gold beads for their favors. I mentioned that to him when I was bargaining my beads for his cloth, and he was suddenly willing to give me three bolts of cloth for a single bead."

His three companions laughed, and Ohaern finally found the will to turn away, his face thunderous. He paced quickly down the dock as the traders cast off the line and began to paddle out into the current. When he was far enough away, he hissed, "That Biriae should sink to such filthy tricks!"

"Almost worthy of the tribe that raised me," Lucoyo agreed, though he seemed much less disturbed by it. "I cannot like the thought of them spreading the worship of Ulahane in their homelands."

"*Our* homeland!" Ohearn snapped. "Tell me again that I should not turn about and go to cut out the corruption as it arrives!"

"You should cut out the source instead," Lucoyo said, but he seemed to recite it almost absentmindedly.

Ohaern looked closely, and sure enough, the half-elf was gazing ahead into the city with longing, his eyes not quite focused. "What ails you?"

Lucoyo sighed. "I could almost wish that I had not offended Ulahane so clearly, Ohaern. Willing women! The thought has great appeal to me now."

Ohaern held himself rigid, shocked all over again. Then he studied his friend's face and finally saw not only longing, but clawing hunger. He did not know which disturbed him more, Lucoyo's lust or the discovery that he had personal reasons for avoiding Ulahane, rather than an affinity for Lomallin.

Lucoyo hurried forward a few steps to a man with a wax tablet, who stood waiting for a boat to pull into the dock. "Man of Cashalo! I greet you."

The trader looked up, and in very bad, very heavily accented Biriae, answered, "Greet you, stranger. What wish?"

"How do I find the Street of Lantern Houses?" Lucoyo asked, while Ohaern stood rigid, unbelieving. "And how do I fare once I arrive there?"

The trader gave him a sly grin. "Find it by going straight from sea gate toward palace." He pointed at a broad street that seemed to sweep in all the dockside area. "Is fifth paved street. Turn left. Once there?" He shrugged. "Offer gold or amber to pimp who owns house, then play with which woman you like."

"Gold or amber?" Lucoyo's face fell. "Well, I shall have to see to gaining that! Thank you, man of Cashalo!"

Still grinning, the trader made a sign that indicated Lucoyo was welcome, and the half-elf hurried off, the hunger naked in his face.

Ohaern followed quickly, his shock receding under concern for his friend. But he hesitated near the mouth of the street, recognizing the trader who had invited the Biriae to Ulahane's temple, and reached out to catch Lucoyo, calling to the trader, "Ho, friend!"

The trader looked up in surprise. "Ho yourself—but I hope we shall be friends. What would you, stranger?"

"Can you tell me if a man can truly trade goods for a woman's favors in the Street of Lantern Houses?"

The trader's mouth widened into a grin, and he punched Ohaern's heavy chest with a knowing leer. "Aye, a big husky lad like you would wish to know that, would he not? Be certain, it is true!"

Ohaern looked away, shaken. "Surely the women must hate this!"

The trader was silent awhile, then said slowly, "I cannot say— only a woman would know."

"No woman would hate what *I* would do to her," Lucoyo boasted. Ohaern tried not to look at him.

The trader shrugged. "I have seen Vanyar traders in that street, and cannot see that any woman could take pleasure in them. The Vanyar are stocky, bandy-legged, and hairy—ugly as jackals."

Lucoyo's head snapped up. "Do you say *I* am as ugly as a jackal?"

"Certainly not, though I would not say you are handsome, either. Of course, a woman might."

"A woman *would*." But in his heart, Lucoyo doubted. Nonetheless, he turned and hurried away, filled with a strange clamoring urgency that he did not fully understand.

Ohaern stood, dazed, then finally remembered himself and nodded to the trader. "Thank you for your information, sir."

"You are welcome." The trader returned the nod. "Enjoy your foray!"

Ohaern turned away—to find that Lucoyo had already disappeared into the crowd.

The broad street from the dock plaza was full of people, and the crowds became thicker as he went along. Ohaern caught sight of the half-elf far ahead and tried to catch up, but soon he was having to elbow and jostle his way through, to a chorus of protest in the foreign tongue—but Lucoyo, slight, slender, and quick, made much faster progress. Before long Ohaern had lost sight of him again.

Then there was an outcry behind him. Ohaern turned and saw a man clutching at severed thongs that hung from his belt, crying, "Akor!" Ohaern decided that the word meant, "My purse!" but more importantly, meant that Lucoyo had passed by. The man proceeded to howl and yell, but Ohaern ignored him, pressing on. Then, ahead of him, another man cried, "Akor!" and began to rant and rave, so Ohaern knew he was on the right path.

On he went, following a trail of protest, dismay, and anger, of severed purse strings and angry citizens—but he did not catch sight of Lucoyo again until he turned into the fifth paved street from the dockside plaza and saw that every hut was large, quite large, twice higher than a man and more—and each had a post sticking out above the door, with a lantern hanging from it. There was Lucoyo, going in under just such a lantern! Ohaern started to follow, but as he came near the doorway, he hesitated. He certainly had no need to go into a place where women gave themselves so casually—well, no, he had a huge need, actually, and a wish so great that it hammered inside him with an intensity that frightened him. He, who had never turned away from any foe that waked fear in him, now paused on the threshold of a house of weak, soft women, a house that promised to fulfill his most secret, but most frantic, desire. Why should he fear ecstasy?

Because of his dead wife.

It wasn't that he feared Ryl's ghost would be jealous, really; it was that she might be grieved, for surely taking the favors that a woman offered to a stranger—a total stranger! And for no better cause than hunger! It would hurt Ryl grievously. For a moment Ohaern pondered why that would be, but could only think that it debased women in some way, though he could not say how.

Then a woman came out beneath the lantern—a disheveled woman, with hair in disarray and clothes awry, yawning and scratching. She looked up and saw Ohaern. A look of distaste flashed across her features and was gone, buried under a sort of shiny hardness that offered a smile, but a smile that was practiced and polished by long and frequent use. It was a heavy-lidded smile, an inviting smile, and her hips circled and thrust as her shoulders pulled back too far.

Ohaern hid his shudder and turned away. Let the half-elf bury himself in pleasure, then. He would be safe, at least in body, and he would certainly know where to find Lucoyo.

He turned away, walking back down the Street of Lantern Houses, out into the broad hard-paved boulevard . . .

And saw the temple of Ulahane looming before him.

CHAPTER 17

Ulahane's temple stood atop a step-pyramid, like all the others—but it was made of a reddish stone, and the edifice at its peak was painted scarlet.

Scarlet, but the war chief's eye could see that the paint covered huge stone blocks. It was a temple, but it was also a fortress—a fortress that soared up into pinnacles from which men could shoot arrows or even throw boiling water down upon attackers; and Ohaern would have wagered that he would find a well within its enclosure.

So much blood color made Ohaern shudder, but so did the number of people climbing up and climbing down. They were no myriad, but there was certainly steady traffic—and they were not only the people of Cashalo, but also Biriae and Myrics, dark men of the south, yellow men of the east, and even some men who were so dark they were almost black! There were many more males than females, but there were enough women to make Ohaern remember what the trader had said about Ulahane's rites, and to make him shudder. If there were so many people as this by day, what would the temple steps look like at night?

He decided that he did not want to know. He turned away, resolved to come here no more—and found himself staring at another temple, obviously much older in both style and wear. It had only four steps, made of a pale stone with a greenish cast—and the smith's eye noted the presence of copper in the stone. The temple itself was low, little more than colonnades supporting a roof, painted the rich green of summer leaves. It seemed more a house than a monument, alive and welcoming.

Ohaern stared. Why had Lomallin's temple been built so close to Ulahane's?

The answer struck him with outrage. Lomallin's temple was the older; Ulahane's worshipers had built him a house as near to Lomallin's as they could, in hopes of stealing his congregation! And from the look of the numbers trooping up his stairs, they had succeeded.

Well, here was one Lomallin worshiper who would not be deterred—or seduced away or cozened, either. Ohaern straightened his shoulders, lifted his chin, and strode proudly up the steps of Lomallin's temple, not caring who saw—and hoping that many would.

After all, he was the only person on that whole expanse of stone.

He came in under the lintel and was instantly enveloped in shadow, coolness, and the heady aroma of cedar. Lomallin's temple seemed modest, but it had been built of expensive imported wood, and its fragrance was like a breath of breeze from a northern forest. He felt as if he were surrounded by a friendly living presence; he felt at home. Looking about him, he saw only a broad expanse of open floor, cleansed by the wind, and at the far end the high reach of a living tree surrounded by bushes, with the vague form of a bearded face seeming to grow out of the trunk, ancient and reassuring: Lomallin's symbol, with Lomallin's face—or as much of it as any living man could perceive. Slowly, he stepped forward before the tree, bowing his head in prayer.

"Who comes to Ranol's temple?"

Ohaern looked up to see an elderly man coming out from behind the tree. He leaned upon a gnarled staff—a branch that had been polished, but otherwise left as the tree had made it. His hair and beard were long and white, and he wore green robes.

"I am Ohaern, a smith and warrior of the Biriae," Ohaern answered. It was courtesy to tell the name of his nation, though obviously unnecessary—the old man had known him for what he was at a glance, or he would not have spoken in the Biriae tongue. His accent was not even heavy. "I greet you, sir—and I beg your pardon, for I had thought I was in the temple of Lomallin."

"You are, though we call him 'Ranol' here. Still, he is the same—the green god, the lover of humanity and defender of all the younger races."

"Are you the priest here?"

"The servant of Ranol." The old man came to peer up into Ohaern's face. "Call me not a priest, for I have no special powers, no more than yourself—though I have some skill in healing."

"I have no need of that, praise Lomallin. Would you deny it if I called you a sage, though?"

"There is some truth to that," the old man admitted, "for I am wise in the ways of Ranol—though I would not claim to know much more than any other man might, at my age. I would rather you called me simply by my name; I am Noril. It is good to see you here, young man. Few come to Ranol's temple anymore."

"Yes, I see that." Ohaern frowned. "Ulahane has stolen your congregation, and I do not doubt he set about doing it quite deliberately. Is all your city decaying to his worship, then?"

"Sadly so," Noril answered. "I could wish we had not become prosperous, for Ulahane's worship seems to grow with our wealth."

"I see that many of your people fish for their living," Ohaern said. "Have *they* become wealthy?"

"Oh, yes, for there are many more mouths to feed, now that there are always two or three thousand traders in the city."

"Two or three thousand! So many as that?"

"Indeed," Noril confirmed. "Most of our people are still fishermen, but the bulk of the city's wealth now comes from the great storage sheds by the water, where the traders barter the goods from both seas."

"I have seen men of the north trading marten pelts and amber for gold beads," Ohaern said, "but those beads shall be of little worth in the cold northern winter."

"Perhaps, but before they leave Cashalo they shall go to one of the warehouses and trade their gold beads for copper pans, fine pottery jars, bronze spearheads and arrowheads, stout cloth, even the spices of the east and the dried fruits and medicines of the south. They shall receive good value for their marten pelts and amber, be sure."

"I can see no harm in that—in fact, a great good," Ohaern said slowly, "if the trade benefits both."

"It is the warehouses that bring it about," Noril explained. "Our merchants take the goods from traders from the Eastern Sea in exchange for goods of Cashalo's making—or for gold beads; that is something new brought from the east, and very useful, for everyone always wants gold."

Ohaern lifted his head as understanding dawned. "So even if your merchants do not have any goods that the folk of the Eastern Sea want, they can exchange for golden beads, and the east-men can exchange those later, when they find the goods they *do* want!"

"Even so," said Noril. "In fact, foreign traders have begun to take gold from the first trader who approaches them, *then* go to look for the goods they seek. It is easier to guard a handful of beads than a whole boatload of cargo."

"But would not the beads be easier to steal?"

"Aye, and they can be exchanged for lavish food and wine, fine lodgings, and entertainments, none of which can be taken home— so foreign traders must need to have strong self-rule if they wish to go away with as much as they brought."

"The goods they seek are those that come from the Middle Sea?"

"Indeed; our ancestors blessed us more than they knew when they built their fishing village between two seas. So, a week or a month after the eastern traders, southern and western traders come from the Middle Sea . . ."

"Not from the north?"

"No; northerners generally come down the Great River. Anon they come, and exchange their southern goods for the eastern goods."

"Or for gold, if the eastern goods they seek are not yet in the warehouse." Ohaern nodded. "But because your warehouses are so big, there is almost always something that the foreign traders want."

"Even so. Thus the eastern ships can spend less time in port—and so can the southern and western and northern—thereby being freed to make more voyages in less time, and to limit the number of golden beads their crews spend in lodging and 'entertainment.' "

"Surely these warehouses are a marvelous invention!"

Noril nodded. "So if the traders of Cashalo keep a bit from each trade for themselves, who could begrudge them? Certainly their labor is worth it! Though perhaps not their entertainment . . ."

"Call it 'vice'—I know the sort of entertainment you speak of," Ohaern said with some distaste. "I have seen your Street of Lantern Houses and have seen that it is so named because each house there has a huge lantern over its portal. Why?"

Noril sighed. "The women light their lanterns at nightfall so that men passing by can clearly see them posing in their doorways, to attract 'customers' who wish to pay to touch them and caress them, even to the ultimate intimacy."

"Women really do such things for gold?" Ohaern felt like the veriest bumpkin, but he could not help staring. He also felt sick to his stomach.

Noril answered, "There are many women who are so poor that they will bed a man for a coin."

"Surely not!" Ohaern said, shocked.

"Unfortunately so." Noril shook his head sadly. "It is that, or starve—for in the cities there is no way to get food by your own effort."

Ohaern looked away, shaken. "Do the Vanyar do worse to them than that?"

Noril was silent a while, then said slowly, "I cannot say—only a woman would know. I hear of men who claim that such women enjoy bedding every man they meet—but I have seen some of those men, when I have gone into that street to try to persuade the women to find some other way to live, and to persuade the men not to despoil them. Of course, the women decry me for seeking to cut off their livelihood, and the men decry me for seeking to deprive them of pleasure—but I cannot believe it can very often be pleasure for the women, for many of those men are ugly as hogs. I doubt very much that any woman would enjoy a night with such a one."

"None who worship Lomallin would so despoil a woman." Ohaern turned thoughtful. "At least, if he did, it would be because his resolve weakened. And no woman who worshiped Lomallin would need to tempt him, for her fellow worshipers would make sure she did not starve." He looked up to see Noril watching him keenly and asked, "The eastern folk have brought more than their goods, have they not?"

"It is even as you say," Noril confirmed. "The traders from the Land Between the Rivers brought us the worship of Ulahane. We had known of him before, of course, but none thought to pray to him. The traders, though, built him a temple, praising him as the source of their wealth and luxury, and many listened. Still, his gathering of a congregation has not been the work of a single night, nor even of a single year, for there are temples to many different gods here, at least one for each of the nations who come to trade. Oh, our ancestors worshiped Ranol, but they were tolerant of other gods and did not mind if foreigners built temples. It is perhaps because there were so many that I did not realize the danger of Ulahane gathering so large a congregation—until I had lost half my own. I should have realized that the Ulin War had not truly ended, only shifted its battleground from the heavens to the hearts of humankind and the other younger races."

"The Ulin War?" Ohaern frowned. "I have heard of that, but only that it did occur. In the north we know only that Lomallin is the god of Life, and the protector of our kind—and that Ulahane is the god of Death, but most especially the death of humankind!"

"That is so." Noril nodded. "When the Creator first made the younger races, Ulahane sought to slay them all—but our race more than any other. Lomallin sought to prevent him and protect us, and they did war."

"Over us?" Ohaern frowned. "Why did beings so great and mighty as the Ulin care about ones so much smaller and weaker?"

Noril shrugged. "Who can tell? The Ulin do as they please, and have no need to explain. My own guess is that they, who had been the only beings who could think or speak, now resented other, younger races being raised up to do even that much of what they could do."

"You do not mean that the Ulin saw some threat in us! In the elves, perhaps, for they have strong magic, or even the trolls and dwarves and dwergs and goblins—but humankind, who alone of all the races have no magic?"

"But can learn it." Noril raised an admonishing forefinger. "Though few wish to devote the time and labor to do so, they nonetheless can. No, I think that for some reason the Ulin saw us as the greatest threat to their supremacy, perhaps because we alone are not willing to keep our place in the order of Creation. We are proud, we humans, and overweening in our pride. Perhaps it is for that reason that Marcoblin was so angered at our creation that he determined to mock the Creator by making parodies of humanity."

"Marcoblin—he was the king of the Ulin, was he not?"

"As much as they had a king." Noril shrugged. "He was their best fighter, though how much use is skill with weapons when everyone else is a wizard, and some more skilled at magic than he? Still, if the Ulin had a king, it was he, even if only because no one chose to dispute the claim."

"Was he wizard enough to raise up mockeries of humanity?"

"No; for that he had need to go to the wondersmith Agrapax. Picture it—think of Marcoblin striding from mountain peak to mountain peak, the earth shaking with his tread and boulders flying loose to go bounding down the slopes . . .

"Ho, Agrapax!" he cried. "I have work for you!"

"I have work for me, too, a great deal of it," the smith replied sourly, and stared pointedly at the boulders that flew from Marcoblin's tread. "You deceive no one with your spectacle, Marcoblin. You are no bigger than the rest of us, and no heavier, so you might as well show yourself as you really are and leave off damaging my mountains."

Marcoblin reddened, a hot retort on his tongue, but he needed

Agrapax's efforts, so he knew he must not deny him. He shrank to only thrice the size of a human, and the earth ceased to shake as he leaped the last peak to land beside the smith's forge with the huge crater of magma behind it, from which Agrapax drew whichever elements he needed to forge his next work. "I did not know those mountains were of your creation."

"They are not." Agrapax knew the king would not apologize, any more than any other Ulin. "But I have improved them. What have you come for, Marcoblin? I have work to do, and cannot labor while I stand here nattering!"

Now, Marcoblin knew that the surly smith had no great love for him—or for any, save his arts—and would not grant him a boon. No, he had need to trick him into it. "I have come to wager with you," he said.

"I do not wager. It is a waste of time." And the smith started to turn away.

"A challenge, then!" Marcoblin cried. "An artifact that you cannot craft!"

Agrapax turned back slowly, blood in his eye. "Something that I cannot make? There is nothing that I cannot make, short of truly living beings, or the world itself!"

"It is living beings of which I speak." Marcoblin sneered. "I thought you could not."

"Oh, aye, of course." The smith turned away, losing interest.

"Not *truly* living!" Marcoblin cried. "Still you cannot."

"I can, if they are not truly alive," Agrapax called back over his shoulder, "but why should I?"

"You cannot! You have never done it!"

"Never?" the smith snorted, and took up his hammer. "Do you not remember the man of bronze I made to afright the goddesses?"

"I remember, and recall also that they only laughed, for it was a man with no genitals! But I speak not of metal, Agrapax, but of flesh! You have never crafted that!"

"No, for flesh lives." The smith turned to Marcoblin, but he looked right through the king, his head rising. "An interesting notion."

Marcoblin's pulse leaped; he knew the fish had taken the bait.

Now, if he could just set the hook . . . "Something like flesh, like something living, but not truly—and formed in the shape of a human!"

"It could be done, perhaps it could be done." The smith nodded slowly. "Let us discover if it can . . ." He turned away, dismissing Marcoblin from his awareness.

"But with genitals, this time!" Marcoblin cried. "One male, one female, for if they cannot reproduce, they are not truly a mockery of life!"

"Yes, there is something in that, though even crystals can make more crystals." Agrapax tilted his head up, thinking. "Perhaps not genitals—perhaps a splitting, and a growing of a new half . . . or a replication, a growing of an entire new being in a sort of prolonged sleep . . . Build it in so that it comes upon them once a year, unawares . . ."

Marcoblin smiled; the fish was hooked, and racing with the line. He turned away, leaving Agrapax to bring in a huge catch.

So they came anon—a troop of homunculi, marching down from the smith's crater, looking as if they had been made out of a baker's raw dough, only roughly human in form—a slab split at the bottom to form legs and slit at the sides to form arms, with a lump of a head at the top. They had only folds for eyes and nose and mouth, and were certainly a very rough parody of the human form.

"Say I cannot make them now!" Agrapax demanded.

"You can, and have done most wondrously!" Marcoblin saw the need to oil the smith's ego. "All these from only two?"

"No, I became enthused with the task and made a hundred— and each of those made another, which made another. But when I saw how quickly they made replications, I modified them so that they will reproduce only once a year."

"But that is too slow!" Marcoblin cried. "I need thousands, tens of thousands! Make more, smith, make more!"

"I tire of it." Agrapax shrugged his massive, lumpy shoulders. "I am bored with them and shall leave them to their own doings."

Marcoblin's face grew dark with anger. "You must make more, many more! I have need of an army!"

Agrapax turned a very frosty gaze on him. "I must do as I please, Marcoblin, no more."

"I shall beat you!" Marcoblin blustered. "Indeed, if you do not do as I say, I shall slay you, for you shall be of no use to me!"

"Slay me? Will you indeed? And where shall you get a new spear when your old one breaks? Where shall you find new armor, if this which you have should burst beneath an opponent's axe? Which it shall, at its maker's death." Agrapax grinned into Marcoblin's face, shaking his head. "No, Marcoblin, I do not think you shall kill me—and if you seek to beat me, why, you shall have to match your sword against my hammer." He hefted the huge tool. "Your sword, which I made, shall turn strangely brittle as it strikes my hammer—turn brittle, and break!"

Marcoblin shook with rage, but there was nothing he could do but glare and clench his fists.

"Oh, fear not, your artificial army shall prove effective," Agrapax said, "for they are very long-lived, immensely strong, and very hard to kill—in fact, they must be cut into little pieces, which must be scattered, if you wish to stop them. But me, I shall not stop. I shall craft many more wonders—but no more of these." Agrapax slung his hammer over his shoulder and turned away. "I am going back to my forge. Do not disturb me again." He marched off, back to his crater of lava and molten metal.

Marcoblin glared after him—but the smith had spoken truly; there was nothing he could do. Well, he would have to manage with a thousand homunculi. He strode down the mountainside to take command of his new army.

"Was the Creator angered?" Ohaern asked.

"If He was, He made no sign," Noril answered. "In fact, for all anyone knew, the Creator ignored Marcoblin and the homunculi completely. Marcoblin grew angrier and angrier, his mood darker and darker, speaking to no one, only marching his homunculi up and down, watching them increase and preparing them for a battle that the other Ulin could only wonder at, and shudder.

"But one Ulin did more. Lomallin was horrified at the blasphemy, and at the inflicting of existence on the poor Agrapaxians. 'You have done wrong,' he told Marcoblin, 'and I fear you would do worse! Would you defy the very Creator Himself?'

" 'It is no concern of yours, Wizard,' Marcoblin snapped—for Lomallin was one of the most skilled of the Ulin in the use of magic. Ulahane was the other, and he was also skilled in arms, second only to Marcoblin.

" 'It is my concern, and that of all the Ulin! If the Creator punishes you, He may punish all of us with you!' "

" 'He is not so unjust, and you know it. If He wreaks vengeance upon me, I alone shall bear it!' "

Which was true enough, but Lomallin still went away filled with foreboding. Unfortunately, he spoke of this to Narlico, who was ambitious. He took Lomallin's concern and spoke of it to all the Ulin, haranguing them into thinking that Marcoblin was about to betray them all, bringing disaster down upon their heads. Many of them took alarm—almost half—and acclaimed Narlico their chief, to lead them against Marcoblin and make him stop.

But the other half of the Ulin hated humans, and applauded Marcoblin for mocking them and, through that burlesque, mocking also the Creator. They drew their line against Narlico and his supporters, calling them human-lovers and demanding they leave Marcoblin alone to do as he would. Narlico, in response, led all his Ulin to Marcoblin, to demand he make all his homunculi vanish—but when they came, they found Marcoblin at the head of all the human-haters, with the sorcerer Ulahane just behind and at his right hand.

"Then the battle began."

CHAPTER 18

"That war must have lasted centuries," said Ohaern, "with gods for warriors!"

"Not so long as all that," Noril corrected, "for the Ulin are immortal only in that they will not die from age or illness—but they can be slain, especially by another as skilled as themselves. Narlico was the first to be slain."

Ohaern smiled. "There was justice in that. He should not have worked up strife as a means of advancing himself."

"Who are you to judge the gods?" Noril demanded, eyes flashing.

It took Ohaern aback, but he rallied. "I judge Ulahane to be evil, Sage. Was Narlico so much better?"

"He was on the side of right, at least," Noril grumbled.

Meaning our side. But Ohaern remembered the dead of his own clan, and the maimed fishermen, and did not say it aloud. "Who, then, took his place?"

"An Ulin named Daglorin, who had all the motives Narlico lacked. He believed ardently in loyalty to the Creator and fairness to the new races."

Ohaern frowned. "What of Lomallin in all this—he who bred the cause for the fight?"

"He stood staunchly at Narlico's right hand, then stood as valiantly at Daglorin's—but claimed he was no fighter, though a great wizard, and no leader to boot. Many Ulin died—on both sides, but more among the human-lovers than the human-haters, and Daglorin turned in desperation to Lomallin . . .

"Build us a fortress, Lomallin," Daglorin said, "for if we have no stronghold, we shall perish. It is an irony supreme that Marcoblin has sent his Agrapaxians against us, when we fight to free them!"

"He has told them we seek to free them from life," Lomallin said bitterly, "by putting them to death. I never said that—I only said that he was wrong to bid the smith make them, and should now leave them free to pursue their own destiny. Is it not ironic that Agrapax holds aloof from all this?"

"At least he has forgone making more weapons," Daglorin said, "but we shall be reduced to throwing stones if we lose many more!"

"Throwing stones . . ." Lomallin gazed off into the distance, then went away, muttering to himself.

He climbed down to the earth far to the south and east, and there raised up mighty stones. He set them in a circle, twice the height of an Ulin, four times the height of a man, and capped their ring with stone lintels. Then he charged each stone with the power of his magic, power that wove an invisible wall between each pair of uprights, stronger and more impenetrable than the stone itself. Daglorin was delighted with the stronghold, and the human-lovers flocked to it, where at last they could rest securely. But their very first night there, a horde of goblins burst out of the ground about the megaliths, yowling and clamoring and beating against the unseen wall—and while the Ulin were distracted in trying to discover why the small, ugly beings were so angry with them, Marcoblin and his host stooped upon them unawares, thinking the sky above the ring was unprotected. But Lomallin had woven his unseen force there, too, and the human-haters struck against it with howls of rage and disappointment.

"Even here they would pounce upon us without warning!" Daglorin shouted. "They have seduced one of the younger races to distract us, and would slay us in our beds! This treachery must end here and now, my kinsmen! Out upon them!" And he led the human-lovers out, ravening for the blood of their own kind.

"Short and vicious was that battle, O Friend, as Marcoblin sought to cut through the throng to slay Daglorin, whom he fancied to be his worst enemy, and Daglorin sought to cut down Marcoblin's bodyguard, so that he might slay the king, thinking he was the keystone of the whole battle. Deft blows grew crude as the Ulin wore one another down, and most forgot magic in their rage, so that it was brute force against rough blows, and as they tired, little enough skill even in that. But at last the goblins swarmed up the megaliths, seeking still to distract the human-lovers, and they did succeed in distracting Lomallin, who turned from protecting Daglorin long enough to send a charge of heat through the stones, burning the feet and hands of the goblins so that they dropped off, shrieking—and since that day, all goblins have sworn enmity to Lomallin, forgetting that their ancestors' burns healed and they still lived, but that many Ulin died. For, while Lomallin was chasing goblins, Marcoblin at last hewed his way through to Daglorin, and the two set to their final battle with edged steel, Daglorin's sword and buckler against Marcoblin's axe and shield.

"Sparks flew from the strikes of blade against axehead, sparks that flew a hundred miles and set fire to whole forests; blood fell, and gathered into a sea, flowing down into rivers. It is there yet today, charred and glazed, a sea of glass, of Ulin blood. But at last Daglorin, wearied, brought his buckler up too late, and Marcoblin's axe bit through his chest. Even as it did, though, Daglorin's great sword severed the king's head. It flew many leagues and fell, striking a huge great bowl in the ground, with a dark hole at its center where the head sank down to the fire beneath the ground— and who knows but that it may have swum up again, to become part of one of Agrapax's new marvels. But Daglorin's body fell down upon the unseen roof of the fortress, and the few Ulin who remained stepped back, lowering their weapons in unspoken truce, stunned by the amount of blood that had been shed and the numbers of Ulin who had died. As the human-lovers gathered up the body of their leader and carried it away into the mountains for burial, the human-haters turned away and, one by one, sought solitude far from mortal eyes—or those of other Ulin—to let their wounds heal, and study peace."

Ohaern frowned. "But there *was* no peace."

"For a time, there was," Noril corrected, "for some centuries."

"But then?"

"Then Ulahane took up the mantle of the fallen king," Noril sighed, "and his cause, also. But Ulahane is a far mightier wizard than ever Marcoblin was, and cares more for seeing the lesser races all slain than for his own glory—so he is a far worse enemy than ever Marcoblin was."

"But Lomallin is equally great in wizardry."

"Equally great, and now schooled in the ways of war." Noril nodded. "Ranol would choose not to fight if he could—but he cannot, so fight he does. But there are few Ulin left now, and fewer of them who wish to be caught up in Ulahane's mad, suicidal cause—so the God of Blood seeks to mobilize all the lesser races against Lomallin. If he can ever strike down the green god, he will turn his powers against the very races that have fought for him— but few of them believe that. They think the notion to be only a lie spread by Ranol's worshipers."

"And will learn the truth only as they die in pain," Ohaern said grimly. "But the Agrapaxians were freed?"

"Freed to seek their own destiny," Noril agreed, "save that they were made without one. But who knows what the Creator had in mind when He permitted Agrapax to craft them? Who knows but that He may have had a destiny in mind for them after all?"

"Who knows, indeed?" Ohaern agreed. "But what of the prophecy, Sage? The prophecy that only by his death can Lomallin become more powerful than Ulahane? How can the scarlet god dare slay him?"

"Perhaps he does not," Noril replied. "Perhaps he seeks only some way to immobilize Ranol, to bind him tight with cold iron and spells that he cannot break."

Ohaern shuddered. "I would prefer a clean death."

"Clean death," said Noril, "is not what Ulahane would give."

Ohaern came out of the temple refreshed in his heart, but also confused. He had never before heard the details of the gods' jealousies. How could they be gods if they were jealous of men? He thought that perhaps Ranol was different from Lomallin after all, or the old priest did not have the story right.

That was all of utmost importance, of course, but not of immediate concern. The current problem was to warn Cashalo of its coming doom—the Vanyar horde—and to help prepare them to meet it.

If they believed him. If they chose to fight.

He went looking for Lucoyo.

He found the half-elf sitting on the steps of the house in which Ohaern had left him, a goblet in his hand, chatting with two giggling, if overblown, beauties. Looking at them, Ohaern was shocked—first by the thickness of the paint on their faces, then, peering beneath it, by the ravages of dissipation—so his voice was sharper than he intended when he spoke. "Ho, archer! What do you here?"

Lucoyo looked up, surprised and ready for a fight—then, seeing it was Ohaern, leaned back with an insolent grin. "Why, drinking the wine of the far south and chatting with two agreeable girls. I have already tasted the grapes of Kuru and of Henjo, borne from afar by industrious trading ships. They are all excellent, though this of Egypt is tart."

"Tart, yes," Ohaern said, with a glance at each of the women. If they were young enough to be girls, he was a bear's father! "But why do you loiter on the doorstep, instead of within?"

"It is hot inside—" Lucoyo paused at the women's giggles and gave them a knowing grin, then turned back to Ohaern. "—and the evening is cool. Besides, I have given them all my gold beads, and the silver, too. I shall have to get more."

"Indeed you must!" said one of the "girls," while the other giggled and tipped the goblet against his lips.

Ohaern felt a thrill of alarm. How many robberies could Lucoyo commit before he was caught? "Then are you not stealing these women's favors?"

"No," said the one on Lucoyo's left, "for we choose freely to come chat with him, and our master thinks we may attract customers."

"But I might steal a kiss." Lucoyo turned his face up to her, and the kiss was long and lingering.

Ohaern reddened and directed a question at the other woman. "How does this town punish theft?"

She frowned at his tone, but answered, "By cutting off the hand that did the stealing."

"Ah! Then you must need cut off my tongue!" Lucoyo turned his face to her.

"I would never dream of it," she said huskily, "for it brings me too much pleasure." But the way she kissed him, and moved her body as she did, made it clear to Ohaern that she was more concerned with inflaming him himself, not Lucoyo or any other passerby.

There was no point in this badinage—at least, not for Ohaern. As the woman broke the kiss, he reached down and yanked the half-elf to his feet. "Come! We have much to do!"

Lucoyo frowned, shaking himself free. "What is your hurry?" Then he glanced at the girls. "Though I must admit I see some urgency in finding more trade goods, too." He picked up his quiver and bowcase and slung them across his back again. "Farewell, girls! Remember me to your 'sisters'!"

"Would you leave us so soon, then?" one of them asked, pouting.

"Only so that I may return to you sooner!" Lucoyo leaned over for one last kiss to each, and each gave him a last giggle and wriggle. He caught his breath, more for effect than from any real longing, then turned away with a wave.

Ohaern stalked beside him, throttling the desire to ask how he could so quickly have forgotten his Biri love. Instead he asked, "How old are those two?"

"The one is seventeen," Lucoyo answered, "the other twenty."

Ohaern walked beside him in numbed silence. Beneath the paint, both women had looked to be in their thirties. How hard a life did they live?

As they came out of the Street of Lantern Houses, Lucoyo veered into a shop as if he had known where to find it on the instant. Ohaern followed and, looking around, saw many small tables with groups of people sitting at them, drinking from fat pottery cups. Several were also eating, and the aroma reminded him how long it had been since he had tasted food.

"Mid-afternoon, and time enough for dinner." Lucoyo sat at a table near the wall. "I have drunk freely, but eaten little."

"And how shall we persuade them to give us food?" Ohaern asked, sitting across from him.

Lucoyo drew out a silver bead. "I lied to their mistress—I had a few beads left."

A passing woman, bearing a tray, saw the gleam of silver and veered to the half-elf. "Would you trade that for food and beer?"

"I would," Lucoyo said, "though I would expect some copper beads with the platters. Two of each, if you will."

The woman nodded and turned away, threading her way between the tables toward a doorway in the wall. Lucoyo followed her with his eyes. "Underneath the sweat and grease and disheveled hair, she is pretty enough."

"Can you think of nothing else?" Ohaern said impatiently.

Lucoyo started to answer, but the whole room froze at the sound of a shout from the doorway. "There!" They looked up and saw five soldiers marching in behind an old man who pointed at their table. Lucoyo paled and reached for his long knife—but Ohaern stopped him with a hand on the pommel. "No fear—it is the priest of Ranol."

"Priest?" Lucoyo swung about to stare at him. "A whole morning in a city where every pleasure you can imagine is at your beck and call, and you spent it in a *temple?*"

Noril and the soldiers filed through to their table, and the patrons leaped back promptly, pulling their tables clear. As they came up, Ohaern rose, nodding to Noril. "I greet you, Sage."

"And I greet you, Ohaern." Noril returned the nod. "These men with me are the king's soldiers, come to invite you to his royal hall."

"Under the circumstances, I can scarcely refuse," Ohaern replied, with a quirk of humor to his lips. Lucoyo stared at him as if he were insane, but he went on. "May I ask why the king finds us worthy of his interest?"

"You are late come from the north," Noril explained, "and the king has this day had disturbing news from that quarter."

Lucoyo swiveled to turn the alarmed stare on the priest.

Ohaern nodded, guessing the nature of the alarming news. "We will come, and gladly. Will we not?" he asked Lucoyo sternly. "Or would you not be a guest of the king?"

Lucoyo stared at him, as much surprised at Ohaern giving a double meaning as at the thought itself. The big barbarian had a point—if he kept on stealing, he was likely to be the guest of the king in any event. "Why not opt for the better chamber?" he said, affecting a breezy manner. "Let us go!"

They followed the soldiers out the door. Behind them the room broke into a hubbub of wild speculation.

"I can guess how you found me," Ohaern said to Noril as the soldiers formed a knot about them, "but how did you learn of the news?"

"The king sent word to all the chief priests of all the temples, asking if their gods had told them anything about the danger," Noril said, "and I thought that perhaps you might know something of it."

"Is the danger a vast troop of men with light-wheeled carts drawn by horses, on their way south?"

Noril stared at him. "Then you do know something of them!"

"That is why we have come to Cashalo," Ohaern said, "to warn you against them—but I did not know how to do it."

"The king's scouts have done that for you," Noril told him, "and the barbarians are still several days away, if they travel no faster than they did when the king's spy saw them as he came south."

"Then there is time to do *something*, at least." Ohaern nodded. "What does the king intend?"

Noril replied slowly. "I think that is what he means to ask *you*."

The king was a tall man, almost as tall as Ohaern, and built as heavily—but he wore royal robes instead of a fur kilt, and had the beginnings of a potbelly. "You are a chieftain, then," he said as he pressed hands with Ohaern. Lucoyo had made certain the monarch knew that.

"I am," Ohaern replied, "and I am gratified that you know our language, O King!"

"You are gracious." Perhaps because Ohaern was a chief, the king spoke to him as to an equal. "Our traders deal frequently with the tribes of the Biriae, and I strive to know the tongues of all the nations with whom we trade—though I know my accent must be as heavy as sand."

"You are better than me in that," Ohaern returned, "since I speak your language not at all—though I think my companion may have learned a word or two."

Lucoyo reddened and cleared his throat, looking away.

"But those are not words to be spoken in a king's presence?" The monarch smiled. "Never fear, my friend—I know them all." Then he frowned, looking at the half-elf more closely. "Are you truly a Biri?"

"Only by adoption," Lucoyo said, "but I, too, have seen the Vanyar."

"Vanyar, yes, that is how they are called." The king turned back to Ohaern. "How closely have you seen them?"

"We have fought them," Ohaern replied. "They are tough and hard, and take a great deal of beating."

"Alas, then!" The king turned away, wringing his hands in agitation. "My scout said they covered the plain as far as he could see! Surely they must outnumber my poor army a hundred to one! How shall we stand against them?"

"In the first place," Ohaern said slowly, "they travel as a tribe, not as a war group only—so perhaps a quarter of those you saw were warriors."

"Only a quarter? Much better, much! They shall only outnumber my men twenty-five to one!" The king shook his head. "Not enough, my friend, not enough! How shall we stand? Or should we surrender?"

Lucoyo spoke up. "If you surrender, they shall rape all your women, enslave those of your children they do not kill, and slay all your old folk along with most of your warriors—or men who are of an age to be warriors. Those they let survive, they shall castrate and lame." He shook his head. "It may come to the same in the end—but I would fight."

"Indeed," said Ohaern, "if it will come to the same in the end, why *not* fight?"

"Well thought—and well said." The king nodded, frowning. "What else can you tell me of them that will help us to beat them back?"

"They serve Ulahane," Ohaern said slowly, "so you must set a close watch on the temple of the Scarlet One, and on as many of his worshipers as you know of."

"You do not think they would fight against their own city!"

"Oh, surely not!" Lucoyo smiled. "But why chance it?"

"True." The king nodded heavily. "What else?"

"We have heard the Vanyar boast of villages being easy meat," Ohaern said, "because they have no walls."

"Yes," Lucoyo said, "they say they can ride their 'chariots' right into the center of the village, slaying as they go."

"Then we must build a wall!" The king frowned. "But how, in only a few days?"

"Every man must work," Ohaern told him—and, with the surety of a tribal chieftain, "and every man must fight. You have a great strength that you know not of, O King—for every ablebodied man in your city can become a warrior at need, and every woman can make arrows for them."

Lucoyo nodded. "Let them work at the wall for two hours at a time, then send them to me for a rest—and I will train them in archery."

"Yes, with Biriae bows!" Ohaern's eye caught fire. "The Vanyar bows are powerful, but their range is short! If you can find two hundred archers who can become accurate with the Biriae bow, they can fell a great number of Vanyar before they come close enough to strike!"

"But where shall we find so many bows in only a few days?" Lucoyo frowned. "Wood must have time to cure!"

"Many of my people already have bows," the king said slowly, "for they still shoot fish in the shallows."

"That is scarcely what I call a long range, but they might suffice. Tell me, are they made of long staves? Or of two horns joined by a foot of seasoned wood, like the Vanyar bows?"

"They are made of the bones of the whales of the Middle Sea—limber and strong, but not wooden."

Lucoyo stared. "Fish-bone bows? Nay, this I must see!"

"Do you think they will shoot as far as the ones you speak of?" the king said anxiously.

"I will delight in discovering the answer!" Lucoyo caught Ohaern's arm. "Come, smith! There is much to do!"

But the king caught Ohaern's other arm, staying him long enough to stare into his face with a sudden wild hope. "Smith? You are a smith, then?"

Ohaern nodded. "I am."

"Do you know magic?"

"Only a few spells, and those for proving and tempering the iron and bronze," Ohaern cautioned.

"That may be enough." Noril came forward, eyes glowing. "In the temple of Ranol, that may be more than enough."

CHAPTER 19

The fishermen, of course, knew how to use a spear, though theirs had three prongs—they were accustomed to spearing fish, with a cast rarely longer than two yards. A spear cast is a spear cast, though, and they learned quickly to hurl a leaf-bladed spear—but more importantly, to thrust with it. Ohaern and Lucoyo discovered that, because of the old art of fishing with a bow, the people of Cashalo were skilled archers; in fact, it was their favorite sport, and evenings saw men and women alike assembled in the parks, shooting at straw targets tied cleverly to resemble huge fish. Lucoyo had only to stand the fish upright, and it approximated the shape of a man. He was quite pleased with their bows, too—apparently the whales who had contributed so generously from their rib cages had exceptionally long, limber ribs, and the bows were naturally curved at the ends. Their range, though not as good as Lucoyo's bow, was nonetheless far greater than that of the compound bows of the Vanyar.

They were also avid wrestlers, almost as enthusiastic about grappling one another at close range as they were at shooting straw fish at long range. But that was the extent of their fighting skills; they knew nothing of any other forms of combat. Ohaern taught them the use of the staff which, when combined with thrusting, made excellent spear-play—but he shied at the thought of these peaceful fishermen and merchants, with only a few days' training, bearing swords against seasoned warriors. Instead he taught them how to turn aside a sword stroke with their staves, and he set the smiths to shoeing and binding those staves with iron. That was all the time he could spare before he went into seclusion with Noril, learning magic.

Lucoyo stifled the urge to protest, and went on training archers. By good fortune, Cashalo had many experienced builders, with warehouses full of tree-trunk logs from the north mixed with costly rare woods and building stone from the south. The king silenced his merchants' cries of distress by reminding them that they would have nothing left at all if the Vanyar took the city—nothing, most likely including their lives, and their wives and children's virtue. They opened their warehouses, grumbling about repayment and recovering their goods when the crisis was past. So the merchants, fishermen, and laborers alike took their turns on the archery field, then on the wall, and the builders directed them in raising what was surely the most expensive barrier ever to surround a city—the bulk of it being ordinary fir and pine, mixed in with granite and basalt from the nearby quarries—but adorned here and there with marble and cedar and ebony.

All this time, the king's agents were very busy, though seldom seen. Many of Ulahane's worshipers disappeared—they were later found, outraged but unharmed, in the cellar of the king's hall—and the one priest of the scarlet god who set foot outside the temple was found lying in an alley, his own blood pooled about him. The other priests showed very little desire for an outing after that.

While all this went on about them, Ohaern and Noril were seen only as passing silhouettes behind the columns of Ranol's temple. Clouds of vapor issued from those colonnades, though. Odors sharp and pungent alternated with exotic perfumes. Everyone wondered what magic the sage and the smith were brewing together, but the only people curious enough to sneak close to look, disappeared into the shadows. They were in the forefront of those

later found in the king's cellar, still loudly protesting their innocence—but since they bore the jackal's-head tattoo of Ulahane's
ardent worshipers, the king heard their pleas with a skeptical ear.

When the scouts reported the Vanyar horde only a few day's
march from the new city wall, Ohaern left the magic to Noril and
Rahani's priestess—who had joined them because Noril trusted
her, and she had offered to help. So Ohaern left the two of them to
stew in their own magic, and picked a small band of the king's soldiers to lead out against the enemy.

"Why should you lead us?" demanded the Captain of the
Guard. "We have been soldiers all our lives! You, you have only
been a soldier when it pleased you!"

"I have been a *warrior*," Ohaern corrected, "and still am. Biriae
are always warriors, even when we are hunting or fishing—or forging iron. And a warrior of the forests knows ways to come upon an
enemy that a soldier of the field never learns."

The captain set himself, eyes narrowing. "You are audacious to
say that to our faces!"

"I will do more than that," Ohaern promised. "I will prove it—
but only to those of your men whom I have chosen, not to you.
You know the ways of the city far better than I; you must stay
here to guard."

The captain's lip curled. "Is that your strategy? That you should
lead troops outside the wall, while I command them here?"

"Part of it," Ohaern confirmed, "though Lucoyo must command the archers."

"I, stay here?" the half-elf cried. "I am twice the sneak you are,
huntsman! Twice as deft, twice as slight!"

"Twice the archer," Ohaern countered.

Lucoyo set his jaw. "You know only the forests! I was raised
to follow the great herds! Surely I will know the way these cow-
drivers think far better than you!"

"I know them well enough," Ohaern returned, "for I can say
where their chariots will roll. You must stay, Lucoyo. When it is
time to lead out the archers, you may sally forth."

Then Ohaern went.

He went with a band of twenty, out along a watercourse that

had worn its way down ten feet below the level of the plain. He went north, toward the place where the Vanyar had been sighted—and as he went, he taught his men how to hide among the rocks and bushes, so that by the time they came to the Vanyar, they could disappear in seconds. A good tracker could still trace them, and a warrior who knew that an enemy might be hiding near could have found them—but the Vanyar would not.

As soon as they could smell the smoke of the Vanyar's fires, they went into the shadows of the bank and moved from bush to bush and rock to rock, as Ohaern had taught them. They were still visible, but did not catch the unwary eye—and the Vanyar slave women who clambered down the bank to fetch water were not wary at all. The warriors froze, then edged back out of sight and waited until the mutter of bitter and dispirited talk faded above them as the slave women climbed back up the bank. Then they edged forward, until they could smell the stench of too many horses in too close a space and went to ground, invisible to all but the most experienced eye. There they waited until dark, until the singing and stamping and quarreling were done, until the camp was quiet above them. Then Ohaern beckoned his men forward, gathered them together, and breathed, "Seek for sentries, and take them first. Then loose the horses."

"May we not slay them?" whispered one fiery-eyed youth.

"Only as you leave the camp," Ohaern answered.

Then up they went, up and out of the watercourse, slipping silently through the night past tents full of snores and past slaves who slept fitfully on hard ground. One by one they came up behind the sentries; only one managed to cry out—and that cry was strangled quickly—before the garrotes did their work. The volunteers were all guards who had killed before, when criminals had attacked them; now they were grim and hard-faced at having to kill from behind, the more so as the Vanyar thrashed and twisted furiously. Ohaern had warned them that the Vanyar were hardened to pain and took a great deal of killing, and he was right—but at last each pair of soldiers lowered its victim to the ground and crept toward the circles of horses.

Here and there a beast whinnied with uncertainty as his hobbles were cut and his picket rein, too—but the soldiers were almost done before they heard a sleepy voice demand something in the Vanyar tongue. They froze, all looking toward Ohaern—but he nodded and pantomimed a slap, and they all turned to whack the horses on the rumps, filling the night with shouts and bloodcurdling howls. The horses screamed and burst out of their circles, bolting in fright for open ground.

The Vanyar rose like bears from a winter's sleep, roaring and famished and thirsting for blood. The soldiers gave it to them, slitting throats and slashing with their swords as they passed. No Vanyar sought to bar their way—they were too busy jumping back from terrified horses, and the soldiers followed in the animals' wake. Here and there a Vanyar leaped in after a horse had passed, howling in anger, and a soldier met his axe with a short sword—while another soldier slipped around behind and split the Vanyar's head. Then on they ran.

Finally, with the camp in an uproar behind them, the soldiers met at the rendezvous point—a huge rock that thrust up out of the plain, midway between the camp and the city.

"How many are we?" Ohaern gasped.

The soldiers turned to tally one another, panting, then reported. "Las and Odro are missing, but all others are here."

"I saw Las fall with a Vanyar spear through him," one trooper reported.

"I saw a barbarian split Odro's head with his axe," another added grimly. "They shall pay for that, five times over!"

"They have already," Ohaern assured him, "but let us not count our kills until we are safely back in Cashalo."

A scream split the night, and a horse, crazed with fright, charged down at them. The soldiers leaped back with cries of alarm, but Ohaern cried, "Catch him!" and threw himself at the beast's lead rope. He caught it, but the horse yanked him off his feet and dragged him bumping over the plain. The soldiers jolted out of their surprise and ran after—and Ohaern's weight slowed the beast enough for them to catch it. The beast plunged and reared, but soldiers helped the smith back to his feet and, bruised but still game, he pulled the horse down, making soothing noises. The other soldiers caught the sense of it and joined him, crooning as they would to their dogs, and finally petting the beast until it had calmed enough to follow on a lead rope.

"Why?" asked a soldier.

"Because I saw some of you daring souls cling to their backs in escape," Ohaern answered. "If we can all learn to do that *without* falling off, we may be able to hand the Vanyar a very unpleasant surprise—*if* we can steal enough of the beasts! I shall take this animal to Cashalo. The rest of you, back into the ditch!"

But they were not willing to let Ohaern risk capture alone, so a handful of them trotted with him and the horse, out across the plain. The Vanyar were slow restoring order to their camp and catching and calming their mounts, so Ohaern and his band were just coming back in through the new city gate when the lookout atop the wall sent up the alarm, as he saw Vanyar chariots appear on the horizon.

The barbarians drove up, shouting in rage and hurling spears that struck only wood and stone, then shaking their fists at the Cashalites as they swerved the chariots past the wall and rode away. An archer bent his bow, grinning, but Lucoyo laid a hand on his shoulder. "No. Do not let them know our range until they come in force."

"Give me a bow, Lucoyo!" Riri said fiercely, his eyes burning in the moonlight. He sat atop an upright tree trunk behind the wall, with his two friends to either side. "Let me see the color of Vanyar blood!"

"You shall have your chance, fisherman—I promise you that," Lucoyo said. "But not tonight."

Riri went back to fletching the arrow he was making, snarling, "One Vanyar shall die for each arrow I can shoot!"

Only one? Lucoyo thought, but he did not say it aloud. He could have sworn that the intensity of the cripple's hatred could have slain a dozen Vanyar by itself.

It was Riri's great regret, and that of his friends, that they could not go out to help slay Vanyar—but it was Ohaern's great relief, for he knew the lame fishermen would not have been able to wait to wreak their revenge until he gave the word, and would have given away the attack. But he led five more raids, then finally heeded the demand of the Captain of the Guard—backed by the king—that he was too valuable to risk. By that time his commandos were experienced enough to raid by themselves. Ohaern agonized over them while they were out, and mourned each one lost—but he could not avoid the press of the work in Cashalo. He consoled himself with the knowledge that of the raiders who died, each took ten and sometimes thirty times their number with them to the Afterworld.

By the time the Vanyar came in sight of the city, their numbers had been reduced by a thousand. More importantly, their morale had been reduced far more sharply than that. They were angry and burning for revenge—but they were also nervous and, for the first time, a little uncertain.

But they affected nonchalance. They pitched camp on the horizon, in sight of the city walls, and strolled about while the smoke from their cooking fires darkened the sunset. Ohaern and Lucoyo walked the length of the wall, calming their archers and spearmen and promising them blood on the morrow—but telling them not to waste arrows tonight, or to press for a sally. Ohaern did send his commandos out, with the result that the Vanyar had scarcely settled down to sleep when their camp erupted in an uproar. And scarcely had they settled down from *that* when the night erupted again, and again. Cashalo lost a dozen trained soldiers that night, but the Vanyar had little sleep—so it was a surly, snappish horde that took the field at dawn the next morning, red-eyed and nervous from lack of sleep. When they attacked, it was by marching forward till they were just out of bowshot, for what good were their proud chariots against a high wall? But they centered on the wooden section of the wall, and many of the Vanyar carried firepots.

"Nock!" Lucoyo called, and arrows rattled against bows as they were laid to bowstrings all along the wall. He glanced up at Ohaern, who nodded, and the half-elf called, "Pull!" Bows bent in a row of curves, and Lucoyo called, "Loose!"

Hundreds of shafts hissed against staves, and arrows darkened the air, then fell among the Vanyar with murderous effect. The howl of surprise, fear, and anger rose clearly to the wall. The Vanyar churned like an anthill in a flood, pressing away from the deadly hail. But those in back did not understand the press and were slow yielding—slow enough for two more flights to sting and stab, and by the time the Vanyar were able to pull back out of bowshot, they left hundreds of dead to mark where their line had stood. Once they were safe, a low and ugly rumble swelled from their lines—the sound of the lust for revenge.

"They would have tortured you for their pleasure even if you had not slain any of them," Ohaern told the archers as he paced their lines. "They shall not hurt you worse for having slain some of them. But even if they could, your only escape would be to slay every one—or so many that they flee in terror."

"Loose!" Lucoyo yelled, and the shafts filled the sky again. The Vanyar howled with fright and rage as they discovered that the bows of Cashalo had even greater range than they had thought. They ran back in such haste that for a few minutes they turned into a jostling, shouting mob and retired very far indeed. When they turned about, their rumble built toward rage.

"Hold your arrows nocked," Lucoyo ordered. "They will charge in an instant."

They did. One huge Vanyar howled, waving his axe aloft, then charged toward the wall. The others echoed his howl, charging behind him. In three long, ragged lines, thousands of Vanyar came pelting toward the city with bloodcurdling ululations.

"Hold!" Lucoyo snapped. "Wait until they are closer, much closer . . . Pull! Loose! Now!"

This time the arrows flew down in a dense cloud. The Vanyar whipped up shields with yells of defiance. Arrows thudded into leather and wood—but other arrows found living targets. Vanyar went down, and other Vanyar tripped over them and fell, rolling. The lines behind them tried to hurdle the roiling obstacle; some succeeded, but others tripped and rolled in their own turn, and were trampled by the third line as often as they were spared.

"Still they come!" Riri cried, bending his bow again.

"Let us see how well they think!" Lucoyo cried. "Every third man, fire straight into them! Every first and second man, fire into the sky, to rain upon their heads!"

There was a moment's confusion while everyone worked out who was first, who second, and who third.

"Third archers! Pull!" Lucoyo cried, then, "First and second! Pull! Third, loose! First and second, loose!"

A scattered flight of arrows shot straight toward the Vanyar, and the barbarians snapped their shields up to catch them. Points thudded into leather and wood, and the Vanyar let out a shout of vindication and contempt—which changed to shrieks of horrified surprise as more arrows rained down upon them. Most who had not already fallen had the presence of mind to pull their shields up overhead. The others simply turned and charged back into their own lines, and the horde churned into chaos.

"Well done, half-elf!" Riri crowed, and a cheer went up all along the wall.

Even now, the spark of outrage flared in Lucoyo, to be called "half-elf"—but he realized that Riri had not meant it as an insult and turned to grin at the lamed fisherman. "It will not work a second time," he cautioned, "at least, if they are as smart as they are ferocious."

And the Vanyar were proving their ferocity, for they charged again with a low, ugly roar. The front line bore its shields before them, and the men behind held them overhead.

"Smart indeed!" Lucoyo snapped. "Shoot for their feet!"

Bows thrummed along the wall, and Vanyar fell rolling—but their mates, prepared for this, leaped over them and came on, lowering their shields. Fallen men scrambled out of the way, trying to regain their footing; some of them succeeded.

"Shoot their feet, too!" Lucoyo cried, but he knew his part of the battle was almost done, for the human wave was rolling closer and closer. Bows thrummed, arrowheads bit ankles and shins, Vanyar fell—but more came on.

Still, the warriors who hit the wall were far fewer in number than they had been.

"Archers back!" Ohaern roared. "Pikemen to the fore!"

The archers leaped down off the ramparts, and the spearmen scrambled into their places. Those spears were long—eight feet long—and they stabbed downward as the Vanyar clambered atop one another's shoulders, forming a human ladder in an attempt to scale the twelve-foot wall. That only required three men, the third leaping over—but even as that third man scrambled up, an eight-foot pike stabbed the second man. All down the line the second man fell back with a cry choked by blood, and the third toppled with him. Here and there the third man came up fast enough so that the spear struck down into him; even more rarely, the third man brought his shield up in time to ward off the spear point, and managed to leap over the wall. The spearman stepped aside, and an arrow struck into the Vanyar's chest. Even then the barbarian warriors kept fighting, hewing about them with their swords as Death pressed its cuneiform into their faces, until they finally fell from the parapet, where other spears transfixed the dead bodies through the chest, just to be sure.

Here and there spears broke; here and there the barbarians were just a little too quick, and the spearmen died, their chests ripped open, falling from the parapet, their bodies striking hard against the invaders, knocking them askew even in death. Their wives caught up their fallen spears, shrieking in grief and rage, and struck downward again and again, until sword points took them and they died with one last stroke.

Then, suddenly, the fight was done. The Vanyar were retreating—not running, but pulling back, gathering up their wounded as they went, driving their chariots forward to take away the bodies of their dead. Slowly, their lines moved away, with much shaking of swords and shouting of curses, calling down the wrath of Ulahane on the heads of the people of Cashalo—but move away they did.

The defenders stared, scarcely believing their eyes. Then a huge cheer erupted, tearing along the wall until the whole city seemed to be howling with joy and victory. The Vanyar heard and raised their swords, answering with a shout of murderous rage.

"They threaten that they shall yet capture the city," Riri translated.

"I do not doubt it," Lucoyo said grimly, "and I fear they may be right."

"If they come again, we shall slay them again!" one of the Cashalo traders said, grinning.

"Will you indeed?" Lucoyo turned to him. "Are you willing to pay the price?"

The trader frowned. "What price is that?"

"Constant drill," Lucoyo answered, "constant training in the weapons of war—and not just bows and spears, but *all* the weapons of war—slings and swords and shields and axes. Constant, and early—raising your sons in the Way of the Warrior from their earliest days, aye, and your daughters, too! Their earliest toys must be wooden swords, their earliest games mock battles. Will you pay that price, peaceful trader?"

The man stared at him, appalled. Then his face hardened, and he said, "Aye—for must we not? We have no choice."

"Oh, yes," Riri told him, "you have a choice. Just look at me."

Farther along the wall the king clapped Ohaern on the back, crying, "We have won, War Chief, we have won! I scarcely thought we could, but we have won!"

"Aye, we have won." Ohaern could not restrain a grin. "But do not relax your vigilance, O King—the Vanyar shall return!"

The king sobered at once. "Aye, they will not leave it at this, will they? No, we must be watchful indeed."

Ohaern gestured at the writhing bodies below the wall. "And what shall you do with their wounded?"

"What of *our* wounded!" The king turned to bark at the Captain of the Guard. "Send out men to see if any of our people who fell outside the wall still live!"

"Guard that party well," Ohaern advised, "from the ground, but also from the wall."

The Captain of the Guard nodded and turned away. The king turned back to survey the wounded Vanyar, who sat or lay, clutching bleeding wounds or the stumps of limbs, white-faced, but with lips clamped tight to hold in cries of pain. "Indeed," the king said heavily, "what shall we do with these?"

"Geld them!" Riri cried, face lit with savage joy. "Hamstring them! Do to them as they have done to us, to all their captives—as they would have done to you!"

Silence fell about them.

"There is justice in what he says." But even Lucoyo could find no enthusiasm for the idea.

"If we gave only that justice, though, we would be no better than they." The king lifted his head with decision. "We shall bind their wounds, we shall see them healed—but they shall serve us as our slaves!"

Riri's face flamed with anger, and he pointed with a shaking arm. "Geld that one, at least! For he is a chieftain."

Everyone turned to stare.

The captive in question set a hand against the wall and pushed himself to his feet, though one leg hung useless, still bleeding freely. "He speaks truth," the man said in barely understandable Cashalan. "I am. What shall you do with a Vanyar chieftain, O You-who-call-yourself-king?"

The people all turned to stare at the king, holding their breath as they waited for his answer.

CHAPTER 20

The king said slowly, "If he deemed himself the highest of the high, he shall become the lowest of the low. No, we shall neither geld nor hamstring him, for that is how you treat a beast, and if we pretend that he is less than human, then we shall become less than human. But he shall fetch wood and draw water, and do all the things that any slave does."

The Vanyar chieftain stood stiffly against the wall on his one good foot, stiff in outrage, crying, "I am no common man, but Ashdra, a chieftain of the Vanyar! How dare you treat me as a slave!"

"By the fortunes of war," said Ohaern, his face hard, and the king agreed. "We treat you as you have done to defeated rival chieftains in your own turn. Be glad we allow you life."

"I would sooner have death!"

"Keep on with such impertinence and you may find it." The king lifted his head to look out over his people. "All the Vanyar who live shall be slaves of the king! The others I shall sell to the merchants— but this one I shall keep for myself; we can spare him this much token of respect. Take him away! Take them all away to the cellar of my castle and see they are tended till their wounds are healed. Then they shall set to work indeed, helping us strengthen our wall!"

Ashdra gave an incoherent shout, but guardsmen held spears to his throat and heart. As they laid hands on him he turned, striking out at them with hard fists—and the guards struck back with the butts of their spears. When the tussle was over, one or two guardsmen were picking themselves up with black looks, rubbing the places the Vanyar chieftain had bruised, while others bound his unconscious form to the shafts of two spears and bore him away. His tribesmen fought as he had, and if they did not fight as well, they certainly fought well enough to knock out several of the fishermen before they were finally borne down, then borne away.

"They are beaten!" the king cried. "Hail Ohaern and Lucoyo, who have showed us the path to victory!"

"Hail, Ohaern!" the people cried. "Hail, Lucoyo!" And they surged forward to seize the Biri and the half-elf, bearing them up on their shoulders and parading in triumph to the king's hall.

Lucoyo looked about him in amazement, holding hard to the shoulders of the men who bore him. He could scarcely believe that he, the outcast, the stranger, the man who was always an alien, could be acclaimed as a hero!

Ahead of him Ohaern was taken aback, too, but quickly recovered his poise. He began to smile and to wave to the people about him, calling, "Thanks, brave fighters! All thanks, valiant people of Cashalo! Valiant bowmen, valiant archer-women! It is you who have won the victory, not I!"

But the people cheered him all the harder, for they knew the truth.

At the doors of the castle, they set the outlanders down beside the king, who grinned widely as he waved at the cheering throng. When their noise began to ebb, he called, "Tonight we shall feast, though two hundred must offer to fast and guard the walls so that others may rejoice!"

"Your scouts must be out and about," Ohaern muttered.

"Scouts, you must be scouring the countryside!" the king called. "All others, come to the central circle, to roast fat meats and pour out wine! We have earned our jubilation!"

The crowd roared their approval, then began to move away to the fire pits in the great open space before the king's palace.

"Come." The king led Lucoyo and Ohaern through the great

portals and into his hall. "While the cooks make ready the festival, let us have wine—and rest!"

They came into a large room with heaps of cushions. The king called, "Ho! Bring wine!" Then he sat down and leaned back against the softness of fine cloth over down as women appeared, bearing wine and platters of fruits. Ohaern stared for a moment, unable to conceal his surprise. The women he had seen in Cashalo all these past two weeks had been clothed decently, if lightly, but these handmaidens of the king were in cloth so fine that he could see through it, though not clearly, and wore only skirts and bodices, with their midriffs left bare. Moreover, each was a beauty, very obviously selected for grace and form.

"They are lovely, are they not?"

The king's words brought Ohaern out of his reverie with a start. He tore his gaze away—and saw Lucoyo, his eyes so wide they nearly bulged, staring at the women and hissing, "Yessss—O King! They are comely indeed!"

"This office has heavy burdens," the king told him, "but it has its pleasures, too. You see now why I thought it best to fight— these butterflies are worth defending."

He said it in a joking tone, but Ohaern caught the seriousness beneath it and knew that this king would have defended any woman, young or old, pretty or ugly. "Your people are, indeed, worth defending," he said. "Therefore I think it unwise that you put the captive Vanyar in your cellar with the priests and worshipers of Ulahane."

"Why? Think you they will brew mischief together?"

"I do not doubt it for a moment."

"Nor do I," said the king, "but I also think they will find ways to come together and brew mischief even if we let them free—so it is better to have them where we can watch them all and have spies among them, while we may."

Ohaern stared; the king was more subtle than he had realized, " 'While you may?' But what could prevent you?"

"Peace," the king sighed, "and the worshipers of Ulahane whom we had no reason to imprison. When we are sure the threat is past and the Vanyar have passed on, I shall have to let them go free again."

"What?" Lucoyo tore his gaze from the nearest handmaiden and fastened it on the king. "Wherefore? You are the king! Is not your word law?"

"No," the king replied. "There is the ancient law of the fishermen, handed down from parent to child since time began—and we have added to it the laws of the foreigners with whom we trade, if those laws are simple and blend well with our own. If I flout those laws in my judgments or commands, the people will be discontent—and if I do it too many times, they will pull me down and choose a new king in my place."

"So," Ohaern breathed, "you are not so different from a tribal chieftain, after all."

"Only in state, and the number of people I lead," said the king, "but I cannot force them all. Indeed, I can only guide the force that comes from all, against those who break our laws."

"But there are ways of gaining power over all the people!" Lucoyo leaned forward, frowning. "You have guardsmen, and surely there are many of your fishermen who would be glad to join their ranks, now that they have learned something of fighting! Pay enough of them, and you could force all your people to your will!"

Ohaern stared at the half-elf in horror. Had Lucoyo always been like this, and he had never seen it?

"No doubt I could," the king agreed, "and do not think I have not toyed with the notion. But I wish to lead, not to rule—to judge, not to force people to obey my whims. That is not my way, not what I think should be the way of men who know the customs and history of their people, as all folk should. No, I think we may leave your tyranny to the Vanyar."

"So." Lucoyo's eyes gleamed as he leaned back among the cushions. "Yes, I think we may—to them, and to the nomads, who raised me and cast me out."

Ohaern sighed with relief. Lucoyo had only been testing the king.

Hadn't he?

If he had, he might as well have tested the whole people—but the new Vanyar slaves were doing that, and quite well, it seemed.

• • •

In the next few weeks, as Ohaern walked among the people, he saw young men gather around the Vanyar whenever they had a few minutes' rest between tasks. "What is it like to ride in a chariot?" they would ask. "How do you fight with a sword?" And the Vanyar were glad to tell them, expanding visibly, basking in the admiration.

"This battle seems to have kindled a taste for warfare in the young," Lucoyo told Ohaern, frowning.

"Yes, and I could wish for better ways to satisfy that taste than to ask the Vanyar," Ohaern answered. "We must begin a school for swordplay, Lucoyo."

But even that did little good; the Vanyar slaves seemed to find ways to be given chores that brought them to overlook the central circle when Ohaern and Lucoyo were teaching. Aftertimes, Ohaern would overhear them telling the young men what Ohaern was teaching them correctly—and the many more things that he was teaching them incorrectly.

Actually, there was little enough doubt as to how the Vanyar were being assigned to the circle at practice times—the king, receiving word from his scouts that the Vanyar horde had driven on to the east, bypassing Cashalo in favor of easier prey, had released the priests of Ulahane and their most ardent worshipers. When he sold the Vanyar slaves, many of them were bought by those self-same priests, and the rest were bought by the ardent worshipers.

"They conspire against you," Ohaern warned the king.

"Surely my spies will bring word of it," the king replied.

Ohaern was worried that the king seemed so complacent—and worried more when one of those spies was found in a waterfront gutter one morning with his throat slit. But the king was more concerned that so anonymous a murder could be done in his city than he was about the identity of the victim. He recruited more guardsmen and doubled the watch about the docks—and did not seem to notice that the new recruits were all from the young men who had so ardently listened to the Vanyar slaves.

Then Ohaern chanced to come into the king's hall and find him surrounded by his handmaidens—but with the Vanyar captain firing the brazier, for the nights had become chill. "But why should the builders fill the places where the ebony and marble have been taken out of the wall?" the Vanyar was saying. "Your people fared well enough without such a bulwark for all ages past, and surely your young men have learned enough of fighting to be a wall in their own right."

"Do not believe it!" Ohaern cried. "Yes, O King, your young men have been diligent in practice at swordplay—but they can not yet stand against men who have studied war from their cradles!"

The Vanyar captain turned a venomous gaze on Ohaern. The smith returned it with a look that should have frozen the man and shivered him to pieces, and for a moment the women drew back, frightened by the unspoken menace in the air.

The king disrupted it quickly. "I will not forbid a man to speak, Ohaern, even if he is a slave."

"Laudable," Ohaern grunted, "and I forget that you have the sense to know when not to listen."

"Indeed I do," the king returned, "but I know also when to hearken, and I have learned that grains of wisdom may be hidden even in the prattling of a child. Are you so wedded to your wall, Ohaern?"

"So long as there are Vanyar roaming the valleys in their chariots, and people in Cashalo to tell them when the roadways are clear? No, O King, *I* am not wedded to the wall—but Cashalo should be wedded to its freedom, and the wall is the ring that is the sign of that marriage!"

"Do you accuse me of treachery?" The Vanyar rose, every muscle taut.

"No," said Ohaern, "I accuse you of loyalty—to your own tribe!" He turned to the king. "He profits nothing by giving you good advice, but regains his freedom and his rank by counseling you falsely!"

The Vanyar captain took a step closer, his eye glinting, his lips parting in a snarl. Ohaern's face froze and he stepped toward the Vanyar, drawing his sword.

"No!" the king cried, but Ohaern only reversed the sword and held it out to the Vanyar. The captive snatched it with a cry of delight—and Ohaern drew his long knife.

"Now I say *no!*" the king thundered, and both men hesitated. "Give back the sword!" he commanded, on his feet and moving toward them both. The Vanyar glanced at him out of the corner of his eye, then reluctantly reversed the sword and handed it back to Ohaern. The smith snatched it, sheathed both sword and knife, and turned away, simmering.

The wall began to come down, and the lumber of which it had been built returned to the warehouses. Ohaern watched it go with misgiving, but the merchants to whom the materials belonged seemed relieved and quite satisfied.

"Is it not ironic," asked Lucoyo, "that the slaves who tear down the wall are Vanyar?"

"I see no irony at all," said Ohaern, "only a threat."

The irony came when he heard one of the Vanyar slaves telling some youths, "Oh, you people of Cashalo have been noble and generous, to be sure! But you have left us, your captives, able to rise up and strike against you."

"Not that we would, of course," said another Vanyar slave, and the first nodded. "Now, we Vanyar would have cut a captive's hamstrings, so that he might not stand against us—and gelded him, so that we could be sure that any children born could only be our own!"

"Besides," said the second, "it makes a captive more docile, more ready to obey, less likely to rebel."

The young men listened, eyes wide, nodding, hanging on the warriors' every word. "Do you say we should treat you thus?" one asked.

"Oh, nay!" the Vanyar said quickly, and his partner chuckled. "We are glad indeed that you are so merciful! But we did expect, at the least, some curses and kicks, to remind us who was slave and who master."

"How would you have treated women you captured?" asked another young man.

"Why, what are women for, youngling?" the slave returned, and his friend gave a lascivious chuckle and answered, "They are for any man—who can pay the price!"

"Would you sell them for bed-slaves, then?" The young men seemed horrified, but held by morbid fascination.

"Aye, if the price were high enough," the slave said, "though since every Vanyar has two or three such, none would buy, unless the woman were amazingly beautiful."

"Which are few, once enslaved," his friend said judiciously. "It is for that reason that the beauties are treated more kindly—but we get our money from letting a man spend an hour with the woman for a fee. Strangers, of course, though even some of our own nation find the notion appealing enough."

"A man who owns a beautiful slave can become rich indeed," the other said, and Ohaern turned away, sickened. He knew he should have beaten the Vanyar for speaking thus, no matter what questions they were asked; he knew he should have rebuked the youths for asking—but he also knew it would have done little or no good, no, not even if the king himself had done the rebuking.

Instead he went to the Street of the Lantern Houses and hauled Lucoyo out of the wallow of delights that were now his for the asking. The half-elf squalled protest, but Ohaern dragged him out onto the street, Lucoyo in one hand and his bow and quiver in the other, scarcely giving the half-elf time to finish pulling on his trews. "You have reveled long enough, archer! We must be on our way!"

"On the road again?" Lucoyo bleated in dismay. "Go by yourself, Biri! I like it here!"

"Will you like it when the Vanyar come galloping down this street in their chariots, slaying all they see?"

Lucoyo froze in the act of belting his tunic. "So. You have seen that, too, have you?"

"If you have, why have you stayed so long?" Ohaern looked up at the cries of protest and saw the half-naked women denouncing him—but one began to beckon, and several others laughed and joined her. "No, I see why. Well, I must be your will, Lucoyo."

"My will *not*, rather," the half-elf muttered, cinching his belt. "But how if the Vanyar do not come back?"

"How if the winter does not come back?" Ohaern grunted. "Though the Vanyar have no need to—the men they have left as slaves will do it for them! This city may yet be delivered up to Ulahane, archer, with or without the Vanyar—through no weapon sharper than foul advice and depraved teaching!"

"No weapon sharper, indeed." But Lucoyo cast a guilty glance back at the caroling women. An oafish grin creased his face for a minute, and he lifted a hand to wave.

"Then, too," Ohaern mused, "there is the question of what fate awaits the man who has offended Ulahane personally, in a city that Ulahane's minions have taken."

Lucoyo's hand stilled in midair, then began to wave good-bye. He turned resolutely away. "Pleasant as they are, no woman should be constrained to such a life—especially since I have seen what use they are put to when they have lost their beauty. Although I had begun to realize that I could become rich by—" He slapped his own face. "No, you have the right of it, hunter. We cannot save this town by staying." He looked up at Ohaern with haunted eyes. "Perhaps we cannot save it at all."

"Perhaps not," Ohaern said grimly, "but it shall not be for lack of trying! We must go, Lucoyo—to find the source of the evil that seeps into this place through its very stones!"

"Yes," Lucoyo said glumly, "we must go."

The king was distressed to find them determined to leave and asked what he could do to induce them to stay—but when Ohaern told him it was nothing less than cleansing the city of all who worshiped Ulahane, the king became sad, for his ancient law would not permit such a thing without proof of cause. He decided, therefore, to give Lucoyo and Ohaern a farewell befitting a hero, even a king—but Ohaern, realizing that would be as good as painting them green for all the minions of the scarlet god to see, refused, claiming the simple life to which he had been reared forbade such vanity, and he bade the king farewell with heartfelt wishes for good fortune—wishes which he sadly feared would do no good at all. Instead, he and Lucoyo slipped out of the city in Riri's canoe—the fisherman was glad to make them a gift of it—and drifted past the borders of Cashalo in the last rays of the setting sun.

As darkness drew in, they beached the canoe on a spit of sand—but before they could step out to draw the craft up, big hands at the ends of long arms laid hold of the bows, and a small gnarled figure drew the craft high on the bank. "It is good to see you safe!" cried the dwerg. "I feared that sinkhole had swallowed you up!"

Lucoyo overcame his surprise. "It nearly did," he said, and climbed out of the boat. "It is good to see you again, my friend." He stretched, looking about him. "Suddenly I feel clean of a soil I had not known I had accumulated, O Smith!"'

"I feel it, too." Ohaern threw his head back and drew in a deep breath of the cool air of evening, then exhaled sharply and said, "I shall build the fire."

"No, I shall!" Lucoyo said quickly. "There is dross in me that needs to burn away."

"Neither of you shall," the dwerg chuckled, "for I already have. Come! There is only one hare roasting for my dinner, but I can quickly find two more."

So they spent the evening beginning to live again as hunter and nomad should live—in the open by a campfire, with talk of simple things, but with a being for whom simplicity was always under-laid by complexity. By bedtime they had finally learned the dwerg's name—Grakhinox—and his rank, which was only that of smith—which was to say, an ordinary dwerg, a very ordinary per-son, for he came of a people who were all smiths. And he was young, for his kind—scarcely more than an apprentice, only a hun-dred fifty years old.

As they paddled away into the morning mists, Lucoyo mused, "It would seem that Ulahane is as much at work among the city folk as he is among the barbarians."

"Or as much at work among the barbarians as in the city," Ohaern rejoined. "Do not forget that his stronghold is Kuru."

"A telling point." Lucoyo grinned. "What will happen, I won-der, when Ulahane's city of Kuru is beset by Ulahane's barbarian Vanyar?"

"Whatever occurs," Ohaern returned, "you may be sure that the Scarlet One will delight in every second of the carnage."

"True, true." Lucoyo nodded. "After all, no matter who loses that fight, he wins."

CHAPTER 21

"Is there no end to these plowed fields?" Lucoyo stared at the endless rows of green shoots. The companions had been watching them drift by ever since they had left Cashalo. They would have wondered who farmed them if they had not passed two villages of mud huts with thatched roofs, or seen the occasional farmer out in a field, bent over a hoe. But as the day aged toward evening, they began to see the farmers trooping home, their mattocks over their shoulders. The men were closer to the shore now, and looked up as they saw the travelers pass—looked up, and grinned, and waved. Lucoyo waved back, albeit somewhat hesitantly—he wasn't sure it was the wise thing to do.

"Always return goodwill, Lucoyo." Ohaern waved back at the people on shore with a broad if somewhat insincere smile. As they drifted farther, a village came into sight, with a sloping ramp of earth going down into the water. The farmers waved, then beckoned to them.

Ohaern's smile gelled, and he asked Grakhinox, "You have roamed the countryside while you waited for us, have you not?"

"Aye," said Grakhinox.

"Do you know anything of these people?"

Grakhinox shrugged. "If they are like the folk who live hard by Cashalo, they trade with the city. Those folk fled when the Vanyar came near—those who could. Many were caught."

Ohaern did not ask what had been done to them; he was fairly sure he knew.

"These have not been caught, and have not fled," Grakhinox finished.

"That is because we travel east, and the Vanyar came down from the north. Do you think we can trust these people?"

Women came running down to the landing, waving and calling. Most were young and wore only skirts. Lucoyo's breath hissed in as he watched.

"They seem friendly enough," said Grakhinox, "and I have heard nothing against the farm villages that give Cashalo its food."

The young women were beckoning now, gyrating their hips as they moved in a dance. Drums and reeds had begun to sound.

"Oh, they are friendly indeed!" Lucoyo said. "Surely we will be safe here, smith—safe, and more! Let us stop for the night!"

"Safe? You only wish to be at peril! Of your virtue, that is." But Ohaern nodded and turned the canoe's nose toward the shore. "They look soft enough, at least."

"They do indeed!" Lucoyo breathed.

"If they seek to trouble us, we should have no difficulty winning free."

"Who would want to?" Lucoyo replied. "Surely being free of such as these would not be winning!"

"Does he always speak in riddles?" Grakhinox demanded.

"Only when he wishes to be understood," Ohaern explained.

As their prow plowed into the mud, a dozen willing hands laid hold of it and pulled it high up on the bank. At least half of those hands were female, and Lucoyo gave a glad cry as he leaped out of the canoe. The women responded with trilling mirth and closed about him, caressing his shoulders and chest and pressing his hands to their own. Lucoyo gave an even gladder cry, and the women laughed gaily, echoing his delight.

Grakhinox gave them a jaundiced eye. "I will disappear awhile, I think, O Smith. Call me at need."

Ohaern turned to protest, but the dwerg was gone already—he might have been speaking from the sand beneath the boat! Ohaern had no chance to look, though, for another half-dozen women surrounded him as he stepped from the canoe, and there were hands, nothing but hands all about him, touching, stroking, caressing. He was alarmed to feel a ravening hunger awaking within him, and he caught their wrists with more brusqueness than he should have— but at the looks of astonishment, he forced a smile. "You honor me, good women, but I am a man who has wedded." He chose the words for strict truth. The young women frowned and shook their heads, puzzled, and Ohaern tried again in the halting phrases he had learned in Cashalo. This time the women understood, and lifted their heads, mouths forming O's, and they stepped back— but only a little, only enough for an elder woman to step forward. "Your wife will never know, stranger," she said in the tongue of Cashalo—accented, but recognizable.

Her skirt covered her down to the ankles and up to the shoulders—rank, Ohaern wondered, or modesty? Or perhaps aesthetics . . . "It is nonetheless not the way of our tribe, Grandmother." Ohaern hoped the term was an honorific here, as it was among his own people.

"I am a grandmother, yes, but I am also the priestess Labina," the old woman said.

"I am Ohaern, a simple hunter." He wondered at the jaundiced look Lucoyo gave him. "I intend no disrespect, priestess, but I must live as I have been taught."

"Well, we would never press a man who thought it wrong." Labina gestured to the girls, who lamented, but turned away quickly to Lucoyo. Most were as tall as he, and some taller; their circle parted for a moment, to show the half-elf locked mouth to mouth with a pretty lass, and desire clawed up inside Ohaern again.

Labina saw. "You need not stick so tightly to the ways of your people, young man. You are our guest, and should try our ways."

"But it is not a thing I can undo," Ohaern said, as if each word were being forced out of him. He understood, in some way he could not have explained, that for him, accepting the favors of women he did not know would make him less than himself—and he needed all his strength of soul just now, especially when he was among strangers.

An old man came up—older than the farmers, at least, but still straight and limber, though his beard and hair were white. "You stare at our simple village as if it were something rare and new, young man. Have you never seen a farmers' hamlet before?"

"No, I have not," Ohaern admitted, "nor has my friend. I am a hunter, and my wife gathered the fruits of the earth while I sought game. My friend is a nomad, whose people followed the great wild herds of oxen. We worship the gods of the hunt, though we worship Lomallin the human-lover above all."

"I have not heard of Lomallin." Labina frowned. "Did you worship no goddesses?"

"Oh, yes, as many as our gods. Rahani was foremost among them."

The woman shook her head. "I do not know of her."

Somehow, that troubled Ohaern—but he assured himself that he would find they did worship the goddess, though under another name. "She is Lomallin's friend, war ally, and councilor."

"But not his mate?" Now it was the old man who frowned.

"Not his, no. Lomallin has no mate."

Labina stared, visibly shaken. "A god without a mate! How immoral, how wrong! How wasteful!"

"Lomallin is a wizard," Ohaern explained, "one forced to be also a warrior."

"Ah." The woman's face cleared. "He shall mate when he has won his reputation, then. Enough talk of gods, young man. You look hungry." She took his arm. Both elders smiled and nodded. "Come." They led Ohaern away.

"What goddess do you worship?" Ohaern asked as they led him toward the center of the village. Somehow, from the last interchange, he was sure their highest deity was a goddess.

"Alique, the Great Mother," said the woman, "Alique, and all her children."

Ohaern frowned. "I do not know of Alique. Tell me about her."

"We worship her in two aspects," said the woman. "The one is young, the other mature."

"Ah!" Ohaern nodded, recognizing two familiar goddesses rolled into one. "The maiden, and the mother."

The old man gave a single laugh that never quite opened his mouth, and Labina said, "We do not worship her as a maiden, but as a young woman who receives many lovers."

Ohaern tried not to look shocked. "And bears many children?"

"Yes, though we do not worship that in her as the love goddess, but as the mother. She feeds her children with the bounty of her breasts, then with the fruits of plenty that she draws from the land."

"And heals them, and gives consolation?"

The old man frowned as if at a new thought, and the old woman said, "She must do that, too, I suppose. Surely she is the giver of all good things, with all her little children about her."

"If we worship her with full ardor," said the old man, "she gives us a good harvest."

Ohaern glanced past the village to the fields of green shoots that stretched out as far as he could see. He remembered his own northern forests and the game that was there year-round, with the host of berries and fruits and roots in the summers. "If you do not have a good harvest," he said slowly, "you die."

"Even so." The old man nodded. "The harvest is vital to us, young man, absolutely vital!"

Now Ohaern glanced at the village and realized how many more people it held than his own tribal camp at the edge of the great wood. "Surely, though, even with so many people, you cannot eat all the food you grow!"

"No, we do not." Labina looked up with a smile. "That is the source of our wealth, though, in all things other than food." She swept a hand toward the village. "See the fine ornaments our women wear, the soft fabrics of their skirts and the fine woods that adorn our doorposts! When you dine with us tonight, you will taste wines from far-off lands, and fruits and spices that never grow in this country!"

"Surely your fields do not bear such delicacies!"

"No, but we give our surplus grain to the traders of Cashalo, and they give us jewels and spices and rare foods in return."

Ohaern was amazed with himself, that he had never before wondered where Cashalo obtained its food. Surely he should have realized that so many people could not all be fed by fish from the river, or even from the two seas! And the sea could not grow grain. But that opened another possibility, one that might be very unpleasant, for he realized that where Cashalo's luxuries went, Cashalo's beliefs must follow. "I must warn you," he said slowly, "that the cult of the scarlet god Ulahane is growing rapidly within Cashalo."

"Is it indeed?" Labina looked keenly interested. "But why is that a warning?"

"Because," Ohaern explained, "if all of Cashalo should turn to Ulahane and his ways, they may try to take by force what they now gain by trade."

Labina threw back her head and laughed merrily. "Oh, I think not! You are a worrier, young man—I knew it the moment I saw you!"

"Cashalo is Cashalo," said the old man, grinning, "and it has many gods. No, lad, I thank you for your warning, but I doubt that the Scarlet One could expel all other gods from so great a city."

Ohaern wished he could share their certainty.

He looked about, suddenly realizing that Lucoyo had disappeared completely, and alarm shot through him. "Where is my friend?"

"He has gone with the young women," Labina told him. "They will treat him well, I assure you. You shall see him at dinner."

"Treat him well!" Ohaern turned to her, puzzled. "Why, what do they do?"

"They seek to imitate Alique," said the old man with a knowing smile, "in her younger aspect."

"They shall welcome you, too," Labina told him. "We have many huts that are small temples to the young goddess. Come, I shall show you." She took hold of his arm.

But Ohaern pulled back, alarmed as he felt desire flare. "I must see my friend."

"He is a man grown, surely." The old man frowned. "He can care for himself."

"I am never wholly certain of that. Where is he?"

Labina gave him a sour look, but a burst of shrill laughter came from a large hut near them. She pointed with her cane. "In there—but do not enter, for you might put him off his stride. Let me see how earnestly he gallops." She went inside, then came back in a moment. "No, he has run the first course, and bathes. Go in and talk to him, young man."

Ohaern brushed past her and through the curtain, alarm cooling to dread. Inside, the hut was dim after the blaze of the sunset, but lamps already flared around a huge pit in the floor, lined with tile and filled with water—scented water, and in it wallowed Lucoyo, naked and leaning back against the bosom of a pretty young woman who held a drink for him to sip, while another rubbed his chest and shoulders with oil, and two more, naked in the pool with him, raised his leg and rubbed the oil into it—oil that foamed as they rinsed the leg and rubbed it, slowly and gently.

Ohaern felt desire boil up within him, and stood mute, holding fast against its tide.

Lucoyo raised his head from the goblet with a sigh of pure pleasure—and saw Ohaern, standing rigid and wide-eyed. "Hunter! Welcome! You have found your quarry!" he cried. "I am amazed it took you so long! Girls, did you not bid my friend be welcome?"

"No, for the priest and priestess were talking to him." The woman who spoke was older than the others, old enough to be a mother of a dozen, but still supple, slender, and fully curved. She came toward Ohaern wearing only a strip of silk about her hips, tied in one loose knot from which a tassel hung down to her knees. "Be welcome among us, handsome stranger!" She reached up to caress the huge muscles of his chest, breathing, "Very welcome."

"Aye, strong outlander!" another breathed in his ear. "Come with us!" husked another. "We must wash off the dust of your journey."

The alarm was almost panic, but Ohaern fought to be civil even now. "I thank you, gentle beauties," he stammered, "but I had only need to be sure my friend was well! I must speak further with your priestess!" He turned and blundered out, moans of disappointment and mocking, delighted laughter ringing in his ears. He could scarcely see for the red haze that darkened the evening, but he stumbled away from the hut, down toward the shore, and plunged into the heaving water, letting it cool his skin, cool his ardor—but still the desire wracked him. He sank down into the ripples, letting its saltiness wash over him, cleanse him. He would not be untrue to Ryl! He would not!

When the longing had ebbed enough, he climbed out and let the wind cool him further as the last rays of the sun dried him. Then he walked through the village in the dusk, chatting with everyone he saw, doing all he could to appear relaxed and easygoing, though he felt anything but. The young women who passed gave him looks of reproach, but did indeed pass by as he talked with the men about weather and crops and what farming entailed—but when the men had all moved on, one young woman came up to him with an inviting smile. "Why do you have so great an interest in farming? You are a hunter!"

"Because it is new to me," Ohaern said frankly. "I have a hunger to learn all that I can, about all that is strange to me."

She stepped closer. "I could teach you a great deal, about matters that seem strange to you."

Ohaern stiffened; his skin seemed to vibrate over every inch that faced her. His answering smile felt false even to him. "I thank you for your kindness, but those matters are not so strange as you might think. My wife died only months ago, and I still mourn within."

"Oh!" The woman's allure disappeared as if a door had shut on it, and she stepped back. "Your pardon! I did not know!"

"Nor should you," Ohaern returned, relieved. "I do not think my friend Lucoyo had time to tell you of it."

She smiled, a little reassured. "No, surely he did not." Then she stepped closer again. "Still, grief must be assuaged, and what is broken within can be healed without." Her allure seemed to wrap about her again, like a garment of spider silk. "If you have need of consolation, be sure that I ache to give it."

Ohaern managed a fond smile. "It is very good of you."

"It is the kind of goodness that I long for," she breathed, "for our goddess Alique has shown me the way. Nay, hunter, if you seek your quarry, I shall not be hard to find." She gave him a slumberous look, then turned and strolled away, rolling her hips.

Ohaern stared after her, then managed to tear his gaze away, drawing a deep and very ragged breath as he sent a wordless prayer of thanks to the Afterworld. Even dead, Ryl protected him.

As they gathered for dinner in the village's central circle, though, Ohaern was surprised to see that the young women glanced at him almost with reverence, though desire was still there beneath it—and some of the men even told him, "It is wrong to refuse consolation in your grief, outlander—but I cannot fault you for keeping faith." Even the old priest told him, "You have the self-restraint that fully becomes a man, O Hunter. Still, I beg you to set it aside; the time for mourning is surely past."

It was a thought that gave Ohaern pause. He consulted his heart, though, and found it was not true.

Still, the desire the young women had raised continued to course through him and make his skin tingle at every touch—and there were many touches of hand and soft shoulder and firm breast, all brushing by in the throng, all quite possibly accidental, but more than enough to set Ohaern burning. He began to long for the meal to be over.

The old priest led him to the seat of honor beside Labina, who was dressed now in rich clothing that made her look much more the priestess than she had during the afternoon. Ohaern had scarcely sat down when Lucoyo strolled up, with two giggling girls holding his arms to keep him upright. He joked with them and kissed them elaborately. He was wearing a villager's kilt, and a wreath of flowers about his head. The girls lowered him down to sit beside Ohaern, who wondered how deeply his friend had drunk—but the gaze Lucoyo turned on him was clear, though abstracted, as if he were elated and still not quite believing his good fortune. "Ah, Smith!" he said, grinning. "I hope your evening has been as pleasant as mine!"

"In its way," Ohaern said carefully. "I confess that I am finding more and more pleasure in learning of new ways and new gods and peoples, Lucoyo."

"So am I." Lucoyo turned away to follow a lissome lass with his eyes. "Yes, I must say that I have learned a great many new ways this afternoon, Ohaern, and I have taken great delight in it."

Oddly, Ohaern thought Lucoyo meant that sincerely. He began to wonder if the half-elf saw more than he did.

Then, suddenly, Lucoyo turned to stare directly into Ohaern's eyes. "The young men tell me you must be mad, Ohaern." Sudden concern shadowed his face. "What is wrong? What pains you?"

Oddly touched, Ohaern smiled gently and assured his friend, "They speak so only because I refuse the women's favors, Lucoyo."

"They are right—you *are* mad!" Lucoyo's concern deepened. "Perhaps their priestess can show us a way to cure this, before it grows worse."

Ohaern was tempted to laugh at his friend's sudden seriousness, but only closed his eyes and shook his head. "It is only grief, Lucoyo—grief for my dead wife. I thought I had purged it by going up against Byleo, then by fighting the Klaja, and now the Vanyar—but I find there is a great deal of it left."

"Why, that is a madness of its own sort," Lucoyo said, low, "but one that is enough akin to my own hatred so that I can understand it. But the women tell me their goddess is one who cures, Ohaern—cures the heart as well as the body. In truth, I could believe her devotees may cure even *my* bitterness!"

Ohaern stared in surprise. "Why, I pray that is so!"

"Do, and I will thank you," Lucoyo said gravely. "So if a goddess offers you healing, Ohaern, I pray you—do not refuse it. That would be wrong, that would be very wrong!"

Ohaern just stared into his friend's eyes for a minute, then nodded slowly. "You are right, Lucoyo—it would be wrong indeed. Nay, if a goddess does bring balm for my heart, I will not turn away."

Lucoyo smiled with relief, then clapped his friend on the shoulder with a grin. "Come, we grow too serious! We must rejoice!" He turned to catch up a wine cup and push it into Ohaern's hand. "Drink! Let us rejoice, for we are alive!"

Ohaern unbent enough to celebrate with him, and with them all—to drink, though not too deeply, just enough to feel the slightest bit giddy; to eat a little of each luscious dish; to marvel at the whirling, sinuous dances of the young men and women, and not to throttle the desire they raised. But when the meal was done and half a dozen young women sought to guide him back to their temple, he politely refused them and went instead to the small hut kept ready for visitors. He would not refuse joy, he would not refuse life—but he was not yet ready to embrace it completely, either.

So, all in all, the goddess still took him by surprise when she appeared to him in his dream.

CHAPTER 22

Ohaern dreamed—and, strangely, knew that he dreamed—and his dream was a sunburst, a silent explosion of light. Against it there appeared a form, a feminine form, but so completely, ultimately feminine that any mortal woman who had dared come near would have been unnoticed. Wisps of clothing drifted about her, but nothing that could hide the luxurious curve of hip and breast, or the profile of elegance and rapture. She was at once alluring and remote, elegant and voluptuous, compelling and seductive. She was the ultimate, the ideal, of feminine sexuality—and that, even though all Ohaern could see of her was her silhouette. But the long-pent desire broke loose and raged through him, hammering in his veins, shaking him with its intensity.

"Ohaern!"

Her voice was within him as much as all about, emanating from everywhere at once, but with no doubt that she was its source—and he knew, with wonder and awe, that he was in the presence of a goddess.

"Ohaern!" she commanded. "Come to me!"

The remembrance of Ryl passed through Ohaern's mind, and he

might have hesitated had he not remembered the promise he had given Lucoyo—not to balk if the goddess came to heal him. "I come, lady!" he cried in his dream-voice, and he strove to run toward her—but his limbs seemed sluggish, as if he strove to wade neck-deep through a mire, so that no matter how he strained, he could make little progress. He would have looked down to see what held him, but he could not take his gaze from the goddess. It was almost as if he had no body, or that it mattered nothing whether he did or not—almost as if the desire raged through his soul alone. "I come, lady!" he panted. "I come!"

"Too slowly," she answered, and waved a hand, a gesture of dispelling that ended in beckoning. Suddenly, Ohaern was freed, and he shot toward her like a bird in flight—no, not "like"; he *did* fly, somehow he knew it!

But fast as he came, she receded faster. "Why so slow, O Hunter?" she teased. "You shall never catch me that way!"

"Tell me how I shall, then," he panted.

"By laboring long in my service," she answered. "By chasing me through hazard and woe, through hardship and chaos—but if you persevere, you shall come to me when you have finished the fight."

"Must I battle my way to you, then?"

"Do you fear to?" she taunted. "Or is the effort too great?"

"I fear neither danger nor labor!" he cried in his dream. "Whom must I fight?"

"Ulahane, for he is my enemy. Best him, and you shall find me waiting."

"I shall, though I die in the attempt!"

"Even then, you shall find me—but only if your death comes in trying." She moved, and her slightest shift of posture inflamed him even more. "But before you attack Ulahane, you must fight the two-faced goddess."

"What—the goddess of the villagers?" Ohaern cried in surprise. "Are you not she?"

Thunder crashed, and lightning split the sky behind her. "I am not, and the question rasps upon me as harshly as it would wound you if I were to ask if you were a Klaja!"

Ohaern shrank in alarm—and in fear of losing this ultimate object of desire. "Forgive, O Lady! I did not know!"

"Then learn, and never forget. Here is your riddle—why is the goddess of the villagers only wanton, then mother, but never more?"

"Why—because the villagers have no need of that aspect?"

"A good answer," the goddess purred, "for this village goddess is only a mind's toy, a thing of story, invented by the villagers themselves at Ulahane's inspiration. But if you press them, they shall admit Alique is a grandmother, too. Ask why they do not worship her grandchildren, and see."

"I shall! But will that bring me closer to you?"

"No, but the battle that follows shall."

Ohaern frowned, puzzled. "Why should a battle follow so harmless a question?"

"Because the two-faced goddess has a third face. But there will be time enough for her later, O Smith! For now, come to me again, come!"

And Ohaern strove—with every overdriven fiber of his being, he strove to overcome the unseen viscous medium that held him back—but for every inch he advanced, she receded two, laughing gaily. Anger churned within him, swelled into rage, and the goddess finally relented. "Poor man, poor limited mortal man! No, I shall not tease you further, though you have not yet won through to me. But I shall give you this, as a promise." She extended a hand; a beam of green light shot from her finger to bathe him in its aura, and the desire flared in him hotter and hotter as her form turned luminous, then seemed to explode and surround him with nothing but light, pure light without form, as if he were wrapped inside her very being, and ecstasy took him, poured through him, blended with him, became him, and did not end, but only slackened and dwindled and faded, leaving him adrift in a sea of ruby light, light such as one sees when brightness strikes closed lids, and he opened his eyes to see the morning sun spreading glory into the sky beyond the sea, and a vagrant voice seemed to whisper on the breeze, *That is only a taste of me. Remember.*

Remember! How could Ohaern ever forget? He lay looking out the door of the hut into the rosy disk of the newly risen sun as the melted, spread-out substance of his being seemed to gather itself back together, and he lay realizing that Ryl would only be a beautiful and fragrant memory now, for he had a living woman to strive for—or if not a woman, at least a living female.

A female Ulin.

Ohaern lay watching the sunrise, dazed and appalled by his own temerity—but there it was, and if he was to be honest with himself, there was no denying it. He had a new reason for living now—not hatred or revenge, but the need to earn another audience with that living, more-than-human presence. He faced it squarely and admitted to himself that he desired an Ulin woman.

A flirtatious girl brought him a bowl of porridge and a mug of beer, but Ohaern scarcely noticed her beauty, only thanked her absentmindedly, nor noticed the indignation with which she stalked off; his mind was still filled with the glory and the dazzle of the half-seen goddess of his dream.

But as the sun rose higher he noticed that the farmers had not gone out to the fields. Instead they gathered in the central circle, laughing and joking and building a pile of straw. Curious, Ohaern finished his bowl of porridge and strolled into the plaza to see if he could discover the cause of the festival atmosphere. "What occurs today?" he asked one young man.

"Why, it is the feast day of the goddess Alique!" the young man answered. "There will be feasting and dancing and drinking, and then—" His smile became knowing, confiding. "—then worship of the goddess!"

"Indeed!" Ohaern exclaimed. "How fortunate we are to have arrived in time for it!"

"No, no!" The young man shook his head. "It is *because* you have arrived that we celebrate her feast!"

Bemused, Ohaern wandered away to look at the other preparations. The roof over a long dais, on the east side of the circle, was being rethatched, and fires were being lighted in the two huge roasting pits. The men were just finishing the butchering of one huge boar as the women prepared an enormous sow for roasting.

Other men were rolling out great ceramic jars, which Ohaern assumed held beer. It was indeed going to be a lavish festival! Ohaern went to find Lucoyo, but found a dozen women about him, anointing him with oils and decking him with flowers. Ohaern found it odd that the sight did not spur desire in him again—but after that vision of the goddess, how could anything merely mortal arouse him?

The festival began as the sun rose to its highest, with nibbling at barley cakes, drinking of beer, and vigorous dancing. It seemed to be a sort of contest, for the dancers came only two at a time, a man and a woman, with interlocking gyrations, whirling and leaping, never touching, and the villagers shouted their approval. The drums beat, the double-reeds droned, and bangles chimed. Looking about him, Ohaern could see the glazed eyes and fixed smiles that meant the villagers were working themselves into a sort of mass semitrance. He had seen the same effect when the shaman of his own village had led the people in the hunt dance, but there had never been so many people, so very many, and there was some quality of anticipation, of hunger, even craving, in them, that made Ohaern turn cold inside. He resolved to drink much less than he seemed to, and to keep his head clear and his knife loose in its sheath.

The chill of caution made him remember the words of the goddess, and he turned to Labina and the old man, who were seated beside him. "Tell me more of Alique," he said. "You have told me she had many children—but has she no grandchildren?"

Labina looked up, surprised, then frowned as if she were less than pleased. The old man stepped into the gap. "We honor the children separately, and Alique when she is old, past childbearing and past the need for lovers."

Ohaern did not like the notion of a woman having a need for lovers, other than love. "Surely she still cares for her brood!"

"When we worship her as the mother-goddess," Labina said slowly, "she is bounty itself, nursing many little children from never-dry breasts."

"*Little* children? She is never a grandmother?" Ohaern pressed.

"Several of her children have children," the old man reminded Labina.

"Well, yes, she is a grandmother," Labina admitted, "but that is a matter for her worshipers only. You must excuse me now, for I must prepare to take my part in the ceremony." She stood, gave him a nod, and hobbled away, effectively ending Ohaern's questions—which sent a rasp of alarm along his nerves and made him all the more determined to stay alert. Looking around him, he saw that the sun was setting, its golden light turning to the red of blood; the afternoon had passed quickly, and the sun itself seemed to honor the Scarlet One. Men were lighting tall, standing torches, and several couples at a time were coming out to dance. As darkness fell, young women began to bring platters of roasted pork about, with tall cups of beer. Ohaern, as honored guest, was served first, and the old man with him. The pork was good and the beer heady, so he ate lightly of the one and drank sparingly of the other. The old man noticed and pressed him. "Come, a great frame such as yours must need an abundance of nourishment! Do you not feel well?"

"It is the heat," Ohaern said apologetically, "and the long afternoon."

The old man nodded, understanding from his own experience. "At least drink the beer, then. It is nourishing in itself, and lies more easily on the stomach."

Caught, Ohaern lifted the tall cup and swung its bottom high— but he contrived to spill far more down his chin than into his mouth. He set down the cup with a cry of disgust. "How clumsy of me! You must think me rude indeed, good sir!"

"Not at all." The old man chuckled, reassured, and a young woman materialized to wipe Ohaern's chin, lingering perhaps longer than was necessary over the spill on his chest. "We all grow clumsy," said the old man, "as the evening progresses."

The young woman gave Ohaern a languorous, inviting look as she turned away. He smiled, then glanced about, noticing that most of the villagers had beer dribbling down as they drank and were smearing themselves with the fat of the pig as they ate. At first he thought it only bad manners; then began to realize that it was, in some way, a part of the ritual.

As the meal ended, the drums beat louder and the dancers came out into the ring of packed earth again. Now there were a dozen couples, twenty, thirty. The movements were slower now, and the bodies came closer, brushing one another with thrusting hips and lingering caresses. Ohaern began to feel the effects of the beer, little though he had drunk of it, and could only imagine the dancers' walking stupor. But it was a trance as much as intoxication, and as the drumbeat quickened, so did the dancing, hips gyrating against one another, then the whole lengths of the bodies, grins growing wider and more fixed, until Ohaern was amazed they could stand at all.

Then, suddenly, the drums stopped and a huge gong rang. The dancers cleared away as if by magic and crouched around the edges, chests heaving, hands caressing, glazed eyes fixed on the center of the circle of beaten earth.

Out came two maidens clothed all in blossoms, with Lucoyo's arms about them. The half-elf still wore a kilt wrapped about his loins, but otherwise wore only flowers—a flower wreath about his head, flower rings about his neck hanging down to cover his chest, ropes of flowers twined about his arms and legs. One look and Ohaern could see that Lucoyo had eaten and drunk as well as any of the villagers, and from the dazed look in his eyes, he had been dancing as they had, too, though more privately.

Now, though, the drums began to beat again with a slow, throbbing rhythm, and the two young women stepped back, leaving him swaying alone—but not for long. A girl stepped out from the ring of watchers, dressed also in flowers, dancing, feet stamping, hips swiveling, hands clapping above her head, lips parted and breathless, eyes wide in wonder and anticipation.

A murmur went about the ring, half whisper: "The virgin! The goddess's virgin! Alique is within her!"

Ohaern thought it more likely that a good deal of beer was in her, but not enough to muddy her movements. She stamped and gyrated closer and closer to Lucoyo, who grinned slowly and began to match her movements, hands clapping with hers, knees bending with hers, hips churning with hers. Closer they came to one another and closer, while the villagers hung on their every movement, eyes wide and rapt, breath rasping, bodies jerking in time to the dance—and Ohaern suddenly realized toward what event this dance was building.

The girl began to turn about and about, moving closer and farther from Lucoyo as she did. The flowers began to fall off her, one by one, two by two, then in fives and tens as she spun faster and faster, revealing a beautifully curved and unblemished body. Lucoyo matched her turn for turn, and his flowers began to fall off, too. When only a few rings remained about the girl's hips and breasts, she stepped closer to Lucoyo, plucking the remaining blossoms from his chest, his arms, and he, gallantly returning the favor, plucked away those remaining to her, but letting his fingers linger and glide as he did, so that the girl began to gasp and shiver with desire, her movements becoming uneven, even clumsy.

All sat with their eyes glued to the spectacle—all but Ohaern, insulated from the fascination by his sense of alarm and by the lingering dazzle of his goddess' beauty. He watched not just his friend and his friend's intended temporary mate, but the whole of the torchlit circle, and even the shadows beyond—so he caught the movement in those shadows, and instantly focused his attention on it. He saw silhouettes moving there, coming closer, until the fringes of the torchlight revealed four men carrying a palanquin high on their shoulders, with a figure crouching atop it. As the dancing couple pressed closer, the bearers bore the palanquin closer, too, until the figure was revealed in the torchlight . . .

It was a statue, an idol—but it was a figure out of a nightmare, too, a wiry bloodred form seated cross-legged amidst the bones of pigs, a parody of the female form, with sunken breasts and bony arms and a stark white skull for a face, from which snaky ropelets of hair straggled. Ohaern sat frozen with horror, for he felt the presence of Ulahane in that statue, felt it so strongly that for a moment he thought he must be staring at the Scarlet One himself!

Then he remembered that Ulahane was male, so this caricature of the Scarlet One could not be his image, but must be that of one of his servants. But it was an image that moved! The horror returned, for he saw the death-hag lift a huge curved sword as Lucoyo snatched away the girl's last blossom and she plucked at his kilt. It fell away, and the crowd shouted with delight, then began to chant as the girl pressed herself against Lucoyo, pressed her mouth to his as his arms came up about her and they sank to their knees, intertwined, and the sword rose higher above them as the bearers, too, sank to their knees . . .

Then Ohaern realized that the figure was no statue, but a living being, masked and painted—and saw what the only full ending to this ceremony could be. With a shout of warning, he leaped out into the ring, drawing his sword. The girl pulled Lucoyo down, but he looked up in surprise at Ohaern's shout, looked up and spat a curse—then saw the huge sword falling upon him, the skull face screaming curses that overshadowed his by far. Lucoyo rolled aside and leaped to his feet, bleating protest, but Ohaern leaped past him to parry the next stroke, shouting, "As you burst into ecstasy, she would have cut your head from your neck!"

The girl cowered away, huddling in on herself, crying.

The bearers set down their burden and rose up against Ohaern with a shout, but he kicked them aside as they rose, then yanked the mask loose, to reveal Labina's face, contorted with rage and screaming, "Curse you, outlander! You have ruined our sacrifice, and the goddess, angered, will yield us no harvest!"

The villagers, horrified, rose up with a shout of anger, but Ohaern held his blade to Labina's throat and shouted, "Back, or your priestess dies!" The villagers froze, and Ohaern pricked the hag's neck, demanding, "When strangers came, you had someone to sacrifice! At the climax, you would have struck off Lucoyo's head, but not hers, because she is one of your own! Is it not true?"

"True," the hag spat, "and she would forever after have been sacred to Alique. Now, thanks to your meddling, she shall be forever cursed, and no man shall touch her!"

The girl wailed.

"A great many strangers must have died," Ohaern said, "for so many young women to be eager to worship your promiscuous goddess! Or do you force a boy of your own, if no stranger comes in the spring?"

"There are always men who think it worth their lives to bed Alique's virgin," Labina spat, "but there are always springtime strangers, too, who are eager to bed any woman who is willing!"

Ohaern stood frozen a moment, then snapped, "And if I had accepted their favors? Would I, too, have been marked for sacrifice?"

"Aye, but now you will go in place of your friend, for you have desecrated the ritual, and only by slaying you can we avert Alique's anger! Nay, slay me if you wish, for there is a matron ready to assume my office!" Then Labina screeched to her people, "Slay him!"

The villagers charged Ohaern with a roar.

He threw the priestess from him, but Lucoyo was already beside her, twisting the sword from her hand and turning to slash at his attackers with a shout. He pressed his back against Ohaern's, and they cut and wounded man after man—but when five lay moaning, the others pulled back, and men at the edges turned to run for weapons.

"You cannot pass us," one big man growled, "and when we have our blades, we shall slay you!"

"You shall not!" cried a voice like the grating of a cell door, and men howled in fright as they suddenly shot up off the ground in a wave that moved closer and closer to Ohaern. The dwerg pressed inward, hurling men out of his way with his huge, long arms—and behind him, guarding his back, came a human form with a jackal's fur and a jackal's head!

Ohaern stared, amazed at the sight of a Klaja coming to his aid. Then he shook himself into motion, taking advantage of the villagers' fright, and leaped toward Grakhinox, bellowing his war cry, sword flashing. Villagers howled and leaped aside until there were none left between Ohaern and his rescuers.

"Do not let them escape!" Labina shrieked. "Stop them, or Alique's wrath shall fall upon you!"

The villagers rallied, especially as voices at their outer edges cried, "Blades! Blades!" and the rattle of copper and flint told of weapons arriving. One man spun to face Ohaern's sword with a copper sickle. Ohaern laughed and knocked it spinning from his hand—but suddenly there were twenty copper sickles, with flint-toothed scythes beside them, and whirling flails all descending on the hapless four together. The Klaja howled and struck about him with his pike, but for each man he transfixed, two leaped at him before he could wrench his blade clear. The dwerg caught those two and hurled them aside while Lucoyo and Ohaern fought madly, beating back blade after blade, but their breath came ragged already, and they knew that within a few minutes the villagers must drag them down by sheer weight.

"HOOOOOLD!" a voice cried out all about them, a single voice, but it seemed to come from all sides with the sound of a gong. Everyone froze, wide-eyed, but kept their weapons high and their gazes fixed on their opponents. Ohaern risked a quick glance back, and saw . . .

A tall figure holding Labina up by the throat, her face turning purple, obscene red-dyed body thrashing—and the tall figure behind her seemed to burn with green fire, to be surrounded with it, and the villagers cowered away, moaning with superstitious fear.

But Ohaern stared with wider eyes than any, for he recognized the figure. It was Manalo!

"Your goddess is overcome!" He did not shout, but his voice echoed all about them. "The power of Lomallin has exposed your false Alique for what she is—only the invention of a diseased mind, only a perversion and a mockery of the figure of the Lady Rahani of the Ulin!"

The whole clearing held rock-still as he dropped Labina to the ground. She looked up at him, at the terrible wrath in his face, and cried out, curling herself into a ball.

"But there is power in Alique!" the old man cried.

"It is the power of Ulahane!" Manalo thundered. "It is the power of death! He sent the priestess Labina to you at a time when the harvests were increasing by themselves! He sent Labina to debauch your young women and slay an endless procession of strangers!"

He looked about at the villagers, staring into each pair of eyes one by one as he said, "Turn from the worship of Death to the worship of Life! Only Lomallin and Rahani can give you increase of your crops!" Then, to Ohaern and his friends, "Turn and go!"

The aisle the dwerg had plowed reopened as if by magic. Ohaern knew better than to run—he marched down that aisle, head high, with Lucoyo behind him, glowering about, and Grakhinox behind the half-elf, with the grinning sharp-toothed Klaja bringing up the rear. As they passed the edge of the crowd, Manalo followed them, looking sternly at each villager, commanding them, "Turn away from this death-bringer Labina! Scorn her false goddess Alique! Turn from the goddess who is only a nightmare tale, to the Ulin Rahani!"

But as he passed the far edge of the circle and stepped beyond the last hut, Labina came alive behind him, screaming imprecations, howling at her people to go, to bring down the blasphemers, or their crops would die, their babies be stillborn, and all their cattle barren. The crowd moaned with fear and bent to habit. They went charging after the strangers, and as they ran, the moan of fear turned to the full-throated bay of the hunting pack.

Ohaern did not need Manalo to tell him what to do. He ran.

CHAPTER 23

"Quickly, aside!" Ohaern dropped into an irrigation ditch. His companions followed him, none paying much attention to the shallow water and mud in which they knelt. The villagers thundered by, shouting and cursing, a ragged line of copper blades flashing in the light of torches.

Manalo leaned over to Ohaern and whispered, "Catch me one!"

Ohaern looked up in surprise, then turned back to the running file of villagers, eyes narrowed as he judged his moment. The body of pursuers passed, with only three stragglers puffing along behind. As the last came by, Ohaern surged out of the ditch and caught the man about the chest, pinioning his arms with one hand while he clapped the other over the villager's mouth. The man struggled, thrashing and gargling—but little noise could escape Ohaern's hand, and struggles were futile in the arms of the big smith. Ohaern turned to drag him down into the ditch, but Manalo had emerged, the hem of his robe clotted with mud. He turned, beckoning. "Come!"

Ohaern followed, hissing, "Lucoyo! Follow!" The half-elf bolted out of the ditch, heedless of the fact that he was still naked, but with a nervous glance behind at the Klaja. The jackal-head showed no sign of enmity, however, and the dwerg was between them, so Lucoyo only hurried after Ohaern, cursing the hour they had stopped at the village.

Manalo led them to the shadow of a large, round, squat structure, out in the middle of the field. There, he turned to face the captive. "This granary will do to hide us for a few minutes," he said, "and it is far enough from the village so that none will hear you if you cry out. Still, Ohaern, you had best keep him gagged."

The whites showed all around the man's eyes in fear. Ohaern frowned; such ruthlessness did not seem like the Teacher he had known.

But Manalo turned away, spreading his hands toward the village and beginning to chant. The green glow began again, highlighting his hands, then growing to surround them. Ohaern felt a chill in the pit of his stomach. What magic was the sage brewing?

Manalo turned slowly, so that he faced one field after another, even pacing around the granary to cast his enchantment over the fields it hid from the village. Ohaern watched, the spell seeming to prickle up his backbone and spread out over his skin. He began to wish he could be somewhere else, anywhere else, for he did not want to see Manalo take revenge.

They came back to their starting place, and the green glow died as Manalo lowered his hands. For a moment he slumped, exhaling a long and exhausted sigh, then squared his shoulders, looking down at the villager. "Your harvest is saved," he said, "and that without slaying a stranger, nor even one of your own. Tell the priestess, tell the priest—but first tell all your fellow villagers."

The man stared, amazed that he was not to be harmed. Ohaern stared, too. Manalo nodded at the smith. "Release his mouth."

Ohaern took his hand away, and the captive drew in a shuddering breath. "You—You shall not harm me?"

"No. You are here only to take word of my enchantment back to the village." Manalo raised a forefinger. "But your crops shall grow well by the power of the Ulin Rahani, not by any strength of your make-believe goddess Alique."

The villager shrank back, glancing at the ground as if expecting a fireball to shoot from the earth and strike down the blasphemer—but nothing happened.

"Rahani does require a sacrifice, though," Manalo said severely. "You must plant your seeds in hills, and in each hill you must place a small fish."

"A fish?" The man's eyes were so round that he might have been one himself. "Only a fish?"

"One for every half-dozen seeds," Manalo qualified, "but it is the sort of sacrifice Rahani wants—food for food, not life for life."

"If you say so," the man said, and gulped.

"I say it, and it shall be so," said Manalo. "Plant as I have told you, pray to Rahani, and you shall see that even if the plants already green in your fields should die, the new planting shall increase enough to yield a rich harvest indeed. Nay, more—the shoots that already live shall grow, not die, and your harvest shall be twice rich, even thrice. When you see this is so, turn away from the make-believe three-faced goddess and turn to the worship of Rahani. Go now, and tell what you have seen and what I have said you shall see in the future!" He nodded at Ohaern, and the big smith released the villager, who stood a moment, glancing about at them, then suddenly broke and ran, dashing away across the field like a gazelle.

"Will he truly take your word?" Lucoyo asked.

Manalo nodded. "But he will also lead the hunt after us. Come, we must be gone before he returns!" And he turned away, leading them off into the night.

He finally let them pause five miles from the village, where a grove of trees grew up by a small watercourse.

Lucoyo threw himself on the ground. "Thank all gods for sweet rest!"

"You have need of a great deal," Ohaern said sourly. "You have exerted yourself steadily for two days, I doubt not."

A slow smile spread across Lucoyo's face. "Ah, but what sweet exertion!" He levered himself up and looked down at his naked body. "I must find a sheep, to steal its skin—and my weapons! Where shall I find a new knife?"

"Where would you have found a new life?" Ohaern retorted.

"It is true." Lucoyo sobered. "I must thank you for saving me again, O Smith. I owe you another blood-debt."

"Or is it I who owe you?" Ohaern rejoined. "I have lost count. But we both owe our lives to the sage." He turned to Manalo. "I thank you from the bottom of the blood-well within me, Teacher, for it would not still be within my skin if you had not saved us."

"Yes, great thanks," Lucoyo agreed, "thank you for every square inch of my skin, and to show that I mean it, I show it indeed!"

Manalo smiled, amused. "It is nothing, Lucoyo."

"It is to me! But how is it you happened by when we most needed you? And how is it you came—" He glanced at the Klaja. "—accompanied?"

The sage shrugged. "I had finished my wanderings, alerting the leaders of all the nations to Ulahane's assault. That done, I conjured a vision of you two to see how you fared—and saw that you would soon be faring most dangerously indeed! I sped to where I knew you would be, and on the way I was attacked by a band of Klaja. They were few enough to be easily dealt with—but I discovered that another of their kind had come up to stand beside me, dealing out blows. The defeated ones howled at him, accusing him of leading them to me, and he did not deny it, though it could not have been true."

"No, it could not." The jackal-head grinned. "But it did me no harm to let them think so."

"Why did they chase you?" Ohaern asked.

"For a crime, for the sin of pride. I dared ask my fellows by what right the Ulharl drove us, and when none could answer, I determined not to obey the giant anymore. That meant death, of course, so instead I fled from my own kind. They would not have it; when the Ulharl discovered I was gone, he sent them after me, to punish disloyalty with slow death."

Manalo nodded. "No wonder a Klaja who turns against Ulahane is unheard of."

"And the enemy of our enemy should be our friend," Ohaern said slowly.

"Or at least our ally." Lucoyo looked up at Manalo. "But what of these who treated us so well, yet would have shed my blood, Teacher? What sense is there in that?"

"In their view, you marked yourself for sacrifice when you were willing to copulate with the women who served their make-believe goddess," Manalo explained. "That meant you would be willing to initiate their newest acolyte—and, in their minds, ought to pay the price."

Lucoyo shuddered. "Who perverted their minds thus?"

"Labina," Manalo told him. "I recognize her kind by the fruits of her labor, and by the idol she sought to become by paint and mask—the third aspect of the made-up goddess, the hag and destroyer. She is a worshiper of Ulahane, sent forth by him to pervert the worship of Rahani and turn humans away from Lomallin's teachings. She took Ulahane's parody of Rahani, twisting her image from something life-giving and nurturing into something that debased men and women alike. For worship she debased an act of love into a public spectacle of physical sensation only— which, like all physical sensations, palls as the pleasure seekers become jaded; they do not realize that the rapture they truly seek is of the heart."

"Cheapened by stripping it of intimacy," Ohaern murmured.

"Yes. Then she glorified death." Manalo sighed. "The villagers kept the hag-face secret, of course, or you would have fled from her devotees—yes, even you, Lucoyo; the hag's purpose was plain."

"But who is this goddess whose image they perverted?"

Manalo looked up at Ohaern keenly, hearing the urgency of the question in his tone—but he did not comment on it, only answered, "She is Lomallin's ally. At first she held aloof from the quarrel between Lomallin and Marcoblin—her interests were otherwise."

"What interests were those?" Lucoyo asked.

Manalo sighed. "She is greathearted but, more importantly, very tenderhearted—so if she saw anyone who needed consolation, she was quick to offer it—and she was very beautiful."

"So the consolation the men asked was physical," Lucoyo inferred, wide-eyed. "Do we speak of human men?"

"No—or not often. By the time humans began to appear on the earth, she had been hurt often enough by the Ulin men who took her favors, then turned away with callous disregard, so that she had curtailed her promiscuity, or at least reduced it greatly. In this she was aided by the counsel of Lomallin, who urged her to keep her self-respect by keeping her favors. She hearkened to him, for he was one of the few men who had never sought her bed."

"He did not find her attractive?" Lucoyo asked.

"That was what she feared, but he assured her most earnestly that he did, but would not treat her lightly—and she believed him, though she did not respect him greatly."

"Why was that?" Ohaern asked.

"Because he was a wizard," Manalo said sadly, "not a warrior. In truth, he was one of the least combative of the Ulin, and she saw masculinity as linked to fighting, so she viewed Lomallin with great fondness, but also fond contempt." He shook his head, mouth twisted with wry reflection.

"Still she listened to him when he bade her refrain?" Lucoyo asked in surprise.

"Listened to him, yes, but watched him, too, and found another object for her tender heart. She saw him teaching Agrapax's homunculi, or trying to."

" 'Trying to'?" Lucoyo frowned. "They seemed smart enough when we met them!"

Klaja and dwerg looked up, startled, and not a little frightened.

"Now, yes," Manalo agreed, "but when they were new, they all were both ignorant and innocent. They had little mind and less initiative, but only wandered aimlessly with no purpose, unless they were driven. So Lomallin gathered a dozen of them and sought to teach them. Once he sparked interest in what little minds they had, those minds began to grow. He made a language for them, a very simple language, then began to teach them the history of the Ulin, and why and how they had been made. Each of them went out and taught two more, so three dozen came back to Lomallin to learn further—and thus, by doubles and quadruples and octuples, the homunculi developed minds and knowledge."

"But what did Rahani see in this?" Lucoyo asked.

"She saw creatures who needed love and care, and joined Lomallin in their teaching." Manalo gazed off into the distance, a smile playing upon his lips. "For a century and more she labored beside him, until all the Agrapaxians had learned as much as they could."

"And during all that time," Lucoyo said, grinning, "the male Ulin fretted and fumed for want of her favors, and cursed Lomallin?"

Manalo smiled with him. "Indeed they did—and cursed harder when Rahani, having learned her bitter lesson, ignored them still and turned to the human race to fill the void in her, that needed something to care for and love. Indeed, she became the most ardent of human-lovers, and Lomallin's most staunch ally."

Lucoyo frowned. "Did her regard for him not rise when she saw him turn to fighting?"

"If you mean, did she invite him to her bed, the answer is no. Perhaps she needed him too much as a friend, perhaps his being her ally precluded his being her lover—who can explain the minds and hearts of women?"

"Not even female Ulin?"

"Them even less." Manalo glanced at Ohaern, who stood stiff and wide-eyed, drinking in every word. Something changed in the sage's eyes, and when he turned back to Lucoyo, he spoke not of love and the goddess, but of war. "Because of their efforts, humankind began to thrive and multiply—for Lomallin taught them to hunt and fish, then learn the use of the bow and net, which brought them more and larger game. Rahani taught them which roots and berries were good to eat, so that they might gather them, and even taught them to plant seeds, so that they would have more to eat in the next year. Moreover, she taught them healing, so many of them were cured of diseases that would have slain them in childhood. Marcoblin was not there to see, but his lieutenant Ulahane witnessed humanity increasing in vast numbers and took this as a threat to the pleasures and hegemony of the few Ulin who had survived the war. He hated Lomallin and Rahani— since they were all that were left of the leaders of the human-lovers—and blamed the whole war on him."

Ohaern came out of his trance. "Blamed him for the war? How?"

Manalo shrugged. "In Ulahane's eyes, it was not Marcoblin's cruelty that had given cause for fighting, but Lomallin's sympathy for the Agrapaxians and humans. Therefore did Ulahane beget a son upon a human woman—"

"One who did not wish it?" Lucoyo guessed

"One who most definitely did not wish it—neither the son, nor Ulahane's embraces! But he hated humankind so deeply that any woman who *had* wished his attentions would have given him no pleasure. No, it was rape, pure and simple. Thereafter he kept the woman prisoner until her son was born, to ensure that she would not seek to abort the child nor to slay herself in despair—which she did, when Ulahane loosed her after the birth."

"Did he care?" asked the dwerg.

"Not in the slightest," Lucoyo said. "She had served her purpose—for him."

Manalo nodded. "Thus was born Kadura, reared with his father so that he should become used to Ulahane's service and accustomed to obedience, or to instant, dire punishment for disobedience. Thus grew the first of Ulahane's many Ulharl children, reviled and taunted by the Ulin—"

Lucoyo frowned. "Did not his father protect him from that?"

"Wherefore? To Ulahane, Kadura was little more than a servant, and one who was tainted by human blood besides. When he was grown, Ulahane sent him out among humankind to teach them to worship Ulahane out of fear, a fear very like Kadura's own. For worship, they were to capture others of their kind for sacrifice to Ulahane—and in the early days, when there were few, Ulahane came in person to torture those given to him and delight in their agony."

The dwerg shuddered. "Why did they worship him if he did such things?"

"Because if they gave him victims for his pleasure, he would spare them, his worshipers." Manalo looked down at the ground, frowning at the thought. "Thus was a religion of fear born among humankind, and thus came war, as other nations banded together, seeking the protection of Lomallin and Rahani and their allies, and defending themselves against the assaults of Ulahane's devotees."

"But did not Ulahane's slaves realize there was escape for them if they fled to the temples of the human-lovers?"

"They did," Manalo said, "so it was then that Ulahane had to begin blandishments and bribes—sexual pleasure and wordly success—"

"Even like these villagers from whom we have just escaped!" Lucoyo cried.

"Even like them." Manalo nodded. "Labina's preaching was

only Ulahane's old cant, dressed up with a make-believe night-mare goddess, to seduce away the folk who worshiped Rahani. This is why I say Alique is a mockery of Rahani, a perversion." He looked up at Ohaern. "What troubles you?"

So he had seen the turmoil in his breast! Ohaern thought. He asked, "Are there other Ulin who would bind a man to their service by the promise of passion?"

"Many," said Manalo, giving him a penetrating look, "but only Rahani would do it without some measure of cruelty. Indeed, only Rahani would enchant a man with love—though not such love as she might feel for a man of the Ulin."

"I see," said Ohaern with a sardonic smile. "Only such love as one might give a favored dog, eh?" It helped, the awareness of his own absurdity.

"More than that, far more than that," Manalo assured him. "Beware your dreams, Ohaern. You know what is right or wrong—do not follow any who would have you do evil!"

"That is not my case," Ohaern assured him. "I only need beware those who bid me do right."

There was relief in Manalo's glance, and—could it have been envy? Or jealousy? Or even both? Whatever it was, it was gone quickly, and his smile warmed as he said. "Then you need not beware, O Hunter—any more than you would with any quarry. But come, we linger too long! Let us go, before the villagers find our trail!"

He led them away, and Ohaern followed, reflecting that at least the sage had not told him to beware as if he *were* the quarry. He decided that he would exercise such caution anyway.

Not that it would do him any good.

By dawn they were far down the coastline, and Manalo had led them out along a peninsula of stone that formed a natural harbor. They camped there among the rocks, warmed by the sun and eating the fish the Klaja speared. They slept through the day, all except Manalo, but when they woke at evening and Manalo showed no sign of again taking up their march, Lucoyo became restless. "When shall we go, O Sage?"

"Perhaps tomorrow," Manalo answered, "perhaps the next day, or the next."

The half-elf frowned. "What do we wait for?"

"A ship." Manalo turned to Ohaern. "We cannot find that sheep he wished for, but you might seek a gazelle or such. Do not wander far, though."

"I shall not," Ohaern promised. "Come, Lucoyo!"

They were back within an hour, with wood for a bow and arrows, and a dozen rabbits. Ohaern allowed them a small and smokeless fire of dry wood, to roast the catch; then Lucoyo set to chewing the skins and sewing himself a fur kilt. He, at least, found occupation.

But just before nightfall, a ship appeared, coasting along near the horizon. Manalo gave an exclamation of satisfaction and stepped up to the highest rock, where he recited an incomprehensible verse—which Ohaern memorized, consonant for consonant and vowel for vowel—as he waved his staff in some very strange gyrations. The ship sailed closer, much closer, until it dropped anchor, apparently having decided to pass the night in their little harbor. Manalo waved and called, and after a while a small boat put out from the ship with several men aboard. They shared the rabbit stew and bargained for the amber Manalo pulled from his pouch, and the upshot was that when the ship put out to sea at dawn, Manalo and his whole little company were aboard.

They sailed along the seacoast for days. Lucoyo grew restive, for there was only so much work he could do on his bow in a day. He eventually became so hard put as to help the sailors in their endless washing of the ship. Ohaern, though, was content to watch the waves and the passing coastline, letting his mind roam free. The Klaja and the dwerg seemed to share his serenity, though their ease might have simply reflected a massive patience in both. Manalo took advantage of the time to teach Ohaern a few more spells, then a few more beyond that, and perhaps another half-dozen. Ohaern felt as if he were nothing but a memory on two legs by the time Manalo finally sought out the captain and told him to put them ashore.

"Here?" the captain cried in dismay. "It is nothing but a barren desert! You will die of hunger and thirst!"

"Then give us sour wine to carry with us, and water skins,"

Manalo replied. "Fear not—we shall find shelter. But it is here that we must land."

So the sailors rowed them ashore, with Ohaern wondering if Manalo were leading them to their doom, but careful not to let it show in his face.

Lucoyo, however, had no such inhibition. He let it show indeed, and when that did not bring forth any explanations, he insisted on knowing. As the sailors rowed away, he demanded, "*Now* how shall we live, O Sage?"

"Fear not, Lucoyo; my knowledge will be your shield—also your coat and hat." Manalo beckoned with his staff. "Onward! for where we must go is a long and arduous distance, and we must be there when the moon is full!"

He turned away, and Ohaern followed, with Lucoyo behind him, grumbling, and the dwerg and the Klaja bringing up the rear. Ohaern watched their guide and leader with concern, though. It might have been his imagination, but he could have sworn he had seen lines of care in Manalo's face—care, and growing apprehension. What could there be so mighty as to make Manalo fear?

CHAPTER 24

T hey wandered through an arid waste where only tough, sparse grass grew—perhaps enough for a few goats, if they were not terribly discriminating in their diet. What water they would have found for drinking, Ohaern could not see—but the sage forged ahead with a steady, tireless gait and seemed never in doubt as to where he was going.

The Klaja was the first to grow weak with the heat. "Must rest," he informed them, and sat down right where he was.

It still amazed the smith to hear so bestial a face utter words that were so human. He turned back to urge the poor creature to its feet. "You cannot rest here, friend! The sun will grow hotter, and you have no shelter."

"Cannot," the Klaja lamented. "Too hot."

"Here, cool yourself." Feeling prodigal, Ohaern spilled a precious handful of water over the Klaja's head. The beast looked up in surprise, then licked the wet fur about its mouth with a long pink tongue. "More!"

"Only a few swallows." Manalo had turned back to help. "Then you must fight your way to your feet, O Klaja, so that we may journey onward to a bit of shade."

"What if there *is* no shade?" Lucoyo glanced at the sun fearfully; like most northerners, he had never thought it could be a source of danger.

"I know of a place," Manalo assured him.

"Know?" The half-elf pounced on the word. "You have been here before, then?"

"Only a little farther," Manalo urged the Klaja, and it pushed itself to its feet, already panting and slobbering again. Lucoyo looked up in irritation and was about to repeat his question when Ohaern's slight shake of the head caught his eye. He frowned with resentment—what right had Ohaern to tell him what not to do?—but subsided. Still, he wondered how the sage could be so sure as he followed Manalo deeper into the waste.

They did indeed come to a rocky outcrop into which the wind had carved niches where they could find shade, and even some coolness stored in the stone from the night. They shared a meager meal of hard biscuit and dried meat, washed down with carefully measured mouthfuls of water, then tried to sleep a little. As the sun swung low, Manalo shooed them out and led them off toward the east again.

They marched till darkness fell, then lit a fire, for the heat of the day was followed by an amazing chill. Ohaern went hunting and found nothing—but the Klaja came back with two hares and refused to eat any, claiming to have already devoured a third. At last they slept—deeply, due to exhaustion—but Manalo rousted them out as the sky began to lighten, and set them on their way again.

That was the pattern of their days, for a week. Manalo refused to tell them where they were bound, or how he knew where to find shade and, every few days, a pool welling from the rock, or a small rivulet. Not understanding why, the companions nonetheless trudged through the dreary waste, their minds numbing and emptying to nothing more than overcoming the dreariness and heat till the next resting place. Around them the grass grew ever more scarce, and patches of sand and bare rock grew more frequent. Then Manalo's next spring turned out to be only a powdery basin of dust, and the companions had to force themselves to go on and on, with only occasional mouthfuls of brackish water as their water skins grew lighter and flatter. Finally, the Klaja refused to rise when the sun dipped, and his friends stood in consternation about him. They would not leave him, but they no longer had the strength to carry him, either.

Then the dwerg fainted.

Lucoyo sat down on the ground with a cry of despair, clutching his head. "The heat drives me mad, it makes the blood pound through my temples, awaking an ache with every passage! Sage, make it stop!"

Manalo laid a hand on his head, muttering an ancient formula. The half-elf sagged with relief, then slumped back against the rock, and Manalo stepped aside, motioning Ohaern to follow. "They can go no farther without water," he told the smith in a low voice. "Here, take my water skin. Guard them and measure out the liquid. Give them mouthfuls of the sour wine as often as they will take it, for it quenches thirst better than water."

"You speak as if you will not stay," Ohaern said, frowning.

"Quite right; I shall seek help. There are folk who live in this waste, and one tribe is near. I shall find them and return—no, do not seek to stop me, Ohaern! I shall be well. Only guard those I leave in your care!"

Ohaern did—he measured out the water, though the clamoring thirst within urged him to drink it all himself, and immediately, but there was perhaps a day's supply left for them all. He hunted that night, and the blood of the hare and the three large lizards he found was a welcome addition to their liquid resources. A foolish snake tried to bite the hunter and was roasted for dinner himself in return. None of them felt any need to be fastidious when it came to the menu.

As the heat built in mid-morning of the second day, and the Klaja lay on his side, panting, ribs heaving, Ohaern found himself on the verge of despair. Surely the sage would come too late—if he was not already dead, himself, of exhaustion and heat! Or if he did come back, surely he would find only four desiccated bundles of skin and bones!

A voice hailed him from far away.

Ohaern looked up with sudden hope. There, dark against the sky, came half a dozen strange, lanky beasts that looked to be moving in a leisurely gait, but were actually running. He stared, never having seen such animals before. They were long-legged, long-necked—and were those humps on their backs? Indeed they were, humps, and atop the humps, men! Men wrapped in long robes, in this blazing heat! But they did not even seem to notice, pounding toward the companions with amazing speed for such a leisurely seeming gait. Surely their mounts were the most ungainly creatures Ohaern had ever seen—but also the most beautiful, at least right now, when they might mean relief from the baking heat, even life itself! Ohaern cried out, clasping Lucoyo by the shoulder and pointing. The half-elf turned in surprise, levering himself up on one elbow, then stared in amazement. His mouth worked, trying to force words out past a leathery tongue as Ohaern laughed and slapped him on the shoulder, then caught up the dwerg and turned him so that he, too, could see.

"Such awkward animals!" Lucoyo cried. "And with men atop them!"

"Yes, it is amazing!" Ohaern agreed. "How could they ever have thought to ride on such animals? How could they balance on top of those miniature hills, especially as they jostle and sway? What manner of men are they?"

"Are they men at all?" Lucoyo asked, suddenly apprehensive.

Ohaern stared, then felt the chill of dread make his skin cold. Lucoyo was right—those robes might hide anything!

Then he saw who rode in the lead, and almost fainted with relief—and heat. "Teacher!"

Lucoyo stared, then leaped to his feet, waving and cheering—until he staggered, and would have fallen if Ohaern had not caught him. His weight almost dragged Ohaern down, too, but he held on until the huge splay-footed beast slowed near him and Manalo smiled down. "Hail, Ohaern!"

"Hail, Manalo!" But thirst overcame politeness, and Ohaern stretched up a hand. "Have you wat—" But the skin was already dropping into his hand. He drew the stopper and splashed a few swallows into his own mouth, then a few more into Lucoyo's.

Only a few; then he lowered the half-elf to the ground and went to administer a dose of water to the dwerg, then to dribble a few drops onto the Klaja's nose. The jackal-man's tongue slapped out to soak them up; then his mouth lolled open, and Ohaern poured in just a splash. The fanged jaws snapped shut and the Klaja swallowed. Then they opened again, and he reached for the skin—but he had not the strength to reach high enough. Ohaern poured a good measure between his jaws, deliberately splashing a little over the half-furred face. The Klaja swallowed, gave his head a shake, and reached out for more. Ohaern poured another mouthful, but one of the new arrivals called out, and Manalo translated, "He says to give the Klaja no more, or he will founder."

Ohaern nodded and turned back to give Grakhinox another drink, while the Klaja barked in protest, levering himself up. Manalo called out in barks and yaps, and the Klaja looked up at him, growling, but saw the sternness in his face and subsided.

Ohaern gave Lucoyo another drink; then the man atop the beast called, and Ohaern reluctantly held up the water skin. But the man shook his head and spoke another phrase.

"He says that you must drink more," Manalo translated.

"Tell him I thank him for my life," Ohaern said, and poured water into his own mouth, swallowing, until the rider called again. Ohaern did not wait for the translation, recognizing the words and guessing their meaning. He stoppered the skin and passed it up. Revived now, he took a closer look at their rescuers. They were hard-faced men, their visages gentled a bit by the sight of distressed travelers—and undeniably human. They wore long robes, and their heads were covered with a sort of light shawl.

But one in particular drew Ohaern's eye—a mild-looking youth, only one among many, gazing down at Ohaern with a half smile and a look of such serenity as the smith had only dreamed of. "Who is that man who seems at peace with the world?" he asked Manalo.

Manalo did not even look; he only smiled his approval and said, "His name is Dariad. He is only another man of his tribe; no one yet sees anything remarkable in him, save that he lacks ambition."

"I see," Ohaern said slowly, gaze still lingering on Dariad's face. The young man smiled placidly in return. Then Ohaern remembered his manners and turned to bow to the rider beside Manalo. "I thank you for this rescue, O Generous One."

The man seemed pleased and gave a reply which Manalo translated as, "He says he and his companions are honored to offer aid to good people, and invites you to return with them to their camp."

"We will, and gladly!" Ohaern said with relief. He turned to help the Klaja stumble to his feet, then turned back to Manalo. "I shall have to carry him, Teacher."

But Manalo was already clucking to his mount, and it knelt, squalling protest. "You shall not carry him, but this camel will." Manalo reached out his arms. "I shall have to hold him in place."

Ohaern helped the half-jackal over to the camel, who brayed its distrust of the Klaja and tried to bite him—but Ohaern saw the teeth looming and managed to sidestep, weak though he was. He laid the Klaja over Manalo's knees, then turned to find that several of the camels had knelt, with indignant objections. "You shall all ride," Manalo informed him, "for these Biharu say you could not live if you tried to walk the distance—and I will tell you they are right."

"If it is more than a hundred feet, I will tell me that, too," Lucoyo replied. He went over to clamber up behind a Biharu, holding onto the man's saddle for dear life. His eyes were wide with fright as the camel climbed back to its feet, protesting now at having to carry double weight—but he stayed on. The Biharu who carried the dwerg eyed his passenger askance, but made no objection, only snapped a command to him as the camel rose.

"He says that since your arms are long enough, you should hold on about his waist," Manalo translated, and Grakhinox gratefully complied. Then the sage turned to Ohaern. "They are safely stowed, O Smith. Do you ride with Dariad."

The bland young man smiled at his name and waved. Ohaern went to him, reflecting that Dariad's face was bland only until you looked at his eyes. He climbed on behind, holding to the saddle for dear life as the camel pushed itself to its feet, grumbling, and began to sway as it moved off after its fellows.

"You from north?" Dariad asked, looking back over his shoulder at Ohaern.

Ohaern stared in surprise. "How is it you speak the language of Cashalo?"

"Cashalo men come trade two, three times year," Dariad explained. "I no speak good."

That was true; his accent was so thick that Ohaern felt he had to force his way through it, and his vocabulary seemed limited. Nonetheless, he said, "You speak it better than I speak your language. Yes, I am from the north."

"How speak Cashalo tongue?"

"I dwelt among them for a month and more," Ohaern explained, "and had to direct them in a battle."

"One month? Learn fast!"

That was true, now that Ohaern thought of it. At the time, he had only been glad he could make himself understood quickly enough to direct the battle. "I wish to learn fast again," he told Dariad. "Teach me your language."

The nomad grinned. "Happy do. This is 'camel.' " He pointed to the beast.

Ohaern nodded, already having learned the word from Manalo.

"This be *demija*." Dariad plucked at his robe. "This be *nisij*." He pointed at Ohaern's sword. "What?"

"Sword," Ohaern told him, and drew his dagger. "Knife. What are those?" He pointed to the reins in Dariad's hand.

"*Ilshna*," Dariad answered, and they rode on to the Biharu camp, trading words as they went.

The nomad camp was bleak, only a collection of tents in a rough oval around a small pond, which supported some grass and a few palm trees. A few goats drank, while many more grazed outside the ring—but to Ohaern and his companions, it looked like Paradise. They were welcomed with the hospitality of those to whom the arrival of strangers is a major event—but even through the feasting and the singing and dancing, Ohaern and Dariad went on exchanging words. Manalo only watched, and the glitter in his eye went far beyond amusement.

In spite of his exhaustion and weakness, Lucoyo tried to strike up conversations with the young women, but won only giggles and flirtatious glances. He sighed and admitted to himself that language was indeed a barrier to more kinds of communication than one.

Within two days Ohaern and Dariad had enough words in common to be able to converse quite freely. Neither of them seemed to notice anything strange in such rapid learning. Later, looking back, Ohaern wondered at it, and decided they both must have had a rare gift for languages. Either that, or Manalo had aided their learning with a spell or two—and that, Ohaern decided, was a very definite possibility.

"Why do the Biharu live in so barren a waste?" Ohaern asked.

"Because it is our home," Dariad explained simply. "Drought has been spreading out from the Sand Sea since our grandfathers' time. Many have despaired and have left, but we have remained steadfast in our fathers' land, and have learned to wrest a living from the dryness and heat."

Ohaern frowned. "What is the Sand Sea?"

"A desert," Dariad answered, "a wasteland that makes this borderland seem lush. There is no water, no moisture of any kind, save that which a man brings with him—and if he is foolish enough to go there, he is foolish indeed. It is all sand and rock and hard-baked clay—and is still growing. As it grows bigger, we move back, to find pasture for our goats and camels."

Ohaern shuddered at the thought of living in such a place. "You must have faith indeed in your gods, to believe they will sustain you here. Do you worship Lomallin?"

"We honor him," Dariad allowed, "but we worship none but the Creator Himself, the God Who Made the Stars—and the Ulin, and us, and all else besides."

Ohaern frowned. "But none have ever seen the Creator! It is rumored that he may not even resemble a human being, even as much as the Ulin do!"

Dariad nodded. "None knows His face or form, or even if He has either. Nonetheless, He is the Source of All, and must needs be the most mighty."

He said it with such serenity that Ohaern had to suppress an urge to reach out and shake him in an effort to shock him awake. "Would it not be better to worship a god you can comprehend, at least in form and heart? Would it not be better to turn to Lomallin, the chief of the human-lovers?"

"None loves humankind more than He who made it," Dariad rejoined, with ineffable assurance. "There is none equal to the Star-Maker; trust in Him."

"Do you not fear Ulahane?'

"Yes, but we know that while we dwell in the shadow of the Star-Maker, Ulahane cannot defeat us or destroy us."

It occurred to Ohaern that Dariad was mad. Oh, perhaps the Star-Maker was indeed more powerful than Ulahane—or Lomallin either, for that matter—but how likely was he to step in and strike down the Scarlet One? Never, so far as Ohaern could guess. Surely He had not intervened in the Ulin War!

But then, Ohaern had never before met a people who worshiped the Star-Maker, either.

"Ulahane is not truly a god," Dariad explained, and Ohaern frowned, hearing an echo of what Manalo himself had spoken. He paid close attention as the nomad went on. "We who worship the Star-Maker know that Ulahane is only another one of the Star-Maker's creations—a flawed one, a bad one, but nonetheless one that the Star-Maker is as loath to eliminate as any other thing He has created—and ultimately loved."

Ohaern stared. "You cannot mean that the Star-Maker loves even so cruel and depraved a creature as Ulahane!"

"Does not a parent love even a naughty child?" Dariad countered. "Nay, I have seen it myself—a young man of our clan who grew to be cruel and violent, so much so that he raped a young woman, and was executed for it by our judge. His parents wept, though they knew him to be wicked—aye, and had suffered his outbursts of anger themselves, though suffered them in patience." He shook his head. "I can understand that the Star-Maker still loves even Ulahane, though He doubtless deplores the evilness of the Scarlet One."

"Surely you do not deny Ulahane's power!"

"Neither his, nor Lomallin's, nor that of any of the Ulin. Indeed, we would be foolish to ignore even the power of another human being. No, we know that the beings you call 'gods' are far more powerful than mere humans—but we also know that they are not omnipotent. They are an elder race, a more powerful race—but they are not truly gods."

And what could Ohaern say, when his own teacher had told him the same thing?

He could change tactics, though. "If you know the Star-Maker to be the most powerful god, do you Biharu not feel you should extend His rule over all the world?"

Dariad shook his head, smiling. "He already rules the whole world."

Lucoyo did not understand how Dariad could say such a thing, when Ulahane strove against Lomallin so harshly, and with such determination to bring about the suffering of all humankind, not to mention the rest of the few surviving Ulin. He said as much, he strove and argued and pointed out the contradictions inherent in believing in only one god—but his doubts did not bother the young herdsman at all. He proceeded to answer each of Ohaern's arguments with a placid demeanor, even though some of his ideas must have been inspired at that moment.

Oddly, his imperturbable, unshakable belief in his God did not ruffle Ohaern, either; he understood what the herder meant, though he could not explain it to Lucoyo when the half-elf complained that a world with only one God made no sense. Ohaern was not skilled with words, as Dariad seemed to be, and anyway, this went beyond language. All he could say was, "I cannot see that it makes much difference, Lucoyo. Greater men or lesser gods, what matter?"

In similar fashion, Ohaern could not explain why he knew that Dariad, who seemed so simple in his serenity, was really a very important man. Perhaps it was because, in his very simplicity, he was so completely dedicated to Goodness and Rightness, and was so greathearted, so enthusiastic and compassionate, that his personality was staggering. But Ohaern knew him for a marked man, marked for Ulahane's destruction. He was an excellent fighter, though, and Ohaern quickly realized that his simplicity was that of a completely unified, harmonious soul, and had nothing to do with intelligence. Indeed, Dariad was very intelligent, but had found no occasion to use his capacity. He was so easygoing and so clumsy in his happy abstraction that he came in for a great deal of good-natured teasing. The rest of the clan seemed to view him with fond condescension.

So the companions passed an enjoyable, if quiet, five-day convalescence and were just beginning to feel strong enough to follow Manalo further in his mad quest, when the caravan came winding its way through the wasteland toward the oasis where the herders were camped.

CHAPTER 25

$\circledast$

The Biharu greeted the caravan with delight. The traders, initially wary, let go of the axes and swords that hung on their saddles and climbed down with broad grins to exchange greetings with the nomads, and trade wine for water. They pitched tents of their own, lit campfires, and settled down to some serious bargaining. Ohaern was amazed at the trade goods the Biharu brought out—bracelets and jewelry of fine workmanship, and rugs and carpets of intricate design and vivid color. Eavesdropping shamelessly, he learned that nearly every Biharu was an expert crafter, making these wonders in leisure hours stolen from the hard business of survival. He was even more amazed to discover that the Biharu were shrewd bargainers, exchanging their creations for an equal weight of raw metal and dyes, plus polished gemstones, wines, and other luxuries.

However, he also noted that only half a dozen of the forty traders actually did the bargaining, while the others strolled about the camp, surveying the Biharu entirely too casually. He began to stroll himself, suspicion growing—then crystalizing when he saw three of the traders standing in a tense group, muttering to one another and casting furtive glances at one particular nomad . . .

Dariad.

It was reassuring to know that someone else thought the man had special qualities, but Ohaern did not think he liked the nature of their interest. Accordingly, for the rest of the evening he made sure he was never very far from Dariad. When the fire was lighted, the meat roasting, and the wineskins passing, he brought Lucoyo to a place near the tranquil nomad, ostensibly to have a better look at the dancing; and when the Biharu and the traders reeled unsteadily back to their respective camps, Ohaern contrived to keep Dariad in sight as he strolled back to his tent.

So he was very near when five traders appeared from behind the tent and fell on Dariad in coldly ruthless silence.

Ohaern shouted an angry warning and ran toward the fracas. Dariad whipped about, and Ohaern saw a knife gleaming in his hand just before three of the attackers fell upon him. Then the other two fell upon Ohaern, one leaping for his head, the other coming in low with a dagger. Ohaern shouted in rage, drawing his own knife in a broad sweep, and the lower attacker had to pull back for a moment—just long enough for Ohaern to catch the jumper by the throat. A fist rocked his head, and the night scene was shot with tiny points of light, but he threw the man from him, straight into his companion, then fell back in guard stance, shaking his head to clear it. The attackers unsnarled themselves and came for him again, but more warily this time, one advancing while the other waited to strike from behind, still in that uncanny silence.

But if they would not shout, Ohaern would. "Biharu! Help! Your kinsman is attacked!"

The merchant forgot caution in his haste to silence Ohaern and leaped forward, thrusting with his knife. Ohaern caught his wrist and bent it outward. The man's mouth opened wide in a silent shout of agony; then Ohaern's knife fist cracked into his chin, closing his jaw for him, and the smith threw the unconscious man into his friend, who was just pivoting in to thrust. The knife caught his companion in the back; then Ohaern caught the assassin, and his knife hilt slapped into the base of the man's skull. He longed to use the point, but was afraid of starting a war with the traders. He threw the unconscious pair aside and stepped forward, frantic with worry for Dariad.

The nomad stood breathing heavily, a rivulet of blood marking his cheek just below the eye and another streaking his forearm— but he was grinning a wolf's grin, and three men lay at his feet. Blood pooled from one and painted another. Their slayer looked up at the smith. "Thank you for my life, Ohaern. I do not think I could have struck down all five—they were very good with their knives."

Ohaern could only stare. Was this really the tranquil, mild-mannered young man who had spoken so calmly to him about his God?

Then the shouting registered, and he spun about, side by side with Dariad, ready to defend—but it was the nomad's tribesmen who came running up, swords and daggers at the ready. "Are you hurt, Dariad?"

"Only a scratch," Daraid panted, "thanks to Ohaern."

The Biharu drew up, staring down at the assassins. "The traders? Murderers among the traders?"

"Murderers trained for it." Ohaern knelt and pried one man's jaws open, then another's and another's. "Their tongues have been cut out to be sure they would attack in silence and could not say who had sent them."

The nomads stared, aghast. Then one asked, "But were they *of* the traders, or only traveling among them in disguise?"

"Assume they are as much traders as any!" The Biharu leader drew his own sword, whirling about. "Protect your wives and children!"

The Biharu stared in amazement, then gave one massed shout as they ran toward the traders' campfires.

"Beware treachery!" Dariad cried. "These men strike from behind!"

Without breaking stride, a score of his tribesmen fanned out on the opposite side of the camp, following Dariad. Ohaern stood in the center of the Biharu camp, looking about him, not knowing which way to turn.

Lucoyo came running up, Labina's sword in his hand. "Ohaern! The traders! Look!"

Ohaern did look, just in time to see the traders casting aside their robes to free their sword arms—and the campfires showed them standing in the harness and kilts of soldiers, leather and cloth dyed the scarlet of Kuru—of Kuru, and of Ulahane!

"Archer! Your bow!" Ohaern cried.

"Useless now!" Lucoyo swung about, back-to-back with Ohaern. "They are too close! Five of them for every one of us, Ohaern!"

"Five at the least!" Ohaern agreed, just as a Kuruite soldier came charging down on him, howling a battle cry and swinging a sword as if it were an axe. Ohaern blocked the blade and kicked him in the belly. As he fell back, two more surged up in his place. Ohaern blocked and parried in a whirl of dagger and sword, then ended one life with a slash and another with a thrust. Four more came at him, half a circle; two tripped over their fallen fellows, one fell trailing a ribbon of blood from Ohaern's sword—but the other opened the smith's chest before Ohaern beat him back. In battle-frenzy, he did not feel the pain, scarcely knew he was wounded at all. He blocked the blows of the next two, scrambling back to their feet now, and the two charging up after them.

Behind him Lucoyo's battle cry cut clear and high above the bull roars of the Kuruites, heartening Ohaern as he cried, "Fall down!" and enforced the command with edge and point. A spear thrust at him; he leaned aside in the nick of time, then slashed the hands that held it. The Kuruite fell with a howl—but his spear point was red. Ohaern paid it no heed, only ducked under a thrust from his left. The Kuruite stumbled, falling against Ohaern's shoulder, and the smith brought his dagger up under the enemy's breastbone. The man gave a single sharp cry; then Ohaern was surging up, throwing the man off, slashing to block a sword coming from his right, counterslashing, then circling his sword around and stabbing. The man's eyes bulged as he leaned forward over the sword, then dulled as he fell. Ohaern yanked his blade free and glared about him, chest heaving . . .

The frenzy parted for a minute, and he saw Grakhinox and the Klaja back-to-back, each striped with blood but still fighting valiantly. Then the churning melee hid them from view again; all about him nomad robes whirled as they stabbed and slashed at Kuruite cross belts and kilts. Ohaern stared in amazement, for each of the

Biharu stood in a loose ring of bodies, three or four to a man. Even as he watched, several of the nomads dispatched the last soldiers who faced them and turned to help their tribesman. In minutes the battle was done, and not a single Kuruite was left standing. The Klaja and the dwerg emerged from the melee, blood-marked but walking, and the Biharu spoke to them with respect and friendship.

Dariad came up, breathing hard, his teeth still set in a feral grin. "They are good fighters, these Kuruites. Three of my tribesmen are dead, and a dozen more are wounded too sorely to ride. Indeed, we shall have to stay at this oasis a week longer than we had intended."

"I do not think that is wise." Manalo appeared out of the darkness. "The Kuruites know where you are now and may send more against you. It is time for your people to disappear into the sands."

Dariad frowned. "Will the judge say so?"

"I shall confer with him." Manalo went off to find the tribal leader.

But Ohaern's brow knit as he looked out over the battlefield at the robed Biharu who prowled among the bodies, suddenly stabbing down, then pulling the sword loose and prowling again. "What do they do?"

"They are finishing the wounded," Dariad answered sadly. "It is hard, I know, but we live too close to the bone to be able to feed and water a score or more of wounded enemies."

"It *is* hard." Ohaern was appalled.

"It would be more cruel to leave them to a slow death under the baking sun," Dariad countered. "Besides, remember that they came in treachery and deception, and would have slain us to a man if they could have."

Ohaern remembered how the five mutes had fallen upon Dariad, and held his peace.

"Those who can walk, may—they may even take their camels—but if they seek to turn and come back at us, we shall slay them in their tracks."

A shout went up from the soldiers' camp. Dariad snapped, "Hajpheth, Zera, Haba! Guard our wounded!"

"Who appointed *you* chief?" one man demanded, annoyed.

Dariad shrugged. "If you doubt me, do as you please!" He turned to run toward the source of the shout. Ohaern followed close, with Lucoyo behind him—but he glanced back and noticed that the three men stayed to do as Dariad had bid. There was something about the young nomad that induced compliance.

They came to a halt amid the Kuruite tents, to find five traders huddled together in fright. Ohaern recognized the men who had done the actual bargaining.

"Beneath their robes are only loincloths," one of the nomads was telling the judge, "no Kuruite harness—and they bear no weapons."

"The soldiers would not allow them to us," one of the traders explained.

"So these are the real traders." Ohaern stepped up. "And the only traders, I doubt not. Why did you lead the soldiers here?"

"We did not lead them—they brought us," the trader explained.

"They said there would be rich trading," another said, "and that we would risk no goods of our own—they would provide all."

"But you knew they were soldiers." Dariad frowned. "Did you not think you should warn us? We bargained in good faith, we gave you bread and salt!"

"As we neared your camp," the first trader explained, "they set swords to our throats and said they would slay us if we told."

"And you had no great reason to protect us," Dariad said with disgust. He looked up at the judge. "What shall we do with them?"

The traders stared up in fear.

"This is my judgment," the leader answered. "They shall go free with one camel each, and swords to protect them from robbers—but no more."

"Thirty camels at least!" Another nomad looked about him. "A score of tents, and a dozen bags of trade goods! We shall gain something by this, at least."

"But we have lost kinsmen's lives," Dariad said, frowning.

"Death comes to us all," the judge reminded him, "and our kinsmen died in glory. Their deaths were not the fault of these deceived traders. They should have told the truth, yes, but they have not enough guilt to be slain."

"That is generous," Lucoyo said with a scowl, "but also foolish. Will they not bring the soldiers of Kuru down upon you?"

The nomads glanced at one another and grinned. "They will," Dariad said, "if they can find us."

"Can you discover the trail of the blown sand?" another nomad asked. "Can you track the sirocco?"

"Where the Biharu have passed, no one can tell," the judge explained. "We leave no traces, and when we choose to hide, none shall find us—unless we wish it."

"But these soldiers found you once!" Lucoyo objected.

"That is true," said the judge, "but we were not in hiding. Indeed, we wished to be found—if the finder was a traders' caravan."

Lucoyo subsided, baffled and angry, but Ohaern said, "These soldiers knew where to find you, and I doubt they were seeking any desert tribe at random."

"Perhaps they followed you," a nomad suggested.

The Biharu stirred, muttering, with uneasy glances at Lucoyo and Ohaern—and Manalo, who came striding up. "They may have—or they may have sought someone who, they knew, was here among you."

"Dariad!" Ohaern's head snapped up; he stared at the young nomad. "It must be Dariad, for they came in disguise, to win your trust and lull you into lowering your guard!"

"Aye." Lucoyo glared angrily. "What need for stealth if they only sought us? They could have come openly as soldiers, and only waited until we had left your camp and gone on alone, then leaped upon us from hiding."

"There is sense in what they say," the judge said heavily.

"But . . . Dariad?" one of the older nomads protested. "Little *Dariad*?"

The other Biharu turned to look at their comrade, puzzled, but Manalo confirmed it. "It is Dariad indeed. There is a quality of uniqueness about you, young man—a sense of great power within. Any of Ulahane's sorcerers could find and follow that aura of destiny in an instant."

"There was a priest of Ulahane with them," a trader said.

The judge frowned. "Where is he now?"

The trader looked about, at a loss. "He stayed here near us, where the guards were."

"I saw him disappear," another trader said, his voice shaking, "fade to nothing and disappear!"

"It is Dariad." The judge frowned. "We must hide, indeed, and arm ourselves to protect our kinsman."

"I will not imperil you!" Dariad exclaimed. "I will lose myself in the desert!"

Even before the judge could object, Manalo said, "Lose yourself with us instead. We must go into the Sand Sea. You can lead us to its edge, at least, and wait for us to come back—and I shall weave a spell that will cloak you from even the best of Ulahane's sorcerers."

The Biharu stared and pulled away, muttering fearfully, and the judge demanded, "Are you a sorcerer, too, then?"

"A wizard," Manalo corrected, "and one equal in power to any of Ulahane's priests."

Lucoyo frowned. "How is it the chains of Byleo could hold you, then? . . . Oh."

Manalo turned to him and nodded. "They were forged by a sorcerer equal to me in power. It was Ohaern's strength that broke that deadlock, not mine." He turned back to Dariad. "Will you come with us, then?"

"If my going will preserve my people from the danger of the soldiers? Of course."

But the Biharu muttered angrily, and the judge said, "We do not leave our own to face peril! If you go to the Sand Sea, Dariad, we all go!"

The young nomad stared, alarmed and touched at the same time.

"Fold your tents and flee like your windblown sand," Manalo advised, "for when these soldiers fail to return, more will be sent to finish what they have begun."

The judge spat in contempt. "We fear no soldiers—and we will not abandon our kinsman! If you go to the Sand Sea, Dariad, we will go with you!"

Dariad gazed about at them all with gratitude and love that faded to concern. "I would not be the cause of the deaths of any more of my kinsmen!"

"And we will not leave you to the soldiers," said another nomad, and they all called out in loud and angry agreement.

"It is well that you do follow him," Manalo told them, "for Ulahane is abroad in the land and draws in his minions to strike down all that is good and brave in humankind, that he may enslave the weak and wicked to abuse for his own corrupted pleasures. Foremost among these are the soldiers of Kuru, for Kuru is a city that is wholly and completely dedicated to Ulahane, aye, worshiping him as a god and having no other gods but the Scarlet One!" He turned to Dariad, and his voice rang out. "I tell you as one who knows, for I am a sage, devoted to Lomallin! I tell you that the Green One has work for you to do, for the glory of the Star-Maker! Aye, you, and all who will follow you!"

Dariad stared at him in awe. Then he recognized the truth of Manalo's words and straightened with inner certainty. Indeed, the young nomad seemed to grow right there before their eyes. "Yes, I can feel the rightness of what you say, and see that fighting for Lomallin is the only way to save my tribe!" He turned to his tribesmen, calling, "The sage speaks truth! Lomallin requires service of us, service for our god and all that is good! Kinsmen, I would not ask you to die for my own vain glory—but the glory of the Star-Maker, and the survival and freedom of all humankind, is a cause worth every drop of blood in our veins!"

The Biharu answered him with a shout, swords waving on high, and the judge said, "If these soldiers come from Kuru, and if Ulahane shall wreak such destruction that no one will be safe from Kuru's soldiers, then Kuru must be destroyed!"

"Aye," Ohaern shouted, with the memory of Ryl's dying face before him, "Kuru must be destroyed, and Ulahane with it!"

The Biharu answered with another shout of acclaim. Any other people would have shrunk in fear at the thought of seeking to destroy a god, but these Biharu did not believe the Ulin *were* gods. Admittedly, they were beings much more powerful than themselves—but the camels were more powerful than humans, and were tamed to the will of the Biharu—so why should not one Ulin be slain?

When the companions left the oasis an hour later, Dariad rode with them, and his whole tribe followed with grim resolve, the Klaja and Grakhinox among them, and the only ones who shied away from them now were the camels.

But Dariad seemed to have shrunk back to an ordinary and rather uncertain mortal as he glanced behind to stare at his tribe, then turned to Ohaern. "How can I possibly be worthy of their trust?"

"Because you are," Ohaern answered, and he watched the young nomad square his shoulders, straightening his back and riding with his eyes fixed ahead. The big smith reflected wryly that leadership of the Biharu seemed to have passed from the judge to this young seeming-simpleton, and no one felt need to comment on the fact!

When they came to the edge of the Sand Sea, though, Manalo turned to Dariad and bade him, "Hide among the sands, as only the desert-born can. There is a meeting I must attend deep within the Sand Sea, and I wish that none of humankind had need to witness it."

"If there is need, I shall go!" Dariad said instantly.

Manalo's smile showed that his heart was warmed, and he clasped the young nomad's shoulder. "I know that you would, and I thank you—but I need to know that you are here, to guard and protect those who come out. Only Ohaern may come with me—and Lucoyo with him."

The half-elf looked up, incipient panic in his eyes, but the judge scowled and said, "There is nothing within the Sand Sea, O Sage, nothing at all—save an accursed ruin which even the Biharu shun! I beg you, do not go, for you shall die of thirst before you so much as come near that evil place!"

The tribesmen clamored their agreement, imploring the teacher not to go, but Manalo said inexorably, "Nonetheless, I must go," and apprehension shadowed his face. "There may be nothing amidst those sands yet, but the one I must meet shall be there at the appointed hour. I must go." He turned to Ohaern and Lucoyo. "You need not come with me if you do not wish it."

"I wish it," Ohaern said instantly, catching Lucoyo with his mouth open.

The half-elf closed his lips and scowled up at the big smith. Who was Ohaern to humiliate him and make him look like a coward? He had been about to say that he did not wish it, indeed—but with Ohaern being so stupidly courageous again, Lucoyo knew he could not stay behind without loss of face—and that, Lucoyo could not tolerate at all! After all, what woman would look at a man who had virtually admitted he was a coward? "Oh, I will go, too," he grumbled. "Take camels at least, though, Teacher!"

"Camels you shall have, and all the water we can spare," the judge said, and minutes later their camels waded into the Sand Sea, burdened with water skins and ridden by fools—or so Lucoyo reflected sourly as his mount followed Ohaern's and the sun sank slowly behind them.

CHAPTER 26

As they rode, Manalo summoned Ohaern up beside him and said, "I have seen the signs of the drought spreading, Ohaern, as I have gone the length and the breadth of the steppe, warning the tribes and giving each a sign, that they may know when to march. The high plains themselves are dry enough, but they do at least support much grass. Still, the farther south I came, the more sparse the growth became, until it was all waste, as you saw in the Biharu's land."

"They tell me the desert is spreading," Ohaern replied. Inwardly, he was still recovering from his shock at the idea that the sage had traveled so far in only the few months it had taken himself and Lucoyo to travel from the land of the Biriae to the land of the Biharu.

"It is indeed spreading," Manalo told him, "and will engulf all these southern lands if it is not ended."

"It is Ulahane's doing, then?"

"It is," Manalo confirmed.

A flicker of movement at the corner of Ohearn's eye caught his attention. He turned to look, but it was gone. "Perhaps it is my vision that falters, O Sage—but I keep seeing something move, and when I turn to look, it is gone."

"It is not your vision," Manalo returned. Again Ohaern felt concern, for that usually gentle face was pale and grim.

"No, it is not," Lucoyo said. "I kept watch, and *I* saw it this time. It is a lion with the head of a man—if a man had double mouths filled with four rows of pointed teeth."

Manalo nodded. "The beast is called a 'manticore.' It is a creature of the open plains."

Ohaern glanced apprehensively off to his left; again, something flickered at the edge of sight and was gone. "What are they doing here, in the desert?"

"Ulahane has sent them after us, of course!" Lucoyo snapped. His face was filled with dread as he glanced to left and right about him.

"You have sharp eyes, Lucoyo," Manalo said, "sharp and quick. But do not fear—the manticores will not attack us until we have come to our destination."

"How do you know?" the half-elf demanded, but Manalo only answered "I know."

"What *is* our destination?" Ohaern asked.

"The ruin that stands at the heart of this sea," Manalo said.

"The *accursed* ruin?" Lucoyo demanded, staring in fright. "It will kill us!"

"It will not, and it is not accursed," Manalo answered. "It is there we must go. You may go back if you wish, Lucoyo. I will not force you to come—no, not in any way."

Lucoyo was on the verge of turning his camel right then, but Ohaern caught his eye and he subsided, muttering. The big smith and he had saved one another's lives too often for him to leave now—at least, not if Ohaern stayed.

The journey was only three days, but the heat became so intense that even the camels began to falter. Ohaern suggested night travel, but Manalo warned them against the dark, telling them that the creatures of Ulahane could come upon them more easily when the sky was black. He saw to it that they rode only in the hours between first light and mid-morning, and between sunset and darkness. When they lit their campfire, he sprinkled strange powders into it, reciting words they could not understand—but as always, Ohaern memorized the sounds, even though he could not comprehend them. Whatever they were, whatever powders the sage used, they kept the manticores at bay and fended off whatever else sheltered in that waste—Ohaern heard the ominous padding all about them and saw the glitter of eyes reflecting the firelight, but none dared come within its circle.

"Sleep, Ohaern," Manalo bade. "Sleep, Lucoyo. None can come near this fire now." And, miraculously, they did sleep.

But as the fourth sunset faded to twilight and their weary camels plodded protesting over the sand, a glittering column rose up to their left, hissing like a hundred serpents—and well it might, for a serpent it was, though with a woman's head and breasts. The face was beautiful, with huge long-lashed eyes and full, wide, bloodred lips—but those great eyes were staring mad, and the perfect lips opened to reveal fangs. A forked tongue flicked out to sample the air, tasted men, and the monster slithered toward them over the sand.

The camels bawled and bolted. Ohaern rocked, almost thrown from his saddle, and Lucoyo *was* thrown, but caught an arm about the camel's neck as he fell, and managed to scramble back on. Manalo's camel fought and curvetted, braying terror, but the sage held on and channeled its fear into flight, after Ohaern's.

The smith's camel was running faster, though, and would have run itself into the ground had not another maddened female face lifted itself out of the sand straight before them. The camel bawled again and whirled about to run back—but it saw strange leonine beasts with multiple jaws coming up in the distance, and it stalled.

Manalo caught up, snatched the reins, and turned the beast aside. Together they ran from the monsters with Lucoyo's beast right behind them—but a third snake-body reared up with a beautiful face framed in wild, windblown hair above perfect breasts, and Manalo's camel leaped aside. It ran north until a fourth head reared up, then turned back to the south, but a fifth snake-woman rose, and hissing seemed to surround them, enwrap them, enfold them, as their camels ran through an inceasingly narrow corridor of snake-women, streaming in now from all sides, until a great rock structure loomed up before them, ghostly in the moonlight. The camels galloped between two huge uprights, and suddenly Ohaern was filled with a sense of limitless power, of unimaginable strength. He knew there was nothing he could not do, nothing within the realm of a man—even the slaying of an Ulin. But as fast as he thought it came the realization: this was the power of the stones, not of himself.

Manalo pulled his beast back hard. The camels slowed to a halt, bawling, but the sage's chanting overrode the sound. Corruscations of blue light sprang up around all the huge stone columns and across the lintels that bound them together, and the air between each pair of columns shimmered with energy. The snake-women and the manticores reared back, shying away, filling the air all about with hisses of rage and roars of disappointment.

Lucoyo leaped off his camel and went running toward the monsters, drawing his sword and shouting, "Away with you, foul creatures! I shall slay you, I shall slay you all!"

"Lucoyo, no!" Manalo cried. "Ohaern, stop him!"

Ohaern tapped his camel, crooning, and the beast lumbered into motion again, swerving around to block Lucoyo. The half-elf shouted in anger and veered around the beast—but Ohaern jumped down on the far side and caught Lucoyo in a bear hug as he came around. "No, archer! The power that keeps them out must keep you in!"

"I can slay them all, slay anything born of Ulahane's foul magic!" Lucoyo raved, thrashing about. "Let me go, Ohaern! At last I can strike back at him who saw me made!"

"No, Lucoyo! The power that thrums within you is not your own, but that of the stones about you! Give over, for once out of this ring, you will be only yourself again!"

Lucoyo stilled, then hung his head and said heavily, "So that is why I suddenly felt that I could fell the Tree that upholds the sky! Oh, let me be, Ohaern! Nay, I shall not seek to do more than I can!"

Ohaern set him down and opened his arms warily, but the half-elf only sheathed his sword, cast a disgusted look at the snake-women, then lifted his head with a look of exaltation coming into his eyes. "I can enjoy that heady feeling, though."

"You can indeed," Manalo told him, "but the manticores and lamias cannot. They are creatures made by Ulahane, and cannot enter here without great pain."

"Is that what the snake-women are?" Lucoyo asked. "Lamias?"

"That is what they are called," Manalo answered.

Ohaern looked up with sudden understanding. "So to them, this ring *is* accursed!"

"Is that where we are?" Lucoyo stared about him in sudden terror. "The accursed ruin?"

"We are," Manalo said, "but as Ohaern has noticed, it is not accursed—to us. Nor is it a ring, but a rectangle. It once was a fortress with a wooden roof, but the boards have long since fallen in and turned to powder."

Lucoyo glanced apprehensively at the dust under his feet, but Ohaern's eyes were on the pillars. They were perfect cylinders, soaring so high that they seemed to taper at the top, and the lintels linking them bore strange carvings that he could not make out for the blue light that played all about them. "Why do men think it accursed?"

"Because Ulahane has put that rumor about through his human agents," Manalo explained. "He does not wish any human to come here, for fear they may find a way to use the power of this ancient fortress to oppose him. So he has threatened to curse any man who approaches, and has surrounded it with devastation to keep them away."

"Why is it abandoned?" Lucoyo asked. "Only for fear of the Scarlet One?"

"That is reason enough, for most men," Manalo told him. "This was the fortress of the human-lovers in the Ulin War. The roof sheltered them from spears and bolts that Marcoblin's forces might rain down upon them. But at the last, Marcoblin broke the roof and fell upon Lomallin and his allies with steel and fire— though it was the human-haters who were burned and slain as often as the human-lovers, for within these pillars and their walls of magic, there was no room for an army to maneuver, so it quickly became Ulin against Ulin, in individual combat."

"And the Ulins were all equal in power," Ohaern whispered.

"Even so. When Marcoblin was slain, and Ulahane saw he could not win, he rallied his forces—what few of them there were—and retreated. Lomallin and his few surviving allies stayed, singing praises for their survival as they scrubbed away the blood, and their goodness and gratitude made it a shrine. Their power endured even after they left."

"Did not Ulahane seek to wreak vengeance upon the place of Marcoblin's death when it was no longer protected?"

"He tried to destroy, he tried to desecrate, but found he could not," Manalo replied. "Equal numbers of lovers and haters died here, so hate was balanced by charity, and the goodwill of the human-lovers for their stronghold turned that balance. Ulahane can only turn it back by slaying an Ulin here, a human-lover."

"Would not he have to slay Lomallin himself to overcome so much goodness?" Ohaern asked.

"Something of that magnitude," Manalo admitted.

"Is that why we have come here, then?" Lucoyo asked, his voice small in the vastness. "To witness the death of an Ulin?"

Manalo stood still long minutes; then he nodded. "A combat to the death. Yes. And there must be a human witness, and two will stand a greater chance of escaping to tell all other humans about it."

"Cannot you bear word yourself?" Lucoyo asked.

"No," Manalo said shortly. "Never mind why. The time is appointed, and the hour approaches. Go to hiding, you two." He pointed to the side, where a column had fallen with a lintel stone leaning across it. "Go there and lie down; when you kneel up in the shadow where the two stones touch, you shall be able to see."

Lucoyo objected, "But you must also—"

"Go!" Manalo snapped, not looking at them. "Go hide, and when this night's work is done, go out secretly from this temple, and hide until you will be safe in traveling! Dariad and his people will wait for you; they will not despair and turn away no matter how long the vigil—and you must survive, because this whole war hinges on Ohaern, and Ohaern's life hinges on Lucoyo. Go!" His arm was an iron rod pointing to the fallen stones, and his face was livid.

Never before had they seen such tension in the sage. Lucoyo felt a perverse surge of desire to defy, to bait, but he looked into

Manalo's face and forced that urge back down. He fell in beside Ohaern and lay down between the stones.

Then they waited. Now and again one of them would lever himself up to glance at Manalo—but always they saw him standing as they had left him, still as the stone columns about him and every bit as straight, his hands holding fast to his staff.

Then, when both had their heads down, a huge blast of sound rocked the ancient temple, a blast followed by booming, harsh laughter that echoed off the stones. Ohaern sat up, peering over the top of the fallen lintel, and Lucoyo edged his way up beside him, then froze in fright, for he saw a giant, three times the height of a man, with a face twisted with hatred, cavernous eyes, and a mouth filled with pointed teeth that gleamed in the light from the stones as he laughed, head back and high. He wore a kilt and armor, all scarlet, and the helmet on his head was shaped like a skull.

Ohaern and Lucoyo both knelt rigid. It was the Scarlet One, it was Ulahane himself!

"Now the hour has come," the Scarlet One boomed. "Now can you hide from me no longer! Now comes the hour of confrontation, when you must fight me hand-to-hand and self-to-self, with none of your puppets nor your puling allies to save you!"

"Now comes the hour indeed," Manalo replied, "but who shall save *you*?"

"I need no saving, foolish green-sick one!" And Ulahane drew a knife from his belt to send it flashing toward Manalo.

Ohaern gasped, rigid, but Lucoyo clamped a hand on his shoulder, holding him back.

The knife changed as it flew, turning to fire, becoming a bolt of ruby light, but Manalo did not even raise his staff to ward it off. It struck him in the chest, and Lucoyo gasped while Ohaern clapped a hand over his mouth to stifle a cry of anger. But the sage still stood, tall and straight, as his body absorbed the ruby bolt and began to glow, first orange, then yellow, even as it began to swell. His robe ripped and fell off, his staff was dwarfed as the hand about it grew. Manalo's form glowed with a nimbus of green light as he grew taller, wider, and taller yet, until he stood, clad only in a loincloth, the staff now seeming a mere wand in the hand of a giant. His face was still Manalo's face, bearded, wise, and gentle—but now Ohaern recognized the face he had seen on statues.

"He—" Lucoyo cried, before Ohaern's hand clapped over his mouth. He did not need to complete the sentence, after all. Both of them could see: their friend, the gentle sage, was in truth the Green One, Lomallin.

Ulahane bellowed with rage and drew a sword that was half again the height of a man. He advanced on Lomallin, and the ground shook with his tread as he swung that terrible blade, blazing with red fire. Still calmly, Lomallin met its stroke with his green-glowing wand—and incredibly, Ulahane's sword jolted to a stop against it. Ulahane bellowed again, swinging the sword up and about, and it *was* fire now, red as blood and smoking. Again Lomallin met burning sword with green wand, and again the two clashed and jolted still. Ulahane howled and kicked Lomallin in the groin, and the Green One cried out, falling back, staggering, but kept his feet. His wand lowered, though, and with a cry of triumph Ulahane swung his sword high in a circle and chopped down. It struck Lomallin where his neck joined his shoulder and went on, sheared through muscle and bone halfway down into his chest, and Lucoyo and Ohaern leaped to their feet with cries of horror—but they went unheard, for Ulahane's bellow of victory shook all that stone square and filled the night as Lomallin's body convulsed, whipping upright, then bending back in an arc, so far that he seemed almost a half circle. Green light streamed from his wound, green light that filled the sky, crackling among the columns as the Ulin's body disintegrated, turning to dust, and the dust turned to glitter as it fell, glittering light that dispersed and rose and blew away into the heavens, while the blue light that had crackled along the columns and lintels dissipated and died with the one who had made it.

The manticores charged in with a roar from the south and west; the lamias arrowed in, hissing, from the north and east.

"Find them!" Ulahane roared. "Find these insolent mortals who dared accompany an Ulin and call him friend!"

But he had done too well in breeding monsters of malice. The manticores pounced upon the lamias, and the lamias threw their coils about the manticores, and the night was filled with hissing and roaring.

"Run!" Lucoyo cried, and Ohaern jolted out of his paralysis of horror and turned, running with every ounce of his strength, running to get away from that horrible place where he had lost his strongest friend and seen a god die.

Behind them, Ulahane waded into the melee, roaring and cursing and striking out, knocking his two kinds of monstrosities apart. Finally, he sent them leaping and gliding out into the night, and Ohaern heard their howling and hissing as Lucoyo passed him, running for more than his life—for the half-elf had no illusions as to what his fate would be if Ulahane caught him and there was no Lomallin to shield him.

CHAPTER 27

It was a long night of hiding and running and hiding again. Several times, when the monsters were near, Ohaern recited one or another of the spells he had heard from Manalo—no, Lomallin! But Ohaern was not an Ulin, and the spell that should have kept the monsters beyond the light of a campfire let them come close, within five feet of the dry creek bed where the two men lay with fear in their throats. Of course, Ohaern dared not stop long enough to light a fire, dared not even show a light, and certainly did not have the powder the sage—and Ulin!—had thrown into the flame. So perhaps the spell did work after all, for the monsters never found them, though they came close enough to have caught their scent easily.

Finally, as the chill of the darkest hour reached through to their bones, they staggered into the shelter of a huge boulder that rose abruptly from the sand, and blundered into a cave hidden under its low-curving side. Ohaern dropped down and leaned back against a cold stone wall, chest heaving, eyes closed, face pale and drawn. Lucoyo was equally winded, but still tense with the energy of fear; he looked about at their new refuge. It was low, not high enough for even Lucoyo to stand upright, and cylindrical, running back into the boulder farther than they could see, almost as if it had been the track of some giant worm that burrowed through on its way to richer fare underground. Lucoyo eyed the depths and decided to avoid them. In fact, he decided to be very wary about them, period.

And apparently he was going to have to be the one who worried, for Ohaern dropped down to lean back against the stone wall and did not move. Instead his body began to go loose, muscle by muscle, and tears welled from beneath his eyelids.

Panic seized Lucoyo, more intense than any he had ever felt before. Ohaern had become the rock of his life ever since he had left the tribe that had raised him, so seeing the big smith reduced to jelly and tears shook him even more deeply than watching Manalo shed his disguise and emerge as Lomallin, only to be slain by the Scarlet One. He dropped to one knee and said in as soothing a tone as he could manage, "It will be well again, Ohaern."

"It will not!" the smith groaned, in the voice of heartbreak. "Ryl is dead, Manalo is gone, Lomallin is dead, and nothing shall endure to uphold hope! It is vain, Lucoyo—all the world is vain and hollow, and life is without meaning!"

The panic stayed, deepening into the horrible feeling for Lucoyo that he was confronting fate. "There is hope, there must be!" Inspiration struck. "Remember that the sage said I must care for you because you are the key to this war! It is you who can slay the Scarlet One!"

"What purpose?" Ohaern groaned through his tears. "What purpose, when he has slain Lomallin?"

"Revenge! Confound you, man, is your nature so kindly that you do not even crave revenge?"

"What matter? We are doomed, we are all doomed! How can I take revenge on Ulahane? How could anything kill him, now that he has slain Lomallin?"

Clear as if he were there beside them, Lucoyo heard Manalo's remembered voice. He said, "The legend! Ohaern, remember the legend! That only after he has been slain can Lomallin become stronger than Ulahane!"

"What a deal of nonsense!" Ohaern cried with building anger. "How can any man become stronger after he is dead?"

"He is an Ulin, not a man."

"Was! Do not say 'is' to me, Lucoyo!" The anger was building toward rage now. "Lomallin is dead! I saw him die with these eyes! Do not pretend he still lives!" Suddenly the smith lashed out, striking a blow that sent Lucoyo flying down the cave and crashing into a wall. "Go away! Leave me! Stop plaguing me with your words of brightness! Leave me to my grief and let me die in peace!"

"All right, if that is your wish!" Lucoyo cried in anger of his own. He leaped up, cracked his head on the roof, cursed, and strode out of the cave, leaving Ohaern to his tears and his wallow of despair.

Ohaern wept long, deep racking sobs that shook his whole frame and drew from him every dram of energy he possessed. At last, worn out, he fell over, lying long on the cold stone of the cave floor, and wept the last few sobs, which were devoid of tears. Finally he quieted, and sleep enfolded him, a sleep that shrouded him in gray mist, a fog such as had lain over the grass when they buried Ryl.

But it was not Ryl who made those mists part—it was golden light, and as the mists burned away, Ohaern saw against it the silhouette of the voluptuous, translucent-veiled female form of his dream, and knew he saw the goddess, the Ulin, again. He dared to breathe her name: "Rahani."

"Come to me, Ohaern." The veiled arm beckoned. "Seek through the world inside and come to me. Come, and you shall have comfort, you shall have consolation, you shall have ecstasy such as mortal men only dream of—if you can find me . . . if you can reach me . . . if you can touch . . ."

But her arms were moving, waving, as her hips churned in a dance, and the veils were enfolding her, hiding her, turning to mist, to fog, in which she disappeared.

"Rahani!" he cried in the tearing voice of despair, and reached out to grasp, to draw, but his hand closed on rock, and the gray of the mist was hardening into stone, a stone that seemed to warm, to turn yellow, and Ohaern realized he was seeing sunlight on rock, a lump of rock swelling out of the cave wall.

He stilled, his eyes flicking up and down, discovering that he was in the cave and that his body felt like lead. He pulled himself up sitting, but hung his head, muttering, "I am awake."

"Yes, praise the gods!"

Ohaern looked up, startled, to see Lucoyo holding out a water skin. In his amazement, Ohaern did not even think to ask where it had come from, only took it and squirted a few swallows into his mouth. Then he handed it back. "I thought you had left me."

"So did I." Lucoyo shrugged. "But I stepped out into that freezing, barren night and realized I had no place to go." He sighed. "I might as well die here with you, as die fighting a manticore or being squeezed to death by a lamia. Unless, perhaps, you have decided not to die?" He did not seem very hopeful.

Ohaern was silent a moment, then said, "I do not know, Lucoyo." He looked up, looked directly into the half-elf's eyes and said, "You see, I have fallen in love."

Lucoyo stared back, then said, "That is not usually a cause of death."

"No," Ohaern agreed, "but she whom I love is a goddess, an Ulin."

Lucoyo stared again, his eyes wide and round. Then, in tones of pain and regret, he breathed, "Oh, Ohaern!"

"Yes," Ohaern agreed. "To worship a goddess, to give her devotion, is all well and good—but to be in love with her?"

"What shall you do?" Lucoyo whispered.

"I shall find her." Ohaern straightened with decision and pulled his legs under him, folded to keep him upright as he set his back against the stone wall. "I shall find her again or die in the seeking, and if it is to be only in dreams that I may discover her, then in dreams I shall lose myself. She bade me search for her through the world inside."

"The world inside?" Lucoyo frowned. "How shall you do that?"

"As shamans do. I have spoken with the healers of our clan well enough to know that they must sink into trance and journey far, though their bodies sit still. I shall sit here until I sleep, and bring up a waking dream—for I know, more clearly than I have ever known anything, that I must find her or die."

Lucoyo bit back the words; Ohaern did not need to be reminded that they would probably die in any case. Well, it was better to die in this cave, of starvation and thirst, but without knowing it, than to die between the jaws of a manticore. Perhaps it was even better to die here knowing you were dying—and keeping a friend's body alive as long as you could. "Sleep then, Ohaern. Though you wake, find your sleep—if you can."

"I shall—or my body shall dry up and lie forever in this cave." Ohaern closed his eyes, leaning his head back against the wall. In truth, he felt that if he could not find the goddess, he would prefer to find death rather than face a life devoid of Ryl and devoid of Rahani, or to confront the fact that Ulahane was laying waste to the world and torturing humankind to extinction for his own twisted pleasure.

Lucoyo stared at his impassive face, still as the stone behind it, and reflected that it was, at least, better than seeing that face distorted with pain.

The eyes opened and Lucoyo nearly jumped back in fright, it was so unexpected. "That was a short dream!"

"I am in the wrong place." Ohaern climbed to his feet.

Lucoyo stared. "How do you know?"

"That, I do not know—I only know that I know." Ohaern prowled to the mouth of the cave, stepped out, went a few paces, then stopped, shaking his head. "No—I am farther from it now." He came back in, sat down in a different spot, closed his eyes, then opened them and shook his head. "Not here, either." He went farther back in the tunnel, sat down again, shook his head again. "Nor here." He rose again, went farther back, tried another spot and another. Heart in his mouth, Lucoyo followed the big smith into the very bowels of the cave . . .

Where it suddenly opened out.

It was no cave, but a cavern, and to judge by its size, the whole of the giant rock must have been hollow. From very high up, nearly at the ceiling, the sun's rays slanted down through long slits in the rock, striking reddish highlights from the stone, so that the whole cavern had a ruddy glow. It was amazingly clean. Lucoyo found it hard to believe that not even one animal had ever made its den in so fine a shelter, but so it seemed.

Ohaern was busy sitting down, closing his eyes, then rising with a shake of his head and walking slowly over the ground until he found another place that felt possible. Finally, after a dozen more tries, he settled down near the wall, leaning back against it and closing his eyes. There he stayed, immobile, save for the rise and fall of his chest. Lucoyo began to feel concern and sat on his heels next to the smith, peering at him closely in the reddish gloom. He could scarcely see any sign of breathing any more, and—surely it must have been his imagination!—Ohaern's limbs, torso, and face seemed to have hardened, to have turned into wood. He stayed long by his friend, feeling the alarm grow, assuring himself that Ohaern could not just sit down and die. Finally he reached out to touch the smith, then to squeeze, and the alarm flared, for Ohaern did indeed feel as if he were made out of wood.

For Ohaern, though, things were very different. He sat still and thought over all he had seen, letting his grief well up, overflow, and empty out—and realized that he still mourned Ryl. He was not truly aware of having closed his eyes, but only of the reddish glow in the cavern seeming to grow thicker and thicker, until it seemed to be reddish mist. He felt a massive disappointment that the goddess had not appeared, but he was bound and determined that he would not stir from this place until he found her again. Presently he began to feel thirsty, but strength flowed from the cave floor to fill him, and his thirst ceased. So did hunger. He hung suspended in ruby mist, with a growing sense of anticipation. Somehow, he knew that something was about to happen, though he had no idea what.

Then he began to hear the drum.

First he heard only one double beat, slow and heavy, the second beat louder than the first. He thought he must have been mistaken, but after a while it came again, then again and again, always a double beat followed by a pause, coming closer and closer until its sound seemed to beat all about him, filling the world. With sudden apprehension, he sensed that something was coming, something dreadful. Rising slowly, he braced himself for combat—and realized that the sound was not a drum beating at all, but footsteps, limping footsteps, giant, heavy, and slow.

The mists parted and a huge, monstrous form emerged from them. It was like a man, but a man almost as wide as he was tall, with pillars for legs and arms knobbed with muscle. But his face was worst of all. It seemed half human, half that of a giant lynx, with great round slit-pupiled eyes and tusks that thrust up from a snarling mouth. It carried a great war club set with spikes, a club that swung down at Ohaern as if to drive him into the ground, while that tusked mouth opened to give a growl that swelled into a roar.

Ohaern leaped aside at the last second. The huge club smashed down right where he had been. Then he leaped in and seized the haft of the club before the monster could draw it back, throwing all his weight against it, all his smith's strength. The monster roared in anger and yanked the club up—but it would not go; the tug jolted Ohaern, but did not move him. The monster bellowed in wrath, set itself, and hauled with all its might, but Ohaern held fast, jolting off the ground, then sinking back to it, his muscles bulging and veins standing out as if they would burst. With a howl of desperation, the monster let go of the club with one hand and slashed Ohaern from shoulder to hip with a great sharp claw. The smith gave a shout of pain, then set his jaw—feeling the blood flow, but determined not to let go while there was life in him—and pulled harder. The club came free from the monster's hand. The creature howled in despair as it fell back into the mist, and the sound of its passing faded into the huge limping footstep sound as it disappeared back where it had come from—a limping sound that reverberated, becoming the double drumbeat again.

Ohaern stood leaning on the club, his chest heaving even as it poured blood. He could not believe he was still alive, could not believe he had managed to wrest the club away from the monster—and least of all could he believe that he still moved, still breathed, while his chest blazed with pain and oozed blood without stopping. Hesitantly, he lifted the club to see if he had weakened—but it came up off the floor as lightly as a leaf.

Then suddenly it seemed to leap in his hands, dragging him around in a half circle, straining to be away, to pull him along with it. Ohaern stood a few moments, reasoning. Surely the monster had been a sort of guard to keep evil mortals from the goddess! Would not its club show him the way to her, then? Slowly, Ohaern followed the direction of the club. It pulled steadily, wanting him to hurry, to run, to tire himself, but he held it fast and kept his pace deliberate, trying to time his steps to the pulsing drum that seemed to beat all around him—a beat that quickened as he went along, becoming once again the sound of limping giant footsteps. He followed the club, dread welling up in him once more. It was another guardian that approached him, surely—and would it not be worse than the first?

There it came, shouldering the mists aside—a monster with a bird's head, elongated, stretched out. A bird of prey it was, with a long hooked beak and huge, round, maniacal eyes. It stood half again the height of a man, spare and lean, as if made from rope, seeming to have no joints save for a leg that looked as if it were made of wood—a stout oaken staff, ending not in a foot, but in an axe head—and a wooden arm that ended in a spiked ball of iron.

The beak opened to let out a great raucous cry—a cry of anger, a challenge at the small, soft being that dared invade the path to the goddess. Then it pounced.

Ohaern swung the war club, but it clanged uselessly against the spiked ball. Then the axe foot knocked the club aside, and the spiked ball swung in a short, vicious arc that ended in cracking against Ohaern's head. He reeled back, seeing only red mist, feeling the holes where the spikes had pitted his skull, and could only think, *I am dead. My head is broken. I must be dead.*

Dead or not, he still moved, even managed to raise the war club again just as that terrible ball swung down at him with the full force of a long, curving swing. Ohaern swung back, feeling an amazing quantity of strength pouring into him from some unknown source, into his arms and his legs as he swung with all his might—and spiked club met spiked ball. Iron clashed against iron and sparks flew—sparks that struck the wood. Leg and arm burst into flame, and the beak opened in a cry of pain and terror.

Ohaern realized he had taken the initiative. He swung again, sheering through a wooden arm weakened by fire. The iron ball flew, to crack against the wall, and the monster spun and hurried limping away, squawking in rage and fear and pain. The reddish mists embraced it, cooled it, soothed it—swallowed it, and Ohaern stood alone again, chest heaving with exertion, blood running down over his scalp, flowing out of his chest, amazed at his victory, amazed that he still lived, and certain that he was dead, for surely his body could not have held so much blood!

But if he was dead, this was the Afterlife, and he could shed an endless amount of blood, for a ghost had no need of it. Slowly, he took up the club again and held it out. Of its own accord, it swung around, and he swung with it until it stopped but quivered in his hands, pulling. Step by step he set off once again, following the pull of the club, that endless, relentless, double drumbeat sounding in his ears and filling his head.

Again the drumbeat became clear, but with a scratching. Out of the mist came rolling a huge ball, but it was a ball with chicken's feet that pounded the ground with each turn, pushing the ball on again.

Ohaern stopped and braced himself, the club up and ready.

The ball rolled onward, faster and faster, huge and purple, showing no sign of having seen him. Closer it came and closer—but much wider than he was tall. He could see veins pulsing across its surface now. Naked and obscene, it rolled down on him. At the last second he leaped aside, and the ball rolled by—but it swerved and came rolling back, slowing now. As it neared Ohaern, a tube lifted off its surface, a tube that narrowed from the full width of the ball to a rounded end only half again as wide as Ohaern's head, a rounded end that split and rolled back into two full, moist lips that opened to reveal serrated teeth.

The ball rolled, and struck down at Ohaern. He leaped back, swinging his club up from under, jamming its end between those side-shifting sawteeth—but saw they did, down through the club's wood as the ball rolled back. Ohaern, in a panic, held to the club, trying to pull back—and the huge clawed feet came up to rip out his belly. He screamed with pain, letting go of the club and leaping back—but his legs would not hold, and he fell.

The end of the club disappeared between those grinding fangs, and the lips struck down, teeth savaging his vitals, chewing down, down through his groin. Then they lifted, and the claws came up, ripping away all his viscera, tearing the gash in his chest wider and emptying out all within, then rolling away to let the lips come at him again. But a sudden notion inspired him, and with his last ounce of strength Ohaern caressed one lip, then the other, tracing its soft flesh with his fingertips—and incredibly, the lips shivered and the teeth broke, broke clean away, so that there were no stubs, no trace of them left. He caressed the lips again and again, his strength fading, but all the teeth fell loose now, tumbling slowly, and the gashes where they had been healed over, the soft lips touching him tenderly, touching his torn chest—and drank, drank of his blood, but with a caress that made him shiver with delight that obscured his pain, and consciousness faded into the red haze, letting him finally relax into death, knowing that he had given all that was within him, given of his blood and his essence, and would no longer have to face the horrifying prospect of a world rent by Ulahane, a world bleak and barren and devoid of all love.

But after a timeless interval, he felt stirring, felt touches on his viscera, felt them moving, being placed back within him. The touches were caresses, the organs were all replaced; he felt whole again, and his sight cleared, to see a woman bending over him, smoothing away the last of the rents in his skin.

It was she. It was the Ulin woman he had seen in his dreams, but already standing back, moving away, incredibly no taller than he, but beckoning, beckoning, and Ohaern rolled up to his feet and took a clumsy, awkward step . . .

Too clumsy. He glanced down, not willing to take his eyes from the woman for long, and saw . . .

Fur.

He was covered with fur, fur over short, bowed legs. He lifted his arms, found paws on the ends, paws with claws, and realized, with a shock, that the goddess had made a bear of him!

Yet she was beckoning, still beckoning with that curious, enigmatic smile, and he felt a stab of sensation in his groin, felt almost as if it was there that she pulled, and he followed, waddling on two feet, then realized that he could go much faster on four and dropped down to run after her, for she was fleeing ahead, fleeing and laughing through the mist, disappearing. The bear that was Ohaern roared in anguish and galloped to follow, galloped till the mist lifted, and there stood the goddess, still smiling, amused but charged, by the base of a tree, a huge tree that swelled out of the ground all about, filling the world, so thick it was, and the goddess was rising up the tree and up, beckoning, and the bear that was Ohaern roared in a panic that she might leave him, abandon him, and struck the tree with claws extended, struck and climbed, walking up the tree as if it were level ground, up and up through red clouds, pink clouds, white clouds, as the trunk narrowed and narrowed until it was scarcely wide enough for his footing. Finally he began to tire, finally each step weighed heavily on his limbs, but the goddess still beckoned and still he followed, until the white mists wrapped all about him and he felt solid footing under his hind feet again. She glowed through the mist, only a silhouette now, and Ohaern followed, heedless that the footing beneath him might cease, until the mist lifted again and he saw, under the shadow of the Tree that still lifted high, a bower, a castle of intricate tracery spires that lifted high.

Ohaern went in through the doorway—and felt man's feet slapping the soft, warm floor beneath. *His* feet. He looked up, discovering he was walking down a tunnel with an arching roof. Holding up his arms, he saw that they were man's arms again; glancing down, he saw he had his own man's body, but naked now. He would have stopped to stare, marveling at his unblemished skin, but her voice rose in lilting song from the end of the hall, song that stirred an answering chord within his vitals and pulled him, tugged at him, and he followed, breathing hard, to the end of the hallway, through its pink scented curtains into a huge curving chamber that was roofed and walled in pink padded satin, floored with a sea of cushions and in the center she stood, still beckoning, her veils floating about her.

"Divest me of my veils," she breathed, "for I cannot see you through them."

And he went to her, unwound the veils from her one by one, his breath hotter and harder and heavier, unwound veil after veil until she stood before him, seeming to glow, her eyes holding his as her hands moved about him, and he fell to his knees, finally come to his goddess, who claimed her worship of caresses. He gave that worship with all his heart, all his being, as she sank down beside him, and this time the ecstasy was of the mind and the body both, yes, and of the heart and spirit, too, as he gave of himself to her, all that he was, all of himself, and she gave back as much as she received and more, and he hung suspended with her in a formless, timeless sea of pure sensation, conscious only of transcendent delight and a wish that it never end.

CHAPTER 28

"I must go," Ohaern said, and moved to rise—but a dainty hand held him with strength that his huge smith's muscles could scarcely have matched. "What," said Rahani, "would you taste of my pleasures, then leave me without a thought? I assure you, you may not treat a goddess so!"

"I could never leave you without a thought!" Ohaern said fervently. "Indeed, you would ever be in my thoughts and in my heart, and I could not leave you for long! If I had to brave the agony your guardians inflicted time and again, I would do it!"

She laughed, the tinkling of wind chimes, and withdrew her hand. "Brave words, O Smith! But if they were true, you would never wish to leave me."

"I do not," Ohaern admitted, "but I have made promises, even though I may not have spoken them aloud. I am concerned for my friend Lucoyo, who guards my body—if it is still in the cave."

"It is," she assured him. "This is your dream body—well, not a dream, really, but the term will do. You are immersed in a shaman's vision, Ohaern, and you have become a shaman—*my* shaman, and you are singularly blessed to be allowed to approach me!"

"Oh, so blessed indeed!" he said, more fervently than ever, and reached out a hand to touch her, ever so lightly, still not quite believing that she was real, that he had come to her, that she would allow his caress.

She laughed again. "You have great daring, O Smith, but it is rewarded—for know that I take delight in your embrace too, though the other Ulin would call me twisted for it. Still, it is not in my caresses alone that you are blessed, but in the lore that you are learning and the cause in which you are privileged to spend your life."

Ohaern wondered in what sense she meant "spend."

"In both," she answered, and nodded at his start. "Of course I can read your mind. Am I not a goddess?"

"Not as I was told by Manal—" Ohaern flushed. "Lomallin."

She did not take offense; indeed, her eye twinkled with approval. "It is true, O Smith—I am no goddess, but only an Ulin woman. Yet the Ulin have great powers and are gods enough for most mortals. Do you not fear me?"

"Yes," Ohaern said frankly, "but the fear is overcome by the desire."

"Only desire?" She tilted her head to the side, gazing at him quizzically.

"Oh, I love you, and you know it!" he said. "Though it is beyond arrogance for a mere mortal to love an Ulin. But I do not think the love by itself would overcome the fear."

"No, but it reassures you that the fear is wrongheaded." She nodded. "An honest man. You have no idea how rare you are."

"I am only a smith and warrior of a forest tribe! And one who is concerned for the friend who remains among the living."

"You need not be," she assured him. "Your friend and your body will be safe in the cavern, for it is under my protection, and my magic hides it from the sight and scent of the monsters and the Ulharls who drive them—so let your heart be easy and your mind be at rest." She lay back, eyelids growing heavy, smile growing sultry, and beckoned. "Come—if you have strength enough."

Ohaern had—but when their breathing had slowed again and she was tracing slow circles with a fingertip that left a wake of sensation on his chest, she said, "I am not goddess enough for you, though I would be for any other man."

"No," Ohaern said frankly. "If I truly believed you were a goddess, I should never dare to touch you."

"And probably *could* not do anything more," she agreed. "Precious little use would you be to me then!"

"I shall be of whatever use you wish!" he cried, rolling up on one elbow.

"Bravely spoken," she said with approval, "but the service I require is the bringing down of Ulahane."

Then she waited, while Ohaern lay rigid in shock. When it passed, he breathed, "If you wish it, I shall strive for it with all my might—but how could I triumph against an Ulin?"

"You could not," she told him frankly, "but you could bring him to the brink of doom—for know, O Smith, that it is not only Lomallin and Rahani who survive of those who opposed Marcoblin, but other Ulin, too, though not many—and some among them might be induced to take arms against the Scarlet One."

Then she told him of the twilight of the Ulin.

When the Ulin War ended, Lomallin tried to assemble all the Ulin who found Ulahane's cruelty and blasphemy distasteful, tried to persuade them to band together to protect the humans. The homunculi joined Lomallin, and would have made the perfect sort of unquestioning soldier, to be sent against the enemy and slaughtered by the hundreds—but knowing how helpless they were in all ways except carrying out specific tasks as they were commanded to do, Lomallin set them instead to building strongholds to protect the humans and the other younger races from Ulahane's predators.

"Then there are other Ulin who will battle Ulahane to save my kind?" Ohaern asked.

"There are other Ulin," she said noncommittally.

Ohaern frowned. "But they will not fight?"

She sighed. "When the war ended, there were so few Ulin left that they could no longer fight one another with expectation of anything but the extinction of their kind. It is for that reason that Lomallin has sought out humans of strength and courage, who may lead their people in defense against Ulahane's hordes."

"Such as myself," Ohaern whispered.

"Such as yourself," she confirmed, "though you will meet others when you go up against Kuru, and have met one or two already."

Ohaern suspected she spoke of Dariad. "And is it for this reason that he has gone among us in disguise—to find those who may act for him?"

"There is that," the Ulin woman admitted, "though it is even more because he has far too soft a heart for his own good, and tries to alleviate the misery that Ulahane visited upon you humans with his magic."

"Surely the Scarlet One could not have objected to such labor!"

"He objected most strongly! You still do not understand the depth of Ulahane's hatred. He may have been Marcoblin's follower, but when he inherited leadership, he surpassed his master in every way, most especially in cruelty and malice. No, he responded to Lomallin's kindness by imitating Marcoblin and again outdoing him. He ingratiated himself with Agrapax, then dared him to make a creature out of a nightmare, and watched while he worked. When the construct was made, Ulahane went away and set himself to making monsters of his own, and to breeding them out of living ones." Her face turned to a mask of loathing and anger, and Ohaern had to fight to keep himself from shrinking away. "Ulahane used his magic with gloating cruelty to breed monsters out of humans and animals together," she said, "and did not hesitate to use rape, and cutting and stitching aided by magic, no matter how painful or degrading it may have been. It was this that persuaded me to work among human folk even as Lomallin did—though not in his fashion—for I could not let pass the atrocities Ulahane worked upon human women and females of all races."

"What of the other Ulin who remain?"

"The rest of the few score of us still living," she said, "whether they be human-lovers or human-haters, have imitated Agrapax, going off by themselves where it was safe, to eke out what pleasure they could without danger, refusing to be drawn into the conflict between Lomallin and Ulahane. Now and then these lonely Ulin will take a human or two for their own amusement, or for servants or laborers. Some have even set themselves up as gods—no difficult task, since human folk think us to be such, anyway—and stir up their own cults to ensure a steady supply of human services. Like Lomallin and Ulahane and myself, they have vast powers, when they can be induced to interfere in human affairs—though they are far more likely to lash out at humanity in jealousy and spite."

Ohaern marveled at the notion of an Ulin being jealous of a human—but then, the younger race had taken the Ulin's place.

As he did, even now? He wondered how many Ulin would long to rend him limb from limb and visit unspeakable tortures upon him, simply for the audacity of approaching Rahani. "But you, at least, went out to work among us humans."

"Went out to you, or brought you here." She turned a lazy, slumberous gaze upon him. "I have tasks for you, O Smith."

"I shall do them," he said without a moment's hesitation—or even a thought as to whether or not the labors she required would be possible. "Is it you alone of all the Ulin, then, who work among us humans?"

"Yes, though I rarely go about in disguise, as Lomallin did. It is too easy for Ulahane to find me and to counter my power with his own, leaving me to the mercy of your kind—and some are less than kind indeed."

Her face hardened again momentarily, then cleared as he said, very carefully, "You are truly alone in this, then."

"Not while I have you." She squeezed his hand, smiling again. "But you speak of Lomallin's death. Know, O Smith, that his death deprives us only of his body. His spirit still moves among us—no, do not be so surprised! Even your kind leave ghosts upon this earth now and then, and certainly an Ulin would, if he had not sickened of existence. Lomallin has not, for he has work yet to do—and though his spirit may not perform the work of hands, it is much stronger now for no longer being lumbered with flesh."

Ohaern's eyes widened. "So *that* is the meaning of the legend!"

"That is its meaning," she agreed, "and Ulahane knew it well."

"Then for him to dare to slay the Green One . . ."

"Means that he is very sure of victory." She nodded. "After all, there is a great deal of the work of hands still to be done. Lomallin's power may counter Ulahane's, but the younger races must themselves counter the strength of the Scarlet One's monsters."

Ohaern thrust himself up to his feet. "I must go, I must gather armies, I must—"

"You must learn." She reached up to stay him with a touch. "You cannot yet fight Ulahane and have even a chance of victory; you must learn magic, that you may fight with arms and with wizardry both."

Ohaern felt despair mushroom within him. "But how can I learn so much, when I must learn so quickly!"

"I shall teach you." The gentle touch became stronger, more demanding. "But first I wish to be cherished. It has been long, yes, very long, since I have been worshiped as a goddess should be."

Ohaern paid the price of his learning—or was rewarded for the labor of it. If it was a price, he was glad to pay it, and if it was reward, he reveled in it. But learn he did, and labor he did. She led him into trances within the trance, and showed him the richness of the spirit world that had lain about him all his life, unseen; he saw the faces in the smoke and the wind, heard the voices in the rocks and the trees, felt and touched the contours of the spirits in the earth. She made him known to all of them, too, and taught him the words of power that would bring them, and all who depended on them, to his aid. She also showed him the malignant spirits and taught him words of power that gave him dominion over them—except a few who were far too strong, and there she taught him how to call up beneficent spirits and weave them into a net that could hold and compel any evil one, a weaving in which they were the woof threads, but he was the warp. She taught him the virtue of every herb and the poison of every creature, and the countering of the one with the other; she taught him the dances and songs and instruments with which malignant spirits could be commanded or banished, and beneficent spirits summoned and beseeched. She made the spirit world as much a home to him as the living world—but now and again, in all these visions, he caught sight of an old man with gray hair and beard, dressed in black robes and bearing a staff that was intricately carved. Several times he turned a glance that was fierce and angry on Ohaern before he strode away into the mists—but she would not tell him who this was, only that he would know when the time came.

At last she confronted him with the spirits of the iron and copper and tin to which he had sung all his years as a smith. Terrible they could be, but gentle they were by nature, and welcomed him as a friend long known.

But always and ever, when the day's work was done, she called him back to her bower, where duty was privilege and homage was cherishing.

So there was respect in both of them when at last she took him out beneath the night sky and bade him go to bring about the downfall of Ulahane.

"But how shall I induce these strange Ulin, who have gone off by themselves, to move against Ulahane?" Ohaern asked.

"That is my task," she told him. "It is for you to bring the tribes of men against the city of Kuru and defeat the soldiers of that cesspit."

"If you command it, I shall do it," he averred, "but when it is done, may I return to you?"

She gave him a melting smile and reached out to touch. "You have learned how to walk in the spirit, Ohaern. You may always come to me in that form."

But that, he knew with deep-plunging sadness, was not what he had asked of her. Still, she had only told him what he could do, not what he could not, so there was yet hope.

She told him, "Do not be sad, O Smith, though I tell you we will never meet again until you have brought down Ulahane, for I shall ever be with you—" She touched his chest over his heart. "—in here." Then she gave him a last transporting kiss, turned away, and was gone. The mists folded about her, swayed with her movements and eddied where she had been, then enfolded Ohaern, caressing him with her perfume, with currents that seemed a last vagrant touch, then enwrapped him and chilled him to the bone. He began to shiver, then blinked to dispel the fog from his eyes— and it dissipated, blowing away. He looked up at the darkened sky again—and saw that it was not truly the sky, but the ceiling of the cavern, ghost-lit by moonbeams. Yet it must have been a sky, for across it stars were falling. He followed their paths and saw that they were truly sparks rising up from a small fire, a fire whose light played upon the features of a gaunt face that bore pointed ears, and Ohaern realized that he had come back to the real world, the world of living men and human women, and though he could not say how or why, he knew that Lomallin would triumph in the end, but that it would be a hard fight, a very hard fight.

More, he understood something about himself now, understood that Rahani would always be with him in some way, but not only her—his wife Ryl, too, for he had taken her into his heart, and she would always be there, smiling, and rejoicing that if she could not care for him, another would. He knew now why he had been so often morose, and knew that he would never be so again.

Looking up, he saw Lucoyo watching him anxiously. How thin he had grown! Ohaern moved, amazed at the stiffness in him, but it was a stiffness that faded even as he brought a hand up in greeting and said, "Thank you, Lucoyo!" But it came out as a croak, from a throat long unused and long dry.

The croak was enough, though; Lucoyo gave a cry of delight and leaped up to clasp him by the shoulders, crying, "You live! Ohaern, I feared you had died and would be forever a statue!" Then he instantly shifted to anger. "You idiot, you death-seeking fool! Cold was your body—and colder your heart, for leaving me so to fret! You would not drink, you would not eat—you have nearly starved yourself to death!"

Ohaern looked down at his body, but saw no lessening in his bulk—though each muscle and ligament did seem to be only now softening, turning from bonelike hardness back to flesh. He looked up to smile with great fondness at his friend. "I cannot thank you enough for having guarded my body throughout this ordeal, Lucoyo. I assure you, I will be well from now on."

Another face rose next to Lucoyo's, and Ohaern blinked with surprise. "Grakhinox! But you were to wait for us with the Biharu!"

"We worried, the Klaja and I, when you did not come back," the dwerg answered in his rusty voice. "We had to see that you lived."

"We?" Ohaern looked up, and heard a slow, slurring yap from

the entrance to the cavern. Turning his head, he saw the Klaja standing, spear in hand, in the tunnel mouth.

"He has guarded us," Lucoyo said, "not that we seem to have needed it—the manticores and lamias have not come near, though the Klaja followed our trail straight to this cave."

Lucoyo seemed puzzled, but Ohaern smiled. "It is because the goddess Rahani has taken us under her protection. She has warded this cavern from the eyes of the Ulharl and their herds."

The Klaja's breath hissed in sharply, and the dwerg stared—but Lucoyo's eyes narrowed. "Why, Smith, how do you know that?"

"Because she told it to me in a vision," Ohaern explained. "She told me many things, Lucoyo, and taught me, too. Call me 'Smith' no longer, for she has made a shaman of me."

The dwerg and the Klaja gave cries of mingled fear and delight, but Lucoyo only said, " 'Smith' you have been to me since I first met you, and 'Smith' you shall be to me always. As to your being a shaman, there is nothing so strange in that, for I have seen you learning all the magic you could, whenever Manalo worked a spell." His face clouded. "Yes, you are a shaman, are you not? For you have learned the magic of the gods themselves!"

"The Ulin," Ohaern corrected. "They are not gods." Somehow, he had come to see that the distinction was important.

Lucoyo was still narrow-eyed. "And why should the goddess do you this boon?"

"Because I will have need of magic in the work she demands of me," Ohaern replied.

"I was afraid of this." From the look on his face, Lucoyo was apprehensive indeed. "What work is that?"

"Only what we had set ourselves to do already," Ohaern said, his tone reassuring. "To go up against Kuru."

"No, there is more!" the half-elf snapped. "The goddess did not need to make a shaman of you only to do a warrior's work. What else?"

"That is all that we are to do," Ohaern insisted. "The goddess will do the rest."

"Which is?" Lucoyo was liking the sound of this less and less.

Ohaern sighed, caught by the half-elf's insistence. "To challenge Ulahane himself and bring him down, even as he brought down Lomallin."

The dwerg cried out, and the Klaja growled, every hair on his neck and scalp bristling—but Lucoyo only whimpered once before he said, "I had feared as much. Well, then, O Weapon Forged by the Goddess Herself, O Spear of Rahani, what shall we do?"

"Rest a few days." Ohaern reached out, stretching cautiously. "I have grown stiff and weak in this trance. How long have I sat thus?"

"Three weeks," Lucoyo said in disgust. "I wonder that your joints have not rusted tight, that there is still flesh on your bones!"

"And I, that there is flesh on yours!" Ohaern exclaimed, staring. "Oh, my friend! I did not intend to cause you such hardship!"

"It is past, and worth it, from your account." Lucoyo shrugged impatiently. "That I have any flesh upon me at all, you may thank the Klaja for; he has hunted and found small game in a wasteland where I could have sworn nothing lived—and if there is water in me and, aye, in you, too, you may thank Grakhinox, who found where it pooled in the earth and brought it forth. Now and then I dribbled some moisture over your lips, and it sank in—at least enough to keep you from shriveling before my eyes."

Ohaern did not tell him that was far more Rahani's work than his own, or that his trance had taken him into her spell, where she had preserved his body unchanged until it was needed again. He only said, humbly, "I thank you for such faithful nursing, archer— and you for your provisions, my friends. Well then, we shall rest and eat and recover our strength."

"And then?" Lucoyo demanded with a jaundiced eye.

"Then," said Ohaern, "we shall go forth to summon all the bands of beings that will fight for Lomallin and the younger races. We shall summon them all as we march upon Kuru at last!"

"And challenge Ulahane himself," Lucoyo finished, and sighed. "Well, at least I might as well die trying to accomplish something. But first I think I shall finish cooking my stew."

Thus they came out of the cavern, a man, a half-elf, a Klaja, and a dwerg. Thus they came, and marched over the desert by night, the dwerg always leading them to the next pool of water, the Klaja leading them to one escaped and wandering camel after another, until they were all riding again. Thus they came up out of the Sand Sea, three of them riding and the Klaja loping along beside— for no camel would suffer him to ride. Thus they came, and the lone Biharu who saw them swell out of the line where the sand met the sky cried out in alarm.

CHAPTER 29

The Biharu came running up, swords drawn and ready, but when Ohaern waved, and as he came close enough for the nomads to see his face, Dariad cried out in joy—but in disbelief, too. "Ohaern, you live! Lucoyo! Klaja! Grakhinox! You walk, and are not ghosts!"

Ohaern drew rein beside the nomad and clapped him on the shoulder, grinning, "Aye, we live."

"Why so amazed, Dariad?" The judge smiled, amused. "It was you who would not let us leave this barren camp, for no better reason than that the sage had said they would return." And to Ohaern, "It is only Dariad's faith in Manalo's words that has kept us here."

Dariad blushed, looking down at the sand. "That was simple constancy, O Judge, for a Biharu's word must be kept."

"But you did not believe I would truly come back?" Ohaern smiled. "The more praise for you then, Dariad, to have honored your promise!"

"You told *us* they would come," one of his tribesmen objected.

"And I knew they would!" Dariad maintained stoutly. "It is

just that . . . I did not quite . . . believe what I knew." Then, as his tribesman laughed, he lifted his head in indignation. "After all, it has been a month since they followed the sage into the Sand Sea!"

"Where *is* the sage?" asked the judge. "Where is Manalo?"

Ohaern grew somber. "In that, at least, you were right to doubt, O Biharu. The sage is dead."

The tribesmen muttered in consternation, frowning and shaking their heads. Dariad, though, peered more closely at Ohaern and said, "There is something of him that has passed into you, O Smith. What is it?"

Ohaern stared in surprise, then said slowly, "Nothing that I am aware of. He taught me much, and I have his knowledge in my head and his compassion in my heart—but no more than that."

"There is something different in you, though." The judge agreed.

"There is," Ohaern admitted. "I have become a shaman."

Nothing was said; indeed, there was only the rustle of cloth as the wind blew through their robes, and perhaps it was that very silence, that and the upturned staring faces, that made Ohaern realize how much he had suddenly changed in their eyes.

"Tell us the manner of it," the judge said.

Ohaern shook his head. "There is too little to tell, and too much to tell. I sought a vision and found it, as any shaman does. For the rest, I have learned what I was taught."

Now there came a murmur as the Biharu exchanged comments with one another, excited, but fearful, too. Watching them, Ohaern felt a great sadness seize him as he realized that he could never again be just a man among friends, but would always be apart, though held in highest esteem.

Never a man among friends, except for Lucoyo. Ohaern resolved to take very good care of the half-elf henceforth.

"Why have we waited?" Dariad asked quietly.

As one, the Biharu turned their gazes toward the nomad, and Ohaern saw that if he had gained an immense amount of prestige by his sojourn in the desert, Dariad had gained almost as much by his simple steadfast faith and refusal to turn away from a promise given.

No, not at all—Dariad had gained prestige because events had proved him right.

"We must fight the Scarlet One," Ohaern told them quietly.

The eyes swung back to him, and fear was written on every face—then instantly replaced by determination. Ohaern was struck by the courage and hardihood of these Biharu. If he had ordered them to march into a dragon's lair and bring him its head, they would have done so, or died trying.

If *he* had ordered them . . .

For the first time in his life Ohaern realized just how deeply other people clung to his words and were swayed by his mere presence. He wondered if this was also the first time in his life that his presence had been so strong.

Dariad nodded gravely. "Why must we do so?"

"Because the Sand Sea is Ulahane's work," Ohaern replied. "As long as he lives, the drought will deepen and the Sand Sea will spread. Destroy him, and the drought will cease; the desert will gain oases and, in your grandchildren's time, will become moist enough for grazing again. If Ulahane lives, your grandchildren will have to flee to other lands."

"Then we shall do it," Dariad said, and the tribe shouted agreement. Ohaern looked out upon them and smiled.

"How shall we destroy Ulahane?" Dariad asked. "How can a man kill an Ulin?"

"Remember that he is not a god," Ohaern replied. "None of the Ulin are gods, only beings of an elder race, as you yourselves have told me."

"That is true," said the judge, "but they are nonetheless mighty, far more mighty than we ephemeral mites. How could a mortal man slay an Ulin?"

"Leave that to other Ulin," Ohaern told him. "But to prevail against the Scarlet One, they must have minions withheld, so that they may give all their attention to Ulahane. It is to us to hale down Ulahane's packs of monstrosities and the Ulharls who drive them."

"Can Ulharls die?" a tribesman asked.

"They can," Ohaern assured him. "They are half human, after

all, and even an Ulin can be slain. How much more easily, then, their Ulharls?"

"If a man can do it, we shall!" cried a tribesman, and the rest shouted agreement.

"We shall," Dariad agreed, "but how shall we go about it?"

"I must work magic," Ohaern told him. "Do you break camp and load your camels while I do. Then we shall ride against Kuru!"

The Biharu roared approval, then turned and ran back to their tents.

"What magic is this you shall work?" Lucoyo asked nervously.

"The Call," Ohaern answered. "When Manalo visited all the tribes, he gave each of them a call-sign, and when they saw it in the sky, they were to march toward Kuru."

"But how do they know—oh, of course!" Lucoyo said in self-disgust. "Manalo told them in which direction to march."

"And told them what obstacles lay in their path, I suspect," Ohaern agreed. "He taught me the spell that will make all the signs appear—but it will take some minutes to work."

A shrill shout of delight came from the camp.

"What is that?" the dwerg asked, staring.

"It is the women, the elders, and the children," Lucoyo answered. "I suspect they have just learned that they may finally leave this place."

Ohaern nodded. "None are sorry to strike camp." He dismounted from his camel and began to trace designs in the sand with his camel stick. Lucoyo watched, frowning, and the dwerg and the Klaja came up to watch with him.

Ohaern finished the designs and began to move among them, chanting. His chant grew louder and more musical as his movements grew more fluid, more stylized, until he was dancing among images of his own making. Then the dance slowed, and Ohaern finished his chant with a slow turning in place, arms lifted toward each of the quarters of the world. Then he gave a shout and sank to his knees in the sand, panting.

Lucoyo ran to his friend. "Ohaern! Are you well?"

"Aye . . . well . . ." Ohaern panted. "But magic . . . takes effort . . . Lucoyo. Almost, I think . . . more than battle."

"Well then, you have done your fighting, and may rest." Lucoyo took him by the arm and helped him to his feet.

Ohaern shook his head. "There is much to do, and not enough time for it all. As soon as the Biharu are packed, we must go!"

"So must we," the dwerg said, coming up. "The Klaja and I have spoken and agree that we may serve you better by going to raise our own people against Kuru."

Ohern stared at the Klaja in dismay. "Your own kind will slay you—they, or the Ulharl who drives them!"

The Klaja shrugged and said, in his guttural voice, "It may be that they shall—but a life estranged from my own kind is no life. If I knew I could never know fellowship, or embrace a female, I would wish to die. Better to raise a dozen who hate the Ulharl enough to die fighting."

Ohaern nodded gravely. "They will most likely die in any case, for they will be thrown into the forefront of the battle. Very well, go and persuade—and I hope I shall see you again, with an army at your back."

"I hope that you shall." The Klaja grinned and clapped the shaman on the shoulder. "Do not mistake me for an enemy, Ohaern!"

"Well thought." The shaman took off an armband and slipped it over the Klaja's paw. "I shall know you by that token, even if I cannot see it. Never let it from your sight."

"I shall not," the Klaja promised, "and I *shall* see you again." With that, he turned and trotted away.

Ohaern gazed after him, face creased with anxiety. "I hope he shall be well." He turned to the dwerg. "Well, friend, I cannot bar you from going to your own kind—but I hope I shall see you again, too."

"Be sure you shall," Grakhinox promised, "but before you see us, you shall feel us—or our work, at least." Then he stretched out his arms and began to pivot, turning about and about in place, faster and faster, until he sank down into the earth, like a drill into a stone—and into stone he must have gone, for the earth closed over his head and filled in the hole he had made.

Lucoyo and Ohaern stood staring at the small mound, which

was all that was left to show their friend had stood there. Then the half-elf said, "What did he mean—that we would feel his works? Pray he did not mean that swords he made would cleave our skulls!"

"I cannot think that would be so," Ohaern said slowly, "for we have been shield-mates, and we have saved him from bondage as surely as he has aided us. We are friends and comrades. Surely he would not!"

Lucoyo felt a bit reassured to discover that the new Ohaern did not know everything.

Dariad's camel came loping up, and the nomad called down, "The women and children will travel to our summer grazing grounds, while our warriors are ready to march, Ohaern! Which way?"

"Toward the northeast," the shaman answered. "There lies the city of Kuru!"

They marched for several days, the nomads singing with the sheer joy of having left the Sand Sea. But as they came out of the wasteland and the vegetation grew thicker about them, the Biharu quieted and began to grow nervous, as if the alien sight of fertile land made them apprehensive.

"What are all these green stalks in the fields about us, Ohaern?" Dariad asked. "Surely they cannot be grass!"

"A kind of grass," Ohaern answered. "They are stalks of barley."

"Barley! Is *that* where the grain comes from?" And Dariad stared, as astonished and awed as if he stood in the middle of a city and stared about at buildings four and five times his height.

Now and then they spied men working in the fields who looked up, saw them, and stared, as astonished at the sight of camels as the Biharu had been by the sight of barley. But here and there a man would turn and run.

"Do they fear us so?" Dariad asked.

"Perhaps," Ohaern said, but privately he thought otherwise.

Unevenness on the horizon swelled into lumps as they rode, then grew into low mounds, purple with distance.

"Hills?" Dariad frowned. "And not of sand?"

"They are indeed hills," Lucoyo answered, "and covered most thoroughly with trees and grass."

CHAPTER 30

They found the refuge toward sunset, or it found them. Ohaern led them back to the line of hills that seemed to be the boundary of Kuru's territory. He led them up toward high ground.

"This seems unwise," said Dariad, frowning. "Should we not be farther from the soldiers of Kuru?"

Lucoyo shrugged. "He is a shaman. He knows what he is doing—I hope."

It seemed Ohaern did, for a very short, very stocky man with very long arms stepped out from behind a boulder and hailed Ohaern.

Africans and Biharu alike pulled back, and a hubbub of superstitious exclamations rolled out of their ranks.

"It is only a dwerg!" Lucoyo protested.

"Only!" a Biharu cried. He turned to a black man, pointing at the dwerg, and said, "Only! A creature from the netherworld, one never seen by mortal men, and he says 'only'!"

The black man nodded, not understanding a word, and pointed at the dwerg, too, pouring forth a complaint of his own in an indignant tone. The Biharu, also not understanding a word, nodded firmly and said, "That is right!" Then he frowned and looked at the African more closely. "I am Shokla. Who are you?" He pointed to his chest and repeated, "Shokla!"

"Ah!" The black man nodded vigorously and pointed to his own chest. "Burayo!"

They were friends forevermore.

Lucoyo looked closely, but saw the dwerg was not his friend Grakhinox. He was talking to Ohaern quite earnestly, beckoning and pointing farther up the slope. Lucoyo only hoped he could be trusted—though truthfully, he saw no reason to doubt one of his comrade's kind, perhaps even kin.

Ohaern nodded, and the dwerg set off up the slope. The shaman followed, not even bothering to call back. The nomads and hunters muttered rebelliously, but followed.

The dwerg stopped by a huge boulder, set himself, and rolled it aside, revealing a cave mouth. The Biharu and Africans exclaimed in amazement, for it would have taken ten of them to shift that huge rock even half that distance. Then their exclamations turned to doubt and wariness; neither forest men nor desert men trusted a cave.

"Be of good heart," Ohaern called. "There is more than enough room for all of us to stretch out to sleep, and even to stable your camels."

"If there is, then the whole hill must be hollow!" the judge exclaimed.

Ohaern nodded. "It is."

So it was, as they saw to their amazement: a huge dome above them, with light filtering in from cracks here and there. Those cracks admitted enough water to form stalactites and stalagmites, joined here and there to form columns. The few sun rays that penetrated the cave lit it most wondrously, bringing out a wealth of gemlike colors and sparkling gleams from bits of mica and rock crystal.

Where those sun rays pooled, there stood a statue.

"Manalo!" Dariad cried, even as several of the black men cried the same name. Then they turned to stare at one another, amazed.

Surely the statue's face did look like that of the sage—and there was no confusion as to the color of his skin, for it was painted green.

"How is this, dwerg?" Ohaern asked, then repeated it in a language that sounded like gravel being ground under rolling boulders. The dwerg replied in the same grating sounds, and Ohaern turned to his companions. "He says that a nation of hunters carved this statue long ago, to honor the sage who brought them fire and barley, and taught them to plant and hunt. Different tribes of that nation would come here to remember him and pray, then go away. Their great-great-grandchildren worshiped the fire-bringer as a god."

"By what name did they call him?" Lucoyo stared up at the familiar, almost beloved face, feeling his back and scalp prickle in response to the eerieness of the place.

"They called him 'Nimola.' "

"Then this is a temple." The judge clucked at his camel, and it knelt, protesting. "Down, all of you! We worship no god but the Star-Maker—yet this statue is that of a hero, and one of the Creator's most excellent works!"

The nomads climbed down off their camels and faced their judge as he began to chant the praises of the Star-Maker, while the black men faced the statue and began a chant of their own.

But Ohaern went and sat at the foot of the statue, gazing up into that face that he knew so well, marveling all over again that Lomallin could have chosen himself, an ordinary smith of a wild forest people, for a traveling companion—and student! He lost himself in a reverie, asking Lomallin's ghost for aid, for protection from the soldiers of Kuru, asking that spirit to respond, to touch his mind, to answer within his head, to advise . . .

Then he felt the most gentle of touches on his shoulder and heard Lucoyo's voice, very low, very gentle: "Ohaern. Where are you?"

The shaman stirred with regret and looked up at his friend. "Here, Lucoyo—unfortunately." Then he saw beyond the half-elf, saw the cavern in darkness, lit only by small fires here and there, fires that gave off very little smoke but showed him a vast assemblage of sleeping bodies. "I am here," he said regretfully. "I have not left this cavern."

Lucoyo sighed with relief. "It would be hard to keep this host together if your spirit went wandering again! What were you doing?"

"Seeking speech with Lomallin's ghost," Ohaern answered, "but if Rahani is right and his spirit has survived his body, he has a maddening way of not answering when it is convenient for those who call upon him." He gazed out over the sleeping army and nodded. "Well then, they sleep." He tested his own body and said, "I feel as if I have slept, too—this sort of contemplation must be as good a rest as sleep."

" 'This kind'?" Lucoyo repeated. "How many kinds *are* there?"

"Only two that I know of so far," Ohaern answered, "and I must now try the other kind—the one that uses up strength, and does not restore it." He turned back toward the statue, leaned against a pillar and closed his eyes.

"No, Ohaern!" Lucoyo protested, but the shaman shook his head.

"I must tell the other tribes where to march and what to do. For that, I must speak to their shamans, and the only way is to meet them in the spirit world."

"Well . . . do not be long, then." Lucoyo glanced apprehensively over his shoulder. "I do not know how long I can hold them here if you do not come back."

"Be calm, my friend," Ohaern said. "I go not to learn this time, but only to confer. I shall be back ere dawn."

"Good hunting, then," Lucoyo said, but he still watched nervously as Ohaern closed his eyes and his breathing began to slow.

After a while Ohaern began to hear the drumbeat again, and the darkness about him lightened. It was gray mist this time, not red, and it was lighted by moonbeams that lanced down to bathe the Tree in their glow. Ohaern began to move toward it, and as he went, thought of himself as a bear again. Then he tried to think like a bear—and realized his easy gait had become a waddle. Looking down, he saw thick furry legs and paws. He dropped down to all fours and loped ahead, running to the Tree.

Up he climbed, his pulse beating high at the thought of Rahani, even though he knew she would not be awaiting him this time—and he was right, for as he passed through the clouds into the shaman world, he saw not Rahani waiting to lead him on, but an assemblage of beasts—a bull, an aurochs, a panther, a tiger, and a great wide-antlered reindeer.

You are come, one of them said. *We have waited.*

Ohaern climbed down off the Tree and came closer, wondering how he had heard that voice, for it had not sounded through his ears. *Let us show our human forms,* he thought, and the others must have heard him, for their shapes began to change. Little by little they became men and women—and as they did, the Tree groaned with the weight of a huge beast whose nose had stretched out as long as any tail and longer, and whose ears were as wide as wings. Then an eagle flew down to join them, and both began to change as the rest did.

Ohaern looked around and saw pale northern men and women, black men and women—including the shaman he had already met in the world below—yellow, brown—even another Biri, though he did not know her face. *We are come,* they said. *What would you have us do?*

A sudden shyness seized Ohaern, and he protested, *Surely another should answer that! I am only newly made a shaman!*

But made a shaman by a goddess, an old woman pointed out; and, *You are the chosen of Lomallin,* the Biri responded. *We have come at his call, given through the sage Manalo; it is for you to bid us go and do.*

The other shamans murmured agreement, and Ohaern, feeling immensely honored but also immensely intimidated, replied, *Well, then, I shall tell you what I best can. Stop when you come to a curving range of hills, for they form a circle, and Kuru lies in the center of the plain it encloses. Wait there until all have come and are ready.*

How shall we know when all have come? asked a yellow-skinned shaman who wore an elk's-head mask.

Let us meet here every night, Ohaern said. *When all are in place, we shall begin the assault.*

How if Ulahane's minions attack us before that time? asked the black man whom Ohaern already knew.

Then all who are in place must attack, Ohaern replied. *We may strike through to the city, but more likely the Kuruites will split their forces and end the attack so that they may fall back to defend their walls.*

It is well thought, said a brown woman, *but how shall we know if another tribe is attacked?*

We must exchange call-signs, Ohaern replied, *so that if one is threatened, he may summon the others who are in place.*

They did, then clasped arms in a circular, mutual embrace, after which they turned back into animal form and all climbed down the Tree to go home to their people.

Ohaern came back to his body—and was jolted instantly into battle. There was shouting and roaring in the cave. He leaped to his feet—and almost fell over. Lucoyo caught his arms and pushed him back upright, saying, "Sit down, sit down, Ohaern! You cannot come all at once from a trance in which your body is wooden, to fighting condition! Let them be—your warriors will deal with the intruder!"

"But what *is* it?"

The roaring turned into a screaming whistle which ended abruptly. Lucoyo relaxed a little. "It was a snake with horns on its head, as long as two canoes and as thick around as a man. It crushed one warrior and would have devoured him, but the dwerg saw and raised the alarm. The nomads and hunters crowded away from it, but the dwerg broke a spear of rock from the ceiling and advanced on the creature—it seemed no stranger to him. The other warriors took heart and pounced upon it. I saw one black man struck down before the crowd closed around it. I hope we have lost no more."

"I, too! No, do not fear—I feel the blood coursing through my limbs again. I will go slowly, Lucoyo. Only take me to the monster."

Lucoyo led him, keeping a hand ready to catch his arm—but Ohaern kept his balance. As they came, the Biharu and the black men looked up, saw Ohaern, and made way for him. Looking down, Ohaern saw a monster at least thirty feet long, a snake indeed, with sharp horns on top of a scaly head that had long, sharp-toothed jaws. He stared. "What manner of creature is *this*?"

The black shaman came through to the circle, stared down, then looked up and answered Ohaern in the shaman's language.

"What does he say?" asked Lucoyo.

"The head is that of a huge sort of lizard that lives in the rivers where he comes from," Ohaern answered, "but the horns are those of a sort of deer, and the rest of the body is indeed that of a snake. He says snakes do grow to such a size in his own country, but that the giant lizards never mate with the snakes."

Lucoyo shuddered. "May I never have to visit their land!"

"I doubt not they would say the same if they came to *my* forests." Ohaern felt a trace of amusement, with relief. "Were there any others of these?"

Lucoyo shook his head. "Only the one, praise Lomallin!"

"We must post sentries," Ohaern told him, then raised his voice to all of them. "You are brave and noble to have slain the monster! But know that it came from Ulahane ultimately, and that if we had let it escape, it would have gone back to him, and he would have known where we are! If any more appear, they must be slain!"

The warriors all rumbled agreement. Dariad told off sentries from his own men, and the black captain did the same. With guards posted and fires banked, they slept.

They stayed in the cavern five more days, and twice more in that time monsters attacked; both times, the humans slew the foul creatures. Each night, Ohaern met with his fellow shamans and discovered that more and more of them were at the ring of hills—but Ulahane made no move against them. Why not? Ohaern finally admitted to himself that his forces were anything but intimidating—only wandering bands of nomads, and hunters whose lands doubtless bore no more game, come to search for plenty. The fact that there were no herds for the nomads to follow, and scarcely enough game to keep the hunters alive, would only have afforded Ulahane amusement, not given him alarm.

But there *was* enough small game to support the hunters in their thousands, and the nomads, too. Even more surprising, each of them found a pool or stream at the end of each day's march— quite surprising indeed in a land in which the farmers had to dig ditches to water their crops. Ohaern itched to ask the dwerg if his people had dug holes to bring that water to the surface, but the small man had not been seen since they had slain the serpent. Besides, Ohaern suspected that they had only dug a few—and certainly the abundance of game could not be credited to creatures of subterranean dwellings.

Finally the hour came when the last three shamans reported that their people were all in place. Ohaern returned to the world of the living—and sleeping—and began a slow dance, chanting softly as he moved around one of the small fires. Quiet as he was, Lucoyo awoke and watched him, eyes wide. When the shaman had finished, the half-elf asked, "Shall I wake the others now, Ohaern?"

"Only Dariad and his men," Ohaern answered. "The black shaman is rousing his own people."

"Of course . . . What spell were you casting, enchanter?"

"One that will cloak our band with secrecy, to hide it from the eyes of Ulahane and his minions," Ohaern replied.

"Surely he will know where we are as soon as we come out of this cavern!"

"Only if he chances to look upon us himself; this spell will hide us from the eyes of his creatures and his spies. Of course, he knows where all the other tribes are, and must see that he is encircled—but he will dismiss them as of no importance, no threat to himself or to Kuru, and will tantalize himself with waiting while he chooses the method of exterminating them that most pleases his fancy."

Lucoyo shuddered. "How can you say that with such calm!"

"Because we shall strike before he does," Ohaern answered. "Wake Dariad."

Wakened, Dariad set his men to preparing for the assault, and they were ready almost as soon as the Africans. Out into the night they went, following the train of hills back the way they had come five days before.

A camel bawled, and Ohaern said to Dariad, "The camels must be silent. Ulahane has many sentries, and although I have cloaked us with a spell that turns away notice, it will not serve if we attract attention."

Dariad nodded and passed the word back. How the nomads achieved it, Ohaern could not think, but the camels were still for the rest of the journey.

Then the road stretched across their path, white and gleaming in the moonlight. Ohaern turned his camel's head, and they filed in between the hills.

The pass was too wide to make a good ambush, but Ohaern could see sentries up high, silhouetted against the sky. He braced himself and whispered to Dariad, "If we are not already discovered, we will be as soon as we come out from these hills. Bid your men be ready."

Dariad called back softly and was answered by a muted scraping as his warriors drew their swords.

"How can you be so tranquil?" Lucoyo demanded.

"Because we have prayed to the Star-Maker for victory," Dariad answered, and Lucoyo rolled his eyes up in exasperation—but Ohaern felt oddly heartened. Yes, Ulahane was also one of the Star-Maker's creations—but that did not mean Dariad's One God approved of his doings. From what the nomad had told Ohaern of his deity, the Star-Maker had very clear notions of right and wrong, and Ohaern felt sure He would, at the least, not strengthen Ulahane's hand.

But if the Star-Maker did not want Ulahane to cause so much suffering, why did He not intervene and put a stop to it? Of course, that was what Ohaern and Dariad were doing, and if they were the Star-Maker's agents, they would win. Still, it seemed that a deity who could make stars would be able to put an end to Ulahane's misdeeds much more quickly and neatly than humans could—but Lucoyo could almost hear Lomallin's answer within him: they had to do their own work. They were not babies, to have everything done for them.

It was not a complete answer, but it was enough. Perhaps there was more—perhaps they were being forged, as a sword is forged, into an instrument for the Star-Maker's purposes; perhaps they were a part of a grander scheme. Whatever it was, it did not truly matter at the moment—all that did was facing Ulahane's forces and striking through them to Kuru.

It was well he realized that, for as they came out from between the hills, they saw the plain before them crowded with monsters of all shapes and sizes, things part bird and part animal, part insect and part fish, giant arachnids and midget boars with steel tusks, many with human heads or human breasts or human legs. To one side came marching an army of Klaja; to the other, a horde of writhing lamias. Behind them, pacing from wing to wing of that gruesome host, an Ulharl towered, roaring and whipping them on with chains. The monsters shrieked in anger and pain and surged forward, pushing the ones in front of them, and the wave rolled forward until the front rank came charging at Ohaern and his companions.

Ohaern shouted a battle cry, and the nomads charged forth. For a few minutes the shaman disappeared and the warrior came to the fore as Ohaern wielded his sword, leaning low and chopping down at the monstrosities. They shrieked and gibbered and howled in anger as they reached for him with long claws and sharp teeth, lances of flame and coils of scales, but he met each attack with dagger or sword and did not count his wounds. Beside him, Lucoyo chopped valiantly, screaming in terror and strewing the ground with bodies as he hewed and hacked. Behind them the nomads shouted approval and charged in, determined not to be outdone by the Northerner—but behind *them* came an army of forest hunters, determined not to be outdone by mere desert herders! Side by side the black army and the white chewed into the heart of the enemy horde, leaving a wake of slain monsters and writhing headless coils, of bisected giant spiders and beheaded boars roasting in their own flames.

But Dariad ignored them all, screaming in frenzy and chopping his way through the ranks of the monsters with a single-minded battle lust that bordered on madness—though if it was, it was divine madness, for he hewed himself a path straight to the Ulharl who drove the horde.

Ulahane's half-human offspring was so busy whipping on his monsters with his chain that he did not even see the human until Dariad's sword scored his side. Then, roaring with rage, the Ulharl turned on the upstart, swinging his chain high to crush this impertinent miniature.

CHAPTER 31

The chain lashed down, but Dariad was no longer there. His camel stepped to the side, slipped in a gory mass, and fell, bawling. Dariad leaped free and landed on his feet, slashing backhanded at the Ulharl's Achilles' tendon. The blade cut through, and the giant fell, roaring with shock and sudden fear. On one knee, he swung that mighty chain again, a chain that glittered with razor-sharp barbs, swinging straight down toward Dariad. The nomad side-stepped, but not quite quickly enough; the barbs shredded his robe and left red trails. But Dariad ignored the pain and stepped down hard on the chain, holding the Ulharl's arm down just long enough to chop into his elbow. Blood spurted and the giant screamed, but even screaming, he caught up the chain with his left hand and yanked, sending Dariad spinning away. The chain flailed high, hissing down—but Dariad rolled away, and the links only caught his robe. He leaped to his feet, the robe tearing away, and swung with all his strength. The Ulharl brought an arm up, to block with a bronze bracelet, but Dariad turned the sword at the last instant and hacked into the giant's forearm an inch above the band. The Ulharl screamed again, but Dariad swung in from the other side and sliced deeply into the giant's neck. The scream cut off into a gurgle, blood gushed, and the Ulharl fell over, eyes wide in shock. Dariad looked down at the agonized, still-living face, braced himself, and drove his sword straight down in a blow of mercy. The giant's body gave one last convulsive heave—and the chain whipped about in a dead man's blow, cracking across Dariad's shoulders. He cried out in pain, then clenched his jaw as blood flowed down across his back in a dozen streams.

"Sever the head!" the judge cried, following down the aisle Dariad had cut. "Hack it off, that we may be sure he is dead!"

Dariad yanked his sword out of the giant's chest, but another nomad came running up with his sword high and swung it down at the Ulharl's neck. It bounced off, ringing, and the nomad stood staring.

Dariad gathered himself for another effort and swung down. His blade cut halfway through the Ulharl's neck.

"Enough!" the judge cried. "Surely nothing can live so sorely wounded!"

"We must finish what we have begun," Dariad grunted, and swung again. This time the head rolled free, and the nomad looked up to see his tribesmen staring in awe. He frowned. "What? Have you never seen a blow struck home before?"

"Aye," said the judge, "but never a stroke at which another man had failed."

All across the field the monsters howled in terror as word of the giant's death passed. They turned and ran, flowed, and flew. The African war chief cried out in anger, and his warriors pursued, slaying as they went.

"Not all!" Ohaern cried. "Let a few escape, to lead us!"

Dariad called to his men, and a few of them galloped after the Africans, calling to them. The black warriors nodded, though with exclamations of disgust.

Ohaern stared. "When did they learn one another's language?"

"In the cavern," said Lucoyo, "while you conferred in the spirit world."

The Africans continued their slaughter, and the Biharu, not to be outdone, rode in among them and helped when monsters turned at bay, snarling—but all in all, there were a dozen monsters left to lead them through fields and over causeways into the center of the plain, where the walls of Kuru towered in the distance. The warriors, Biharu and African alike, gave a shout of joy and proceeded to ride down the remaining monsters. They turned to fight, pulling into a knot of scales and beaks and talons, hissing.

"Hold back!" Lucoyo shouted, and some of the Biharu relayed the message to the Africans, who hesitated just long enough for the half-elf to shoot a dozen arrows into the knot of monsters. The Africans shouted approval and threw their extra spears. Monsters howled, biting at the shafts; some came roaring out to seize and maul the humans, but more often than not their targets slipped aside, and their comrades chopped the monsters to shreds. Ohaern stood and watched, amazed to see manticores and lamias so quickly cut apart—though it was scarcely surprising, with a dozen battle-mad warriors to each of them.

Then he looked up and saw a horde of monsters approaching across the plain, driven on by whip-wielding giants. More titans came behind them, leading the soldiers who poured out of the gates of Kuru. The shaman shouted, "Pull back! Rally! The defenders come!"

The warriors looked up, saw, and pulled back into their own bands. Heartened, the embattled monsters came roaring after— and died, with a score of spears in each. Lucoyo's arrows found vital spots, and some died with only one shaft buried in a heart or a brain.

Then a roar went up from the attacking army as the largest giant of all shouldered through the gates of Kuru, driving his lesser kin before him. A shout of alarm went up from Ohaern's people, and Lucoyo cried, "What monstrous form is *that*?"

"It is Kadura," Ohaern answered, from his newfound shaman's lore. "It is Kadura, first of the misbegotten spawn of Ulahane, eldest and most hate-filled of the Ulharl."

"Can it be killed?" An African warrior called out in the Biharu tongue.

Surprised, Ohaern turned to him and called back, "As surely as any mortal can!"

"Then we kill!" the African said with determination, and his companions shouted in affirmation. Together with the Biharu, they marched toward the monsters, singing songs of death.

But shouts echoed from all around the city, and looking up, Ohaern saw other troops of hunters and nomads charging into the fray. Monsters and soldiers came pouring out of other gates, and the battle was joined in earnest, all around that blood-colored city.

Ohaern, however, was not about to let his army face the monsters alone. He called out two spells that he had heard Manalo chant, and flame fountained up from the plain in the midst of the Kuruite host. Monsters and men alike screamed and crowded frantically away, and a towering fiery form demanded, "Who calls?"

"I, Ohaern!" the shaman answered, though every nerve in his body screamed at him to run. "I call you by the promise you gave to Manalo! I implore you, salamander, turn upon this host and burn them to ashes!"

The salamander turned its head, pondered the horde of men and monsters, and said, "I owe them nothing, and owe their master spite. I will." Then its mouth opened wide and a jet of fire swept over the creatures below, turning them instantly to ash. They screamed and pulled back, jammed back, scrambled back over the living bodies behind them, and a semicircle of confusion spread inward over the plain even to the city walls as the salamander began its slow, steady advance, charring all before it. Ohaern's troops pulled back in alarm, too—at first, but when they saw that the elemental fought their foes, they began to follow in its wake, slaying those at the circle of its ashen half ring, but giving a wide birth to the creature itself.

Behind them came marching another army, of beings who looked half finished, doughy and soft. Their leader came up and cried out to Ohaern in his own odd language.

"Agrapax's homunculi!" Lucoyo cried. "What did he say?"

"He said, 'You have summoned us by Manalo's call. What would you have us do?' " Ohaern translated, then replied to the homunculi in their own tongue. "Slay those minions of evil!"

The homunculi answered with a shout and turned to charge, clumsily but irresistibly, into the Kuruite host.

"The allies are summoned and the fight is joined." Ohaern drew the broadsword from its sheath across his back. "It is time for me to join them."

"You are too valuable!" Lucoyo cried. "They will fail and be slain if you are killed!"

"Lomallin will protect me from Ulahane." Ohaern hefted his sword. "This will protect me from men. Come, Lucoyo! There is glory to be won!"

Just then, though, Kuruite soldiers erupted into the air, scream- ing and howling, in a curve that expanded outward like a wave rolling in from the sea, and the ground trembled beneath Ohaern's feet—but stopped short of the armies of nomads and hunters and began to roll back.

"The dwerg!" Ohaern shouted. "Grakhinox and his kindred, shaking the ground beneath our foes, sliding it out from beneath their feet! Charge in and slay while you may!"

Apparently all the other shamans heard, for the nomad armies howled and charged in, reaping death about them.

Then a howling rose from the plain, a howling more like that of a wolf or dog than a man, and another army came charging in to slay monsters and Kuruites with whetted swords and sharp fangs, an army that looked to be as much jackal as man, and all through- out Ulahane's horde, knots of similar jackal-men turned on their allies to bite and chew and slay.

"The Klaja!" Ohaern cried. "He has returned as he said, and brought hundreds of his people with him! Who would have thought they hated Ulahane so, or sought revenge upon him for having made them! Come, Lucoyo! Or there will be no glory left for us!"

"I could live without it," the half-elf grumbled, but he followed his friend into the battle.

There followed a timeless interval of fear and panic and stab- bing and slaying, trying desperately to keep sharp fangs and sharper spears from Ohaern's body. Lucoyo followed his friend back-to-back, with frequent glances over his shoulder to make sure Ohaern had not charged away from his rear guard—but he fre- quently did, leaving the half-elf to curse and retreat, parrying and thrusting frantically until his own spine jarred against something that he hoped was Ohaern's back. Fortunately, he was almost always right, and on the other two occasions, the Kuruite soldier was more surprised and less ready than the half-elf—also, it would seem, more mortal. The slaughter seemed to go on and on forever, and only the increasing weight of his sword and the sight of the red slick on his forearms told Lucoyo that a few of his enemies' blades had reached past his own. He hoped frantically that Ohaern was faring better than he.

Then a scream went up all across the field. Fighting stopped as attacker and defender alike paused to look upon a sight that froze them in their tracks.

A city gate burst asunder and a figure taller than the walls of Kuru strode forth—a scarlet figure of death and depraved delight that Ohaern had seen before, a figure with a skull-helmet atop a head whose cavernous eyes glittered with malice and whose fangs clashed with anticipation.

The armies of men, who had stood bravely against Kuruites twice their number and a horde of monsters that would have frightened a dozen ordinary people, now moaned in fear and shrank away from that terrible visage. Ulahane laughed aloud with cruel delight and advanced, sweeping all before him with a chain of fire and a curving sword twice the height of a man.

"Lomallin!" Ohaern cried. "If ever you have stood by humankind, stand by us now! If you do not save us from this paragon of evil, we are lost, and the younger races doomed! Strike now, I pray, if still you exist!"

But there was no answer, and Ulahane's laugh of delight boomed out over the plain, forming itself into words. "Fool! With an army of fools! Lomallin is dead! I slew him myself—as I shall do to you, to all who oppose me! I shall do what all my misbegotten sons could not: slay the defenders of humankind! Slay those treacherous Klaja who turned their hands against me! Even the salamander I shall rend asunder and stamp down deep into the earth, to crush—"

A lance of green light stabbed down from the sky to bathe the Scarlet One in its beams. Thunder rolled as green and scarlet mixed, and Ulahane stood in light-born black, a living, screaming shadow. The scream endured as his eyes fell in and smoke boiled out of their sockets—smoke that swirled up into the heavens to take on the form of Ulahane, even as his body still stood frozen on the plain below, frozen even as the green light receded, gathering itself back up into the heavens, where it took on the form of a man, a giant with a gentle face now creased in sternness, a green and glowing form that cast aside its glowing robe to stand in a loincloth only, hands open and ready for battle.

They stood a moment, while the armies below held their breath—the red ghost and the green, squared to one another and readying themselves for what they knew must be their final battle, for both their bodies were dead now, and victory could be gained only by destroying the ghost that remained. Far below them, men forgot their own battle in their dread anticipation of the ghost-battle above them, between godlike spirits who seemed to tower up into the very stars.

More than "seemed to"—for Ulahane roared and reached for a star. He caught it and hurled it, a flame-tailed ball of light sailing straight toward Lomallin's heart.

Lomallin seized a star of his own and hurled it at his foe—or rather, at his missile. Star met star and exploded in a soundless burst of light that dimmed the two ghosts for a moment. When they became clear again, the watchers saw that Ulahane had seized a string of stars and was whirling it about his head, like an Ulharl with his chain, as he advanced on Lomallin.

The Green One reached out and plucked one star after another, then as Ulahane came close, hurled them into his face. Silent explosions filled the night as star met star and burst. Ulahane fell reeling back, but even as he staggered, he caught the raw star stuff about him, then advanced again, molding the glowing mass and forming it into an axe of light with a blade half his own height. He swung it at Lomallin, but the Green One sidestepped, and the force of the blow swung Ulahane's ghost about. Lomallin stepped in and laid green hands against scarlet skin, only laid them, but smoke boiled up where they touched, and a skreeling scream filled the night as the red ghost bucked and thrashed, trying to rid himself of Lomallin's touch. Finally he dived, leaving the Green One behind. Below, his own men and monsters howled with fear and fought to escape the spot where he seemed doomed to strike—but the Scarlet One turned his dive into a spring, leaping back up into the sky even as he remolded the axe, shaping it into a war club. As he came back level with Lomallin, he hurled the weapon at his enemy. Lomallin reached out and caught it, though its momentum whirled him about in a circle—and as he whirled, he reshaped and modeled and forged. Ulahane leaped in, thinking to take the Green One unawares, then pulled back, as if remembering the pain of Lomallin's touch—and Ohaern cried, "It was true! In dying, Lomallin gained greater strength than Ulahane!"

A moan swept through the army of evil even as Lomallin hurled a spear of light straight at the heart of Ulahane. The Scarlet One dodged and whirled, but the spear followed his every movement until it exploded against Ulahane's chest, flying apart into five shooting stars that fell to earth. One fell straight down toward Ulahane's forces; his armies howled with fear and scrambled to get away, slaying one another and trampling one another in panic—until it winked out, as did the fragments that fell to the east, west, and south. But the largest fragment shot away to the north, trailing fire beyond the horizon, even as Ulahane's ghost broke into a thousand points of light that flew apart, winking out one by one—and below on earth, his charred husk crumbled to dust.

The opposed armies stood spellbound, staring up unbelieving into the night—until the Green One, looking down, smiled, raised a hand in blessing, and disappeared.

Then, even before his armies could shake off the spell of awe that held them, the Ulharls screamed and fled, kicking their own warriors aside in their haste to escape.

Ohaern came alive. "Stop them! Slay them! Do not close, but hurl spears, shoot arrows! If they escape, evil and misery shall pursue humankind down through the ages!"

All the hunters and nomads came to themselves with a roar of alarm and ran to head off the Ulharls, hurling spears and shooting arrows, even slinging stones. The giants roared in rage and panic,

kicking and hurling the humans aside—but they were mortal, after all, and vastly outnumbered, for the monsters were fleeing,
too, and the soldiers of Kuru were running back to the safety of
their city walls.

It was a night of hunting, a night of slaughter, a night of blood—
but when it was over, all but a few of the Ulharls lay dead.
Ohaern told off bands of men to seek them out and armies to
follow, to hunt them down, but only two were ever found—and
neither of them was Kadura, eldest of the Ulharls, and their chief.

Without him, without the Ulharls and the monsters, and having seen their god slain, the people of Kuru had no more heart to
fight. When Ohaern swore a solemn oath to leave them in peace if
they laid down their weapons outside the city and turned to the
worship of Lomallin and the Star-Maker, doing what they could to
right the wrongs they had done in obedience to Ulahane—if they
did all that, Ohaern and his armies would go away and leave them
in peace. The city accepted, and the armies drew back to leave the
Kuruites a wide place to pile their weapons. The heaps grew high,
but when the Kuruites had gone back inside their city and closed
the gates behind them, Ohaern's armies quickly carried away
every pike, every spear, every sword, every shield.

"They will have kept some within, Ohaern," Lucoyo warned him.

"Some, yes," Ohaern agreed, "but not enough to cause anyone
else real grief."

"Especially since you have appointed scouts to haunt these hills
that ring the city?"

"And given them spells to call up the Biharu and the African
nations. Yes." Ohaern nodded. "I think they will abide by the
peace, Lucoyo. Perhaps not at once, but after a few defeats. Yes."

And they did—but sooner than Ohaern had expected, for the
clan leaders within the city came out and asked him to tear down
Ulahane's temple. Dariad feared treachery, so the clan leaders invited him to escort Ohaern with all his Biharu. Reluctantly, he
agreed—and the African shaman and all his warriors held themselves ready to charge the gate on the instant, should Ohaern call
or the great portals begin to close. They stayed open, though, and
Ohaern rode down a broad boulevard between buildings that tow-

ered four and five times a man's height, lavish buildings inlaid with enameled tiles and semiprecious stones in designs sacred to Ulahane—but those designs had already been defaced. Even so, the hair at the nape of Ohaern's neck bristled with the feeling that every one of those hidden weapons was trained on him from the many eyes that watched in secret from windows and rooftops, or even among the throngs of people who lined the boulevard, crying out their thanks for mercy. It was hard for the Biharu to remain stern and glowering under so much gratitude and, yes, flattery, but they held their ranks, looking down from their camels with their swords in hand. Never a missile flew, though, nor any soldier leaped to bar their way, and they rode straight to the wide, wide stairs that led up the giant steps of the pyramid to Ulahane's temple on top. There, an old woman stood waiting for them, and as they came up, she fell on her knees, bowing and crying out, "Thrice welcome, noble shaman! Thrice welcome, valiant warriors! I am Nilo, an unworthy priestess of Rahani! I have lived in secret these thirty years, ever fearing discovery by the priests of Ulahane! Thrice thanks for my life!"

The shaman in Ohaern recognized her words as true. "Where are the priests who kept this temple, O Nilo?"

"Crept away in the night, those who could. Come! I shall show you to those who could not!"

It was to Nilo's credit that she did not gloat over the broken remnants of what had been Ulahane's priests. "When the soldiers streamed back into the city last night," she told Ohaern, "they came first to this temple to tear the priests apart in revenge for their betrayal in turning the city to the worship of the weaker god."

Dariad frowned. "That is not the best reason for abandoning a false god. It is not even a good one."

"It shall serve as a beginning, though." Ohaern turned away to keep his gorge from rising. "If they come to the worship of Lomallin, perhaps they will discover good reasons for their faith—or to worship the Star-Maker."

Dariad shook his head with certainty. "He would not want them to come to Him only in order to gain a victory."

"No," Ohaern said judiciously, "but if He loves all His creations, as you have told me, He will not turn them away, either. Off this pyramid now, all of you! And you, O Nilo! For I must brew a fearful magic!"

He danced then, around a fire that he lit himself, and in which he put certain herbs that Nilo fetched him. The smoke spiraled upward with a sweet aroma as the shaman turned and leaped about the blaze, singing and chanting until, with a tiny grating that grew into a huge rumble and a thundering, the temple of the scarlet god collapsed, falling in on itself till it was nothing but a huge pile of sand. The Kuruites drew back, moaning and weeping in terror—but Ohaern turned away from the sight with grim satisfaction. "I do not think they shall seek to attack neighbors now, Dariad."

"No." The nomad chieftain stared at the rubble, his eyes huge. "No, I think not."

"Rule us, O Shaman!" Nilo fell to her knees, hands uplifted, imploring. "Rule us, O Dariad! For this people no longer knows the ways of peace!"

Ohaern stared in surprise, then sadly shook his head. "I have a home to visit, and a son to care for—if Lomallin leaves me time for it, and has no other tasks."

Nilo glanced up at him keenly. "Or Rahani—for I see it is her you truly serve."

Ohaern frowned. "You see too much for my comfort." Then, quickly, "Let Dariad rule, for he is worthy."

"I am not," the nomad said flatly, "neither worthy nor fit. What know I of a city?"

"Surely you can learn!"

"But I have no wish to," Dariad said simply. "I wish only to go back to my desert and watch it come alive with moisture, now that Ulahane is dead."

"But what shall we do?" Nilo cried, and the clan leaders came up to drop to their knees and join her, imploring, "How shall we fare, who were raised to war and cruelty, but are now beaten, aye, and have seen our god fall?"

Dariad spread his hands. "What can I say to those who have

grown all their lives in cities? I know only the nomads' law, the herders' morality! I could only advise you to return to those truths, that simple code of life and living! I can counsel you to nothing but that, for I know nothing more."

The clan leaders stared, then turned to talk to one another with agitation and excitement.

Dariad stared in return. "What have I said?"

"Perhaps more than you know," Nilo told him. "If your law is simple and stark, it is so much the fundament of life that it will hold true in the city as well as in the desert. Oh, we will need other laws than that, it is true, and soldiers to enforce them all—but you have given us a beginning. Teach us your law, O Nomad!"

"Come out to meet our judge, and he shall tell you," Dariad said slowly.

The judge did. He told Nilo and the clan leaders the Law of the Star-Maker; he told them of government by council, with no king or ruler but God, and only a judge over men in times of peace and a war chief in times of war, both chosen by acclamation of all who were grown. But when the Biharu left Kuru, a stream of slaves followed them out to reclaim their freedom and to return to the desert and steppe from which they had been captured. Kuru lost a third of its population that day and was no longer crowded. There was time to consider, and room for virtue.

Dariad shook his head as they rode away. "They would do best to all leave that moldering pile of stone and mud and come out into the cleanliness of the countryside."

"They would," Ohaern agreed, remembering Cashalo, "but they will not. Cities will always arise where men need to trade, Dariad, so that the surplus of a land rich in grain can feed the starving mouths of another land lean in foodstuffs, but rich in amber and tin—and where folk meet to trade, cities will grow. They can even become a force for good."

"I hope it shall be so," Dariad sighed, "but I shall leave it to you to guide them, Ohaern. For myself, I could not abide to live so hemmed in."

Neither could Ohaern. He suspected that Lucoyo could, and would, gladly—but he was not about to give him the chance.

CHAPTER 32

The land was already beginning to show more life as Ohaern and Lucoyo rode with the Biharu back to their homeland. "Has the drought ended so quickly?" asked Dariad, looking about him in amazement.

"It has," said Ohaern, "for he who caused it and maintained it is dead. The waters he penned up now flow, and infuse the land with life."

They found the truth of that as they came to the summer grazing ground where they were to meet the women, children, and elders—and found a broad river where there had only been a long dry gully. The Biharu halted their camels and sat, staring in amazement.

"How can it be?" the judge whispered. "This is a desert!"

"No longer." Lucoyo grinned. "If you are not wary, O Judge, you shall have hunters encroaching on your land."

Dariad shook his head with certainty. "Not while I live."

"He speaks more than he knows," Ohaern said to the judge, "as usual." He turned to Dariad. "You are the hero who slew an Ulharl. None will dare come near the lands that the people of Dariad claim as their own."

The young nomad looked up at him in astonishment, but the judge said, "Come. Even I, old as I am, long to see my wife again— and the younger men must be frantic."

The camels moved as the men rode for the tents of their families, Dariad musing, trying to adjust to the notion that he was no longer a simple member of the tribe—but the other young men were eager for the welcome due to heroes.

Playing children saw them approaching and ran to tell their mothers. The women and elders came streaming out from their tents, and grinning Biharu slipped down off their camels to fold their wives in their arms as the elders cheered their return and children came running to tug at their robes. Ohaern stood back, watching with pleasure, and a little sadness that deepened to a pang.

Lucoyo saw and gave him a punch. "Ho, Watcher and Waiter! Do not stand and envy! Surely these Biharu can find a woman obliging enough to fill your cravings!"

Ohaern turned to him, puzzled, then smiled, amused. "You know as well as I do, Lucoyo, that if there is one people who would *not* abuse a woman so, it is the Biharu."

"Yes, I do know," Lucoyo said sourly, "so there is nothing here for us, O Hunter Bold. Come! Let us seek out wild game for their victory banquet!"

"Wild game?" Ohaern stared. "In a *desert*?"

"It is a desert that is greening," Lucoyo reminded him, "and if the plants are coming alive, why not the animals that feed on them? There will be fish in that river, at least, and I doubt the Biharu have ever tasted them!"

They had not, as it transpired, and they exclaimed with surprise and delight as each Biharu tasted a fish of his or her own that night. The women were avid to learn how to cook them, and all were eager to learn how to catch them. But when the meal was done and they reclined about the great fire in the central area between the tents, the judge stepped up and called, "Hear, my friends!"

Everyone instantly fell silent, sat up straight and paid close attention to their leader.

"I grow old," the judge said, "and the care of this tribe weighs the people of Cashalo to refurbish his temple and hearken to his advice, bade them all turn to the homage of Ranol and listen to the Biharu leaders as they explained the worship of the Star-Maker. The people of Cashalo listened with quiet attentiveness, then cheered them as they rode out of the city.

"Do they cheer us," Lucoyo asked, "or our leaving?"

"Let us give them reason to cheer indeed," Ohaern replied, and to the armies, "Ride on and away! Give these people the chance to discover a True Way by themselves!"

So they rode homeward, stopping to destroy any temple or shrine to Ulahane as they went, to chastise the rover bands that had broken off from Ulahane's armies to prey upon the weak—and finally they came to the land of the Vanyar.

Word had run ahead of them, and they found a Vanyar army drawn up and waiting for them—but Ohaern called up the dwergs and the Klaja again, and the Biharu proved to be better fighters than the Vanyar, even as the back of a camel proved to be an excellent place from which to strike down at racing chariot drivers. When the battle was done and the Vanyar fled, Ohaern looked upon his Biharu and Klaja, and grieved at the loss of a tenth of their number—but when his armies followed the fugitives home, he found them more than ready to sue for a truce. He left them with a stern injunction to live in peace with their neighbors and steal no more. Then he bade Lucoyo tell them the tale of the battle between Ulahane and Lomallin, and when he was done, advised the Vanyar to abandon the worship of Ulahane, of whom not even a ghost remained, and to turn to Lomallin.

When they left the chastised invaders behind, the word of Ohaern's band of vengeance spread throughout the land, so that the wicked turned away from their cruelties in fear that the shaman or his Biharu might find them.

Finally, by the banks of the northern river that divided the land of the Biriae from those of their neighbors, Ohaern turned to thank his escort, and then sent them back to their homes with gifts of the booty they had captured from the robbers. For himself, he kept none, but Lucoyo bore a pouch of gold and gems. Then the smith and the half-elf crossed the river and made their way through forests becoming increasingly familiar as they came home—until, one afternoon, they came out of the trees, and Ohaern's eyes filled with tears as he readied himself to find the wreckage of his former village.

But his eyes dried with amazement as he saw the village standing as it had been when Ryl had been alive and vibrant in his arms. A young woman, watching children at play, looked up and saw them, then cried with delight and came running.

Lucoyo stared, unable to believe his eyes, then gave a shout of joy and tossed his pack away so that he could run and sweep her up in his arms. Ohaern stared in surprise, too, then remembered that the Biriae had been broken into many tiny bands of fugitives. So Elluaera had lived after all, and Lucoyo had spent his grief in vain!

No, not in vain. The Vanyar were weakened by the loss of the false god who had lent them rage and hatred; they had been chastened by the Biharu and penned within the lands they already held, their vanguards harried back to the main horde, where they would settle to farm the earth like the shamans who would rise to rule them by knowledge alone, and by faith in a god that would not die. Lucoyo had helped to accomplish much in his wanderings.

Ohaern picked up the pack of gold and weighed it in one hand; he would keep it for the half-elf till he was done with the distraction that gave him so much joy. Lucoyo had gained by the adventure in gold as well as experience and wisdom, and had come back rich enough to wed a wife and rear babes, even to see them marry and have children in their own turns.

"Such a woman as yourself?" Lucoyo asked in a dangerous tone.

"No, husband." Elluaera rose, a little stiffly, and came over to clasp his hand. "I have a taste for lighter fare. There was no merriment in him, and I need the salt of humor in a man."

"Well, you found that, truly enough." Lucoyo smiled into her eyes. "You chose that, if nothing more."

"A great deal more." She tightened her hold and pressed his hand against her. "If Rahani's mouth watered at sight of Ohaern, I rejoice—for mine did not." A little lie never hurt a marriage, after all.

"The other boys say that Ohaern's body lies locked in ice in a hidden cave," the eldest boy said stoutly, "but that his spirit has found his goddess, there in the spirit world, and learns wisdom from her lips as he dwells in rapture with her. What is 'rapture,' Gran'pa?"

His mother cleared her throat rather sharply, and Lucoyo said, "Well, I can believe the part about his body, at least."

"Did the goddess fall in love with him, then?" the eldest girl asked breathlessly.

"They say the Ulin cannot truly fall in love," Lucoyo hedged, "for they can love nothing so much as themselves. But I doubt not that she still takes pleasure in—"

His wife coughed.

"—his company," Lucoyo said smoothly, "and keeps him rapt in his trance, teaching him more and more of that which a man like Ohaern most desires—"

His daughter coughed.

"—wizardry!" Again Lucoyo changed directions without the slightest sign.

"So she keeps him entranced, teaching him wizardry and love?" the middle girl asked.

"But when shall he waken?" the eldest boy demanded.

"When humankind needs him," Lucoyo told him, "and be sure that we will, for it is even as Ohaern thought it was when he told me, 'This is not finished, nor will it ever be.' And he was right, for the fight is not done. Ever."

The bear stepped off the Tree and found the radiant woman waiting. "So you have found me at last, Ohaern," she said.

"At last, O Lady—O Beloved!" Even as he turned back into a man, Ohaern fell to his knees, reaching up to clasp her robe.

It came away, revealing a sheer garment beneath, and the woman laughed. "So impatient, Ohaern!"

The shaman stared at the form that seemed to glow through the translucent fabric, and stammered, "How—How can you condescend to embrace a clumsy mortal like myself!"

"You are never clumsy, but sensitive, deft, and caring." She clasped his arms and raised him up. "There is no condescension in it, only desire—though I am sure the few Ulin remaining would charge me with cowardice in pursuing a male whom I could so easily overpower, if I chose."

"You have done so," he whispered, "and without choosing."

She gave him a languid smile, bathing in the flattery, and came into his arms. When they separated, she told him, "If I choose this way to teach you things men are not born knowing and only rarely have need of, who is to tell me I am wrong?"

"None would dare," Ohaern said fervently.

"No, but they would ask why." She gave him a mischievous smile.

"Is this to be my reward for work well done, then?" Ohaern said, with a bitterness he had not known was in him. "Am I to be given pleasure for doing your bidding, for attacking when you commanded and coming at your call? Am I, truly, only your pet? For I cannot understand how I could be anything more!" Then, instantly, he pleaded, "I beg you, do not tell me that I am, for I could not even then summon the pride or the anger to turn away from you!"

"As indeed you should not, with a woman of a race so much older and more powerful than your own," she said tartly. "How, though, if I told you that you were not a pet, but a weapon that I must forge and sharpen to ward me against my foes, in a battle that will come?"

"I shall guard you with my life!" he said instantly and with total devotion. "Bid me attack, and I shall do it—now, or in five centuries, or whenever you wish! Forge me as you will, that I may protect you as you need!"

"Why, so I do," she said, "and this is the manner in which I choose to do it." Then she slid into his embrace again, arms twining up about his neck to draw him down, down, where the luminous mists enfolded them and the wisdom of the Ulin could be imparted to a mind not made large enough to hold it, by love and care and caresses, by lip and touch and fingernails trailing sensation, heart-to-heart and mind-to-mind, and spirit enfolding and sharing itself with spirit.

About the Author

CHRISTOPHER STASHEFF spent his early years in Mount Vernon, New York, but spent the rest of his formative years in Ann Arbor, Michigan. He has always had difficulty distinguishing fantasy from reality and has tried to compromise by teaching college. When teaching proved too real, he gave it up in favor of writing full-time.

He tends to prescript his life, but can't understand why other people never get their lines right.

═══ DEL REY® ONLINE! ═══

THE DEL REY INTERNET NEWSLETTER (DRIN)

The DRIN is a monthly electronic publication posted on the Internet, GEnie, CompuServe, BIX, various BBSs, and the Panix gopher. It features:

- hype-free descriptions of new books
- a list of our upcoming books
- special announcements
- a signing/reading/convention-attendance schedule for Del Rey authors
- in-depth essays by sf professionals (authors, artists, designers, salespeople, and others)
- a question-and-answer section
- behind-the-scenes looks at sf publishing
- and much more!

INTERNET INFORMATION SOURCE

Del Rey information is now available on a gopher server—gopher.panix.com—including:

- the current and all back issues of the Del Rey Internet Newsletter
- a description of the DRIN and content summaries of all issues
- sample chapters of current and upcoming books—readable and downloadable for free
- submission requirements
- mail-order information
- new DRINs, sample chapters, and other items are added regularly.

ONLINE EDITORIAL PRESENCE

Many of the Del Rey editors are online—on the Internet, GEnie, CompuServe, America Online, and Delphi. There is a Del Rey topic on GEnie and a Del Rey Folder on America Online.

WHY?

We at Del Rey realize that the networks are the medium of the future. That's where you'll find us promoting our books, socializing with others in the sf field, and—most important—making contact and sharing information with sf readers.

FOR MORE INFORMATION

The official e-mail address for Del Rey Books is

delrey@randomhouse.com